NONE OF THE ABOVE

A Novel

Michael Cocchiarale

NONE OF THE ABOVE

A Novel

Michael Cocchiarale

For Mary Ellen (1939-2015)

Special and abundant thanks to Lisa Cocchiarale, who read and proofread the novel a saintly number of times, and to Jayne Thompson, who provided valuable feedback and reassurance at a key stage in the process.

CONTENTS

NONE OF THE ABOVE

A Novel

Rite to Remain

(Fall 1980)

In the near-beginning, there was a classroom—small, colorful, radiator warm, backlit by a bank of windows overlooking Fulton Road. In five straight rows of desks were fourth graders of all shapes and sorts. It was mid-October, so a necklace of construction paper leaves dangled from the ceiling. To the left, the pole with the Stars and Stripes stuck like an errant javelin in the wall; to the right was a laminated map of the world, shiny as a grin. Above the chalkboard, a Jesus tear dropped from the cross.

There was a teacher—new and nervous, with large, pink Rorschach arms and loose, laboring lips.

There was a difficult question—one word: "Whyowa?"—and much stifled laughter.

Miss Chumley lowered the mimeograph from which she had been reading. "Frankie," she said in a measured tone. "Slow . . . down . . . and say that again."

"Why," Frankie McGooken said, counting to three with his fingers. "Iowa? Why, I mean, does Iowa get to say what goes for us?"

Miss Chumley blinked through threatening looks for the one that might put this student in his place. Undaunted, Frankie sat straight as a ruler at his desk. The teacher glanced at her mimeograph and carefully explained again the Iowa Test for Basic Skills, the series of standardized tests they'd be taking the following week.

"Shouldn't it be the *Ohio* Test for Basic Skills? Ohio is where we live." Frankie turned his body to the left and then the right. He grinned nervously, playing his clip-on tie like a silky saxophone.

Miss Chumley had blinked through all her options, and then the eyes just sat there—dark Velcro balls on a pinkish dartboard. "The test was invented in 1935," she said, trying another tack.

"But . . . my point . . ."

The teacher moved from the desk, intending a dramatic show of authority. However, the tip of her shoe caught on a nail in the hardwood floor, and she pitched forward, hands falling upon the desk of Bethany Hyde, who scrunched her face in horror. The radiator hissed and popped, the rim shot at the end of a joke. Titters bubbled up from the back of the room.

"Frankie, do . . . do you think Sr. Mary Grace would try to tell the Pope that there were really four persons in the Trinity?" She forced a laugh to underscore the absurdity. "Abraham listened to orders. Moses listened to orders. Even Jesus our Lord listened to orders. Tell me, are you better than Jesus?" By the end of her speech, Miss Chumley stood tall again, eyes wide, blotchy arms crossed, lips sewn up with satisfaction.

Frankie said. "I would like to go on record—"

"I know, I know," Miss Chumley said, patting the air as if it were a pouting toddler's head. "It's not fair." She went on to list a series of grave injustices against humanity: Indian Removal, Jim Crow, the domestic servitude of women, mass murder in Cambodia.

Frankie gave up, folding his hands upon the desktop. And yet, something in the boy's guileless smile, his perfect posture, suggested a triumph of his own. Miss Chumley just seemed grateful to survive the moment. Taking a deep breath, she ordered students to turn to page twenty-six of their spelling books and "repeat after me."

Hunched at his desk on the far side of the room, shoulder blades brushing his earlobes, John Alt chewed his fingernails. The word "Whyowa" continued to float miraculously in the air, like the Wright brothers' primitive plane, which they'd learned about in history the day before. Sr. Regina, proud possessor of her very own pilot's license, told them about that long ago day at Kitty Hawk, when the contraption tottered twenty feet above the ground, if only for a handful of seconds. "Just imagine," Sr. Regina said, hand on cheek, and John obeyed. Imagine: The plane could have crashed into the small crowd below; Imagine: It could have exploded like a cherry bomb in the air; Imagine: Orville could have fallen out and split open his head on the ground. As Mom never tired of reminding him, even a slip in the bathtub could be enough to make one dead.

"Authority," Miss Chumley read with gusto from her book. When she turned for a moment to write a sentence on the board, Dave Baske whispered "Abortion" through fat chapped lips. There was some muffled laughter, but John sat still as a bird. He was deathly afraid of Miss Chumley, who took fierce joy in stashing miscreants in the corner behind the upright piano, where there was nothing to look at but a blank, beige wall. On a dare last Friday, Stinky George Sophronia, desperate to make a better name for himself, crept from his seat to blow his nose on the American flag that sagged from the pole at the front of the room. Just as face touched cloth, Miss Chumley, who'd been next door borrowing chalk from Miss Da Via, reentered the room. Livid, eyes blinking like a TV on the fritz, she dragged the boy to the wall and made him stand there, hands behind his back, straight through recess. Then, despite tears and apologies, she sent him off to the principal's office. Head bowed at his desk, John listened to the boy's sad steps into the hallway, the bone snap of the door as it closed. He wondered if George would ever be seen alive in this world again.

Miss Chumley read her sentence: "The Pope's authority is unquestioned by the faithful."

The students who were still paying attention—the girls, more studious as a rule; Frankie McGooken, disappointed but dutiful; George Sophronia, now just a smelly little yes man; John Alt, of course—responded with a compliant mumble.

When Dave whispered again, "The Human Abortion," there was more stifled laughter. Everyone knew he was alluding to Frankie, the nickname a reference to the steel shaft that rose out of the depths of the boy's Oxford shirt to the metal ring circling his neck like a torture device. A letter describing the boy's condition had been sent home to parents, and Mom read it, nodding knowingly as if she'd worn her fair share of such braces when a little girl. "It's just Scoliosis," she told John. "Everyone has a cross to bear, and if you're a Catholic, you keep your eyes to yourself." John shuddered. "Osis" sounded like something that could contaminate—something that might even kill. Afterward, John had to fight the impulse to hold his breath whenever the boy came near.

This time, Frankie must have heard Dave, for he turned quickly, the brace clunking against the back of the chair. The boy was still smiling, but more strenuously than before. His eyes were small—all lashes and wrinkles. He scratched his hair, a black brush smashed against canvas.

Dave shrank in his desk and pointed with a shaky finger. "Aborrrrr-tion," he mouthed.

"Baggage," Miss Chumley said, oblivious to the furtive drama.

"Baggage," the good students echoed.

Dave had despised Frankie since the first day of the school year, when with just a hint of a posh accent he proudly announced, "I was born in London, England, where my father had a lectureship." This fact—the sheer audacity of having come from not just outside the city limits or across a state line or two, but from the other side of the ocean—amazed everyone. That afternoon, several students huddled by the bright map at the front of the room, chattering excitedly. On the periphery, John tiptoed to observe the island in question. It was small, a mere speck of cosmic dust compared to the Jupiter-like immensity of the United States. But it had the grand allure of elsewhere.

For weeks, Dave wouldn't leave Frankie's "born in London" statement alone, repeating it on the playground with bad accents modeled on the Monty Python shows he was allowed to watch on PBS. Each time he used the line he'd add some physical gesture: a tilt of the head, a bat of eyelashes, a flaccid bend of wrist. As weeks went on and it became clear that Frankie was a force to be reckoned with, Dave went on the attack, focusing on the boy's name. He started with "Hankie" and "Wankie," before latching onto Frankie's last name, bursting with fresh possibilities. "Hey Gook!" Dave said to him one morning as they lined up to enter school. The word seemed to slip out by accident, but then, in the midst of the giggles that followed, Dave sniffed major success. He said it again, this time pointing—"Luke! A Gook!" Naturally, Frankie became "Gook" until the name got old, which took a good week. "Gook," of course, turned into "Chink" turned into "Slant Eye" turned into yesterday, during an afternoon bathroom break, "Ah, Most Honorable AssHo," complete with praying hands and a ceremonial bow. Frankie stood patiently in front of the door to the lavatory, which was blocked by Tim Sager, Dave's weedy right-hand man, and said, "You do know I'm Irish."

"Cowardice," Miss Chumley said, continuing down the list.

As the insults stumbled and spit from Dave's fat lips they did not always make much sense, but John, in front of a urinal on the far side of the lavatory, felt them like direct blows from Larry Holmes. He wanted to strike back—scream "Leave Frankie alone!"—but that would do nothing more than make him visible once again. A target. If Dave didn't simply punch him in the mouth, he might remember

John's given name—Increase—and all the obscene alternatives, which the bully had flung around the year before. No, no, the best John decided he could do was watch and listen, serve as witness.

"David," Miss Chumley said. It took John a moment to realize that this was not another word on their vocabulary list. "David Baske, go to the wall right now. Do not pass Go. Do not collect two hundred dollars."

Dave shrugged, stood up, and took short, robotic steps toward his punishment. Some kids risked a smile, but John did not. He might fail to do many things in his life, but he vowed to never, ever, ever find himself out of options, his face against a wall.

*

The following week, the test booklet from Iowa landed on John's desk like a hydrogen bomb from Russia. By the time he realized he'd been spared incineration, Miss Chumley was half way through the directions. The gravity of her face, the tone of her voice, and now her hair, which had overnight gone from drainpipe brown to frosty, curly blond—all these changes impressed upon him the magnitude of the event.

"Begin," Miss Chumley commanded, her voice strong and deep, as if she were trying to part a sea. When John broke the seal, a noxious flow of words was released. He closed his eyes and held his breath until his teacher came by to say, "You must get to work!" He placed an index finger under each word of the directions before moving on to the questions. He "carefully and fully" began to fill in the ovals on the answer sheet, imagining all the while a crazy-haired Iowan in a lab coat who would feed these sheets one after the other into some monstrous grading machine, crying out, "You like? You like?" while stroking the thing on its hot steel head. Periodically, the machine would snort and spit out a sheet with too many errors. The man in the lab coat, seeing the smoldering paper on the floor, would cackle maniacally. Before coloring in a bubble, John made triply sure he was right. Once, he changed his mind and tried (as directed) to completely erase the mark. As hard as he scrubbed with the eraser, the gray ghost of his mistake remained. Or perhaps it was the right answer after all. How could he know for sure?

Just as John began to develop some kind of rhythm, Miss Chumley cried "Stop!" He dropped his pencil on the desk, and it

16

rolled, gathering steam, until it plunged to its death on the floor. He looked in horror at the answer sheet. He still had seven questions to go—questions to which he would never be permitted to return. In the middle of the room, Frankie sat rigid and smiling, hands folded and eyes trained on the blackboard, empty except for dust swirls below the word TIME all in CAPS. Hatred for the smug boy shot through John like sweater shock. He tried to sustain the feeling but kept running up against the fact that Frankie was not only nice (he'd give you good clues that could be used to solve your math homework) but also disarmingly candid about his own faults ("I'm such a dope at drawing!") and idiosyncrasies ("I always dot my Is first thing").

And yet, and yet—when the next section of the test began, and Frankie began to confidently color his bubbles, John felt he would not be displeased to see The Great and Terrible Osis finish him off for good.

*

At the dinner table that evening, John nervously knocked vegetable mix around his plate. The lima beans—pale, green alien eyes resting in a bed of carrot cubes and forlorn corn—were enough to make him gag.

"How was school?" Dad asked. "How was that test of yours?"

"If he did well," Mom said, "he'd have said so." Mom's brown hair swung pendulum-like on either side of her chin. Her green eyes narrowed, her lips nearly disappearing. She was upset—or suspected she had reason to be—and John would rather face a second helping of aliens than the interrogation that was bound to begin.

"Is it really that important?"

"It's a test!"

"I mean, it doesn't really count for—"

"Every test helps to determine your future."

"That's true," Dad said, reaching for another piece of white bread he could margarine to the edges.

Dad was a slight man—bony shoulders, thin wrists, narrow face, hazel eyes like the glass figurines in Grandma Alt's china cabinet. He was peaceful too, always good for a deferential smile. His job at the faucet company required him to be on the phone for most of the day, so when he got home he wasn't inclined to make yet another sales pitch. He was, in other words, no match for Mom, especially on the subject of education. A semester short of graduation, she had dropped out of college. There had been some problems—a sharp difference of opinion with her parents, a sudden move from Indiana to be with Dad, a subsequent falling out with nearly all her family members. "I'm a living lesson," was about all she would say. "A parable." What she didn't say lent terrible authority to what she did. John knew not to ask questions.

Dad nibbled the edges of his Wonder Bread. "Well, tomorrow's another day."

John glanced at Dad, who flashed a buttery grin. Mom, her fingers dancing like bug legs under her chin, broke into a sigh. On John's dinner plate, the pale green alien eyes stared, daring him to make a move.

*

Although there was no school the following Friday (a reward, he assumed, for having endured the trauma of those Iowa tests), John rose early, ecstatic at the thought of spending the day with Sandro, his best friend since first grade. Sandro lived on Medina Avenue, all the way across the interstate bridge. It was too far to walk—and "far too dangerous," Mom insisted—so Dad drove him over on the way to the work.

Mrs. Gismondi answered the door with a bright lipsticked smile. She wore a red and white checkered blouse and linen pants. Her hair was pinned up, face and neck and ears all fabulously revealed. Regardless of the season, she reminded him of the day school let out for the summer. Sandro came into the living room, dark hair still glistening from the shower. In his hand was a huge Lego spaceship, which he landed smoothly on the dark, luxurious shag.

After a pancake breakfast, the boys headed outside to play cops and robbers. Following a time-honored ritual, John counted on the back porch steps and Sandro scrambled off to hide. Usually, he settled on some place obvious—the crotch of the sycamore, the bed of his father's El Camino. This time, though, John had to search a long time, finding his friend at last under the tarp that covered his father's fig tree. John kicked at the covering until Sandro cried, "Christ Almighty!" When his friend peeked out, John shoved the muzzle of the Tommy Gun into his face, announcing with as much authority as he could muster: "You have the right to remain silent!"

18

Typically, Sandro would put up his arms and march willingly to the dirty prison underneath the front porch of the house. Once inside, he would shake the wooden lattice work and growl, "You haven't heard the last of me," and they would move on to other things. This time, though, Sandro stood up and batted John's weapon away with a hand.

"Anything you say can and will be used against you in the court of law," John said, shocked by his friend's behavior, but committed to the script.

Sandro's full, dark eyes blazed. "You gonna hafta kill me, motha sucka!" he screamed, taking off, head low, in a zigzag across the lawn. Before John knew what happened, Sandro was safely in the house.

John let the weapon fall by his side, the sound of the slammed door still ringing in his ears. Cautiously, he approached the house. A few minutes passed. He stepped onto the first cement stair then back down again. He watched two squirrels corkscrew up the tree. The sun went behind a cloud, and John, despite his jacket, was suddenly freezing cold.

Was this part of the game? Should he call out for Sandro? Should he go inside? Stay put? Maybe he would have to just go home. It was a long walk, though, and he'd have to cross the perilous bridge over the interstate. He could do it—he was almost sure—but then Mom would find out because John would tell her, too nervous and guilty to make up a plausible story. Certainly, the punishment would be harsh: no TV for a week, no dessert for the month. John found himself thinking about those harrowing Iowa tests. There were always four choices—A, B, C, or D—and if you really thought about it (if you weren't, as Dave Baske loved to crack, a "total retard") you could always eliminate one answer or maybe even two. The problem was that, in the end, you were seldom quite sure of the choice you'd made.

At a loss, John sat down on a pile of damp brown leaves. The tears arrived just as the back door opened, and his friend bounded down the stairs, wielding two cold cans of Faygo.

"What's wrong?" Sandro said with a hearty laugh. "See a ghost?"

"I thought," John said, unable to keep a whimper out of his voice. "I thought you were mad or something."

"Oh." Sandro glanced back at the house. "It was all part of the game! See, I was the black man, and you were supposed to shoot me dead when I was running away. Bam, Bam," he said, jerking his head from the recoil of an imaginary gun. "I would've died."

Sandro passed him a can of orange pop. Shoot you dead? John thought. Dead? He heard the word before—of course he did—but this time, for some reason, it poured through him and hardened like the concrete in the patio Uncle Lare put in last week for his parents. John took a long drink, letting the fizzy sweetness burn down his throat to dissolve the terrible mass. He drank again, but the word was still there, a hard, intractable lump. He took a third swallow, but by that point he knew that twelve ounces of pop wasn't going to make the awful thing disappear.

*

Time spent with the Gismondis was a thrill—not unlike those *Choose Your Own Adventure* books John loved to devour; time spent at home, though, was something else altogether. It was "quiet." It was "safe," perhaps, or "slow"—like Grandpa Alt at the checkerboard, knocking out his pipe while mulling his next obvious move. "Predictable" was yet another way of putting it. Every day during the week, Dad arrived home from work at 5:15. If this routine had to be broken, it was usually in order to do something of great domestic importance, like stop for a jar of spaghetti sauce or a four-pack of toilet paper, in which case Dad would call well in advance of the mission and Mom, deftly making the necessary adjustments, would time the supper for 5:45 instead. Afterward, John would wash the dishes and retreat upstairs to finish his homework or read one of his fantasy novels. Dad, still in white shirt and tie, would stick his nose in *Shipwrecks of the Great Lakes*, *Amazing Wonders of the Earth*, or any other of his many tomes of trivia. On the couch across from him, Mom would page through one of her many religious books that she kept around the house: Thomas á Kempis on the coffee table, Francis de Sales on the kitchen counter with the cookbooks, Fulton Sheen on the nightstand on her side of the bed. Each book had been well-thumbed and paper tongued. Recently, though, she'd become especially fond of Thomas Merton, to which Grandma Alt introduced her at Christmas last year with a present of *The Seven Storey Mountain*. "It's a book about seeking . . . and finding," Grandma said, hands pressed together over her heart. Judging by how often Mom placed that one in her lap, there must have been plenty to discover.

At 8 p.m., when he heard the TV go on, John would come downstairs, lie on the floor beside Dad's straight-backed chair, and watch the sitcoms of the night. He could have a snack—two Chips Ahoy! or a modest bowl of mini pretzels. When nine o'clock came, he'd wave goodnight and go upstairs to bed.

On the weekends, a few wrinkles were added to the routine. Saturdays, depending on the season, there was painting or leaf raking in the morning, patio or living room time in the afternoon, grilled meat for dinner to go with the canned or frozen vegetable du jour. On Sundays, long, quiet mornings before a box of plain cake donuts and *The Plain Dealer* comics were followed by mass at St. James the Lesser, where Fr. Nadolny gave homilies rivaling the length of the promised life after death. Following the release ("The mass is ended. Go in peace." "*Thanks Be to God!*")—following the equally torturous front step gossip with women Mom only saw once a week—came the long afternoon spent helping Dad with chores (cleaning out the garage, changing the oil or antifreeze) while Mom puttered around the house or fenced-in backyard.

The slightest trouble would make waves through the house for an entire week: Cousin Cynthia taking a round of antibiotics, Cousin William chipping a tooth during a T-ball game, Uncle Lare in another fender bender. These things would be examined, turned about in the light streaming down on their dinner table. Mom would invariably glean stern morals from such events, and John would take in the supper table adages with his family steak and baked potato and a stab or two of gross wax beans.

Events of larger import had a more difficult time slipping through, but like a fly through a screen door, they sometimes did. On most occasions, one parent or the other would just swat the bug to death; sometimes, however, the fly would be quick and persistent and Mom and Dad would just let it ricochet around until it died on its own. A year ago, John had heard the buzz about Dennis Kucinich, Cleveland's "boy mayor" who let the city tumble into default, a bad thing, whatever it was. And just this past winter, his parents couldn't stop talking about the United States hockey team, which beat the grim-faced Russians who spoke in deep, Dracula-like tones. The buzz followed him to school, where Denise Abney presented a tray of red, white, and blue cupcakes for the kids to consume. Brian Whittier brought his hockey stick and flipped balls of paper into a tipped over garbage can, throwing up his arms and saying, "Eruzione scores!" Sr. Regina, John's teacher at the time, hailed it as a triumph of good over evil, which sounded as right as anything to him.

A particularly huge and persistent fly buzzed into the house at the end of October in the form of a presidential debate—the last before the election. From what John gathered, this TV show was going to be an argument between two famous men about a number of problems facing the country. More thrilling—and the thing his parents could not stop marveling about—was that the debate was going to be held in downtown Cleveland, a mere ten minutes from where they lived. In the days leading up to the event, his parents began reading both *The Plain Dealer* and the *Press*. After Mom read what she wanted, Dad clipped pictures and articles to paste into a scrapbook—for "posterity's sake." John knew little about the two speakers. Ronald Reagan was one, a movie actor from the hard-to-believe days of black and white. With a name like "Raygun," John thought the man should have come from the future, or, at the very least, a galaxy far, far away; however, he looked like someone from the dawn of recorded time. Jimmy Carter was the other—the peanut farmer, the man with the Billy Beer brother, the current president. From what John gathered, the main knock against him was his inability to free some hostages from that country overseas. This had been a problem for a year now or more. Shortly after the Americans were kidnapped, John and his parents had been eating dessert in front of the local news when Gib Shanley burned that country's flag right on live TV. Sliding forward in his recliner, hands pressed together as if in prayer, Dad exclaimed: "Good for him!" Mom, just then walking into the room, said, "I thought you were watching the sports."

John heard little more about the situation until the day before the debate, when Frankie asked Miss Chumley to tell the class something about the people of Iran. Miss Chumley said she wouldn't waste her breath.

"Why?"

"They're monsters."

"They're people!" Frankie cried.

Miss Chumley narrowed her eyes and wondered aloud if he was trying to be a little Ayatollah. Not to be outdone, Frankie said that, in several important ways, she was not unlike the Shah.

"Go to the principal's office!" she cried, jabbing at the door. "Do not pass go. Do not collect two hundred dollars!"

"May I—"

"I don't have time for your little Islamic Revolution. Get out."

John didn't know what "Islamic" meant, but he was well acquainted with the word "revolution." Jefferson, Washington, Adams—from his father, John knew a few neat facts about them all—were heroes, deities almost, who risked their very lives for the great cause of freedom from tyranny. This revolution in Iran—must there have been something "good" about it as well? The question grew in John's mind like a bubble of gum—poof and poof and pop! Then it was recess, and Sandro brought out *Mastermind*, his board game of the week. Each tried to outdo the other, cracking codes in five moves, then four, then three.

"Look at the Terminal Tower!" Dad said now, pointing at the screen. As he took a sip of pop, ice clapped excitedly in his glass.

John pushed popcorn into his mouth and studied the building he had seen so often in person now crammed into the small screen in front of them. The skyscraper looked like a rocket ship ready to blast off. If John wanted to, maybe he could reach out, hold on, climb aboard. It was good to know that, should he want it, adventure was a short, sand-colored stretch of carpet away.

So much of the debate soared right over his head. Health care, inflation, national defense, those American hostages again—this was clearly a show for adults. But John continued to watch because it was happening in Cleveland, at the Convention Center, where he and his parents had been just this past February for the Home and Flower Show. Whenever cameras switched from one contestant to the other, John studied the background closely, trying to recognize some part of the building. Even if he had not been standing where these two men were now, he had been close—he had been in a place that might very well be on TV now. That had to count for something.

John dozed off but woke near the end of the debate, when the men offered closing remarks. The Raygun, his loose face giggling with good humor, zapped viewers with the simple question: "Are you better off now than you were four years ago?" Four years ago, John wasn't allowed to play in the front yard. Four years ago, if the baseball he bounced off the stairs rolled across the street, he had to go and find

Mom or Dad to retrieve it. Four years ago, he had to be in bed—lights out—by 7:30, so early he could still hear his friends on pleasant evenings chasing each other through neighboring yards. Was he better off than four years ago? Without a doubt—YES!

His parents, however, were of a different opinion. Throughout the show, they had murmured affirmatively after almost everything the Raygun said. When Mom went into the kitchen to make another cup of decaf, Dad called out: "There you go again," and she laughed—which was a rarity, like the two of them leaning toward each other for a morning kiss.

*

The day after Thanksgiving, John was reading a fantasy novel on the living room couch when the telephone rang. He cringed. This was usually about the time Uncle Lare, Dad's brother, called to apologize for what he'd done and said, three sheets to the wind, at dinner the day before. Mom would be on the phone for a couple of hours, saying things like "um hmm" and "sure" and "of course" and "we all have our failings." She would be as measured as could be. Afterward, though, she'd always be sharp with John: "Did you make your bed?" "Did you put away those G.I. Joes?" She'd keep grilling him with questions, waiting for the "no" that would justify her anger.

With great trepidation, he answered the phone.

"John," Mrs. Gismondi said, sniffling like she had a cold. "Be a hun and put your mother on."

Relieved, he handed the phone to Mom and returned to his novel, which was about a virus spreading through the country that made people move more and more slowly until they froze in place. The only cure, a young brilliant boy had discovered, was to keep doing different good things for people: buy a meal for a homeless person, give a child your coat, even just say hello to an ailing neighbor. Failing to convince parents or teachers of the solution, the young protagonist had to somehow get to the president—before it was too late. Thrilling as the book was, it was difficult to concentrate because from the kitchen Mom kept saying, "I see, I see," and "Yes, yes, yes, how terrible." When John looked up at last, the phone was back in its cradle, and Mom was staring at him, glistening green eyes between that pendulum hair.

"You," she said, her finger a wand of accusation. "You are

grounded for the rest of the month!" As John rose to protest, she slapped him across the face. Stunned, savaged by shame, he bolted up the stairs to his room, where he fell on his bed and burst into tears. What in the world had he done?

An hour later, when Dad came home from work, John crept down to peer through the spindles of the staircase railing. In a moment, Mom shuffled from the kitchen, kneading her hands under a black dish towel. Quietly, she said, "He is dead. Dead and gone."

Still by the door, one leg crossed over the other above the knee, a dress shoe dangling, Dad looked at her and said, "Good grief, who?"

"Frankie McGooken. The boy drowned last night in Brookside Creek."

Frankie? Dead? Name and concept appeared on opposite sides of John's brain. He closed his eyes, scrunched his face, tried like mad to move them together. The words, though, stayed exactly where they were, digging in heels like children in a fierce game of tug-o-war.

Mom went on with what she knew, and Dad interrupted with all kinds of questions: What time did it happen? When was he found? How deep is that creek? The one question neither of them asked (and the one that loomed before John like some fat-lipped bully) was: What was it like to be gone—suddenly, and once and for all?

*

Sunday morning, standing with a group of mothers in the vestibule of St. James, Mom said, "Just tell me this: What in the world was Frankie doing out there alone?"

"The parents are divorcing, you know," Mrs. Hyde said, as if that explained everything.

"He was collecting something for a science project," Mrs. Frears said. "Frogs maybe?"

"Why? Miss Da Via had the frogs," Mom said, arms two bars across her chest. "Last week, she ordered a whole habitat."

Mrs. Gismondi said if she had to bet, God forbid, which one of the parish children would meet an untimely end, she would have put her husband's paycheck on a boy with a tragic Irish name like Frankie McGooken.

"Lee Ann!" Mrs. Frears said. "What a thing to say!"

But the others, including Mom, nodded in agreement, only

slightly embarrassed that the comment could—or did—carry the weight of moral judgment on the mother and father and maybe even the dead boy himself. Sandro was home sick with the mumps, and beautiful Bethany Hyde stood twirling honey blond hair beside her mother. Ignored by everyone, John put a hand to his cheek, feeling the awful sting of his mother's slap coming back. It was more than enough to keep him in line.

Later that afternoon, John finished his novel, which ended happily with the boy saving the world, receiving a gold medal from the president, and winning the heart of a girl who reminded him of none other than Bethany Hyde. The protagonist acted, took incredible risks, succeeded against all odds. But Frankie was no fictional character. He was a real-life boy who could not stop being curious. He had to challenge every single thing in the world. He pushed his luck; consequently, he paid the ultimate price. Not that he deserved to die. No, no—that's not what John thought at all.

*

Frankie, of course, did not show up to school that Monday, but that didn't keep him from being the center of attention. His name was on everyone's lips, as if he'd done something heroic. The girls were misty eyed, the boys (for the most part) subdued. Dave Baske, much to his delight, was relevant again. With great elation, he unveiled a brand new name—"Frankie McSinken"—and Tim Sager, the weedy boy of few words, followed suit with "McGlubben" and then, even though maybe two kids dared to laugh, Dave added "McDeaden," which seemed to be the final word on the matter.

But Dave had so much more to say. He was just dying to pass along what he heard, the "startling truth" about what really transpired at Brookside Creek. It was recess, a snow-cloudy day, and the boys gathered by the oak tree in front of the rectory, where Dave sat cross-legged, a Bic lighter cupped in his hands—a little camp fire to set the mood. "Frankie sank and sank," he said, "his body was turning around down into the, the . . . the depths . . . the murky depths! And, and he was reaching his hand around to the middle of his back cause there was like a keyhole on that metal cage. He was trying to get the point of the key into the hole—"

"They found him in like a foot of water!" Lance Duda said.

Dave narrowed his eyes. "Like Houdini or something, only he

couldn't do it because he wasn't a magician, he was the one and only—"

"Human abortion!" George Sophronia exclaimed.

"And then, and then, he hit bottom, laid down there, and the minnows swam right through his ears."

"Sick!" Tim Sager said, which most of the boys understood as "Coolest thing in the world."

The wake was the following evening. Mom declared that John was "far too young" to attend and sent Dad as the family representative. John tried to kill any thoughts about Frankie by watching *Happy Days*. When the show went to commercial, there was without warning a long period of silent blackness. John waited. He bit his lip. Suddenly, he found it difficult to breathe. Clutching his throat, he stood up and rasped, "I'm going to die."

"Don't be ridiculous," Mom said, hand digging into a bag of potato chips.

At that moment, the technical difficulty was resolved and a commercial leapt to the screen. "Reach out and touch someone," a voice soothingly implored. Bright-toothed people moved around and smiled. All was right with the world again.

Later in bed, though, the fear came snaking back. Frankie is dead. Frankie is dead. John mouthed the statement over and over, and each time name and concept edged a bit closer together in his brain. He slid the sheet up to his neck, pretending it was the cool lid of a coffin. He closed his eyes and pulled the sheet over his head and lay there holding his breath. He lasted eighteen seconds—an unbearably long time. To be successfully dead, though, you had to hold your breath not for eighteen seconds or minutes or months or even years. You had to hold your breath for all eternity. There was no way he'd be able to do it.

"Frankie is dead," John said aloud, "and I am alive." His chest went up and down. There was the beautiful sound of breath soaring through his nose. "Ha, ha, HA HA ha," he said, hand upon swelling breast. Did it sound like he was laughing at Frankie? That's not what he meant—no, not at all. But the laughter was out there, echoing in the room, mocking his intention. He thought about God in heaven, furrowing his massive brow, crossing his huge, omnipotent arms. Sr. Marie always reminded the kids that the Lord was merciful, but that didn't mean there wasn't a hell where some people, by virtue of their crimes, were going to roast forever and ever amen.

Quickly—there was not a moment to lose—John scrambled to his knees and mumbled long apologies toward the cross that jabbed down at him in the dark. He waited, waited, waited for some kind of response, but there was nothing. Either that was a good sign or it wasn't.

*

A few days later, Denise Abney, fighting back tears, suggested a celebration in honor of what would have been Frankie's eleventh birthday.

"A celebration?" Miss Chumley said, her eyes rising from the mimeograph she was distributing.

Dave Baske sat up, whispering to no one in particular: "He had his day."

"A kind of service, with—you know—cake and stuff."

A joyful murmur made its way around the room. Sandro started a soft little chant: "Cake and stuff, Cake and stuff . . ."

Miss Chumley smiled despite herself. "Yes, yes," she said. "That is a splendid idea."

Every day for the rest of that week, time was set aside to prepare for the event. In art class, students were assigned to draw pictures of "life's abundant sacraments." For Language Arts, students wrote short poems and observations about their classmate. When the class was sent to Sr. Marie's room for Religion, they reflected on passages about life after death. In one of the gospels, Jesus said to Martha, the brother of Lazarus: "I am the resurrection and the life; whoever believes in me will never die." Sr. Marie stopped reading, cast her eyes around the room, and said: "Remember: This is what we as Christians believe." The children nodded. Sr. Marie read about how Jesus told the dead man to come out and so he did, body wraps dangling but pretty much good as new. John thought about Frankie's body. Perhaps the dead boy was soaring somewhere high above, sloughing off his back brace as if it were so much metal underwear for the hamper. Perhaps he was just now touching down on cozy clouds to begin his very own life everlasting.

But hadn't he died already? Wasn't his body in a box in a hole, six dark feet forever from the sun?

*

On the morning of Frankie's celebration, John arrived early at school with a foiled plate of oatmeal cookies. Immediately, he could tell something was wrong. Everyone looked stricken. Most of the girls and some of the boys were in tears that seemed to indicate some fresher, keener pain. John did a quick head count of his fellow students and was relieved to find no one missing. Miss Chumley was busy writing "IMAGINE" in perfect cursive on the board. After dropping the cookies off on a table in the back of the room, John headed for Sandro, who was playing paper football with a group of boys on the far side of the room.

"My dad says they should hang the guy by his balls," Lance said.

Dave said, "Maybe you could just suck——"

"Shut up!" Lance—a big boned kid, at least four inches taller than everyone in class— pushed Dave, and Dave, on tiptoes, put his fat chapped lips up in the other boy's face. They stood like that for a few tense moments, until the smaller boy's smile tore open like a bag of chips. Lance pushed him again, and Dave, with puckered lips, whistled all the way back to his desk.

"What happened?" John asked.

"You didn't hear?" Sandro said, wiping his eyes. "John Lennon's dead!"

The salty snacks and sweets, the heartfelt poems and tears, were supposed to be for Frankie, but John Lennon—the ex-Beatle, the peace freak with the cool round glasses and the long-haired Oriental wife—was dead. Dead and gone forever! Patty Breen, who had not two weeks ago given a report called "John and Yoko: Peace Everyone," was inconsolable. Denise Abney walked aimlessly around the room, clinging to her ponytail like a fraying rope. She didn't know who Lennon was but couldn't stop saying, "I hate his lousy guts!"

When the recess bell rang, Denise opened her desk for the card she made for Frankie. Everyone had to sign it, she announced, before they were allowed to eat anything at all. She encountered no resistance until she approached Dave, who was slouching in his desk, a ball point pen like a snake tongue in his mouth.

"Dead boys get no birthdays," Dave said, flicking the card out of Denise's hand.

Denise clutched the hem of her skirt and howled.

"David, David, I saw that," Miss Chumley said, pointing the knife she'd been using to cut the cake. "Go to the wall this instant. Do not pass go, do not collect—"

"Two hundred dollars—I know. I know!"

"No cookies, no cake. You don't deserve a thing."

Dave took slow, dramatic steps to the wall, his second home at school.

The ceremony began in earnest when Sr. Marie appeared, guitar case in hand. She led them in a short prayer about God and love and life everlasting. Then, one by one, the children came up to the front of the class to offer remarks about Frankie. Some read their poems, more than a few of which rhymed "died" and "cried." Patty Breen started in on a tear-soaked eulogy for John Lennon, and Denise stood up and declared, "Stop that now!" Heedless of her command, the other children rushed out their thoughts. Lance said that "Instant Karma" was the best song ever. Stinky George claimed that Lennon and his wife were "a bunch of nudists." Bernadette Miller, who always chose with great care her moments to be sassy, declared him "a saint." Miss Chumley finally restored order with clapping that sounded like gunfire from a tower.

"This is Frankie's day," Denise said when it was her turn in front of the class. "It's Frankie we're supposed to remember." She drew her ponytail across runny eyes and began to read her poem, "The Boy Who SO Loved the World." She tried three times, but couldn't get past the first line. At last, Miss Chumley escorted her back to her seat, murmuring, "he most definitely did." When John's turn came, he read from a folded piece of notebook paper—"Frankie was good at answers"—and rushed back to his chair.

By this time, Sr. Marie had the guitar slung around her neck. After a few tweaks of the tuning knobs, she began to strum and sing "Be Not Afraid." John felt tears roll down his face; however, since he was not the only boy crying (far from it), he made no move to wipe them away.

After a few short readings, it was time for what all the kids were waiting for. Miss Chumley, standing proudly over twenty-two paper plates of cake, clapped her hands and said:

"Okay everyone, please make a line in the center of the room."

While the kids went up for cake, Sr. Marie strummed "I Am the Bread of Life." Instinctively, the kids bowed heads and folded hands.

John happened to glance at Dave, who was now facing the room, moving his arms up and down against the wall. He looked like a bird, or an antsy Christ.

"Here you go," Miss Chumley said to John, thrusting out a plate of cake with a scripted O on top. Out of habit, he mumbled, "Amen."

Back at their desks, the girls wiped their eyes and blew their noses. Even the boys could only jab half-heartedly at their cake. But soon, sugar worked its miracle, and the children began having the time of their lives. The ceremony had been sad, but John was glad to have been a part of it. The songs, the prayers, the sharing of food—the staples of ritual were so comforting to him, like dinner at 5:15 or communion at 12 o'clock mass. There was something right and true and permanent about the day-in-day-out, the week-in-week-out, the again and again and again—everything like it had been since the beginning of his time, which, of course, was the beginning of all time.

John scraped his plate and let the last of the frosting linger on his tongue. He studied the cut out snowflakes, the crayoned scenes of Christmas, the shoebox dioramas of dinosaurs, of Jesus in the manger. A Kardiac Kids poster made him think of the Browns, 10-4, the Vikings coming up, a chance (Dad had told him) to win the division and go to the playoffs and maybe even the Super Bowl. Red and green lights blinked happily around the back windows. A few real flakes of snow swirled outside, and John, only a little bit itchy in his wool sweater, imagined he was wrapped up in blankets on the couch, munching an iced toaster pastry in front of the first of a long winter morning's worth of laugh-out-loud cartoons.

Never-to-Be

(Fall 1982-Spring 1983)

Mr. Bishop, the brand new teacher at St. James the Lesser, stood in a charcoal suit at the front of the room, reading from the class roster with the intonation of an epic movie god.

"Ce-leste Aar-on."

Each mighty syllable shook through John's bowels. He thought of *The Ten Commandments*, the grand, gaudy voices of God and Moses beside the flimsy burning bush.

"De-nise Ab-ney."

As Mr. Bishop crossed to the other side of the room, John felt his desk vibrate with fear. Instinctively, he sat up straight, then worried he'd be too conspicuous. From the hand that dwarfed the roster sprung fingers that on Dad would have easily served as wrists. Mr. Bishop's eyes, buried in the ruddy cliff side of the face, looked like sinkholes to eternity. Huge pimples of sweat dotted his forehead. Just one of those drops could probably drown John on the spot.

Mr. Bishop put down the roster to remove his jacket. The arms slipped and swung, and Ink flinched as huge shadows seemed to swoop over him. "I'm from Colorado—way up in the mountains," he explained, taking some of the bass out of his boom. "Still not used to all this humidity."

John studied the mouth—the powerful lips, teeth the size of headstones—and imagined his new teacher growing up: the first few years in a cabin in the Rocky Mountains, huge hairy feet dangling over a full-sized bed by the time he was three. His mother, fearing for life and livelihood, cast him out when he started to devour whole cows and pigs for dinner, and so with nothing but the clothes on his back he rumbled up and down the mountains with an oak tree for a club, and slept deep in a cave somewhere beside a three-headed something. Sr. Mary Grace, the principal, ever on the hunt for converts, had thrown a rope around his neck and dragged him all the way back to Northeast Ohio. Holding him down with the help of God, she had clipped his bone hard nails, sheared the excess hair, bathed him for a full week in Lake Erie, taught him the language, and stuffed him into this big black suit so he could stand in front of this group of sixth graders and make them fear for their lives.

"In-crease . . . Alt," Mr. Bishop said, trying too late to hide the incredulous rise in his voice. John splashed his eyes around the room: Bethany Hyde put two fingers over a soft, pink smile; Stinky George Sophronia snorted so hard he had to thumb back snot; Dave Baske, thank God, was slouched at his desk, eyes closed, fat chapped lips mumbling at his dreams. John had had every intention of approaching his new teacher to ask that Increase, his given name, not be spoken aloud for all the class to hear, but when the giant appeared in the doorway, briefcase like a chocolate Graham cracker at his side, he resigned himself to ridicule.

"Is there a boy by the name of Increase on the premises?"

"Actually," he somehow managed to begin, the second half of that word splintering into high-pitched pieces in the air. "It's just . . . John."

"John," Mr. Bishop repeated, trying the name out, as if it were even stranger than the one on the roster.

"You *could* call him Ink," Sandro said, his best friend suggesting a nickname he'd been calling John since the Fourth of July, when the Gismondis had taken him to see a fireworks display. "Ink!" Sandro had cried—a warning about an errant Frisbee bearing down on his skull. "Ink!" he said again, savoring the new name in his mouth. "Oh my God, that's great. A stroke of genius!" His friend grabbed a raw hot dog from the cooler and, placing it on one of John's shoulders and then the other, proclaimed: "I dub ye Ink!" Holding hands across camping chairs, Mr. and Mrs. Gismondi laughed heartily. Francesca, Sandro's moody older sister, offered a grudging, "How cute." It had been a perfect family moment.

And to think he'd almost not been allowed to go. "Something will happen," Mom had declared, making a steeple of her arms at the kitchen table. At a celebration last year, there had been a mishap—a near-tragedy: a woman—a pregnant woman no less!—had been struck in the leg by an errant rocket and had to be "rushed" to the hospital. "And besides," Mom continued, her monologue gathering steam, "Edgewater always draws a hundred thousand people. How can you promise me you wouldn't get lost? Kidnapped?" Mrs. Gismondi phoned to plead her case, and after considerable time, a compromise was reached. They would go to Lakewood Park, which was safer, and had what Mom determined was a "less threatening" display. At first, John had been disappointed, but things, for once, turned out more than well enough.

Mr. Bishop said, "Hmm, is Ink okay with you?"

Ink gulped. He nodded. He was trying to say it most certainly was.

"Increase is an interesting name."

"Buttcrease," a voice like a cool breeze blew in from the back of the room. Eager for the opportunity, the flimsiest excuse, everyone burst out laughing.

Ink turned to see Dave straighten out of his slouch, panicky eyes darting left and right. Someone, to his horror, had beaten him to the punch.

"Oh, we have a funny man—a genuine comedian," Mr. Bishop said. "What is your name?"

"I'm Macho," the boy said, standing up to bow.

Mr. Bishop made a "sit down" motion with his hand. Macho obeyed, but only after flashing a broad white smile around the room.

"People," Mr. Bishop said, clapping to disperse the giggles. "There's nothing funny about making fun of others. Do you want me to respect you?"

Macho looked at him, devilish smile lingering.

"Because I could just write you off as a troublemaker. I could make your life difficult."

Macho offered large palms to the sky. "Mr. Bishop sir, I didn't mean—"

"Please apologize to . . . Ink."

"Lo siento, mi amigo."

"In language he can understand."

For any other student, this would have been a moment of terrible humiliation. For Macho, still grinning away, it was sweet victory, a potent example of both his fearlessness and sensitivity. When he slouched back into his chair, a few girls sighed audibly, the delicious sound of Spanish still tickling at their ears.

As the school year went on, Ink wondered why no one made fun of Macho's name, which was at the very least as ridiculous as his own. When the dark-faced boy appeared the previous fall, why had no one joked about his oversized lips, his gunked up speech? The boy spoke haltingly, sounded like Indians in cowboy movies Grandpa liked to watch; yet from that first day he captivated the boys with his frank talk of sex. He used huge smiles, sensuous eyes, and silky streams of Spanish to dazzle the pretty girls. They were especially in awe of Macho's singular devotion to Jesus, and swooned every time he kissed the tiny gold cross around his neck before casually dipping it back under his shirt.

His allure was enhanced by the fact that he was an excellent basketball player. He had daily occasion to showcase his skills during recess, toying with the boys, most of whom had little control over their bodies. It was not uncommon for five or six of his classmates—the ones, at least, willing to endure what they convinced themselves was just a little good-natured humiliation—to surround Macho on the blacktop, trying to prevent him from getting to the basket. Flexing his brows, he would start from the top of the circle, dribbling right then left, bouncing the ball between his legs if need be before spinning his body through the flailing defenders to score an easy layup. Sometimes, in frustration, Lance Duda or Kevin O'Meara would just grab Macho's shirt in an attempt to hold him still, but he'd make the shot anyway. He'd smile and wag a finger at them, as if they were children who should know better.

To Ink, the most impressive thing about Macho was his total freedom from deliberation. No second guessing, no umms and ahhs, no waiting for someone else to do or say. Walking back from sharpening his pencil one morning, Macho told Bethany Hyde, "You look good." Smiling, her face reddening, she managed to say, "Shut up!" but only long after the boy was back at his seat. By Christmas break, Macho had established himself as both class heartthrob and leader, supplanting Dave Baske, who had no other choice but to remake himself into a brooding loner. Macho's influence, his rapid rise to power, made Ink seethe. He began to fantasize about the ways the dark boy might be destroyed—with bombs, rayguns, laserbeams and anything else his fantasy novels could help him imagine.

Sunday afternoon, the Cavaliers played the Celtics. Earlier, there'd been church and leaf raking, but afterward, Dad suggested they sit down together and watch the end of the game. World B. Free, the only star player for Cleveland, made two jump shots in a row, and the Cavs pulled within six. But then Larry Bird, whom Sandro's father always called The Very Last of the Great White Hopes, began to go to work. A jump shot here, an assist there, a steal followed by a behind-the-back pass to Kevin McHale, another splendid if less spectacular white guy. Slow, ugly, awkward, Bird was nevertheless a superstar, a millionaire, a world champion. Limitations, the lesson seemed to be, weren't the end of the world. In ten years, perhaps, he might be really something, but right this minute, Macho was the unquestioned king of the class while Ink, who'd been at St. James since the very beginning, remained a total nobody.

After dinner, he wrote up a book report for school at the dining room table. Dad had his nose in a book called *The Complete History of Flight*. He'd skip around such obese tomes, uttering cries of appreciation and surprise and meticulously recording his favorite tidbits of information in a small spiral notebook he kept on the end table next to his chair. There were all kinds of categories: "Famous Firsts," "American History," "War," "Out of This World." When the notebooks were finished, he put them in the bookcase for future reference.

"Laura Ingalls," Dad said, as if he were announcing the name of a guest at a ball.

Mom glanced up from her crossword puzzle, mouthing a word that might fit into a long train of squares.

"Did you know," he continued, eyes dipping back into the book to get the details just right. "She holds the record for the longest solo flight by a woman. 17,000 miles!"

"Really?" Mom's said. "The *Little House on the Prairie* woman?"

"No, no. Amazingly they're not related." Dad looked pleased to be able to correct this mistake. "You'd have thought it was someone like Amelia Earhart. Anyway, that's what I would have guessed."

Mom scratched a bit more at her crossword and then, glancing at the mantel clock, got up to turn on *The Jeffersons*. Dad set aside his book and slipped on his wire frames. The show had been on for years, but his parents had only recently, with some trepidation, begun to watch.

Dad had quickly come to love George—his outlandish speech, his pugilistic bobbing—while Mom thought Florence was a riot. To Ink, though, it often seemed like a whole world of Machos running amok. He gave up at the first commercial break, went upstairs with a barely audible "good night."

He slipped into his pajamas and opened his math workbook on the bed. He wanted to get back to his *Choose Your Own Adventure* book, but there were some problems left to do. Greater than, less than, or equal to? The questions were easy, but every time Ink wrote the less than sign he felt an uncomfortable twinge in his stomach. Ink was not greater than, not equal to. He was less than—much less than—just about everyone else in the world.

*

"Halt!" George Sophronia said, thrusting out his orange guard flag as Ink and Sandro approached the crosswalk outside school.

"Wash!" Sandro fired back.

George tried to tap the silver badge without looking down at his shirt. "I can report you."

When Sandro laughed, Ink took the cue and did the same. The WALK sign flashed, and George had no choice but to let them pass. Poor George, Ink thought. He'd been smelling bad for years, and Ink couldn't understand why. There was soap in almost every store you went to, and it didn't cost a lot of money. Sandro suspected it had to do with the weird food he ate. The boy's mother was Turkish, Nina Sissyan explained, to which Sandro said, "gobble, gobble!" When he gave his ancestor report last spring, George stuttered on about the Grecian archipelago before unveiling a pan of homemade Moussaka, which only Denise Abney liked very much. Ink was confused: was George Greek, then, or some malodorous fowl? Or, like some creature of myth, a hideous combination of both?

After school, Ink and Sandro stopped, as they usually did, at Ruby's, a convenience store on the corner of Fulton and Woodbridge. Bethany Hyde and Nina Sissyan were at the register buying bright shapely bottles of Orange Crush. Sandro smiled, but Ink, face fwumping on fire like the pilot light at home, studied the canned soups until the girls were safely past. Back at the beverage cooler, Sandro whispered, "So what do you think of Nina?"

Ink shrugged. For him, there was Bethany, and then there was a

37

huge undifferentiated mass of girl.

"She's a total fox."

"I guess." Ink risked a glance back at the counter to see Bethany bring the bottle to her lips.

"You guess?" Sandro grabbed his arm. "Give me your wrist." Ink let him flop it back and forth. "Just what I thought: You have a bad, bad case of HOMOTOSIS!"

"Shut up!"

Sandro slid open the refrigerator door, and cool, smoky air poured out around them.

"Get this," he said, jabbing a Dr. Pepper in his face. "We're shooting baskets the other day at lunch, me and Lance, and Nina comes up out of nowhere and says: 'You going to play this year?' And I, I was so cool and did not even look at her at first." He laughed. "Anyway, I dribbled twice and just let it go. Swish from fifteen feet! Then I turn to her with 'What do you think?' eyes, and she's smiling, looking at the basket and then at me, and, you know, one plus one equals two!" He pointed the bottle toward the closing door at the front of the store. "Man o man, she's just smiling until that stuck up Bethany comes and drags her away so they can do their giggly stuff."

Ink gritted his teeth. Tall, blond, with brown beanbag eyes, Bethany was the love of his life. He wanted to stick up for her—was almost ready to call Nina an ugly dog, but Sandro, grabbing a *Whatchamacallit* from the candy rack by the counter, said, "Look, if I buy this for you, will you try out for the team?"

Sandro had been playing on the CYO basketball team since the fourth grade, and since that time had been pushing Ink to get involved. It was one thing to occasionally play HORSE in Sandro's driveway, but to join a team and play official games with coaches and referees and people watching and drawing conclusions?—the thought was too much to bear. Then there was the whole problem of uniforms, those tight shorts and sleeveless tops that would expose Ink's skinny legs and pointy shoulder blades; changing with the other boys in the locker room; putting up with his teammates' disgust when he made a costly mistake. And if all that weren't enough, Mr. Bishop was now going to be the coach. Ink shuddered at the thought of the mountain man looming over him from the sideline, threatening landslide at his first false move.

"My mom would never let me," Ink said, and he took some comfort in the fact that he spoke the truth. A year ago, Mom learned during one of her post-mass confabs, that Kevin O'Meara had gotten his nose bloodied in a game. "It could quite easily have been broken" was her official word on the matter. Mom continued on with an impassioned monologue about the danger of unnecessary human activity. She didn't have to say so, but the undercurrent of her talk was Frankie McGooken, the classmate who drowned a few years ago at Brookside Creek. "Why don't you play a musical instrument?" she often liked to wonder. Violin, flute, guitar—the choice would be his. The thing was, Ink had no desire to play an instrument. Nor did he yearn to play basketball. More than anything, what he wanted to do was sit quietly at his desk and learn what his teachers had to teach him. He wanted to complete his homework and pass his exams and move unmolested through the remaining grades of his academic career.

"Baby," Sandro said, punching him in the arm.

"I am not."

"Boys, no fighting in the store," Ruby said. "House rules." Beside her was a TV on a stool; she shook the rabbit ears before slapping it once upside the head.

"Can I beat him up outside?"

Ruby shot them their change and said, "Shoo."

Outside, Sandro didn't let up: "A big fat drooly baby," he said.

"Grow up," Ink said.

Sandro grabbed Ink's clip on tie. "Bird makes the steal!" he cried, pretending to dribble. Ink lunged for him, but Sandro spun away and dunked the tie in the trash bin in front of the store. "And he SCORES!"

"Idiot. Creep!" Ink yelled. By the time he fished out the tie and refastened it on his shirt, Sandro was across Woodbridge with a mouthful of candy bar, and he was gleefully opening his mouth for more.

*

Ink wanted exactly one thing for Christmas. On a piece of legal pad paper, he wrote it all in CAPS: ATARI VIDEO GAME SYSTEM. He cut out a picture of the console from a Sunday circular and stuck it under a magnet on the fridge. Everyone else at St. James had had such a system for years, and if he wanted to play *Asteroids* or *Adventure*, he had to beg Sandro, who these days had moved on to Intellivision, which he declared was "much, much better for sports." How much longer could his parents deny him such a necessity if they wanted to think themselves "good"?

When the Alts arrived at Grandma and Grandpa's on Christmas Eve, Ink went straight to the living room and slid to his knees in front of the blinking tree. Lifting a branch here and there, he read gift tags. He studied the size and shapes of presents.

"Are you going to set up the board?" Grandpa asked, shifting in his recliner.

"I want to open presents." Ink took hold of one that seemed to be the dimensions of a video game system. The tag, however, claimed it was for Mom. "I hope I get what I really want."

"If it's meant to be," Grandpa said.

With a sigh, Ink took the checkerboard from the window seat and placed it on the ottoman. As usual, he made his moves quickly, with little thought about scenarios that lay ahead; When it was his turn, Grandpa scratched for a time at his pepper-haired chin before leaning forward to nudge a piece to a waiting square. Occasionally, he'd ask one of his vague and goofy questions—"How's tricks?" "What's gotten into Charlie Brown?"—and Ink, grateful for an easy challenge, talked through his wish list between double and triple jumps. Grandpa laughed gently at each of his mistakes.

"King me!" Ink cried once, twice, and again. In a matter of moments, victory was his.

While Grandpa set up for another game, Ink went to the kitchen for a refill of pop. Mom and Dad were chatting with Grandma as she finished icing poppy seed rolls at the kitchen table.

"Every year—I don't know how you do it," Mom said, stirring gravy on the stove.

Grandma, as usual, looked like she'd just returned from a five-mile run. She smiled weakly, wiping her brow with the back of a hand. "Me neither."

Dad laughed; Mom pursed her lips. Ink, nervously glancing from one to the other, took a two-liter bottle from the refrigerator, filled his glass to the brim, and slunk out of the room.

A half hour later, with "Happy Holidays" jumping through the old cabinet radio, the front door burst open. Groaning genially,

Grandpa got up to hug Aunt Ruth and Uncle Lare, the latter of whom looked seasonably glum with his unkempt hair and febrile eyes. Dad, rushing from the kitchen, patted his brother's back and tried hard to have a smile large enough for the both of them. He kissed Aunt Ruth, shook hands with her date, a tiny well-groomed bald man with a beard and thick black glasses. Ink was engaged to take the coats, and he dutifully stacked them in the back room. Back at the ottoman, he poured checker pieces into the box and folded the board over them, like he was fastening the lid of a coffin. He was old enough to understand that the warm, cozy part of the evening was drawing to a close.

By dinner time, the front door holiday joy had long since fizzled out. Smiles tightened. Family members spoke at a slightly higher pitch. Aunt Ruth talked at great length about overcrowded malls. Heavy lidded and unkempt, Uncle Lare was drinking again—one glass of wine after the other. To smooth things over, Grandpa raved about his wife's homemade spätzle. Dad declared the brown bird on the table to be the juiciest of turkeys in the whole history of holidays. Ink glanced from Uncle Lare to the tree. Back and forth, each time his throat constricting a little more. Regardless of what happened this evening, he'd still be able to open his presents. However, Ink wanted peace as well. And goodwill. And all that other sweet Christmas stuff.

Ruth's date, doing his best to be pleasant, asked Dad about his job, and Dad, as he was fond of doing, started at the beginning—with a story, with a bit of trivia. He talked about the founder of the company, a bright young engineer who invented the single handle faucet. "Back in the thirties, he burned his hand while washing up in one of those two handled faucets—you know, cold on one side, hot on the other. That won't do, he said. That's not how things should be." He was happy to let everyone know that the company had for years lived up to its motto: "How Things Should Be."

Mom interrupted Dad at that point to inform the table that he was really trying to make a point about vision, about ambition.

Dad nodded. "Now, if you can believe it, our faucets are often called the 'Cadillacs' of the industry."

"It sounds like you truly love your work," Aunt Ruth's date said.

"I'm proud of our products. I believe in them. It may be a cliché, but the customer is number one." The company was growing by leaps and bounds. He was excited by the possibilities for advancement.

Uncle Lare muttered into his wine.

"It's a career," Mom said, looking straight at him. "Lucas helps to provide the world with something people need."

Aunt Ruth, her head swaying—a nervous tick—reminded everyone that her date was a genealogist. With a touch of a hand on the wrist, the amiable man was more than happy to tell the story of a recent job, which took him all the way to rural England in an unsuccessful quest for a royal line. "The husband," he explained, "was convinced he went back to one of the Henrys." The genealogist searched parish records, town registers, wills. Slowly, carefully, he "pasted vibrant leaves to this man's family tree." The end result? No kings, alas, but a handful of distinguished nobles.

Throughout the tale, everyone (except sullen Uncle Lare) paid rapt attention. Ink wondered if the man had encountered danger: poisoned wine, a knife to the throat in a cobblestone alleyway, a high-speed chase past Buckingham Palace. The problem was, with those studious glasses and that bright bald head, he didn't look much like a man who'd be involved in international intrigue.

"So . . . you're a names person," Dad said, wiping his mouth with a napkin. "Bet you'll find this really interesting."

Ink cringed. He knew full well the story that was coming.

"Diane was seven months pregnant, I believe, and she was, forgive me dear, simply huge."

Mom reddened. The genealogist chuckled politely. Ink looked at Uncle Lare, who made not-so-furtive babbling motions with his hand.

"Just huge," Dad said again, determined to wring all possible laughter out of that observation. "I'd been reading this book about the real names of famous people. Did you know John Wayne's real name was Marion—that's right, Marion—Morrison? Can you believe it?"

"That's really something," the genealogist said.

"Anyway, I'm sure you all know Cotton Mather—the witch hunt preacher? Well, his father's name was Increase. Increase—now I bet that's something hardly anyone knows."

"At least you didn't name him Cotton!" Grandpa said. It was an old joke, and the laughter that followed did its best not to be tired.

"Increase—the name has deep meaning. I feel every name

should."

"Of course. So what does it mean?" the genealogist asked, leaning in, elbows on the table. Aunt Ruth squeezed his arm in gratitude.

"Well, if memory serves, his father wanted the name to stand for, let's see, the 'never-to-be forgotten Increase of every sort, wherewith GOD favored the country.'

Uncle Lare, who'd been sulking behind a newly filled glass of Beaujolais, sat up to ask what kind of increase this sorry excuse of a country was enjoying right now. He'd been divorced for two years, and Aunt Judy was getting ready to marry again, this time to a gregarious amusement park manager whom William and Cynthia just adored. To make matters worse, Uncle Lare, fired for pinning a colleague against a wall, had been out of a job for the last six months. This much Ink knew from animated discussions Mom and Dad had while they thought he was in bed, well out of earshot.

"Well, it's not another tax increase, thank goodness," Grandpa said. "I've had it up to here with big government."

Uncle Lare laughed derisively. "Then you must have hated the inauguration."

"Wasn't that your theme last year?" Mom said. Year after year, she complained about having to endure Uncle Lare's boorish behavior during the holidays, as well as his weepy telephone apologies, which inevitably followed. It was, for worse and worse, a family tradition.

"There's your big government," Uncle Lare said. "Sixteen million for a party the public can't even attend."

"Reminded me of the royal wedding," Grandma said. "Pageantry always gives me goosebumps." She looked down her arms to see if the memory was bringing them back.

Mom nodded. "We don't have kings and queens so…"

"Exactly!" Uncle Lare said, staring at Mom. "That's the whole point of America. Not having kings and queens. Somebody help me out here!" He turned to the genealogist, who etched at his skull with an index finger. Maybe he was writing something, Ink thought. A curse word, an S.O.S.

"If only that guy had killed him."

"Lawrence!" Grandma said, hand grasping the apron strap

against her heart.

"Him and the whole damn crew."

"Maybe," Aunt Ruth said, "maybe the table doesn't have to be a place for politics." When she spoke, she had the tendency to sway her head back and forth toward either shoulder. There was always an uncertain lilt to her voice. She didn't voice opinions—she gamely tried words out, like new foods on a plate her mother set before her.

"Politics is not a separate thing. It's out there," Uncle Lare said, waving wildly toward the kitchen, the living room windows. "It's in here. It's swirling. In and out and in between." He looked to the right and left. He took another gulp of wine.

"It's Christmas Eve," Mom said.

"Oh Jesus!"

"That's right, Larry. For once, you're exactly right."

There was peace—a delicate détente—until dessert, when talk shifted to travel. Ruth and the genealogist had been to New York earlier in the month to see *Joseph and the Amazing Technicolor Dreamcoat*, and Grandma wished aloud that she would one day be able to go. Maybe, she suggested, on their wedding anniversary. Grandpa scratched his stubble. "Too big," he said. "I'll take you to Playhouse Square. They get the Broadway shows sometimes."

"Wouldn't it be nice, though," the genealogist said, "if Cleveland had a little more going on? Ruth and I drove downtown the other day to see the lights, and I was shocked to see how little is there. So many boarded up shop fronts. Halle's is gone now. Higbee's won't be far behind. How many people shop at the Arcade? I was in Chicago last—"

"These days, everybody's moving out of town," Dad said. "West. East. South. Out, out, out. I wish we could afford a place in Lakewood, or Rocky River."

"I love your neighborhood," Ruth said.

"We used to. But it's changing now, almost on a daily basis. A few doors down there are these noisy people—these, well, not that it matters, but they are Puerto Ricans. They just moved in two months ago, and I can't for the life of me figure out how many of them actually are supposed to be living in that house. Diane's home all day, and there's this constant stream in and out of the door."

Mom nodded grimly. "And their cars. Loud, rattle trap things…"

"Are you sure they're Puerto Ricans?" Uncle Lare asked. Everyone was drinking coffee now, but he had just opened a new bottle of wine. "They could be Mexicans, or Dominicans. Wouldn't it be something if they were Spaniards?"

"They're Puerto Ricans," Mom said.

"Please," Grandpa said, hands patting the air before him. "Grandma has been working hard in the kitchen for the last two days. Let's show our appreciation by finishing the meal in peace." He bit into a golden wedge of apple kuchen to show everyone exactly how it was done.

"Here, here," Dad said, a teardrop of sweat sliding down each sideburn.

Uncle Lare performed a livid drum roll on the table before standing up and swaying toward the bathroom. In his absence, there was only the clinking of coffee spoons and the mumbled requests for dishes to be passed.

"Anyway, the point is, before we . . ." Dad said, trying to restore normality. "With the name, I was just thinking more in personal terms, how our son here, after so many years, filled us with never-to-be-forgotten Increase."

"A beautiful sentiment," Grandma said.

Dad swiveled in his chair, as if expecting Uncle Lare to pounce on him from behind. "I hope, too, that he'll increase something in the world. Increase the good." He patted Ink's shoulder. "Is that too much to ask?"

Ink wished for the courage to plug a napkin in Dad's mouth.

Grandma said, "There's never enough good in the world."

"Here's to good works," the genealogist said, raising a glass of wine.

"And faith," Mom added. "Faith and good works."

"Amen," Aunt Ruth, swaying her head back and forth.

"Amen," said everyone else.

*

January, February—daylight an incredulous eye blink, snow every other morning, the wind gnawing through coats, ski caps, and gloves. Then one day, improbably, it was March and so warm that the sidewalks and streets became gray channels of slush. Ink was thrilled that time decided to wake up again, and he was standing behind the telephone pole in front of Ruby's, dodging snow balls hurled by Sandro and Lance. When he managed to take Sandro's hat off with a well-placed fastball, his day was made; he didn't even mind when his two friends chased him down and blasted him at point blank range. With his Eskimo coat, he was impervious to their fire.

While the three pooled money to see what they could buy at Ruby's, Macho came loping up, deftly stepping over puddles that yawned across the sidewalk. He smacked them all on the shoulders in that way he had of making everyone seem like a good friend, when all he was looking for was an audience for what he had to say.

"You've got to hear this, man," he began, bright white teeth between those big, brown lips, shoulders going up and down as if even standing had to be some kind of dance. Sandro and Lance returned the smile, thrilled Macho had chosen them for confidantes. Ink despised the cocky boy, yet right now even he could not keep his lips from curving up.

So what they had to hear, what was so amazing and important, was the story of how Macho had gone back up to the classroom to get a book he'd forgotten and Bethany Hyde was all alone, washing the blackboard. On his way back out, he walked past and, on a whim, flipped up her skirt with a pen. She said, "you pig!" and threw the wet rag at him, which he caught with no problem before moving toward her to say, "Where do you want it?" To which she said—get this— "Wherever you want to put it."

"No way," Lance said.

Macho punched him. "Calling me a liar?"

Lance held his arm, as if it might otherwise fall out. "I'm just...ow! She really said that?"

"Want to hear the best part?"

Sandro and Lance were laughing, eyes ravenous for more. Ink wasn't surprised at Lance, who'd laugh at a door if you told him it was funny. But Sandro, his best friend in all the world—how could he encourage such vileness? He knew Ink worshipped Bethany. There were times when Ink felt his eyes physically dragged from the board upon which Mr. Bishop was scribbling out some math problem and toward those tender lips, the brown beanbag eyes, the blond hair spilling around creamy cheeks. Last week, she'd caught him staring, and she looked right back—at him, through him—her beautiful face unmoved.

Macho was in the middle of talking about some kind of dance he and Bethany had done in that empty classroom, the rag in his hand, both of her hands wrapped around his wrist in order to keep the sloppy thing at bay.

"Aw man," Lance said, eyes beginning to glaze.

"You shouldn't talk about her," Ink said.

Macho smiled. "Man, I'm not talking about her. I'm just telling you what she did." He turned back to Sandro and Lance to say in a low, slick voice, "And what she let me do." To give them a better idea, he put a finger through the tight hole he'd made with his other hand. He pulled it out and pushed it in—in and out and in and out, the hole growing wider until Lance and Sandro roared.

Ink heard the rush of something coming down from a small, black room behind his bones. At first, he thought it was the rush of fear; however, when it arrived, there was only anger—a white scald of wind like he'd never known before. It melted the triple bolted door he kept himself behind in one terrific flash, and the next thing Ink knew he was saying, "You . . . You . . . prick." He looked into the boy's dark face, fixated on that flattened nose. "You," he said, the next word teetering like a Lego tower on his tongue. "You . . . spick!"

Macho's lazy smile disappeared, replaced by a slack-jawed blankness. There was a twitching of the cheek, a flaring of the nostrils, an ominous inflation of eyes. The boy's breathing grew and grew and grew and just as Ink began to think how much the sound was like his bicycle pump he found himself flat on the ground. It took him a few moments to realize that Macho had been the cause.

Only then did Ink become aware of the utter stupidity of what he had said. Macho stood over him, fists clenched, breathing pouring out of his mouth. Lance and Sandro inched away, eyes blinking. Ink decided that the simplest, most sensible thing to do would be to just get up, dust himself off, and walk quietly home. However, Macho's hand met Ink's chest as he tried to rise, and he found himself again back on the sidewalk. He tried to get up again, and the same thing happened. Instead of giving it another go, he remained on the ground, fingers probing a somehow bloody lip, absorbing the machine gun splatter of Spanish from above.

"Get out," Ruby's cried, appearing out of nowhere. "Get out of here—all of you!" The woman struck Macho twice with a broom on the head, and he backpedaled, stumbled, eyes filled with pain and surprise. "I don't want your business." No one was near Ruby now, but she kept ripping that broom through the air. Below her on the ground, Ink felt each swoosh of air like the cool wash of relief.

"And just so you know," Macho said, retreating down the side street, "I'm a nigger too!"

"I'm telling," Ink cried. "I'm telling what you said!" Macho was across the street already, stomping away, hand in the air as if flinging Ink from his back. Lance ran after him, patting the boy on the shoulder, spewing consolations, as if *Macho* were the injured party.

"Forget about it now," Ruby said, lifting Ink up with one hand under his arm. "Get home to your mother."

After Ruby went back inside, Sandro inched back across the street.

"Are you ok?" he asked, still at a distance, but with a hand out now to help.

"Go away," Ink cried. "Go chase your little faggot friends!"

Sandro pursed his lips. He walked away without a word. After crossing the street again, he even seemed to pick up the pace, closing the gap between himself and the other two boys. He didn't run, though—Ink had to give him that. At least he didn't want to make his treason obvious.

On the way home, Ink began to feel good about himself. After all, he'd struck a serious blow to Macho and made the smooth boy lose his cool. He thought of Lance and Sandro, "wimp" and "chicken shit" scrawled across their faces, and licked his lips, grateful for the blood that had been drawn. He chewed long and loudly on that powerful word he used: "spick, spick, spick." Each utterance was crisp and delicious, like a chunk of Easter chocolate snapping off into his mouth.

When he came in the front door, Mom was folding towels on the living room couch. "My God, what did you do?" she cried, running to him, grabbing his arm. It was a simple question, but it brought back all the shame and horror of a half hour before.

"There was this boy . . ." he said, and already she was dragging him to the kitchen, pulling off his ruined shirt, dabbing at his face with a dish towel and asking, "Why did he hit you?" in a voice that unexpectedly seemed to inch to his side. Before he knew it, he was leaning hard against Mom, crying, "I don't know, I don't know," resigned to the fact that she'd find out the whole sordid story from one of the mothers after mass. If only Dad could lose his job and be barred for some reason from every working in the city again. Then they could pack their bags and move—to Youngstown, to Western Pennsylvania (even Pittsburgh, if need be), to a place where he could be a no one once again. As usual, though, his father came home at 5:15, more tired than usual, but still gainfully employed.

"Goodness," Dad exclaimed, slipping off his shoes. He sat down with Ink on the sofa, eyes full of empathy. He was happy to have someone else to tell the story to. The second time through he told it much better, clarifying the sides, doing a better job of making Macho out to be the monster that he was. When he finished, Dad smiled and put a hand on Ink's shoulder. "Well," he said. "I have a good feeling this will all blow over by Monday."

It was the weekend—for that, Ink thanked almighty God. But Monday, of course, would arrive soon enough; by then, everyone in the world would know what happened. Dave would probably be waiting at the classroom door with some new detestable nickname for him. Bethany, ignorant of Ink's motivation for the fight, would cut him to the ground with one dismissive slant of those big brown eyes. Macho, upon seeing Ink's wounds again, would be inevitably reminded of the word Ink had punched him with. Who was to keep this combustible boy—this, this spick—from shiving a number two pencil in Ink's spine when Mr. Bishop's back was turned? Surely not his fellow students. In fact, Sandro and Lance would probably crowd in with everyone else for a great big belly laugh.

And that would be Day One! What additional horrors would be in store for Tuesday? For Wednesday? For the rest of his grade school days?

Late that night, Ink sprawled in his beanbag chair playing Pitfall on his Atari. He'd received the console for Christmas—a dream come true—but already this game was a total bore, just an endless series of jumps over quicksand and scorpions. After twenty dull minutes, he decided to see how quickly he could kill himself off. He pushed reset and ran headlong into a log. Then he sprinted into a hole. Finally, he jumped into the mouth of a chomping gator. He killed himself like this for a good long time, images of the afternoon fight splicing through his thoughts.

Later, Ink climbed into bed and found himself chewing again on the word he'd left out of the story he told his parents. Where had it come from? His parents often said things like "The neighborhood is changing" or "They don't know how to behave themselves," but they would never be caught dead using such a word. Mr. Gismondi, perhaps? There were times when Ink was visiting when Sandro's father would come into the room, a beer in hand, and speak with great passion to his wife about the bad influence of "the blacks and browns" on American society. Perhaps Ink had just breathed it in—like airborne particles from the steel plants in the Flats. He tried out his word again, mouthing it at first and then speaking it clearly into the darkness. His face crunched up. Suddenly, it didn't taste so sweet anymore.

Trouble, Mr. Majeski's beagle, began to yap, as if seconding the thought. Ink bent back the blinds and watched the dog run his nose back and forth against the fence. Just about anything set that animal off: the cry of a child, a car starting up down the street, an ice cream wrapper skittering across the driveway. It was always something, especially if it was nothing.

Ink tossed and turned. He put a pillow over his head. The word he used was bad—there was no question. But hadn't Macho said much worse—the N-word, for God's sake! Never in a million years would Ink utter anything as terrible as that.

Trouble continued his yapping, and Ink, at wit's end, yanked open the window and tried to stare the animal down. Oblivious, the thing kept going: yap, yap, yap, yap, yap. Ample food and love of owner and plenty of room to roam—what in the world did the animal have to complain about?

"Shut up!" Ink screamed at the top of his lungs. "I hate your guts!"

The dog looked up, cocked its head as if trying to determine just what it was dealing with. Mr. Majeski's back door opened, and the old man came out, bathrobe flapping.

"Hey, girl," he said gently, in a tone he often used with the wife he no longer had. "What's say we call it a night?"

Ink eased down the window, let the blinds fall. Why couldn't he have even the modest pleasure of putting an animal in its place?

Back in bed, the words continued to swirl around him: spick and nigger, spick and nigger. Was it true that Macho was black as well? Puerto Rican *and* black? Ink closed his eyes and covered his mouth, trying to shut out the words but they—and many others, like guilt and shame—were still there, throbbing inside his body. Spick, spick, spick, spick, spick—each thought was now a stab of pain, forcing itself upward through the skin until he could bear it no more and he kicked off the covers, mashed his face against the pillow, and cried to God, "I'm sorry, I'm sorry, I'm sorry," even as he understood that the only real escape from the pain would be through the cold, dark crucible of the confessional booth.

*

St. James was empty and echoey, quiet and warm. Ink slid into a pew in the back, kneeled and crossed himself. Glancing back at the confessional, he noticed the red light above the door, which told him Fr. Nadolny was busy hearing the sins of someone else. It was good to know that there was at least one other guilt-ridden person in the parish.

Waiting in the pew was like the final hours before a test: abject dread, memory-erasing panic, failure like a shovel of dirt thrown over his body. Ink focused on the altar—the long table clothed in simple, immaculate white. He imagined Fr. Nadolny standing behind it an hour or so from now, the host transforming before his very eyes. Yes, he would stay for five o'clock mass. He would place the wafer on its tongue and let it do its healing work.

The confessional door opened, and Ink was surprised to see Mrs. Gleeson—bingo volunteer, occasional lector, and recent widow— doddering out of the booth. What sins could this woman have committed? How terrible would his own sound juxtaposed with hers? He was tempted to just get up and go, but if he did, he'd have to pass Ruby's, the site of his humiliation. He could go the back way home, of course, but there was the Doberman on 38th that sometimes got loose in the neighborhood. Even were he to make it past unmolested, he'd come through the front door and be teased by the wonderful smell of family steak he would not, in his guilt, be able to enjoy. If he did not now tell the priest all—especially the word, the terrible word— his day would be hellish.

51

He crept into the booth and softly closed the door, praying Fr. Nadolny would not hear him. Perhaps if he just stayed in this room for a certain length of time—a minute, maybe, or even ten—he would be magically absolved.

"Hello," Fr. Nadolny said after a seemingly interminably time. "Yoohoo, anybody in there?"

"Uh, yes Father. Bless me Father," he said, actual audible words slipping through the screen. "Bless me Father for I have sinned, and I feel so bad about it" and, just like that—hard, copious tears. Could life get any worse? Could Ink sink any lower in the eyes of the world—in the eyes of God hovering in the darkness that entrapped him?

"I called someone a name . . ."

"A name?"

"A terrible name."

"What was it?"

"A . . . a . . . spick."

"I see," the priest said. To Ink's relief, he sounded more concerned than shocked. "Why did you do this?"

"I wanted to hurt him. To punish him for . . . for something."

"Did you hurt him?"

"I think so."

"Did it make you happy? To hurt this person?"

"For a second. And then he . . . *we* beat each other up." This, of course, was not close to the truth. It was another sin, perhaps, but one Ink could live with.

"Fighting too? These days, everybody's fighting."

"But he used a name too. A worse one!"

"Hmmm, whose confession is this?"

"Mine, father."

"Ok then. Name calling, fighting—tell me, is this the kind of world you want to live in?"

"No."

"How do you feel now about what you've done?"

"I am ashamed."

"And are you really, truly sorry?"

"Yes, Father. I am sorry."

There was a silence. Ink dutifully awaited his penance. Five Hail Marys he figured—because that's what it had always been in the past. Maybe Fr. Nadolny would add two more for the gravity of this sin, but Ink could manage that; in fact, he couldn't wait to get started.

"Tell me, are you going to see this person again?"

"Yes father. We go to the same school."

The priest cleared his throat. "In that case, your penance is to apologize to him."

"What about the Hail Marys?"

The priest chuckled. "Oh, I'll give you some Hail Marys, don't you worry about that. But I also want you to go up to this person, look him in the eye, shake his hand, and say: 'I'm sorry I hurt you.'"

Ink couldn't imagine ever looking Macho in the eye again, much less telling him how sorry he was.

"Can't I just say the prayers?"

"Make God happy. Make yourself happy."

"I want to be happy," he said.

"Will you do this then," Fr. Nadolny continued, "and sincerely mean it? Because if you aren't going to mean what you say, there's not much of a point in your being here."

Saying no to God's intermediary would be no different than saying no to God Himself, whom he imagined was sitting in his throne directly above him, arms crossed, impatient for an answer. A "yes" would immediately release him from one burden only to heap another upon him—the burden of meeting the angry eyes of Macho, of groveling before him, of begging for forgiveness. No, yes, no, yes— either way seemed terribly hard.

"Yes, Father," he said.

"I am happy for you, son. Our Father in heaven is happy for you."

"Thank you, father."

"Now, is there anything else I can help you with?"

Ink wanted desperately to say that the whole thing had been Macho's fault. Macho Maldonado, a sixth grader, the basketball wiz who lives over at 11332 Woodbridge Avenue. Yes Macho: that's spelled M-A-C-H-O. He was the one who started everything with that crude story about Bethany Hyde. He was the one who was always dirty and lewd, and no one—not even Sr. Mary Grace—seemed to care at all. He could have said all this and more, but he heroically bit his tongue and forced a "No, Father" through the screen.

"Life's not easy, but if you can do your best to say 'yes' to our Lord every single moment for the rest of your life, you'll be just fine."

"Yes, Father."

"Go apologize to this person . . . and, while you're at it, say Three Hail Marys and two Our Fathers. Think you can do that?"

"Yes Father."

"But just don't say these prayers. You need to let each word enter into your soul. "Hail Mary, full of grace . . .""

And Fr. Nadolny went through the prayer line by line while Ink fingered his knuckles like rosary beads, praying, "let me out, let me out, oh Lord please let me go!"

"Now, and at the hour of . . ."

Now. Now. Of all the words of that prayer, "Now" was the one that donged in his head with church bell clarity. Now he was forgiven. Now, right outside the confessional door, there was his new good self waiting, shiny and clean as a Camaro from a car wash. If he could be this new self this very second and the next and the next after that, by Monday, he would have accumulated such a staggering amount of exemplary moments that he might be too sanctified for sorries. Now, his classmates could surround him, call him names, shove him to the blacktop, grind his face into gum wrappers and glass. Now, he would suffer their abuse in silence. Now, God willing, he could be a martyr for the cause.

Basketballwise

(Fall 1984-Spring 1985)

"It's not like anybody's asking you to serve," Sandro said, giving several preparatory taps to a fat paper football with an index finger. On the other side of the desk, Ink touched thumbs together to form a goalpost. He closed his eyes, imagined tripping over his cassock and spilling wine—no, blood!—across the sanctuary floor.

"I like watching," Ink said.

Sandro flicked his finger and the puffy white triangle spun like a morning star through the air, striking Ink squarely in the forehead.

"And the extra point is good!" Sandro exclaimed. "42, no make that 49-7."

Ink got up and retrieved the football. At the back of the room, a group of excited boys surrounded Dave Baske, who'd quietly let it be known that he was in possession of a *Penthouse*—the Vanessa Williams issue. He was relevant again in a way he hadn't been in years; for a short while, even Macho Maldonado—the school's heartthrob, the basketball star, Ink's sworn enemy for life—had been temporarily reduced to satellite. Ink ignored the buzz, the whispers about where to meet for the clandestine unveiling. It was, of course, the worst kind of sin to look at naked women.

"You've seen me," Ink said. "I can't even dribble."

"Don't need to dribble. Macho dribbles. Lance rebounds. Kevin passes off. Sean sets picks. I shoot. You can come off the bench to wave your arms."

He knew painfully well the consequences of being out of his depth. Last spring, there'd been a field trip to Estabrook. Not knowing how to swim, Ink made sure to stay in the shallow end of the pool but then, somehow, lost amid the splashing and screaming, mesmerized by the sight of Bethany streaking from the diving board in her slick green one piece, his tippy toes lost contact with the bottom of the pool and the water, greedy and opportunistic, swallowed him whole. He flailed in slow motion toward the squiggling legs of classmates.

Frankie, Frankie, he thought—the boy who years ago drowned in Brookside Creek. Round steak, chocolate donuts, Donkey Kong, Mom's perpetual scowl, plaid skirt dancing above Bethany's knees—the images from life spun with his body in the water until two strong hands pulled him by the armpits from the pool and deposited him on a plastic chair. Mrs. Forbes, the gym teacher. "You're okay, you're okay," she said, wiping Ink's face between his tortured coughs. By the diving board, Macho stood, black hair slicked, mouth bouncing like a superball with laughter.

"Or," Sandro said, "you can just ride the bench. It's also the front court seat for the cheerleaders."

For the third year in a row, his friend pressed him hard to join the basketball team. It was yet another invitation to this after school world, a magical land populated by pretty girls—Bethany, of course, and Bernadette Miller, and Nina Sissyan (Macho's "Holy Trinity"—in that particular order) who, like superheroes, disappeared into the locker room before games wearing drab sweatshirts and jeans and emerged in resplendent blue and gold, jumping and kicking along the baseline, pompons in the air, teeth shining, eyes ablaze. At a holiday tournament game last year, Ink saw Macho dive out of bounds for a loose ball and crash into Bethany and Bernadette, who were sitting cross-legged on the floor. The girls laughed, blushed, pushed him playfully away. Macho stood and soaked in the moment before shrugging punkishly back down the court. Ink was not athletically gifted, but even he might be able to throw himself into Bethany's unsuspecting lap.

"And, the thing is, it's not all about the games." Sandro dropped his voice to tell him something he'd been keeping secret since it happened at the end-of-the-season party last spring. Ink had probably been watching *Love Boat* and *Fantasy Island* on that Saturday evening while the cool kids gathered at Lance's to devour pizza and chips and, once Mr. Bishop left and Mr. and Mrs. Duda went upstairs to watch TV, play Truth or Dare. Macho, of course, took the dare and Bernadette, her freckled face coloring, cried out, "Slow dance with Bethany!" Everyone, of course, said, "ooooooh," but Macho just pulled her up out of the chair with one hand and she snapped to his side while Lance cued up "Little Red Corvette" and, get this, Macho was moving his hips like Prince himself, moving his "thing" (here, Sandro had to stop to laugh), his, well, you know into her and she was just laughing and throwing her head back, with that blond hair falling towards the floor. All the while, Ink had been sitting home in low wattage lamplight with a bowl of stale popcorn, watching Tattoo jab a pudgy finger at an incoming plane.

That wasn't the only thing, Sandro said with a wink. Later, Sean foolishly took a dare and had to stay in the laundry room with Marie Katz for three whole minutes and half way through, with everything quiet, Macho said, "Maybe he's milking her," which, Ink had to admit, was pretty hilarious, a definite advancement over the tired nicknames of "Cow" or "Fat Katz." Sandro tried not to laugh much because Nina, whom he thought was cute, had turned away to study the wallpaper design. Like Bethany, he just flashed a smile and shook his head, as if he only barely approved. But make no mistake, when he was walking home with Macho and Lance later on, they laughed so hard about Fat Katz, he thought he was seriously going to die.

Sandro finished his story just as he once again nudged the edge of the paper football over Ink's side of the desk. "55-7," he said. "Man, anybody ever tell you that you royally suck?"

Friendly ribbing from his best friend—he could handle it. But he'd seen enough of organized sports—with the constricting uniforms and set plays and referees and urgent red numbers on a game clock ticking down down down—to understand it for the minefield that it was. He'd seen firsthand the chaos of bodies, the collisions and the cries of pain or outrage, the angry exhortations of coaches as they stomped the floor, the admonishments of parents who cupped hands over mouths to tell sons to "wake up!" and "front your man!" Nothing good could come from stepping on the court.

"What's that now? 62?" Somehow, Sandro had scored yet again and was lining up for another extra point.

"I quit." Ink said. Recess was over anyway, and they had to grab their books to head down the hall for science.

"You can't just cave when you're down. We'll continue tomorrow."

After school that day, Ink leaned against the school wall by the dumpster waiting for Sandro to finish wishing Nina a happy birthday. He handed her something—a square, black box. Slowly, reverentially, she opened it, stroked strands of hair from her face to better see. "It's beautiful," Ink heard her exclaim. Sandro tapped on his lips, and she stood on her toes, that floppy hair hiding his best friend's face. Did she kiss him? Did she really kiss him?

Sandro's eyes were brilliant, his lips wet like he'd just had something cool to drink. Ink waited for the details, but his friend just said, "Did I tell you there's a car wash this Saturday?" It was being held in the parking lot of St. James to raise money for a spring tournament in Columbus. Bethany would be there and maybe Ink could, you know, accidentally squirt the hose at her boobs. Such things had happened before.

Ink smiled. He replaced the image of Sandro and Nina with a brief movie featuring Bethany in denim cut-offs and a flimsy blouse, crunching up her face, saying "Don't you even dare!" as he shot a blast of water from point blank range. She scraped soaked hair out of her face, holding her nose, and . . . laughing, really losing it, thrust her hand in a bucket and sprinted after him with a soaped-up sponge. He grabbed her hands, trying to twist the frothy thing away. Slumped against the rectory fence, Macho burned with jealousy, while Ink, with the beautiful girl's fresh wet face inches from his, gleefully ignored him.

"Ok," Ink said. "Maybe I'll stop by."

"Next thing you know, you'll be trying out for the team!"

"Maybe I will." There was no question: playing basketball for St. James would be filled with pitfalls. But who was to say that, even if he made the team, he would ever see significant time on the court? And even a bench warmer would be able to enjoy the many social benefits. Just as he began to feel a spark of excitement, he thought of Mom— the fused lips, the pendulum hair. "I'll have to see."

For the next few days, Ink replayed his mind's movie countless times, honing it here and there to make Bethany more adorable and Macho more of a pathetic jerk. The only thing he hadn't accounted for was waking up ill on the day of the wash. His stomach gurgled and popped; his bowels rumbled. The night before, Dad had taken the family to a no-nonsense family restaurant on Memphis run by Mr. Krauss, a long time parishioner at St. James. Ink had ordered the tuna melt, and as soon as the first bite he knew it didn't taste right; however, the last thing he wanted to do was cause a scene, especially since Mr. Krauss was one of Dad's few good friends. Now, minutes before the wash opened for business, Ink filled a bucket with water, his stomach turning ominously as the bright suds ballooned to the rim. He tried desperately not to think of the word "mayonnaise" and then of course all he could see was a bowlful of that creamy substance ripening in the sun. There was entirely too much saliva in his mouth. He swallowed, but it didn't help much.

The first hour of the wash was slow—mostly a lot of standing around after the buckets were filled, boys in one group, girls in another. Lance went on about some boy who'd just moved into the area, six feet two, a friend of his cousin's, a "black kid," and he was going to play for St. Boniface. Joey Accorsi, a squat, jovial boy, said "maybe one of us'll have a growth spurt," and Macho, eyes sweeping over the girls, simply repeated the word "spurt," busting up the boys better than Robin Williams. Standing stiff to quell a sudden spasm in his bowels, Ink smiled weakly. He glanced at Bethany, dazzling in a red Indians jersey and bright white shorts. Would a body like that ever give an illness the time of day?

After Kevin's father, only the third customer of the morning, drove out of the lot, Mr. Bishop raised his sunglasses and studied the traffic buzzing down Fulton Road. He scratched his cheek. "Rosalinda," he said matter-of-factly, "you've got legs. Go out there will you and see if you can bring them in."

Standing on the periphery of the chattering girls, Rosalinda Cabrera blushed. She picked up one of the homemade signs leaning against Mr. Bishop's Olds and headed toward Fulton Road. Whenever Ink looked at Rosalinda, all he ever saw was a wide nose and a face marred with acne. Now, Ink saw that, just as Bishop said, the girl had definite legs. They started at pink flip flops and, smooth and dark as a newly paved road, traveled all the way up to and through the daisy print tunnels of her shorts. Until this point in his life, Ink hadn't really thought about legs much beyond their practical use; now, just like that, he became the world's biggest fan.

Ink lasted ten more minutes before he really, really, really had to go to the bathroom. Back in a sec," he told Sandro, trying to be casual about his departure. Once out of sight, he gingerly tapped down the stairs of the church and along the hallway, past the auditorium and to the bathroom door. Then, after another paralyzing assault below, Ink barged into the stall and threw down his jeans. With release came relief, a teary-eyed gratitude that lasted as long as it took him to realize that his classmates in the parking lot would soon be adding up the minutes he was gone. If he did not get back immediately, questions would be posed, foul jokes would be made, girls would giggle and point. The moment would be fat with ugliness. Fat as Fat Katz herself.

He came out of the bathroom and nearly made it to the end of the hallway before his body decided that it wasn't satisfied with what it had just accomplished. In fact, there were palpable signs that its foul ambition knew no bounds. Ink leaned against the wall, wiped sweat from his forehead with the back of his hand. At that moment, Nina Sissyan sandal slapped around the corner. She stopped chewing her gum when she saw Ink.

"Goodness! Are you okay?" she asked, eyes large with concern.

"Yes." He swallowed hard. "Why wouldn't I be?"

"You looked a little . . ."

Ink brushed by her to the stairs. She hadn't said more than a dozen words to him in the past eight years, and now, all of a sudden, she wanted to know how he was feeling? He knew that game. She just wanted to bring some good material back to the parking lot for laughs.

Back at the car wash, legs trembling and self-esteem in ruins, Ink kept his distance from Sandro, seething at the sight of his bright, healthy face, vowing to formally end their friendship at the first possible moment. He avoided Nina as well, although they exchanged glances once before Ink returned to the quarter panel he was scrubbing. Her eyes (he was almost certain) were still brimming with that phony concern. He had half a mind to tell her she should try out for the school play this spring.

By dinner, though, Ink was feeling much, much better. He devoured Mom's Shake-N-Bake, the boxed potatoes, even the canned cream corn. The car wash might have been a near-disaster, but he'd seen enough of Sandro's other world to want to be a full-time resident. He dismissed his sickness as an unfortunate anomaly; healthy now, full of energy, he could almost see how he might be able to handle being on the team. During a lull in the dinner conversation, Ink cleared his throat and took his best shot, declaring, "I want to play basketball this year. On the team."

Dad looked up from stirring coffee and said, "Sounds like fun." Mom, however, chewed her maple roll more and more slowly. There was an audible swallow, a pause, and then a quiet, predictable "I don't think so." Ink resisted the impulse to object. It was enough to have brought the issue to the table. His parents went back and forth about it until Mom, with a sigh, said, "I need to talk to this coach," which she did after mass that Sunday, while Ink listened to Sandro tell him about sleeping over Lance's house. After his parents went to bed, Lance pulled out a VCR tape of a movie called *Porky's* his older cousin had lent him. It was rated R, and there was this one scene when the boys looked through a hole into the girls' shower, and there they were without any clothes at all, the water firing down all over their naked bodies. While Ink wondered about the morality of imagining soap-slathered breasts, Mom quizzed Mr. Bishop about schedules and transportation to games and who would be watching the kids at every possible moment. Mr. Bishop was patient, polite, surprisingly smaller than he seemed when he stood suited in front of the class.

Mom said nothing on the way home from mass. When she got in the door, she took out the lunch meat, the bread, the mustard and the dreaded mayonnaise. Ink tried to catch Dad's eye, but he disappeared outside to fill the bird feeder. It was not until half way through lunch that she turned to him with severe eyes and said, "Don't think you're walking home alone," which was her way of saying Ink could join the team.

"Oh Diane," Dad said. "He'll be with a group of kids."

"Did you know that the police were over on Storer the other night because some man beat up his pregnant girlfriend?"

"Okay…"

"And do you remember the murder—a murder—on Clark?"

"Sure, yes. That was certainly terrible." Dad sucked his lips—for him, a sign of embarrassment.

"It's getting closer," Mom said, a wedge of tomato tumbling from the sandwich she was moving to her mouth. "It doesn't hurt to be careful."

*

Two weeks later, Ink sat with Sandro and the other hopefuls along the perimeter of the center circle of the court while Mr. Bishop pivoted like a clock hand in the middle.

"Basketball is a discipline," he said. "It requires hard work, learning skills, knowing what to do. You go out there without a plan, without control, something bad is bound to happen." One huge tennis shoe rose from the floor and landed with a clump ninety degrees to

61

the right. "Now I'm not one of these win-at-all-cost guys, but I do think it's pretty stupid to put on a nice uniform and embarrass yourself and your entire school with your lack of preparation. So what's say we do some ladders..."

There was a collective groan. Ink nervously tugged at his tube socks.

"Man, let's just play," Macho said, drumming the ball he held on the floor between his legs.

Mr. Bishop walked over to the boy and placed his huge shoe on the ball. "Next time, it will be your head."

Macho got up, made rapid break dance moves, head popping here and there. "Gotta catch me first, Mr. B.," he said, bouding to the wall, in running position, ready to go. Everyone, of course, thought the routine was the funniest thing in the world.

"Ladders?" Ink whispered to Sandro.

Sandro smiled. "Just do as I do . . . and pray you don't throw up!"

At the sound of Mr. Bishop's whistle, Ink sprinted with the twelve other boys to the foul line. The thunder of twenty-six feet against the hardwood floor, the murderous shriek of shoes—the sounds were enough to kill his legs with fear. But Ink kept on going, throwing his hand down to touch the line before backpedaling to the wall. He raced with everyone to the midcourt line, slapped the floor again, and ran backward to the wall. Then came the longer dash to the other foul line and back, then one more all the way to the far wall and back. Much to Ink's horror, Mr. Bishop made them repeat the whole agonizing process again and again and again. After two minutes, there were cries of pain, and Brian Gerbic, a cherubic seventh grader, staggered up onto the stage to shove his head in a garbage basket. George Sophronia, hands like dog tongues at his side, tripped for the fifth time over his own two feet and, heedless of consequences, decided to sit out for the rest of the drill.

"Let's pick . . . it . . . UP!" Mr. Bishop boomed.

Ink struggled to breathe, but fear of the giant rock face kept him going—back and forth and up and down until the whistle finally blew. He'd done it. He'd survived the first test.

"Nice with the backpedal," Sandro told him. "You're a natural!"

Macho put his hands on his hips. He did not look winded in the least. "You got to have heart." He tapped his chest. "La corazon!"

Oh God, Ink thought. He rolled his eyes, but no one noticed.

Unfortunately, ladders was just the beginning. The drill was followed by sit ups, pull ups, and squats; bounce and chest passing; foul shots and lay ups. For "My Hero Week" last Wednesday, Joey Accorsi's older brother had come in to talk about boot camp in the Marines—rising at the crack of dawn, wolfing down horrible food, shaking under the stare of the tyrannical drill instructor, running and running and pushing up until you wanted to die. Discipline, Physical and Mental Toughness—these were the themes he hoped to convey. During the question-and-answer period, Joey's brother began talking quite angrily about Beirut, wherever that was. He had buddies there, good buddies, and, in the blink of an eye, two of them were dead. "I'm still asking, you know, for what? Maybe one of you could tell me when we're going to get out of the Middle East…" The students did not understand what was going on, but they knew, instinctively, that the young man had veered off script. Miss Da Via, with panic in her eyes, leapt from her chair and said, "Let's give Corporal Accorsi a wonderful round of applause!" After an awkward moment, everyone did.

The moral of the story, it seemed, was that things could be much, much worse. As Ink greedily sucked at the water fountain during their thirty-second break, he tried to keep this in mind.

With fifteen minutes left, Mr. Bishop finally allowed them to scrimmage—shirts and skins. Ink, as fate would have it, was told to be a skin. He made a few half-hearted tugs at his t-shirt, exposed his stomach in the hopes that would be enough. Mr. Bishop moved through the boys who had arranged themselves along the perimeter of the jump ball circle. He did some quick addition, and then pointed at Ink, saying "Off." Ink obeyed, but put hands atop his pointy shoulders and touched elbows together to keep the boys from laughing at his unimpressive chest. When the practice game began, he stood self-consciously on the perimeter, the ball whipping around, his heart nearly jumping out of his skin each time Mr. Bishop offered encouraging gunshots of applause. Ink didn't touch the ball during three consecutive possessions, which was totally fine with him.

Then the cheerleaders arrived, bouncing through the side door in cute, chatty clusters. Ink was scrambling back on defense and heard the thrilling voices, caught glimpses of color—red, blue, yellow, and green. Out of the corner of his eye he saw pink and white canvas shoes tapping carefully around the perimeter of the court and up the stairs to the stage behind the south basket. Ink smelled perfume and fruity lip gloss. With the entrance of the girls, there was a palpable change in the intensity of the game. Macho, for one, acquired a sudden bounce to his step. He skipped up court, moving the ball back and forth in his hands, hypnotizing Spider Polaski before rocketing past him to the rim.

Bethany Hyde, Bethany Hyde. The name kept doing ladders across the length of Ink's brain. As he trotted up court, he risked a longer look. The girls were taking off their coats, popping squishy squares of gum into their mouths. He zeroed in on Bethany, scrunchie pressed between lips, hands working her blond wave into a ponytail. He dropped his eyes down to the darkened patch of denim between her legs and thought of that party Sandro had told him about, her hips moving against Macho, wondering what that would feel like until, to his dismay, his body began to respond. All this happened in the three seconds between when he looked Bethany's way and Stevie Troutman hit him with a chest pass full in the face.

"Dream boy," Mr. Bishop said, finger a sideways stalactite at his skull. "Head in the game!"

Ink reeled. He closed his eyes, shook his head, squeezed his nose to see if it was still there. Laughter surrounded him—Macho's, of course, and even Sandro's, if he was not mistaken. The next time down the court, he didn't dare glance back at the stage.

*

Mr. Bishop wasn't any smaller on the basketball court than he was in the classroom. In some ways, the shorts and t-shirt were more intimidating than his dark suits. Ink could now see so much more of that giant body—the thick arms, the pillar-like legs covered with bear-black hair. And, of course, there were his feet in those cruise ship shoes. But Mr. Bishop on the basketball court was also someone very different—funny, human perhaps, maybe even in league with the kids.

At the first official practice, Mr. Bishop explained that "the key to the game is defense. And defense is all about being in position."

He tossed the ball to Macho and told him to dribble up court.

"Ok now, here comes your man. You get up on him. You crouch. Pretend you're sitting on the can. Head down below the guy you're defending. Spread those legs. Hands out and up." He demonstrated.

He stood up again. "Just remember to wipe when you're done."

Generally speaking, the boys loved pretty girls. They loved Nacho Cheese Doritos. But most of all, they loved scatological humor. They roared at their coach's joke; they pounded the floor with delight. Ink, taking the cue from the others, laughed quickly, trying to catch up.

As the practices went on, Ink found it difficult to reconcile the one Mr. Bishop with the other. As a result, he retreated further inside himself, trying to be someone different as well. He paid attention. He passed the ball crisply. He made sure not to cry or complain. When Bishop issued imperatives like "Stonehenge, move those feet!" Ink nodded, did his best not to take the instruction personally. When Macho glared at him for inadvertently stepping out of bounds with the ball, he simply said "My bad," a useful phrase he picked up from those who'd been on the team for years.

Two weeks later came The Day of Judgment. Mr. Bishop, the silver screen God, stood before them, clipboard in hand, ready to separate the sheep from the goats. Ink pulled the collar of his shirt over his nose to wipe off the sweat. The names began to thunder from his mouth: "Macho, Lance, Spider, Sandro . . ." Ink was so busy making plans to deal with the humiliation that would come from being cut that it took Sandro slugging him in the arm to realize he'd made the team. It turned out that everyone did, except for stinky George, who, after a five-second heart-to-heart with Coach, happily accepted a position as Mr. Bishop's personal assistant.

Mr. Bishop gathered the boys at center court. "We're going to be good," he said, and they were going to be good because, most importantly, Macho could dribble the ball expertly with his right hand and his left, a rarity in the world of CYO ball. They would be good because Sean and Kevin—The Double Os—were tall for their age. They would be good because Lance played excellent defense and Sandro, with convincing head fakes and a quick first step, could create his own shot, even if it went in much less frequently than Mr. Bishop would have liked. "The question is," he said, hands out toward the boys. "'How good?'"

"Awesome!" Kevin declared.

"Unbeatable," Lance said.

Mr. Bishop smiled. "Be fearless, be focused, and the good will take care of itself.”

It was settled beyond doubt: they were going to be good. And since Mr. Bishop said everyone on the team was going to play, that meant Ink would have to bear at least some of the responsibility for bringing about this “goodness.”

Afterward, as they waited on the front steps of the school for Mr. Gismondi to pick them up, Sandro gave Ink a few more congratulatory slugs in the arm. “Don’t worry, man. Don’t tell me you’re worried.”

“Heck no,” Ink said. His smile, though, was as weak as Mom’s Kool Aid, quarter cup of sugar per quart. The games were thirty two minutes, so that meant that for as many as fifteen minutes he would have to be on the court. So much time on stage, and so much to do at once: the running and rushing up and down, the complicated plays, the dribbling, the toilet crouching. And, of course, getting to the basket—the goal, the whole point of the game.

Sandro laughed. “You look like you’re going to hurl.”

Ink put his hand on his stomach. He stumbled to the bushes and made vomit noises—as gross as he could manage. He was only half-joking, but his friend didn’t need to know.

To his relief, the first few games were a breeze—easy wins in which Ink displayed an off-the-bench competency that was just this side of invisibility. Macho did most of the work, scoring on acrobatic layups, routinely poking the ball away from the reckless dribblers on the opposing team, finding Sandro or Lance for the easy two. The Double Os gobbled up rebounds on both ends of the court and, for good measure, muscled in a basket every now and then. Generally speaking, Ink was able to stay in front of his man, remembering most of the time to watch the boy’s chest instead of his eyes. He committed a few fouls here and there, double dribbled once, lost a no-look pass from Macho out of bounds. But even the best players turned the ball over. Against St. Stephen’s, Ink amazed himself, scoring three baskets in a blowout win. In the locker room, Sandro’s congratulatory spank glowing on his behind, Ink began to suspect that he might even be coming into his own.

The stakes were raised considerably in the fifth game against Our Lady of Good Counsel, a team that was also 4-0. Because Kevin was out with the flu, Ink, the next tallest guy on the roster, was given the opportunity to start. Standing on the perimeter of the half court circle, he wiped his shoes with his hands. He darted tongue from cheek to cheek, trying to cure himself of an awful case of cotton mouth. Suddenly, the whistle blew, and the ref stepped into the circle to toss up the ball. An instant later, the ball was somehow in Ink's hands and he was off, dribbling, head down, the curiously panicked voices of teammates calling after him. Bishop's voice boomed as well, but Ink blocked him out. When he approached the basket, he looking up and saw on the baseline the open mouths of Bethany, Bernadette, Nina— the blonde, the redhead, and the brunette, a flag for a beautiful country he'd never be able to visit. After his previous game, how could everyone doubt he'd make a simple layup? He looked back down, took one more careful dribble, and made sure to lift off the left leg like he was supposed to.

"No!" Sandro screamed, and that scared Ink's shot right off the rim. Good thing, as it turned out, since he was, to his surprise and horror, standing beneath the opponent's basket.

At the next dead ball, Mr. Bishop took him out. Ink sprinted off court, waiting until the last possible moment to raise his head. Coach stared at him, huge shoulders hunched, hands like serving trays.

"Head in the game," Ink heard as he took a folding chair at the far end of the bench.

"I'm wondering," George said, pencil on a stat sheet, "if I would have done something like that."

Ink narrowed his eyes. "Trust me, you would have done worse."

George shrugged. "You're probably right."

The good news was, St. James won by seven. Ink failed to score, but after the egregious start, he managed to avoid further occasions of sin. The bad news? In the locker room, Macho snapped him in the back with a wet shower towel and gave him a new nickname: "No Think Ink."

*

"Columbus?" Mom said, butter knife an exclamation point in the air. "I'm really getting tired of all these requests."

Ink was sitting with his parents at the kitchen table, crumbs of a store-bought nut roll on napkins before them. Mom and Dad were several sips into their after-supper coffee, and Ink had thought this the perfect time to bring up the spring basketball tournament, which Sandro had called a "once in a lifetime opportunity." Block by block over the past month, Ink had built up the trip in his mind: the boisterous van ride down; the fancy hotel with a pool and cable TV; the dress up banquet; the mixer with all the other teams and their cheerleaders in the ballroom. For the greater part of several consecutive evenings, Ink lay on his bed, Van Halen sizzling through his headphones, conjuring up Bethany in a bathing suit. Blue. No red. A bikini. Yes, why not? Something loosely tied at the neck and hips.

There'd be the games too, of course, and somehow he'd manage to survive them. It was a single elimination tournament in front of big crowds in a totally alien environment. With luck, they'd lose the first one, and Kevin or Sean or—even better—Macho would be to blame. After that, there would be pure, anxiety-free fun for the rest of the trip.

"You want to go to Columbus," Dad said, "We'll take a trip this summer. We'll have a little vacation. Did you know Columbus used to be known as Arch City?"

"But everybody—"

"Last week," Mom said, "a school bus plunged off an overpass outside of Dayton. Two children died." Unlike Dad, she didn't need a notebook to jot down information; if it was something terrible, it remained forever in her head, accessible in an instant.

Ink glanced at his father, who nervously scratched his Adam's apple. After a moment, he said, "There used to be all these lighted arches over the main road—High Street, I think."

Both of them and their stupid facts! Ink pressed and pleaded, but he knew all was lost.

At Christmas, the basketball trip came up again. Aunt Ruth had been talking about her "sojourn in Southern California" to see an old college roommate. On the way back, the plane had been grounded in Denver due to weather. For four hours, she shifted back and forth in a plastic chair, reading silly entertainment magazines.

"This one," Mom said, pointing a fork across the table, "he wanted to go to all the way to Columbus with his basketball team. In the middle of winter!"

"He's a little young," Grandma said, appearing in the doorway with yet another steaming bowl of Brussels sprouts.

"Plenty to do right here in Cleveland," Grandpa announced.

"Right," Uncle Lare chimed in. "As long as it's on the White—I mean West Side."

Grandpa laughed. "I lost my passport years ago!"

As usual, Aunt Ruth swayed her head back and forth, weighing the pros and cons of the Columbus trip in her diplomatic way. "I wonder if that might be something more appropriate for high school," she said at last, eyes twinkling with empathy.

Uncle Lare downed his wine. "Want to know what I think?"

"Not especially," Mom said.

"It's a damn short life. Might as well live it."

"Lawrence!" Grandma said.

Mom made praying hands under her chin. Smiling sweetly, she said, "Are *you* going to tell *me* how to parent?"

Aunt Judy had divorced Uncle Lare a few years earlier, but he was still allowed to drive down to Canton once a month to spend time with Cynthia and William. Last year, from what Ink gathered, his uncle had been pulled over for speeding. He'd been drinking too, a shade over the limit, the kids unbelted in the backseat. Somehow, he avoided jail; from that point on, though, the custody battle became a simple rout.

"No, no Diane," Uncle Lare said, reaching for the Beaujolais. "You're the expert when it comes to family."

"What's that supposed to mean?"

"Christ, can't you take a compliment?"

"Did you know," Dad said. "Did you know that the life expectancy in Canada is seventy-six? In the U.S. it is only seventy-five."

"I'll take seventy-five," Grandpa said. "When you look around the world, it is one disaster after another. Earthquakes in China, floods in Vietnam, droughts in Africa, and now this poison chemical thing in India. Over there," he said, waving his hand at the window, "it's amazing anyone has a chance to grow up."

"It's too terrible," Mom said, closing her eyes. "Please don't talk about it."

"I tell him not to read the news," Grandma said.

Uncle Lare snorted. "God forbid."

"He reads the paper straight through with a cup of coffee, like it's one of those police shows he needs to see the end of."

Grandpa shrugged. Aunt Ruth opened her mouth to say something, but decided against it.

Everyone went back to eating, the stabs of forks and slides of knives a bit more strident for a while, but soon, as usual, the storm passed and skies sweet as iced cookies settled in for the rest of the day.

The next morning, Ink called Sandro to see what he received for Christmas. As usual, his friend got the much better deal: a bundle of the latest video games; a remote control airplane; tickets to see Motorcycles on Ice at the Richfield Coliseum. Ink got history books and monochromatic sweaters. He received *Trivial Pursuit*, which Dad was going to make them play after dinner. Aunt Ruth gave him a writer's journal. At the bottom of each blank page was a quotation by a famous writer, most of whom (for some odd reason) were women.

"This is Kate Chopin," Aunt Ruth had said, pointing at one of the pictures inside the cover. Ink read the quotation: "The beginnings of things, of the world especially, is necessarily vague, tangled, chaotic, and exceedingly disturbing. How few of us ever emerge from such beginning! How many souls perish in its tumult!" He had little idea of what the passage meant, but it scared him half to death. "And here's Willa Cather . . ." Aunt Ruth went through each of the quotations, head swaying back and forth in her easy going way. Blank pages—that was all Ink could focus on. He loved his aunt, but really, what did she think he could do with a gift of almost nothing?

His best present by far was Megatron, a Transformer robot that, with a few twists and turns, could turn into a pistol. All through the fall, Ink had been singing the commercial song—"Transformers!— More Than Meets the Eye." Dad said, "If you're good," and Mom offered a vaguely encouraging "We'll see," but in the end it had been Uncle Lare who'd come through with the prize of the season.

"Yeah?" Sandro said, when Ink told him, saving what he thought was the best for last. "Aren't you a little old for those?" Just like that, the shiny robot felt like a baby rattle in Ink's embarrassed hands.

In the evening, he suffered through an interminable game of *Trivial Pursuit*. About an hour in, Mom, his teammate, stood up to say she had to fold some laundry. "You're on your own now," she said. After all that time, there was one lonely Sports & Leisure wedge in their pie.

"Not as easy as it looks," Dad said.

"This stuff hardly matters."

Dad smiled. He could afford to be magnanimous, since his pie was filled, and he was moving toward the center of the board. Ink dropped the die yet again on the board and plunked his pie on an Arts & Literature square.

"Ah," Dad said. "An easy one for you. Who wrote *Uncle Tom's Cabin*?" He read him the four options.

Ink shrugged. He imagined Sandro sunk into his cushy rec room couch next to Mr. Gismondi, the two of them gloriously lost inside a shoot-em-up video game on the twenty-seven-inch screen before them.

"Think now. It was the number one best seller of the entire nineteenth century."

Think. Think. Ink tried to, but all he could see was Macho's big-lipped smile, his "No Think Ink" reverberating off the walls of the locker room.

"I don't know . . . Abraham Lincoln."

"That's good," Dad said, smiling broadly. "A book about slavery—I could see why you'd say that. But the correct answer is Stowe."

Ink put his head down.

"That's okay. Now you know it." He picked up a brown wedge from the pile and rolled it between thumb and finger. "Now you have one more piece of information in that head of yours."

On his next turn, Dad moved to the center and won the game by answering correctly a question about the American Revolution before Ink could even read him the choices. He was annoyed, but also relieved that the evening's torture had come to an end.

*

The Columbus tournament came and went, and the night the team returned to Cleveland, Sandro called Ink. His friend was distracted, mouth full of something, and it took a few moments for Ink to understand that St. James had won the tournament and Macho (of course) was the MVP.

"And? And?" Ink, who'd been drowsing over a book, sat up in bed, completely alert.

"And what?" Sandro asked, innocent as could be.

"The other stuff. Tell me the good stuff."

"Oh, you know, nothing much to report."

Ink knew full well that "nothing much" was a two-word tarp thrown over a treasure chest of "quite a bit." For the next few weeks, someone or another at school would make oblique reference to the trip. There'd be a snicker, a few lines of an inside joke that would have everyone holding their sides. Sandro seemed to have transferred his attentions from Nina to the suddenly busty Bernadette, while Bethany, to his dismay, had developed more than a simple tolerance for Macho's off-color comments, not to mention the occasional arm around her shoulder. If Ink had been allowed to go to Columbus, how would things be different? What would he know? Which of the girls— Celeste Aaron? Denise Abney? (someone, of course, from the second tier)—would have developed a crush on him? For weeks, the questions danced around his head, sticking out their tongues.

Not until the beginning of the playoffs— "warrior time," as Mr. Bishop declared—did the pain of that missed trip begin to abate. The team was 10-0 and preparing to play Our Lady of Peace, whose team had been decimated by injury and illness; however, Ink was much less excited by the probability of taking the first step toward the city championship than he was about the team spaghetti dinner, which, win or lose, was scheduled for that evening at Sandro's house. It would be nothing like Columbus, of course, but the Holy Trinity would be present, dazzling in their lip gloss and teased out hair. There'd be games and music and dancing, bold talk and crude jokes and—who knows?—maybe an opportunity to brush against a breast when someone flipped off the rec room lights. Come Monday, Ink would arrive on the school playground and nod knowingly at Sandro or Lance, which would be sweeter than a blowout on the basketball court.

The bleachers were packed the afternoon of the game, but Ink's parents weren't among the crowd. Dad, angling for a promotion, had been called into work unexpectedly, and Mom simply could not bear to watch what she called a "violent spectacle." "You better be careful out there," she'd said as Mr. Gismondi pulled up at the curb, her concern (as always) tinged with threat. Dad, apologizing again for having to miss the game, said, "Whatever happens, we just want you to know we're proud of you." His eyes were soft and sad, as if Ink had already been declared the goat of the game.

The game was sloppy at the start. There were plenty of

turnovers—double dribbles, shifting pivot feet, bounce passes where teammates were not. Shots grazed rims or thudded off backboards, when they weren't dropping a foot or more short of the baskets. Midway through the first quarter, Ink was sent in, legs wobbly, mouth a total desert. Guarded by a speedy, silent, and extremely long armed boy, Ink quickly determined he'd be able to do nothing and so did his best to avoid the ball. He moved here and there on occasion to appear engaged, but all his cuts were half-hearted. Soon, he found himself thinking again about the party. Perhaps Bethany would arrive in her cheerleading skirt, and he could watch her legs cross themselves on a couch or, better yet, come apart as she rose for a drink. There'd be music—strong, rowdy beats you'd just have to move your body to. He'd sit down, say "hi" to her. Unable to hear, she'd tilt her head even closer. He'd lean toward that shapely ear, and there would be the smell…the smell of vanilla…

"Next time, get it inside," Kevin said, smacking his chest with a palm. They were moving back down the court to play defense. Ink nodded at him, although for the life of him he could not remember having had the ball to pass.

In the last two minutes of the half, Macho solved his defender, beating him off the dribble three straight times. Spider got a steal for an easy layup. Sandro put back a missed shot as time expired, and St. James was up by ten. In the locker room, the boys were giddy. Sean was demonstrating to Macho how he'd given the opposing center an "accidental" shot to the balls. Lance had Sandro's head in a playful headlock. "Sixteen more minutes," Mr. Bishop said, his face more of a rock than ever. "We've accomplished nothing yet."

In the second half, the game quickly became more physical. Macho drove past his man to the basket and was knocked to the floor by Fifty-Two, a tall, solid block of boy who for some reason was seeing his first action of the game. Macho popped up, got in the boy's grinning face until the referee gave both of them technical fouls.

"This means war," Spider said during the timeout that followed.

"Easy now," Mr. Bishop said, glaring at the opposing coach, who was backslapping his boys. "Be smart out there. Keep your cool."

The Peace coach, despite only having seven players, settled on a game plan of naked aggression. Sandro got elbowed in the lip and had to come out until the bleeding stopped. Spider jammed a finger wrestling for the ball with an opponent on the floor. The poor boy stood up, holding his wrist, finger in the shape of a thunderbolt. The fouls started adding up. One Peace player fouled out. Then another. Their opponents were down to just five players.

With the game tied, Fifty-Two, out of position on defense, stomped on Kevin's ankle as he turned to the basket. Kevin went down on the floor, clutching his hightop, and Mr. Bishop bolted onto the court, waving arms over his head. Play was stopped as Mr. Bishop attended to his player. With Coach on one side and Macho on the other, Kevin limped toward the bench, eyes full of tears, the grimace on his face all the more awful because of his braces.

"Need a sub, Coach," the referee said.

"You should throw that boy out of the game."

The referee shrugged. "Didn't see it."

"Get some glasses."

"Come on, man. I'm one guy."

Mr. Bishop turned away in disgust. "Ink," he growled. "Get in there."

In the fourth quarter, Ink typically sat on the bench and watched Bethany do knee-weakening scissor kicks. Now, the outcome of the most important game of the year was in the balance, and he was being ordered to be the new Kevin—shorter, skinnier, and far less athletically inclined. Would he have to play the rest of the game?

"Goooo!"

Ink gulped. He trotted onto the court. Behind him, George cried, "Don't think the worst!"

With two minutes left, St. James was only up by only two. Ink breathed in and out, reminding himself that it was important—it was vital—to get the ball into Macho's hands. He was their point guard, their general on the court. He hated the boy, but he knew he was the only one who would lead them to victory.

When the whistle blew, there was an awful mess of movement. The thunder and squeak of tennis shoes made him want to run for shelter. Ink glanced up at the clock, where bright red seconds dripped like blood. Without warning, the ball came his way. His nemesis, the long-armed defender, raked at him with a claw. Ink raised his arms to fend off the attack. A second later, the whistle blew. The boy opened his mouth to protest, but the referee shushed him with a finger to the lips. It was the boy's fifth foul, and he was out of the game. For the rest of the contest, it would be five against four.

Disgusted, the Peace coach jammed the fingers of one hand into the palm of the other—the timeout sign. In his own team huddle, Mr. Bishop grabbed his players, each of whom were again overcome with giddiness. "Relax, relax. We've got a real advantage now, but if we don't play smart it means absolutely nothing. Nothing!"

Despite the advantage, the boys from St. James felt the tightening of the knot at their necks. Passes were tentative and mishandled. Shots started coming up short. There was a distinct lack of movement on the defensive end. On the sidelines, Mr. Bishop became apoplectic. "It's five on four," he screamed, throwing his huge hands into the air. "Somebody's got to be open!"

And that somebody was Ink. The pass from Sandro came, a floater that dropped toward him as casual as a bomb. Grab it, grab it, he thought, and he did, a hand on each side, the lines and the dimples right in front of his face. He had an impulse to lay his head upon it— a pillow for sleep. For dreams. For escape.

A gawky kid with clown-sloppy feet charged towards him, eyes wild, hands frantic in the air. Ink froze, but when the boy stumbled, the spell was broken. He saw Macho zipping up to the top of the key and he bounced it to him. Disaster averted.

Macho, Lance, and Sandro played catch on the perimeter. When the defense broke down, Macho zipped a pass to Sandro, who had cut into the lane. He grabbed the ball and put up a shot—a glorified layup—that dripped off the rim and into the hands of one of the Peace forwards, who launched the ball down court to his point guard, who had slipped past the St. James defense. The boy scored to tie the game, and Mr. Bishop called a timeout. The first thing he did was grab Ink by the shoulders. "Why'd you pass? That boy fell down. All you had to do is go right by him."

Ink nodded. He thought of Jesus sweating blood in the garden, hands fused together, eyes to the heavens imploring his father to take the cup away.

"One dribble and you've got an easy basket."

"Fifty Two will smash me in the face."

"Stop thinking!"

"Just give me the ball," Macho said. "I'll drive."

"They're keying on you," Mr. Bishop said. "We've got to win this as a team."

The buzzer sounded. Ball out of bounds under the basket.

Macho, Sandro, and Lance formed a line perpendicular to the baseline. Ink scrambled in behind his best friend until Macho yanked on his shirt and put him behind Lance, where he was supposed to go. Sean took the ball from the referee under the basket.

Only one minute left. He could get through this, he could do it, and then there'd be the raised arms and backslaps and, later, the spectacular spaghetti dinner, where maybe just maybe, without much maneuvering, he would happen to find himself right next to Bethany on the sofa, his leg against hers as kids squeezed in from either side.

The whistle blew again and Sean slapped the ball, holding it over his head. His teammates were on the move, but Ink couldn't remember if they were running out-of-bounds play number one or two. He shuffled into the key, hid behind Fifty Two. Suddenly, everyone was bounding down court—the ball had been stolen. By the time Ink made it to the half court line, one of their guards was banking the ball off the backboard to put Peace up by two.

Mr. Bishop called his last timeout, and Macho tailed Ink to the sideline, spitting something in Spanish. The players huddled around Mr. Bishop. Ink had his head down, pretending he was looking at the white board Coach was using to draw up another play. He felt the heaviness of Macho's shaking head, shame that wafted like sock sweat. When Coach finished diagramming the play, the team walked back on the court. Mr. Bishop grabbed the back of Ink's jersey, pulled him back, placed his huge, mountainous face in front of him. "Be smart. Do what you're supposed to do."

"Do you want to take me out?"

"Do you want me to take you out?"

"Sit him down," Macho said, wandering back towards the bench. "He's going to blow it for us."

Mr. Bishop turned on Macho. "You be quiet or you'll be riding pine."

Never in the history of humankind had Ink heard the boy spoken to in such a way. What a thrill it was for him to see Macho get even a little of what he truly deserved.

"In or out?" he asked again.

"Out."

"Wrong answer." The thunderclap on Ink's behind sent him several feet back on the court, where he felt everyone was watching him, waiting for the one awful thing that was bound to go wrong.

Macho brought the ball up court, flashing three fingers with his left hand. Following orders, Ink ran down to the baseline, setting a pick for Sandro, who came under the basket to catch a crisp bounce pass from Macho. The defender bit on his head fake, and Sandro drove to the middle. Fifty Two came barreling at him, and Sandro flipped the ball up, trying to bank it in off the glass. Instead, the ball came high off the rim and was deflected by an unlikely combination of body parts into Ink's stunned hands. As he stood there, transfixed by the ball's orange dimples, he failed to realize he was all alone, six short feet from the basket until he was double teamed by two waving and leaping defenders. Ink dribbled once, and then knew he was sunk. His teammates screamed for the ball. He wanted to turn to find an opening, but didn't know how to do so without picking up his pivot foot as well. He had to do something, though—something quick. Shoot? The ball would end up in his face. Call a timeout? He was pretty sure they had none left. Out of ideas, he closed his eyes, jumped in the air and threw the ball across the court, where Macho had been last time he looked. The speedy Peace guard, the one who had scored moment before, poked the ball away towards center court. Macho sprinted after it, shoulder up against the other boy, each trying to nudge the other off the ball. His teammate won the contest, but slipped just past the half court line and fell. The other boy picked up the loose ball and dribbled in for the easy score.

Fifteen seconds left. St. James had one last chance. Macho brought the ball up, put his head down, and drove, his teammates staying out of the way.

"Five on four!" Mr. Bishop cried, hands glued to his head.

The zone collapsed on Macho, and he brought his arms up and flipped the ball into the air. It was close—so close—but it popped off the rim and the buzzer sounded before it fell to Sandro, who put it in anyway, with a half-hearted release. Peace players piled on top of each other. Macho stalked off the court, saying "Where's the foul?" and Mr. Bishop's answer was to turn him around to go shake hands.

"Good game, good game, good game," Ink said, holding out his hand to be slapped by each opponent (even that bully Fifty Two) as he passed them in line. Slowly but surely, waves of dread and shame began to crash and curl inside him. He'd blown the game, hadn't he? He panicked, threw the ball away because he couldn't stand the heat. But hadn't everyone made mistakes? Spider missed a layup in the first quarter. Lance threw up not one but two airballs and Sandro missed more than a few gimmies. Kevin let Fifty Two crush his foot and, like a coward, decided to hide on the bench for the rest of the game with an ice pack strapped to his foot. Even Macho—the all-star guard, the ladies' man—had his share of turnovers, not to mention that huge missed shot as time ran out. And Mr. Bishop—why in the world didn't he listen to Ink when he said he should be taken out of the game? Ink didn't know much, but he was keenly aware of his limits.

In the locker room, the boys slumped on benches, dragging sweaty tops over their heads, eyes soaked with tears. Mr. Bishop gathered them around, spoke with trembling voice about pride, about holding one's head up high, about giving it everything you had. "You were warriors out there today," he said, huge hand to his heart. "Each and every one of you." The boys nodded, but didn't—couldn't—take their eyes off the floor.

After the boys showered, Mr. Bishop was waiting in front of the vans, congratulating each player as he climbed in. "Good year, good year," he said. When Ink approached, Coach held out his massive hand, and Ink, embarrassed, took it, expecting his own to be crushed. The shake was gentle, though—the hand more like a tissue paper than a falling boulder from a cliff. Thankfully, the first van—the one with Macho—was already closed up and ready to go. Ink climbed in the second and slumped down next to Sandro, who was thumbing to death a hand-held video game.

"Last year, last game of the season," his friend said without looking up from the screen, "ten seconds left, we're down by two, Macho passes me the ball in the corner, and I dribble the ball off my foot. Game over. Afterwards, Coach tells me maybe I have a future in soccer."

Ink smiled appreciatively.

"I cost us a regular season game. But you—*you* killed our championship dreams!" Sandro dropped his jaw and shot Ink dead with horror movie eyes. As the van lurched into motion, Ink fell against him, playfully pummeling him in the chest. Kevin, still wincing in pain from his ankle, said, "Hey, homos—knock it off." The van filled with laughter. The two friends didn't come near each other for several long days after that.

*

The food was lined up on the bar: a heaping bowl of pasta, a pot of homemade sauce filled with eggy, oblong meatballs, crusty bread, an iceberg lettuce salad, two huge bags of rippled potato chips, several plates of triple fudge brownies that were under no circumstances to be touched until the "official go-ahead" was given. Mr. Gismondi had brought everything down one item at a time, and when the girls (who adored him) volunteered to help, he waved them away. "Tonight," he said, "parents work. Kids have fun."

Ink enjoyed a grace period at the party while everybody tore through the food. In between stabs at his rigatoni, he kept his eye on Bethany. For a moment, she was actually alone, sitting on a folding chair, pulling up a fuzzy pink sock, bright bangles embracing delicate wrists. Her underwear was just ten feet away, behind crossed legs and under that skirt. White? Black? Red? Ink had passed through the lingerie department at Sears enough times to have a good idea of color and shape and (when Mom was looking elsewhere) even texture. He thought about going over and sitting on the coffee table beside her, which might be low enough to sneak a peek between her legs. But she would be suspicious. And besides, it would not be right. And besides, she would blame him for the loss. And besides, Bethany—the actual fact of her—scared him half to death.

While Ink was lost in thought, everyone else was having fun. Sandro slapped *Born in the U.S.A.* on the turntable. Lance was showing Nina how to throw darts. Spider, the school's widely acknowledged shark, was knocking in balls on the pool table, screwing the chalk into the stick after every blast. By accident, he poked Celeste Aaron in the behind, and she dropped her cup of pop. Spider laughed but helped her blot the floor with napkins. Macho and Sean approached George and asked him, for once and for all, why don't you ever take a bath?

"This isn't the Third World," Sean said.

"I hope you both die of AIDS!"

"You're the faggot, George," Macho said, opening his arms for embrace. "Why don't you show me how?"

79

Laughter. For eight years, George had made valiant attempts to get the best of fellow students in verbal altercations. Recently, though, he'd learned, after a little token resistance, to take his defeats with equanimity. "Good one," he said now, and this response worked like magic, diffusing the tension, making Macho smile instead of going for the kill. Maybe the enemies saw through the strategy. It would have been hard not to, given how practiced the response soon became. But as long as the enemies got the last good dig, they seemed to be satisfied to let George have the last word.

Francesca, Sandro's seventeen-year-old sister, stomped downstairs, a dark sponge of hair bouncing back and forth on her head.

"Where's my Madonna tape?" she whined.

Sandro said, "Madonna is a skanky two-bit whore."

Francesca took a fat hairbrush from behind her back and whacked Sandro in the ribs. Sandro cursed her and tried to take a bite out of her arm. She threw him off, and, disappearing back up the stairs, expressed her sincere wish that he'd drop dead. Not to be outdone, Sandro told her (when she was safely out of earshot) to go shave her mustache.

"Which one?" Macho said, spinning like a top on the barstool behind them.

There was a moment of silence before the boys began to howl. Ink, dimly aware of the nature of the joke, smiled like a boy whose dinner hadn't agreed with him.

After the feast, the mood of the party changed. The loss really began to settle in, heavier than pasta and fudge brownies in their stomachs.

"So Stink," Macho said. "I wanted to tell you something."

Ink lowered his head, bracing for the assault.

"You are not a bad guy."

Ink looked up, a glimmer of hope on his face.

"But you screwed things up," Kevin said. He'd been brooding in an old Lazy Boy all evening, seemingly waiting for this moment.

Ink looked to his best friend—the host of the party—for help. Sandro, however, stood with his head bowed behind the bar, record album like a shield against his chest.

"Basketballwise," Macho said, "you are an idiota. Estupido."

Kevin laughed. "He doesn't know Spanish."

"They're compliments, I think," said Bernadette, always eager to get in on the fun.

Mrs. Gismondi spared Ink by appearing in the stairwell: "You kids need anything?"

This got everyone talking: No, no, nobody needed a thing. The pasta was terrific. Totally awesome brownies! Thank you, thank you, thank you! Sandro, sensing a second wind, took the opportunity to slap Duran Duran on the turntable. Nina woo-hooed, tossing one hand in the air and grabbing Bethany with the other. Together they spun and shook around the pool table, others quickly joining in behind them. Ink tried to smile, but he was still smarting from the blows that had rained upon him.

*

Later, out of the blue, Denise Abney sighed. "In three months, we're all going to go our different ways."

There'd been another lull in the party. The chip bags and pop bottles were nearly empty. Sandro was behind the bar sifting through his tape box to find the one that might save them from this funk.

Denise continued: "My dad said the other day: 'You ready for the big world?' And I said, um, no."

"It's pretty scary," Nina said, hands on her lap. "High school…" her voice trailed off.

"In a few months, the whole gang is just going to break apart." Denise's eyes watered.

Years ago—was it fourth grade?—Denise had organized a memorial for Frankie McGooken, the boy who drowned in that shallow creek. Since then, she'd cried in front of everyone at least one hundred times. Once, after she learned Ray Kroc died, she was especially disconsolate and Sandro called her "our designated bawler." Kevin, outracing Macho to the first crude comment, said under his breath, "I'd ball her." It was a good one—most everyone laughed, although Lance said he pitied the boy who would claim such a thing about "Flabney," even for the sake of a joke.

Ink expected a smart comment from someone, but no one smiled or said a word. It was ten minutes to ten, and the party was a breath

81

away from dead. It was just as well, Ink thought, since Dad would be coming soon to take him home.

Just then, Bethany slapped her lap and said, "I want to do something crazy, something, you know, that will be remembered."

"Take off your underwear," Macho said. He pointed to the deer head mounted on the wall. "Hang them on the horns."

The room came to life with "ooooohs" and "aahhhhhhhs" and two distinct "no freaking ways." All eyes turned to Bethany. Sandro crept half way up the stairs to gauge the location of his parents then popped his head back into the room, flashing an "all-clear" smile. Another round of "oooohs," this time softer, everyone understanding the dire consequences of too much commotion.

It was difficult to figure the look on Bethany's face. Clearly, she adored the attention. Her eyes glinted, tips of knives on a pristine table cloth. She looked across the room at Bernadette, who gave her a comradely nod. She remained seated, arms tightly crossed against her scarlet sweater, her knees frozen together. She toed the Styrofoam plate at her feet. She opened her mouth, but nothing came out except the shy tip of a tongue.

I'll even take them off for you," Macho said with a smirk. He stood in front of her now, arms crossed, eyes bright with challenge.

The room erupted. Sandro, still standing on the stairs, pounded the railing and chanted, "Oh man oh man oh man!"

Bethany looked from right to left. A smile crept across her face. She bounced right up, thumbs like a cowboy in the waistband of her skirt. "Sure," she said. "Go ahead." She was a tall girl, maybe an inch or two taller than Macho. They looked each other in the eye, grinning because they'd reached the point of no return, and there was nothing to be done.

"John," Mrs. Gismondi's voice again intruded. "Your father is here to pick you up."

Bethany was in the middle of making ground rules, when Ink tore up the stairs, promising Sandro he'd be right back. Without a word, he passed the Gismondis in the living room and bolted to the street where Dad's drab brown wagon idled. He knocked frantically at the passenger side window until his father, face lost in a book, leaned across the seat to roll it down.

"Dad, Dad. Hi," he said, smiling, struggling for breath. "Can I stay a little longer?"

"We all agreed on ten."

"But it's just getting fun!"

"You heard what I said." His voice was as firm as half-chilled Jell-O, and his eyes shifted with uncertainty.

"Please!"

"We're not going to have an argument."

Ink opened the door and slammed it as hard as he could.

"Is that the behavior of a nice young man?" This was a new disciplinary technique with Dad—the asking of questions for which the answer was patently obvious.

As the car rolled away from the curb, Ink didn't care about being nice. He wanted to know what was going on in that damn basement. Bernadette had said the lights should be off, and by now they probably were. What color were they? What did they feel like in the hand, fresh and warm from the soft skin they covered? What if Macho was doing something insane like using his bright, big teeth to draw her underwear down? Why Macho—always, everything, for Macho? He hated the boy for trying to blame him for the loss. He was nothing more than a . . . spick—that's right, spick, and he didn't care if God heard his thoughts or not.

When he burst through the front door, Mom glanced up from the sofa. "Well, did you win?" she asked.

"No."

"Have fun at the party?"

He stumped upstairs without a word. Fun? Fun? He was fourteen and only tonight had he been able to get a tantalizing glimpse of what that meant. And now, unbelievably, there were just three months to go before he'd have to adjust to a completely new world. Sandro would be going to St. Ignatius with Ink, but Kevin would be going to Ed's, Lance to Padua, Nina and Bethany to St. Joe's, Bernadette, Macho, and Sean to Central Catholic. It would still be 1985, but come fall, nothing would be the same. He studied the calendar hanging next to the mirror. All the squares for days were like blocks upon a board game. Dad's favorite: *Trivial Pursuit*. Roll the die. Move to the end of August. Listen to yet another question whose answer he'd never be able to guess.

Iceberg Queries

(Fall 1986-Spring 1987)

Ink swiveled on a stool in front of the split open frog. With each glance, he drew a deep breath. The blur of organs and sinew and bone thoroughly convinced him of the ingeniousness of skin.

"I don't see the gall bladder," he said.

"It's there," Joel Stein said, tapping with the tip of his pen. "That green thingy. Helps when you look."

Since as far back as he could remember, Ink had been a firm believer in textbooks. The glossy covers, the bone-hard binding, the authoritative words, the detailed diagrams—everything about them seemed enduring and irrefutable. Lowly sophomore that he was, he was not going to doubt what the biology book said about the three chambered heart and a liver and, yes, a gall bladder, which once had been responsible for squirting acrid juices into the frog's small intestine to help the body digest all the flies and bugs and whatever else the creature consumed. He did not need empirical evidence of what was going on inside all God's creatures.

"Don't be a puss," Anthony Gigante said.

Ink braved a peek, but the view was not improving. He took another deep breath. The formaldehyde was starting to give him watery eyes that he hoped the others would not mistake for tears.

"Hey, you'll never guess what," Rick Maconichie said.

"You're a fag?" Ant said, snickering.

It was a good guess—really it was. Rick appreciated the deep thought behind it. However, the thing that they would probably never guess—the thing he just had to tell them about—was an outside-the-classroom sighting of Miss Keane, English teacher and the collective wet dream of twelve hundred college prep boys. It was just before the dinner rush last Saturday night, and Rick was folding napkins on a back table at Lucille's, the restaurant his father owned over on 117th. In through the archway she strolled—high heels, black dress, spaghetti straps, cleavage, the whole nine yards. She went right up to the bar, squeezed between an elderly couple like an old pro. "She was smoking, I tell you—hotter than hell." Rick touched thumb to forefinger and waved them both in the air.

"Excellent," Ant said. It was hands down his new favorite word. He used it as if it were a personal invention, some hard-earned discovery the product of years of assiduous trial and error.

Rick went on to say that Phil ("he's the bartender") leaned toward Miss Keane as she asked a question. She frowned and looked around while Phil scratched out something on a receipt and gave it to her, jabbing a forefinger north toward Lorain. The music stopped just as Phil said, "I'm sure he's there." A few moments later, she passed by the window, glancing back into the bar, as if she hadn't believed what she'd been told. "Honest to God," Rick said, "I used one of the napkins to wipe my watering mouth."

"Dude, wait. Rewind," Joel said, taking off his glasses to knuckle his eyes. "You didn't even say hello? Buy her a drink? For Christ's sake, your dad owns the joint!"

Ink looked at Rick. His face was bedeviled by freckles. He had jagged auburn hair and braces in which chewed up bread always became stuck. He was, in a word, ugly. But what did that matter? He was someone to sit with at lunch—someone he could count as a friend.

"I would've given her directions!" Ant said, tossing thick eyebrows meaningfully into the air.

"Yeah, yeah," Joel said. "That's a pretty good one."

"Kneel down…"

"Ant, we get the idea. You may now give it a rest."

The story, with its savory details, its tantalizing holes, was enough to send Ink into another daydream about his English teacher. She was walking down to Lorain. She got into her pinstriped Fiero and ran reds down Lorain to Denison, Denison to Fulton. She squealed onto his street, braked hard in front of the house, and got out—no, emerged— face radiant in the moonlight. For the first time in forever, his parents were out of town. Standing on the tree lawn, she looked down again at the receipt Phil had given her. Yes, this was the place. She tossed her hair, which silvered under the luminous moon. He appeared bare-chested at the window. She rushed to the door and tried the knob— one way then the other.

"Okay," Joel said. "Let's find us some ovaries!"

Ink chanted to himself: corpora cavernosa, tunica albuginea. He tried to quell the uprising below with the homeliness of Latin. When that didn't work, he crossed his legs, pressed down like a spatula on a grilled cheese sandwich. Too late—the thing was wide awake and sawing mightily at his briefs. It demanded a peek and a poke at the woman Ink's febrile imagination had brought to life.

"Mr. Alt," Fr. Kirby said, stopping at their table. "You do not appear in the least bit well."

He wiped his tearing eyes. "I'm fine." He squeezed some more. He conjured up health class—an ugly cluster of veins, a penis engorged with blood. As recently as last week, that had been enough to sicken him into softening.

"Father," Ant said, "This assignment has been really hard on him."

"Maybe you should take a trip to the loo in order to refresh yourself."

Ant grinned. Oblivious to Ink's epic struggle, he was just thrilled he'd slipped another dirty joke past the Jesuit censors.

"I'm okay," Ink said. No way in hell was he was going into a bathroom with that straight edge lodged in his slacks. No way could he be alone and unzip to adjust without Miss Keane floating into his mind again, her body like the capital S of sex sashaying up the stairs, to the door, her hand firm upon the knob.

"To think we'll all be like this one day," Joel said. "Stiff, lifeless, pumped full of chemicals."

"We'll still have our souls," Rick said.

"I came here for the academics, not for the fairy tales."

A tweezer of doubt pinched Ink's heart. He sat up, one leg falling from the other, an image of himself sliced open for the world. Vital organs preserved with chemicals—what if this was the best the afterlife could do? Abruptly, the monster in his pants shrank back, like a vampire from morning light. He was relieved. Also, he was doomed.

*

On Monday, Miss Keane—minus the black dress, the high heels, the bare shoulders, the knee-buckling pinch of cleavage—began class by asking them to turn to "Young Goodman Brown," a story they'd been discussing in the previous class. Ink, still burning from the shame of last Friday's fantasies, kept eyes glued to his spiral notebook.

"So," his teacher said, hands on hips. "Does Brown see a witch meeting or not?"

Silence.

"Which is it? A or B?"

"Neither," Timothy Bashour said. "Hawthorne won't tell us for sure."

"That's right. Now why? Is this just a case of sloppy writing?"

"No," Jerry Parrington exclaimed, jumping all over the softball.

"Okay, things are not what they seem. Give me a word for this."

"Complicated," Jerry said.

"Sure . . . anything else?" Miss Keane stood there palms out, lips parted, eyes the color of hotel pools.

"Ambiguous," Timothy said.

"Exactly!" She smiled at Timothy while Ink slouched at his desk, kicking himself for being afraid that "ambiguous" would not be the word his lovely teacher was looking for.

"Remember," Miss Keane said, "Brown is totally out of his element. He's left his home and, most importantly, his Faith. He gets lost in the wilderness, which in early America, was certainly frightful and dangerous. In the Puritan mind, it was the complete opposite of the safe, civilized, Christianized world of Salem."

"The forest is a key symbol," Timothy said, only afterward remembering to raise his hand.

"Yes!" she said, eyes blazing with gratitude. "That's exactly where I was going."

Behind Ink, there was soft giggling. He heard Alex Wright's lispy whisper: "The foreth is a thimbol!"

"The forest is a literal place, but it can also be understood as a kind of moral wilderness." Miss Keane went on, and heads bobbled vigorously in their sockets. Ink closed his eyes and tried to conjure up again a picture of her in her Friday night finery. Where did she go after she left Lucille's? Who was she trying to find? What moral wilderness might she be thrashing through right now as she lectured this class of lust-crazy boys? Perhaps she had simply gone to the wrong place. But what if she'd been stood up? No, no, what if she just learned that she was pregnant and was looking for the man who was already running away?

Miss Keane told them to take out their journals and write about a real-life symbol from their own lives. "A symbol, remember, is a person, a place, an object that has come to mean more than what it actually is." Ink was tempted to write: "Miss Keane is the symbol of ideal beauty," but he quickly lost himself in thinking of her shedding clothes one silky article at a time. In eighth grade, Ink used to go over to Sandro's every Saturday afternoon, racing slot cars on the track they built over the rec room pool table. MTV was on in the background and when Van Halen's "Hot for Teacher" galloped onto the screen they would just freeze, squeezing controllers until their Formula Ones flew to the floor. "Man," Sandro said, as the scantily clad educator strode across desktops. Ink nodded, unable to muster even a syllable of assent.

"I'll give you five more minutes," Miss Keane said, moving past Ink as he stumbled from his reverie. He glanced at her behind, but it was hidden today in a loose-fitting skirt, beige and boring as could be.

Ink returned to his notebook. He tapped pen to paper. Symbol, symbol, symbol. Person, place, or thing. Frankie—the name, buried in his memory, popped to the surface. Frankie McGooken: the awkward, outspoken boy who wore a back brace that made him look like a botched abortion. For some reason, he drowned in a foot or two of water. Still dead after all these years, perhaps Frankie was, as Mom once suggested, the symbol of the consequences of ambition—a boy who failed to learn his place in the grand scheme of things. Wasn't it true that everyone had his limits? Wasn't it important to be smart enough to recognize them if you didn't wish to come to a bad, untimely end? Ink wasn't sure what he thought, but he wrote it out anyway, in the process softening his judgment on the boy a bit, lest Miss Keane think he was unchristian. He titled the piece "Sagacity" because it sounded like a place where smart people like him might go to live. Miss Keane would be sure to appreciate the essay's depth, feel the pathos of a sensitive young man's close brush with a tragedy, marvel at how the experience opened up to him a wisdom beyond his tender years.

*

Wisdom had been a motif since the beginning of the semester, when Uncle Lare, already on his fourth beer, accosted Ink at Grandma and Grandpa's Labor Day barbecue with the question, "So how's my favorite fool?"

Ink looked at him, confused, afraid, cursing himself for being unprepared for such an assault.

"Okay, wise fool. Sophomore." Uncle Lare smacked his beer into Ink's plastic cup of pop. "Christ, you're almost an adult."

"Really?" Impatient for eighteen, for twenty-one, Ink still saw himself as a little boy, especially at these family functions, where he was always the youngest by decades. Uncle Lare stared with crinkly eyes that reminded Ink of the paper bag he used and reused for lunches at school. There was a crease like a laceration across the chest of his too tight polo shirt. Unemployed for years, his uncle now worked thirty-five hours a week in the Men's Department at J.C. Penney. "Measuring fat chumps for suits, helping them squeeze into their jackets," he said. "Big time stuff." The stability, such as it was, had done little to curb his drink and temper. At family gatherings, he would brood and burn eyes at everyone until a switch flipped and he railed against Reagan. Last Christmas, when he was especially drunk, he said, "What I'd give for someone to take another shot . . ."

Later, when Ink's uncle was passed out in the guest room, Mom said that he should not be allowed to come to family gatherings. Grandma, though, was surprisingly firm: Under no circumstances could family ever be turned away.

"Hey, you want to go for a ride?" Uncle Lare pointed to the driveway, where his new car—a black Trans Am—rested behind Dad's bland brown wagon. It was tempting, but there was something a little too desperate in his uncle's voice.

"We're going to eat pretty soon, I think."

For some reason—perhaps because he knew his uncle now owned a gun—Ink thought of child abductors, crazies who drew you in with candy, dragged you into the woods to bury you alive. He was relieved when his uncle didn't make much of his refusal, less so when the man grabbed another beer from the back porch cooler and followed him to the lawn chair under the thick-armed sycamore. With a grunt, his uncle plopped on the grass beside him. Ink tried to lose himself in thoughts of girls, but going to an all-boys school, the only ones he saw these days were those who shopped at Parmatown, the mall to which he and Ant bussed on Saturday afternoons. The girls arrived in his mind the same way they strolled through the place—in sweet, fragrant dazzling clusters. There were pretty faces and big hair and taut behinds filling out shorts or designer jeans. Out of nowhere came the image of Bethany Hyde, a girl Ink adored all throughout his grade school years. He hadn't seen her now in over a year; to his dismay, he had trouble recalling anything beyond her long blond hair.

"Sometimes, you know," Uncle Lare said, wincing at a sudden shaft of sun through the leaves. "I think I could just kill myself."

Dad had just tossed hamburgers onto their uncooked backs, and smoke and fire spit from the grill. Ink was twenty feet away, but he swore the flames were licking his face, melting his nose and eyes.

"You're the family sage. What's the best way?"

"Uncle Lare, I don't know . . .

"You mean you don't think about it? You haven't thought about it even once?"

Ink said, "You really shouldn't…"

The Blue Angels suddenly streaked overhead—four sleek jets in a perfect diamond, silent against the pristine sky. Everyone looked up, shielding their eyes, and then came the roar, like a grand celestial cheer for what they'd all just seen.

Uncle Lare smiled and placed a hand on Ink's shoulder. "You think I'm an idiot? I was testing you." He tapped an index finger to his temple. "Just say no, right? Like Nancy says." He got up and shambled to the cooler, the neck of his empty swinging between two fingers.

In a daze, Ink wandered back to the grill, where Dad was talking to Aunt Ruth about a minor plumbing issue.

"You have one of those rotary ball faucets?"

She shrugged and smiled. "I think so."

As he slid juicy cheeseburgers onto a plate, Dad tried explaining. "The cap probably needs tightening. You have a hex wrench?"

She laughed. "Is this repair going to involve witchcraft?"

Dad smiled and handed the plate to her. "I'll just come over next week. I'm sure you don't need a new one . . . but don't let my boss hear that!"

When Uncle Lare returned home this evening, would he close the garage door and just leave the sports car running? Take a steak knife to his wrists? Slide his newly purchased gun into his mouth? Should he tell Dad now? Call the police? Call Aunt Judy and tell her to remarry this sad, volatile man?

Ink gulped down two burgers and drank several cups of orange pop. However, he did or said nothing. In the days that followed, he frequently broke into a sweat, dug fingernails into his head in an attempt to scrape away the worry and guilt. To his astonishment, Uncle Lare lived on, and sophomore year continued, dropping upon Ink with full force after the Labor Day holiday and giving him something more important to do with his time. He'd had a full year to adjust to the rigors of a college preparatory high school, but this year was like starting over in so many ways. English was still pretty easy for him, but there was Biology, which made him anxious about what was going on underneath his own skin and bone; French, with its irregular verbs and unpredictably gendered nouns; and Algebra II, the sequel to the freshman year horror show he barely survived. To make matters worse, he seemed to be on his own. Sandro, his best friend from grade school, became even busier with soccer and band, not to mention that play he was in at Magnificat, the girls' school in swanky Rocky River. Those boys who did pay attention to him were geeks desperate for any kind of legitimacy or, worse, Cro-Magnons like Andy Crabb who, among other things, derived great pleasure from pressing finger to nostril to blow shiny emeralds of snot onto Ink's unsuspecting shoes.

Despite these challenges, Ink was determined to succeed. He wasn't going to flunk out. He wasn't going to brood in obscurity or become the subject of gruesome abuse. He swallowed his pride and became friends with Anthony Gigante, who was crude and occasionally insulting (he'd call you "cunt" or "compadre," depending on the time of day), but he was a wiz in math and science. Just as important, the boy had friends like Rick and Joel who didn't mind him sliding in among them so he could eat his salami sandwich.

So with one brilliant alliance, Ink solved two major problems in his life: he became a better student, and he found a home of sorts at school. However, there was no such simple remedy for Sophomore Service, a community-focused course that was a requirement for graduation. For the first few weeks of the semester, they learned about something called social justice. They read an essay called "Men for Others," the title of which was also the motto of the school.

"Love of God, love of neighbor," Fr. Harter said. "We all are familiar with that commandment. But Arrupe says that, in order to love, you must respect that person—you must grant him his dignity as a human being." Harter smiled—he was nearly always smiling. Even the wrinkles on his face—sides, top, and bottom—were deep curves and curlicues, fabulous parabolas that made everyone think him the personification of all earthly joy.

Arrupe's reasoning was all well and good, but it did little to improve Ink's attitude about the next phase of the course, which involved weekly trips to a nearby soup kitchen to treat the local homeless with the aforementioned dignity and respect. Every Tuesday morning, he'd meet with classmates at the front doors of the Administration Building and, with the jovial priest leading the way, follow the brick path through the golf green knolls of campus to Lorain, that grimy road whose only saving grace was the Wendy's directly across the street. Each time they approached the shelter, Ink could feel an anxious rumbling in his bowels. Sometimes, he really really had to go, but there was no amount of layering that would make it safe for Ink to sit upon the toilet seats these people used.

In the kitchen, Ink gouged eyes from potatoes, splashed soup into plastic bowls, slapped ham and cheese and tomato between slices of white bread. He tried not to laugh when Alex Wright, working beside him, peeked through the window to the dining area in order to find fodder for his lunch period soap opera, *The Dirty and the Vile*. Occasionally—and this was the thing that rattled him the most—Ink would have to go out into the dining room, where they all sat at long tables, boisterous and smelly, their shifty eyes darting this way and that. Each time, he held his breath, as if his head were being dunked under water.

Once, he got waylaid by a blob in a Browns jersey. His first impulse was to run, but Fr. Harter had admonished them about this again and again. "You should talk to the clients. You need to. After all, they are human beings."

"I know Bernie Kosar," the blob announced, tapping the cracked white 19 on his jersey as if that was all the evidence he needed.

Someone behind them said, "Oh, you don't even know your mama."

Ink turned around, saw men laughing gently over scraped-empty plates.

"We go way back. Gave me four seats to the Steelers game. Fifty-yard line."

"Really," Ink said, wiping down a table. He looked up, saw Alex's face beaming through the kitchen window.

"Let's see them," one of the table men said.

"Oh yeah, right. You'll take them. You always do."

"Hey Denny, my man," said another one. "You know I used to play for the Browns?"

"No!"

"Sure. Got tired of the bright lights, though. The women and the money. Now I'm just keeping it real, one bowl of soup at a time."

"What position you play?"

"You don't recognize me? Damn, what kind of fan are you?"

More laughter. Ink turned and nearly ran into another one. He was tall and thin, his hair slicked back over his head. He wore a bowling shirt with a name in script above the heart. Cliff.

"God be with you!" he said.

Ink nodded. He began rolling the dish cart back to the kitchen.

"What I mean is thank you very much."

Ink turned. "Okay," he mumbled.

"You keep up with that school." The man tapped his temple. He winked. "Nose to the grindstone."

When he made it back to the kitchen, Ink wanted to faint into someone's arms.

"Dude," Alex whispered as he passed. "They surrounded you out there. Like fricking zombies."

Ink smiled. Alex was often a real ass, but his comment now was like a hand pulling him back on board a ship.

A few days before Christmas, Ink was holed up in his bedroom, trying to complete a reflection essay on his experience with the homeless. "It's like a parallel universe," he wrote. "An underground world. You don't see it if it isn't shoved in your face." Shoved, shoved—that was certainly what he felt, but he was smart enough to know that a word with such negative connotations should not be used in this situation. He scratched it out and wrote: "If you don't have the opportunity to see it for yourself." There, that was better—much better. "Opportunity" was the kind of word that would cause Fr. Harter to break out into half a million smiles. Now, he needed a final sentence—something that would really demonstrate the nature of his growth. He wrote, "I am more conscious about poverty in the Cleveland area." Good, good, he thought, but it was not until he added "and in the world at large" that he felt the piece was ready to be typed.

He interrupted Mom's puzzling at the dining room table in order to show her the final product. For the entire semester, she'd bitten her tongue. "I'm sending you to school," she'd said more than once. "Not out onto the streets." But she'd been powerless—the one time in his life when he wished that she wasn't. Now that she had tangible evidence of the end of this reckless adventure in her hands, she was visibly relieved. After carefully reading the piece, she smiled and said, "Well done. I think you should be really proud."

*

How much better was the next semester, when, the service course was replaced by a theology class that went by the wonderful name of SEX? Sure, "Sex and Morality" was its full title, but Ink was sixteen, and, like the rest of the boys in the course, he had trouble getting past the orgy of images that the glorious three-letter word conjured in his mind.

The teacher was Mr. LeMonde, a young man with long hair and a jeans jacket with "Zoso" in fire red stitched across its back. He drove a motorcycle to school, buzzing helmetless by the boys who were heading into the Administration Building to start their day, swaying to the left and right into a parking space, hair fluttering like bad ass wings behind him. Mr. LeMonde taught with the same reckless attitude, and Ink entered class every morning with great anticipation. When Mom noticed the course on the schedule at the beginning of spring semester, she wondered aloud: "Is this a Catholic school or what?"

Dad, looking up from the most recent edition of *The Guinness Book of World Records*, said: "They must know what they're doing."

Mom was not convinced, and she phoned the principal, demanding an explanation. At the supper table that evening, she stabbed hard at her cube steak and canned green beans, a clear and glorious sign that she'd suffered another defeat.

The day before Valentine's Day, Mr. LeMonde stopped the lesson early and said, "Before we finish, let's talk a few minutes about

94

tomorrow. Show of hands: Who here has a date lined up?"

A few boys raised their hands and then several others, after worried glances around the room, put theirs up as well. Ink added his hand at the last second in a lame effort to save himself from conspicuousness.

"Ok, ok. And what are your plans? What are you going to do?"

"You mean *who* are you going to do," Andy Crabb said.

Mr. LeMonde looked up at the drop-down ceiling, waiting until the laughter died away. "The goal of life, you know, is to be more dignified than dogs on the street. That should go without saying, but with you horny grunts, I can't take anything for granted."

More laughter. Andy snorted like a swine. Besides playing middle linebacker for the junior varsity football team, it was (Ink thought) the one thing the boy could do better than blow his snot.

"Let's see," Mr. LeMonde said, putting a finger upon his lips. "I bet you're going to take your girl some place fancy—like Denny's."

The boys laughed.

"You'll get her the double cheeseburger, a chocolate sundae—the works. Then you'll go watch *Lethal Weapon* or *Robocop* and hold her hand and maybe, just maybe, when there's a bad guy blowing up on the screen, she'll rest her pretty head upon your shoulder?"

Murmurs and chuckles.

Mr. LeMonde sat back on the desk and folded his arms. "What I'm getting at—what I want you to focus on is the end of the evening, the two of you alone in the car in the theater parking lot or on some tree-covered dead-end street a few blocks from her house. Say that, against all odds, you're getting lucky: she's kissing you, she's sliding hands down your back, whatever. In response, you get a little overzealous. After all, including the box of candy and the long stem rose, you're probably out fifty bucks. It's simple justice, you might think, when you slide your hand under that skirt."

Around him, Ink heard a few dirty whispers. He glanced at Ant, but he was busy putting the finishing touches on a three-headed dragon he'd been drawing for days inside his notebook.

"And let's just say, to complicate things, she starts really getting into it. She appears to want it bad."

"Sounds good to me," Crabb said, glancing around for the

support he knew he'd find.

Mr. LeMonde placed his right hand on his left. "Tell me boys: What does this right hand represent?"

Someone in the back mumbled, and the boys around him exploded.

"Come on now. Pretend you are young men, actual human beings at a certain advanced stage of emotional development."

The boys grew quiet. Mr. LeMonde had been letting them have their fun; now, they were expected to indulge him for a while.

"It's the hand of God! But look—it's not there to stop you. No, it's just His way of letting you know He's there before you go one single step further."

"Okay, okay," Crabb said, rubbing at his smirk like it was a smudge that wouldn't come out. "What's really the problem, Mr. LeMonde? You want it, she wants it. It's there for the taking."

"You're not going to hurt anybody," Jerry said.

"For starters, you're going to hurt God."

"But if you love each other . . ."

"Don't you think there are better ways of showing love than by having a feeding frenzy in the front seat of your Chevette? I mean, for one thing, how much do you really hope to accomplish with bucket seats? And what are you going to tell your family proctologist when he asks how you got a gear shift stuck in your behind?"

The boys laughed again. They were having the time of their lives.

"Sexual intercourse is not just a bodily function," Timothy said. "It's a sacrament."

Mr. LeMonde put a finger on his nose. He pointed. "Someone gets it! There is at least one human among our ranks." He stood up. He crouched in front of Crabb, looking earnestly in his eyes. "Here's what you do: You zip up and say goodnight. You are a good boy. A Christian."

Crabb was grinning, but he was nodding too.

"And, when you get back home, feel free to crawl into bed and give yourself a hand for a job well done."

The boys nearly fell out of their chairs.

Mr. LeMonde stood up. "Here's what I always tell my kids: It's ok to *have* the biggest dick in the world . . ."

Terrific explosions of laughter.

"Just don't *be* the biggest dick in the world."

Thumping on desks. A series of triumphant hoots.

"Mr. LeMonde," Connie Hendricks said, squirming in his chair. "You probably shouldn't talk like that." A few other boys nodded in agreement.

The teacher shrugged. "If I don't, how are you all going to hear me?"

The boys were quiet now, faces pinched with confusion.

"You know, Ignatius of Loyola was not unlike you once: young and self-absorbed and horny as hell. And then came the big change. Metanoia. Write that one down because I do believe I'll throw it on the test. Means spiritual conversion. A total redirection of your life. A move from self to other. Sometimes, as with St. Paul, it comes with a bolt of lightning. Sometimes, as with our own dear Senor López, all it takes is a flaming cannonball between the legs."

The students groaned. The boys, well versed in slapstick comedies, could empathize with the guy who endured even a close call to the balls.

"Men for others. It's the Jesuit way."

The bell rang.

"We're not like those selfish bastards from Ed's."

More laughter, the thunk of books, the thunder of chairs. The boys standing around Ink seemed like trees in a dense forest. Ink looked down at his notebook. Forty-five minutes of class, and the only thing he learned was metanoia. He wondered what else they'd be responsible for on next week's test.

*

A few days later, Sandro called out of the blue to say he'd gotten his driver's license and, as if it were some sweet package deal, Cindi Lewes, a girl from that play he was in at Magnificat, agreed to go out with him. She insisted, however, upon a double date. The other girl was already lined up—her cousin Donna, a junior at Augustine. All they needed now was a willing and able boy.

"Just think: an older woman!" Sandro said.

Ink hadn't seen much of his friend lately. The only class they shared this year was French, and Sandro sat three rows away, trading doodles with Dmitri Bukosky, his new soccer pal, and the JV's star striker. He was grateful for the call, giddy and nervous in fact, as if Sandro were not his long-time friend but some pretty girl he'd been admiring from afar. But a part of him was angry as well—angry about the neglect, about not (he was almost certain) having been the first boy on his list.

"I don't know," Ink said, trying to salvage some pride. "What's she look like?"

"She looks fine. She looks great. Hair, boobs, butt—it's all there, man."

"I bet you've never even seen her!"

Silence for a heart-stopping moment. Did he hear a sigh? Was Sandro going to withdraw the offer?

"Come on: Playoff basketball. Pepperoni pizza. Maybe a sweet hand job good night."

Ink laughed. He was really not in the position to press the issue of her looks. "Yeah, yeah, sure," he said, as cool as could be. "Count me in."

And just like that he had a date—a date and a whole host of worries about what to wear, what to say, when to make a move (and what, for that matter, a move looked like), and what to tell his parents so they'd never even know.

*

For some reason, Miss Keane was not in a good mood. Crabb had come in a few minutes earlier, pretending to be David Byrne, hiccupping lines from "Burning Down the House" and she said, "Not today," her eyes bright and sharp. Around Ink, speculation was rampant. Jerry wondered if it had anything to do with their last exam, which he was sure he bombed. "Her boyfriend finally dumped her," Joel suggested. "Man, she's just on the rag," Ant said. Alex smirked, shrugged, and drew what was for him the most obvious conclusion: "Once a bitch, always a bitch."

"Okay now, lots to get done today," Miss Keane said as soon as the bell rang. "Page 402. Hemingway. An American master. What's going on here?"

A cough. A snicker. The scud of a desk.

"The man and the woman are having a conversation, right?"

The furious clicking of a pen.

"Jerry," Miss Keane said, hands on hips. "Sounds like your brain could use a tune up."

Light laughter.

"Come on, people. Focus! What are the man and the woman talking about? What does the man want the woman to do?"

Crabb opened his mouth for surreptitious fellatio with a thumb.

"He wants her to get an abortion," Eric Chevalier said. Although only a sophomore, Eric was already considered the official "tortured artist" of the entire school. He had thin black hair that stuck at all kinds of bad angles to his face. To Ink, his lips were like a blob of blood you'd squeeze from a pinpricked finger.

"Yes. Right. Exactly!"

Ink paged back through the story. He didn't remember seeing that word. No—it definitely wasn't there. How could Eric have known? Did his book have some special answer key in the back?

Miss Keane drew an iceberg on the board. A boat too—one that looked like a toothless smile impaled by a pennant. "Seven-eighths of the thing is below the surface. Hemingway uses simple words and sentence structures, but there's so much more going on than ever meets the eye."

Baffled by the story, Ink had nothing to add to the class discussion; however, he could listen with the best of them. He wrote down everyone else's questions and observations. When Eric said, "The man looks at the suitcase labels because he just wants to continue with their traveling way of life," Ink starred the point in his notebook. It gave him great satisfaction to fill up a page with notes—with real knowledge. Later, he would go over the ideas at a leisurely pace to test them against any thoughts he might in the meantime come up with on his own.

Miss Keane launched into a lecture on the Twenties, the decade during which the story was published. It was, without question, a most interesting and exciting time. Women had, at last, the right to vote. They were going to college, to work. They were becoming sexually liberated. But it was still a patriarchal society. The men, in other words, were still in control. And almost seventy years later? There were still many battles to be fought. Equal opportunity. Equal pay. Women, she said suddenly, were not objects. She put the book on the table and began moving back and forth across the room. Ink thought of her in that black dress at Lucille's, alone and unknown, searching for the man who'd stood her up. Maybe this was weighing on her now. He thought of her pushing through the apartment door, bags of groceries in her hand. He saw her chopping vegetables, scraping sticky rice from the edges of a pot. He saw her later that night, alone before a TV, sweats, face shorn of makeup. After a while, a bucket full of tears, sleep at last in a narrow bed, *The Sun Also Rises* hugging her lap. Ink tried to get her up and lose the clothes. He tried to put her in the shower, with soap bubbling between breasts. He tried hard, but for some reason, his imagination wasn't up to the task.

"So," Miss Keane said, picking back up the textbook. "All of this is a long preface to what I think is the story's most important question: What does this woman want?"

Silence again. Crabb buried a smile under his hand. A moment later, the bell sounded.

"Okay people," Miss Keane said, raising her voice over the packing of book bags and the scuttling of chairs. "For tomorrow, give me 500 words on what the woman wants."

Crabb glanced around the room. He was desperate now to tell his joke. His cheeks bulged from the weight and size of it.

"Does it have to be typed?" Jerry asked.

"Oh Jerry, it doesn't matter. Just show me you know how to think!"

There was that anger again, flaring out at them all. Chastened, the boys filed out silently, heads down. Ink made sure he was the last one to leave. Alone with her, he hoped to be able to offer a word of comfort, some oblique sign of understanding that would help her with whatever it was she was going through. He shyly approached the desk, where she was forcing notes into a manila folder. When she muttered "Dammit," he changed directions and retreated to the hallway. She might not be a "bitch," as Alex believed, but Miss Keane, he was sad to say, was not half as pretty to him as she'd been at the beginning of the year.

On his bed at home, Ink read back over the Hemingway story. It was clear the man wanted her to have "it"—the abortion, of course (how could he have failed to see this before?)—but he did not want it to appear that he was talking the young woman into it. He wanted her to see it as the best thing to do, the quickest and most efficient way to return to the wonderful, carefree life they had been enjoying.

So what did the woman want? At the beginning, she simply wanted a beer, but that couldn't be the answer. Did she really want the child? The child as a way of keeping her man? Did she want some assurance that their future life together would be strong and healthy, regardless of the decision? An hour later, the words still refusing to arrange themselves satisfactorily on the page, Ink went downstairs for a cookie break. TV hour was over, and Dad had disappeared into the basement to have one more look at the dryer that had been acting up the last few days. Mom sat on the couch, Thomas Merton in her lap. Ink let her read the first few pages of the story while he scraped Oreo cream into his mouth with his bottom teeth.

"So let me get this straight," Mom said, brows narrowing. "They're talking about abortion?"

"Right! But if you notice, Hemingway never really says." He was happy to be able to pass along such important information.

"Abortion is wrong. Life begins at conception."

"I know."

"Then why on earth are they having you read this?"

"It's literature."

"What if we had—?"

"Mom, Mom, what do you think the woman—?"

"I'd hate to think what you'd be reading if we sent you to public school."

Ink gave up. Back upstairs, he pored over the story again. At the end, the woman seemed to want nothing more than for the man to be quiet. Once he complied, she said she was fine. Was this a happy ending? Had the woman gotten what she wanted? Or was this just a brief lull in a larger, losing battle? Questions bred questions, and all Ink could do was write out his various theories and conclude his piece with the words: "I'm just not sure."

Ink woke in the middle of the night to the sound of Trouble, Mr. Majeski's obnoxious beagle. Yap, yap, yap, yap. He pulled back the curtain, saw the thing burrowing its nose at the back door. He would have yelled—he would have told the beast to "SHUT YOUR LOUSY MOUTH!"—but the old man had just returned from an extended stay in the hospital. Blood clot? Bypass? —whatever it was, it was reason enough to cut him some slack.

"Okay, baby," Mr. Majeski said, appearing in a bathrobe on the back porch. "You know I'd never forget you." The dog disappeared into the house and the door closed. Ink thought about his upcoming date, pictured a girl who was a real dog: wide bottom, mop water hair, face purple-pink with acne, mole like a booger tucked under the flabby curve of a nostril. What she wanted more than anything was to be treated decently by a boy. With God's help, maybe he could be up to the task for a night. Who knew? Maybe a little altruism now would pay big dividends later. "Karma," as Joel Stein always liked to say.

Later, returning wide awake from the bathroom, Ink saw a light on under his parents' bedroom door. The door was cold and white— a thick sheet of ice over a deep body of water. An iceberg. Behind it, or below, was the craggy dangerous bulk of the thing. Who was up? Dad? Mom? And was this a new development, or some routine that had escaped his inattentive eyes? He imagined the two of them in low voices going on about important marriage stuff—a new refrigerator, less expensive car insurance, the financial strain of an oft-talked about trip to Washington D.C. How much had they wrung their hands over in the last twenty years? And yet, for all the daily trials, there must have been a real page-turning start to their relationship. He knew they'd met at college, and for their first date (memorialized by a picture framed on the living room wall), he'd taken her to a church picnic. What had that date been like? What had they talked about? What had they done? What had they thought of each other then and later, when she quit school and moved to Ohio with him so he could begin his career? And now? After all their years of better or worse? Ink couldn't dive that deep below the surface. He didn't dare.

*

The morning of his date, Ink was a bundle of nerves at school. Periodically, a stern, robotic voice in his head would declare: "T-Minus X hours until lift off." He thought of rockets billowing smoke on a launching pad, a sun-splashed crowd cheering wildly, the sky an Easter egg blue. Then he thought of the space shuttle, those seven poor astronauts who, despite all the planning, preparation, and precautions, had been obliterated in an instant on national TV. No, no—the girl would not be a disaster. She was Cindi's cousin, after all, and Sandro's date was a thing of beauty. She'd be pretty enough. She'd listen with

102

rapt attention to his incisive dissection of Hemingway. She'd laugh at his self-deprecating jokes. And if all that weren't enough, he'd be seen in public for an extended period of time with someone of the opposite sex. And if, by chance, he botched things badly, Sandro would be there, hands firmly on the wheel; his friend wouldn't simply stand by and watch the night blow up in his face.

In world history class, Fr. White droned on about the British Empire, its ill-fated exploits in Afghanistan. Around him, boys took meticulous notes about Disraeli, Macnaghten, Brydon. He tried to pay attention, but his thoughts wandered again to this evening, which would be history making for him. Tomorrow morning, regardless of what happened, he would rise and be someone transformed, his former self as dead to him as all these obscure nineteenth century Brits.

At lunch, Ant and Alex had another heated discussion about the Browns, what they were going to need to do to take the next step to the Super Bowl. Yards per carry, points allowed, the merits of Schottenheimer's prevent D, John *Fucking* Elway—a swirl of stats and trivia that made them sound like raunchy versions of Dad.

"So what's going on this weekend?" Ant asked. Ordinarily, Ink would have said "same old, same old," but today the question sang in his ears like sweet, celestial music. Here, at last, was his chance! However, if he was going to announce the news, it had to come out naturally, like it was no big deal.

"Nothing much." There. That was a good start. "I've got a date."

Alex smiled. "With your left hand or your right?"

"Excellent," Ant said, nodding his head.

"Does everybody always have to be so gross?" Ink asked.

Joel adjusted his glasses. "Could it be true that our boy here has at last obtained for himself some female companionship?"

Ink shrugged, but it was a losing effort to play it cool.

"Are we sure now it's a girl?" Ant asked, mouth sticky with peanut butter.

Everyone laughed. Everyone was having a gay old time, Ink thought, like the royal faggots that they were.

*

Donna, his date, turned out to be not half bad. Sure, the ringlets of hair hanging off either side of her head made Ink think of chain mail, but the face, with the help of makeup, was on the good side of decent. She wore a loose shirt and jeans, making it hard to determine the quality of her figure, but, all in all, he could have done much worse. However, she paled in comparison to Sandro's girl Cindi with her rich, shampoo commercial hair, full red lips, spandex pants, and crimson high heel jellies. As they all waited in line for tickets, Ink stood behind her, breathing in bubble gum and vanilla. It was all he could do to keep from eating her alive.

The gym was packed, but the four found seats near the far wall, about half way up on the Ignatius side of the stands. It was the sectional final, and Ink was looking forward to seeing his school pound Central Catholic, whose star was Macho Maldonado, Ink's grade school nemesis. Across the way was a large swath of Catholic fans—dark, boisterous, angry-eyed kids who seemed more suited for a fight than to root for their team. Ink had heard many vague, terrible stories about what went on at this other school: a pot ring broken up, a boy stabbed between classes, a teacher pinned against the wall. As the Wildcats trotted out for the shoot around, a gang of boys—Puerto Rican maybe? Black?—congregated near the baseline and began to chant:

> Oh my goodness
> Oh my gracious
> There's those fags
> From St. Ignatius!

On the Ignatius side, two clean-cut male cheerleaders banged the sides of megaphones and cried: "The Wild-cats Will WinThisGame! The Wild-cats Will WinThisGame!"

Sandro said, "You know, they do have a point."

Ink laughed and Cindi smiled, but in a generic way, as if eager to prove the quip had not flown over her head. Donna narrowed her eyes at Sandro. "That's terrible," she said.

A horn blared, and the players assembled around the half court circle. Ink clenched his teeth, recalling eighth grade, Mr. Bishop pushing him onto the floor and towards his doom. He glanced at his companions. Next to him, Donna had hands jammed in pockets and eyes on the ceiling. Next to her, Cindi leaned into Sandro, whispering and giggling. Coyly, she moved back toward her cousin when Sandro went on the offensive. Below them, the game was on: a basket here, a basket there. Macho had the ball now, was dribbling up the court, flashing fingers to call a play.

"Are you a basketball fan?" This was the best question Ink had come up with to break the ice with Donna. During the drive over, Cindi had talked so much about hair care products and Michael Jackson that he hadn't had time to use it.

Donna shrugged. "Off the top of my head, I can name thirty-two more interesting things."

Macho effortlessly sliced through the Wildcat zone for a left-handed layup and a foul. Ink studied the girl's profile. Her chin, he concluded, was too square. Her nose was unappealing, with pores the size of strawberry seeds. Such plainness empowered him to say, "Name one," his voice full of challenge.

"Like, I don't know, the problems with our president? Like wheeling and dealing behind the backs of the American people?"

Every once in a while, Ink made a conscious effort to read the front section of *The Plain Dealer* and tried to connect the world of news with his own world of home and school. He'd read the first paragraph of a half dozen articles and knew the president had been in some kind of trouble for the last few months. But inevitably, within a day or two, his attention had turned to more important matters: an upcoming French exam, an essay about *Dubliners*, a fantasy about a cute blonde who served him a soft pretzel at the Parmatown Mall.

Donna had been especially irritated by Reagan's speech on TV the other night—"'The power of the presidency resides with you'— what a joke!"

Taking a chance that honesty might be the best policy, Ink said, "I'm not sure I know what you're talking about."

The buzzer sounded for substitutions. Ink thought of *Family Feud*, the giant red X when the contestant made a guess that the survey didn't say. He watched a Catholic boy trot off the court, head down, the coach chomping at him as he passed to the bench. Despite Macho's best efforts, Ignatius was up seven.

Donna, after a long pause, decided to educate Ink, and he said "yes" and "uhhuh" until Sandro interrupted to say that he and Cindi were going to beat the halftime crowds to the concessions stand. Donna continued her monologue while Ink watched them walking away, chatting avidly, bodies close. Just as they reached the doorway, Cindi tossed her head to laugh, lifted a heel all the way back to her behind. Donna blabbed on, but all he wanted to think about was sex.

Ink tuned in again when Donna asked him about reading, and, eager to say something, he mentioned a novel by Piers Anthony that (he knew, somehow, not to say this) was giving him wonderful ideas for a *Dungeons & Dragons* module he was creating for the club to which Ant, Rick, and Jerry belonged.

"Hmmm. Don't know him. If I read anything close to fantasy, it's usually Orwell or Huxley. Life is short, you know. I look for the high-quality stuff." Donna went on to talk about the dystopia as a literary genre, hands demonstrating all the deeper levels, the contemporary political implications of individual scenes that Ink knew nothing about since he hadn't read either of the writers in question. "Books like this over the last hundred years—they're warning us. The world is rocketing straight to hell and all people care about is sports and their cable TV."

"Of course I love the classics too—Hemingway, for example," Ink said, scrambling to save some face.

"Hemingway? Seriously? I read him for comic relief."

Eventually, Donna ran out of steam and they watched the halftime show—cheerleaders and pep bands—in silence. After a while, Donna began digging through her purse, reacquainting herself with old coupons and receipts. She pulled out her checkbook and mouthed calculations. She brushed away chain mail hair.

"What school do you want to go to?" she asked, as the second half began. Ignatius led 31-28; Macho, damn him, had ten points already, to go with several assists.

"You mean college?"

She laughed. "You've already done the elementary thing, right?"

"I don't know." Ink shrugged his shoulders. "Haven't given it much thought."

"How do you spend your days?" Her tone was a deadly combination of curiosity and malice. He looked at her, a stupid smile leaping upon his face.

"Let me guess: video games, some of that heavy metal music and a pot of sniffing glue.”

Ink had the powerful urge to stand, to tell Donna to shut the hell up. He longed to let her know that her cousin blew her out of the water in terms of looks and that, if he weren’t doing his good friend a favor, she’d be sitting home alone with her dumb, frumpy clothes and chain mail hair and strawberry nose that no amount of makeup could improve. Of course, he was smart enough to know that such a rant would make Cindi livid, and she would hold it against Sandro, who, as a consequence, might never ever call him again. So he simply said, “Give me a break,” a command that sounded more like a plea.

Donna nodded. “Will do.” She stood, straightened her jeans, and clumped down the bleachers. While maneuvering through the crowd, she stumbled, nearly falling onto a group of guys who were already telling her to get out of the way. Ink smiled to himself. He turned his eyes back to the court and tried to take interest in the game. It was close now, a back and forth contest. Ignatius would hit a shot, and then Macho would bring the ball up the court again, hand in the air, signaling his players where to go. They would do as he said, and, more often than not, he’d either drive for a score or deliver a teammate the ball for an easy basket.

At the start of the fourth quarter, Sandro returned with Cindi. He winked, sprawled on the bleacher, and gave Ink’s arm a squeeze to make it clear just what his absence meant.

“How’s Macho doing?” he asked.

“Hey, who you rooting for?”

“I didn’t say I wanted him to win.”

“Where’s Donna?” Cindi asked.

Ink looked at her as if she were the first question of an impossible exam. He could make something up—“She’s in the bathroom,” “She’s talking to an old friend”—but the truth would come out soon enough. And when it did, Ink would look worse for trying to conceal it.

“I wanted to have a normal conversation,” he said. “She wanted to talk politics.”

Cindi laughed so hard Ink could see her gum. “Oh yeah, that sounds like Donna, alright.”

Sandro did not seem disappointed in Ink, but maybe that was because he had an arm around Cindi, his fingers massaging the skin beneath the chain of her crucifix. Ink’s eyes dropped down to where that skin stopped and the form-fitting top began. It occurred to him that the clothed body—the clothed female body—was a kind of iceberg. How far already had Sandro made it below the surface?

"Oh well, she'll come back," Sandro said. "She needs a ride home."

With the game on the line, Macho's teammates suddenly crumbled around him. Tentative and callow, they seemed like clones of Ink from his ball playing days. The last five minutes of the game was a bore—a series of foul shots, time outs, and substitutions. Sandro and Cindi cheered occasionally, almost randomly, when they weren't speaking soft, private, evidently hilarious things into each other's ears. Ink should have been thrilled to see his old enemy go down, but the best he could offer was a few perfunctory claps. Basketball, after all, was dumb. And so was everything else.

*

When Ink pushed through the door, Mom was casting a stern eye at the weather report.

"Icy rain tomorrow," she said, crumpling her bag of chips. "Turning to snow."

"That's nice."

"Not for your father. He leaves for Omaha in the morning."

Ink nodded, remembering that Dad, just recently promoted, had a kitchen and bath trade show to attend. He'd made it to the stairs; his hand was on the railing.

"I didn't hear the car pull up."

"Oh." Ink had been working the lie over in his mind for hours, but now he felt a rush of panic. "Um, well, Mr. Gismondi just dropped me off at the corner. I told her—I mean him—that'd be okay." For the life of him, Ink couldn't remember the story he'd made up that had allowed him to go to the game.

Mom turned to him with dubious eyes. Ink looked with longing into the dark, peaceful hallway above. He placed a foot on the stair.

"Did you thank Mr. or Mrs. Gismondi for the ride home?"

Briefly, he thought he could make the lie better. He could add another sentence or two, filled with specific details that would leave no doubt. But the fact was that words had not been his friend tonight. On the way home, as Donna held forth yet again, talking about apartheid, about Reagan's lame response to the AIDS epidemic, Ink blurted out, "Are you some kind of lesbian?"

"Noooo," Donna said, drawing out the word as if it were a broadsword from a sheath.

"Then why do you care?"

Ink expected her to go on the offensive, but Donna just glared at him, arms locked against her chest.

"You're something else," Sandro said after a long moment. His voice had an edge to it that might have been real anger, but Cindi's giggly eyes suggested his reaction was a joke.

And now, standing on the stairs, Ink knew he was something else: socially awkward, uncommonly cruel, a liar to boot.

"Mom," he said, swallowing hard. "Sandro drove."

"You're kidding." She laughed. "You lied to me?"

Ink smiled, caught off guard. Maybe she was going to call him a "little devil" and muss his hair and say, "Next time smarty pants, you're going to get it good."

"You lied and you think it's funny? What am I going to do with you?"

The last thing Sandro had said when dropping him off was, "Better luck next time." Cindi's shoulders shook underneath his arm. Ink was barely out of the backseat when his friend roared away from the curb. Ink turned onto his darkened street, ill-clothed for even this short walk home.

"He's sixteen years old. You could have been killed."

"Better luck next time," Ink mumbled.

"There's not going to be a next time."

Ink sat down on the stairs, buried his face in his hands. He saw things clearly now. Sandro hadn't been trying to help him find a girlfriend. His plan had been to embarrass him in the worst way—to finish him off as a friend.

Mom moved closer and so he really turned it on, gasping and heaving and sucking back snot. He was not quite as distraught as the wailing suggested, and this new lie only made him feel worse. Soon, earnest tears arrived to drive off all the tainted ones. "Nobody likes me," he burbled.

"You think this is going to save you?" Mom said, her voice low, surprisingly gentle, and then there was an unexpected hand upon his head, stroking downward once and then, less awkwardly, again. Who was the woman below the surface? Of what was she capable? And who was he? What kind of person—on the surface and below—could he hope to be from this point on?

Seriously

(Fall 1988-Spring 1989)

Fr. Fruehauf, the short, black-clad globe at the front of the room, certainly didn't make things easy. Soft spoken, nailed down behind the podium, he spun out a complicated lecture about places that Ink, despite a course in World Geography a few years ago, would be hard pressed to find on a map.

Ink had point one and point two clearly printed in his notebook, but somehow, Fr. Fruehauf was mumbling through point four. He looked around the room, as if he might catch a glimpse of point three steaming off toward the horizon. To his left, Ant Gigante put the finishing touches on a dragon that breathed thick penile shafts of fire at a naked woman writhing in chains against a rock. In front, Jerry Parrington dropped his chin over the fat knot of his tie. To his right, Eric Chevalier read a Camus novel he had hidden behind his textbook. In the dead center of the room, Timothy Bashour was riveted, but as editor of *The Eye*, it was his job to absorb every last thing.

"That brings us, gentlemen, to point five," Fr. Fruehauf said.

Ink gave up, his mind drifting to his appointment later that day with Mr. Gregory, the college counselor, who was going to ask him yet again what it was he wanted to do with the rest of his life. Over the last few weeks, Ink had tried out several answers: write for a newspaper, edit great books, be a literary agent, teach. None of them sounded right. Seventeen, he thought, was an impossibly early age in life to have to know such things for sure. Why couldn't Mr. Gregory just hand him an envelope with a college name and career? After all, *he* was the professional.

Fr. Fruehauf slapped the pointer against the map. The boys, eager for any excuse, laughed when the stick popped right through.

"Hmm, not bad," the priest said, peering at the map. "Only about two hundred miles from the Kremlin."

More laughter.

Fr. Fruehauf tore out the flap, leaving a thumb-shaped hole that went straight through to the oblivion of the blackboard. "The Cold War continues."

Doug Bale, a tall, expertly coiffed boy across the room, raised his hand to declare that this was the dawn of a new day. As evidence, he hailed last year's speech by Reagan at the Brandenburg Gate. Glasnost was for real. Timothy raised his hand to wonder if the end of the Cold War might create more problems than it solved.

Fr. Fruehauf smiled. "Other thoughts, other thoughts?" he said, moving the pointer like a prison guard rifle back and forth across the room. Ink hunched his shoulders, lowered his eyes, did what he could to become less of a target.

That afternoon, Ink arrived at the senior lounge before the rest of the gang. He unwrapped his salami sandwich, snapped open an orange pop and a tiny bag of ruffled chips.

"Hello!"

It was Timothy—Timothy Bashour—and he stood before him holding a tray with a colorful salad, a seed sprinkled roll, a cup of peaches in syrup. Ink sat up, as if he'd been caught sleeping by Mr. Caprese, the Trig teacher with the three-pound ruler. The boy had the kind of smile that made it seem like he'd been searching you out to tell you the most exciting news. His mouth was big and full of clean white teeth—the epitome of optimism and good health.

"I've been meaning to ask: What do you know about Malle?"

Ink shrugged his shoulders, tried not to look at Timothy's face, which the boys had been discussing the other day at lunch.

"High cheekbones," Joel had said. "That's what you all are noticing."

Alex balled his napkin, gave it a terrible squeeze. "Does make you want to hit him, don't it?"

"Malle," Timothy repeated. "The director?"

Ink didn't say anything. Whenever Timothy looked his way, Ink was flattered, and a little star struck, as if the boy were a major motion picture star. But this feeling, this giddiness, troubled him too because Timothy was, as Ant had told him more than once, "queer as a three-dollar bill."

"*Au Revoir Les Enfants*. Our AP history class went to see it."

"Oh."

"Thought it might have been mentioned in your French class."

"We're doing *The Stranger*. Marcel Mersault," Ink added, stealing one of Joel Stein's jokes.

Timothy's laugh was overly generous, with enough teeth for a mouth and a half. Inwardly, Ink beamed, and he kept beaming all the while Timothy explained the film: France, World War II, the Nazi pursuit of Jews taking refuge in a Catholic boarding school.

"What happens?"

"Oh, you should go see it. It's still at the Cedar-Lee."

"What's that?"

"You don't know about the Cedar-Lee?" Timothy said, incredulous without being accusatory. "They get the only movies worth watching!" The theater was, Ink learned, in Cleveland Heights—on the east side, a part of town for which Grandpa Alt jokingly said you needed a passport.

An awkward pause. Ink looked down at his salami sandwich, which, in the presence of the kind of boy who was in front of him, could not simply be salami, but a symbol, a euphemism. His back became damp, his armpits prickly with sweat.

"Well, enjoy your day," Timothy said, cordial as always. Ink watched him walk to his table in the far corner of the lounge, where his people waited, their smiles bright as the sun.

Soon, Ink's own friends surrounded him, and talk spun around in a loop of sports and music and movies and what Miss Keane may or may not have been wearing under today's short skirt. On the fourth or fifth lap, Ant started in on the musical genius of INXS.

Joel said, "I don't listen to this popular music."

Ant, trying to be helpful, sang the guitar riff from "Devil Inside."

"Yeah, that's a good one!" Rick said.

Alex sneered at the boy. "INXS sucks donkey dick."

A battle ensued: Hutchence against Bon Jovi, pose against pose, song against song, hair against hair.

"You guys just like the ones they tell you to," Eric said. His brother had a radio show at Case. He wanted to know what they thought about the Pixies or the Smiths.

"Gay, gay," Alex said, a finger gun at phantom targets in the air.

Not surprisingly, everyone had a well-informed opinion about what was gay and what was not. Together, they were able to come up with an impressive list, citing rock stars and actors before zeroing in on more proximate examples, one of whom dined on a spinach and romaine salad at the back of the lounge.

"No question," Alex said, mouth full of melted cheese. "Dude's bent like a drinking straw."

"Bent?" Joel Stein asked, toggling his nose. "Is this some kind of anti-Semitic joke?"

Ink, sweating again under the arms, chimed in with his chuckle a good safe second behind the others.

Alex lit a cigarette, blew smoke in everyone's faces. "Seriously, the dude's a homo. A fruitcake." Additional terms and phrases tripped from his tongue, one after the next, as if none quite conveyed what he wanted it to, even the best words pale approximations of the thing that troubled them all.

Ink glanced at the table in the back. Timothy was sitting with Chris Lee, French Club president, and Neil Herring, the school's John the Baptist for *Godspell* two weeks from now. Between forkfuls of salad, Timothy was talking, maybe more about that film (Ink had already forgotten the name), and the other two nodded knowingly, adding comments of their own. They were having a simple conversation, like adults in a respectable restaurant.

Alex went on: "Faggot. Flamer. Fudge Packer. Buttfucker." The boy's ambitious quest for the proper term was encouraged by guffaws from Rick and Ant, mouths full of half-masticated lunch meat.

Joel said, "You speak like an expert in the field."

It was the perfect stroke—the exact same words Ink would have said, if he'd had the courage. Everyone turned to Alex with patient, mocking smiles.

Alex blew more smoke. "Fuck off," he said.

"You say that all the time," Eric said. "What does it mean? How would one even begin to oblige you?"

"By fucking off," Alex said, stabbing out his cigarette in Eric's plate of Turkey Tetrazzini.

At that moment, Guns N' Roses screamed through the cafeteria's PA system. Eric groaned, but Ant said "Awww yeah!" Joel, with only a modicum of irony, made devil horns with a hand. Ink bobbed his head. Rick worked a fret board in the air. Even ornery Alex let a smile slant across his face. It took a while, but at last they had something upon which everyone could more or less agree.

*

The door to Mr. Gregory's office was open, and Ink could hear the man telling a student, "Frankly, that one's out of your league." Sitting down in a waiting room chair, Ink blanched, as if the words were meant for him. He thumbed through university catalogs. For the past year, informational packets had been arriving at his house: several from Ohio schools, a few places near Erie, a Jesuit school in Chicago. Mom went through them meticulously, marking the Cleveland-area schools with a check and almost every other one with an "X." Ink didn't have the numbers, but he remembered that Dad, a trivia fanatic, said Cleveland had been losing population for decades: 750,000 in 1970, 570,000 in 1980, and maybe less than half million by the time the next census rolled around. If so many people were escaping this so-called Mistake on the Lake, why in the world couldn't he?

Now, in the guidance counselor's office, Ink found himself looking for the first time at colleges several states away. The literature bloomed with photographs of rolling greens, stately stone buildings with impressive archways, pretty girls strolling down leafy lanes, cozy in college sweatshirts. But it was not until he picked up a brochure for a school in California that he realized his dream. California—why had he not thought of it before? Ant had an older brother out there in a San that was not Francisco. Always, Ant would return from visits with dream-hazy eyes, saying something like, "oh man, oh man, you would not fucking believe!" Endless sun and spraying surf and famous stars and gorgeous women in bikinis roller skating through oceanside parks. California—it was the world's greatest party and for years it had been going on without him. Ink had never flown before, but he imagined a spacious window seat on a plane, the mad backwards rush of the world as it roared down the runway, the jolt into the air, the carefree tossing away of everything he'd come to know.

The more he thought about it, the more he realized that this was just a new manifestation of an old dream, dating back to Ink's first meeting with Mr. Gregory at the beginning of his junior year, when the counselor wondered if he'd ever thought of studying abroad.

"Seriously?"

115

"Sure. Why not?" Mr. Gregory spread his hands across the desk. "It's exactly the kind of experience that looks great to college admissions committees."

"You've got to be kidding," Mom said that evening, folding her dessert napkin into a tight, lethal square which, like a paper football, she might flick against his face. Dad, his mouth full of maple roll, raised his eyebrows, as if wanting to know more.

"No, I'm . . . not."

"Where in the world would you want to go?"

Ink told her. He told her that the counselor, in his expert opinion, had suggested it.

"England?" The way she said that word was enough to drain his enthusiasm. Something could happen—a crash in an abandoned field, an Arab hijacking, a gaping hole in the fuselage. Mom didn't watch the news very much, but she was an expert on disasters. "England!" she said again, as if no one yet in the long course of human history had ever made it safely to its shores.

"England is a long ways," Dad said, trying to be helpful. "About 3900 miles, if I'm not mistaken."

Ink didn't doubt it. Dad probably had it written down in his book under a brand new category called "Distances."

"I wonder what that is in kilometers."

"John, please don't be smart," Mom said.

"I'm not!"

"Okay, just say you survive the trip. What next? There's three whole months in a foreign place. Anything could happen. *Anything.*"

Mom stopped, letting that word splash like acid all over the happy face of Ink's ambition. Anything. She didn't have to mention Frankie McGooken by name—Frankie, the smart, awkward boy who drowned in a creek when Ink was in fourth grade. Mom's point seemed to be simply this: the boy had died in 1980, and here it was more than halfway through 1987 and Frankie was still just as dead as he was before. Death, in other words, was amazingly resilient. Fine—point taken. But Ink wondered why the word "anything"—a simple, indefinite pronoun—had to always carry such a menacing connotation. Wasn't there a good kind of "anything" as well, one that was powerful enough to break down the door between life as it was and life as it might choose to be?

"Here's another way of looking at it," Dad said, pointing praying hands at his son. "Are more students doing this . . . study abroad than are not doing it?"

The fact was, only a few students—the wealthy ones from Shaker Heights, Westlake, or Bay Village, the ones he didn't even know— were planning to spend time abroad. And finances aside, did Ink really think he had the grades, the work ethic, the courage to be one of those few? Of course not. If he did not die in one mishap or another, he would most certainly embarrass himself in some grave way, and the failure would cling to him like a bad smell for the rest of his days. By the time he went to bed that evening, he was so relieved he nearly gave his mother a kiss good night.

Ink was finally called into the office, where Mr. Gregory smiled and took his perspiring hand. As usual, the counselor was impeccably dressed, and gave off such a powerful scent of cologne that Ink wanted to lean into him for a hug. The counselor sat and slowly turned the pages in his slender file while Ink studied the framed diploma on the wall behind him. The man was an expert; Ink was in good hands.

Mr. Gregory sighed and then, without warning, said, "Time is running very short." The interrogation began: Where do you want to go? Do you know your major? What do you want to do for a career? On and on. While Ink struggled to respond, the counselor looked from time to time at his watch. Ink was overwhelmed. He answered part of one question, then the other, never coming close to making any sense.

"Wait," Mr. Gregory said, holding up a hand. "You want to go to college. You know that much, right?"

"Yes!"

"Good, at last we have a square one." He offered another professional smile. "Most of the boys I see at this point have had a square one for quite some time."

The phone rang, and Ink breathed a sigh of relief. He would be off the hook for a few moments and be able to get his act together. The phone rang again, but Mr. Gregory made no move to get it.

"That, Mr. Alt, is a distraction." Mr. Gregory said. "And distraction has always been the bane of mankind." The phone continued to ring. "So what's your square two? And three?" He glanced over the resume Ink had worked up for the meeting. "This dragon playing club is fine, but I wish I could see some evidence of *significant* involvement here."

Ink nodded and mumbled and, some interminable time later, emerged from the office with encouraging words and a short list of schools he had a good shot of getting into: John Carroll, Case Western, Baldwin Wallace—the local choices, any of which would satisfy Mom. When he'd asked at the door about that school in California, Mr. Gregory shrugged and said, "What do you have to lose?"

That evening, Def Leppard in his headphones, Ink sat on his bed, thumbing through the brochure, trying to figure out how best to present his case to Mom and Dad. He found a pen in his backpack and filled out the first page of the application—name, address, social security number—all the while bobbing his head to the driving beat. Already he felt like he was giving tangible form to his dream.

*

A week later, Ink followed Timothy out of Fr. Fruehauf's class and asked, "Who are the Sandinistas?" He'd been looking for the term in his notes for the last three days, but it was nowhere to be found. Timothy not only gave him the answer—"The Communists, the so-called bad guys"—he also offered to help Ink study for the exam at the end of the month. There was that fresh, open face again, the clean, toothy, smile that made Ink think he ranked among the most fascinating young men in America. Then, out of nowhere, he thought about Alex Wright rattling off that loathsome string of words; suddenly, Timothy's warmth became sickening, like too much candy in the week after Halloween. What to do? What to do? Ink tossed out a few more questions, which gave him time to weigh Timothy's kindness against his designs as a likely homosexual. The problem was, he had no idea what to do with his measurements of each. Finally, he just said "yes" and prayed to God that all would be okay.

At Ink's insistence, they met in the school library—a public space.

"Let me see if I can explain," Timothy said, textbook in front of him, typed notes to the right, a binder of photocopied newspaper articles to his left. Ink couldn't help being bothered by the fact that everything was just so.

"There were some people in our government who sold

118

weapons—missiles and such—to Iran."

"Why?"

"Well, throughout most of the 80s, they were at war with Iraq."

Iraq was new to Ink, but at least he'd heard of Iran. Several years ago, crazy revolutionists had taken all those American hostages. Carter couldn't free them, but Reagan did, as soon as he came to office. Unlike the peanut farmer, the current president was a man who, according to his parents, got things done.

"Why did we help Iran? We hate them."

"Well, we actually supported Hussein back then."

"And he is . . .?"

"Saddam Hussein. The dictator."

Ink opened his mouth.

"He rules Iraq."

"So, over the years, we've helped both sides?" Ink was certain he could not be alone in his ignorance.

Timothy smiled. "American foreign policy is . . . complex."

What Ink appreciated more than the information, more than the glimpse of the boy's deep passion for his subject, was the simple fact that Timothy at no point dismissed him as that chain mailed Donna did during his first official Date from Hell. Nor did he ever refer to him as "dummy" or "asshole" or "dickhead," which Crabb or Alex or Ant would do without the slightest pretext; instead, he just smiled at Ink, more than happy to be of help. It was strange—it was disturbing—such simple kindness from a boy his age.

As Timothy continued the short course on US foreign policy, generously going all the way back to the war with Mexico, a powerful new idea came to Ink. According to the Church, the real sin of homosexuality was not one's sexual orientation; it was the act itself. Timothy was a good guy, smart and destined for many great things. He had so much going for him he didn't have to act on his desires. Maybe—just maybe—Ink could be the one to pull the boy back from the brink. "I owed you one," Ink would say immediately afterward, as they shared smokes like two bandaged soldiers safe from mortar fire. Years later, he would meet Timothy at a class reunion and shake his hand. Next to him would be a stunning wife, a blonde with a slit skirt, and she'd say something like, "You're the one he always talks about!"

Maybe Ink would have a girlfriend or wife himself, and the two women would hit it off while Timothy talked about his job with *The Plain Dealer* and Ink talked about whatever he was doing. At the end of the drink-filled evening, Timothy would lower his voice and express his deepest gratitude, while Ink, embarrassed, would wave him off. On their way out, they'd exchange cards, a firm handshake, best wishes for a life blessed with many beautiful children.

But in the meantime, Ink felt the obligation to say *something* about Middle East affairs, and "They're all crazy" sounded as good as anything else. It was impossible for him to get out of his mind all those images he'd seen in passing on the TV news: the bearded men chanting, the burning effigies of Western leaders, huge tattered banners with those ominous squiggles, like letters too drunk to stand on their own two feet. Was it any wonder why such people were perpetually at war?

Timothy smiled. "Well . . ."

"Serious nutjobs."

When a few of Timothy's teeth disappeared from his smile, Ink knew that he'd gone too far. Timothy dropped his eyes to write something down, and Ink imagined that the comment was going to go straight in Mr. Gregory's file.

"Anyway," Timothy said. "Reagan hates the communists—so much so that the administration took the money we made on the arms deal and sent it to the Contras."

"The Contras?"

"In Nicaragua. Central America. They're fighting the Communists—the Sandinistas—there."

"Okay," Ink said, although he still couldn't see what one place had to do with the other. What he really wanted to say was: "The Communists are bad, right? They are the enemy. For as long as I've been alive, they've been the most dangerous 'Them.'" That, if he recalled correctly, was what the Miracle on Ice had been all about. "What's wrong with trying to defeat the Communists?"

"Well . . . all this was going on behind everyone's backs. The president is our nation's leader, but the executive branch is not above the law. Reagan knew—he had to have known."

The explanation became even more confusing when names started pouring out of Timothy's mouth: North, McFarlane,

Weinberger, Shultz. Ink could feel the boy's explanation bumping over the rolling plains of his brain, around the lake in the middle that all of this stuff was supposed to sink down into, and down a canal towards the opening on the other side of his head. He tried to keep the words inside, tried to sluice them back to that lake, but they were out, gone, whooshing back into the world.

With an obligatory pang of guilt, Ink found his thoughts drifting to the weekend, when he and Ant were going to catch *Die Hard* (again) at the mall. Maybe they would sit behind hair-flicking cuties and make jokes the girls would find hilarious. Maybe he could shake his box of Snowcaps and one of them, the blonde, her arm over the back of the seat, would exclaim: "Those are my absolute favorite!" Afterward, they'd all chat in the lobby and Ant, in his clumsy way, would blurt out "pizza!" and the girls would squeal "yes!" in perfect unison. While they were in the bathroom, freshening up, Ink and Ant would jostle each other as they teased out scenarios for the night. When the girls returned, maybe the brunette would slide next to Ant and the blonde would take her place next to Ink as they all moved toward the glow of the parking lot. And then something big would happen—something that would change his life once and for all.

Timothy was still going on, and finally, Ink had to put up a hand. There were too many characters, too many sides. His explanation was beginning to sound like one of those movies Mom rented from the video store—huge casts in period dress sweeping through history, the landscapes going on and on like the films themselves.

"I think I get it now," Ink said, slapping closed his notebook.

Timothy smiled so pleasantly that it—that he—seemed dangerous, or something. What if, he thought with sudden horror, the boy was not only gay but had also already done what was so expressly forbidden? With Chris, perhaps, or Neal—or, good God, the two of them together! What if Timothy was right now on the prowl for conquest number three?

"Thanks for the help," Ink said.

For a terrible moment, he thought the boy was going to stick out his hand—make a grab for him. Instead, he just said, "If you need anything else," which in its vagueness struck Ink as more frightening still.

*

121

Over the next few days, Ink completed the rest of the California school application. He printed slowly, carefully, certain that good penmanship would indicate maturity, a deep sense of personal responsibility. He typed a draft of the entrance essay, in which he talked about Hemingway and icebergs. "In Ohio," he wrote, "all I've ever seen is the surface of the world. I want to go farther. I want to go deeper." Thinking primarily of Mom, he used his dead schoolmate Frankie as an example of the need to balance one's passion to explore the unknown with caution and circumspection. He even alluded to the Contras, hoping he understood what he meant. Finally, on one Sunday evening, after all of his homework was done, he summoned the courage to act. He paper clipped the essay to the application and went downstairs, where Mom sat on the couch folding laundry. She took the form from Ink, examined it front and back. She did not even glance at the essay. After a few moments, she rubbed her eyes and said, "I'm going to say no." She held out the packet to him, so that, presumably, he might have the honor of throwing it into the wastebasket himself.

When Mom returned to warm underwear, Ink left the room, making sure to keep his cool. Passing through the kitchen, he saw that the back door was open. Dad was on the patio, squatting in front of his telescope—a new purchase to indulge his latest interest.

Last week, Dad had asked Ink if he'd like to go with him while he worked the booth at a kitchen and bath show in Columbus. "It'll be an exciting glimpse into the professional world," he said. Ink, thinking that the sacrifice might pay dividends down the line, said yes. For most of the day, he read on a folding chair behind a cardboard cutout of a state-of-the-art shower head and listened to Dad speak with great animation about the virtues of his company's products to the people who streamed by.

"You were bored," Dad said on the drive home.

"No . . ."

He laughed. "It's okay. I just wanted you to see what I do."

Ink opened the back door and stepped outside. It was a cool night, but startlingly clear.

"Pegasus," Dad said, palms out in invitation. "It's all lined up for you."

"Maybe in a minute," Ink said, sitting on the stairs.

Undeterred, Dad told him all about the constellation. He talked in general about the composition of stars. He didn't ask why Ink had come outside to sit without a coat on a chilly November night. He didn't ask what Ink was holding in his hands. He didn't ask what was wrong. This was not surprising, of course. Dad avoided such directness in the same way he avoided big decisions, leaving them to Mom. Was it simple division of labor? A distaste for conflict? Sometimes—and recently more than ever—Ink wondered if it wasn't fear. Simple cowardice.

"I want to go to California."

Dad stepped back from the scope, blew on his hands.

"There's a school there, and I want to go."

"What did your mother say?"

"She said to ask you."

"Really?"

"No, I guess not."

Through the darkness, Ink could make out the trace of a sympathetic smile. Before his own disappointment became too keen, he thought about his parents—outside, inside, the surface cordiality, the raised voices behind closed doors. Last week, Ink had overheard Mom going on about the insulting indifference of her family, the Fosters—a grandpa and a grandma, an uncle, an aunt, a number of young cousins, all within maybe four years of his age either way. Ink had seen this side of his family a grand total of twice—once when he was four and again when he was eight. Each time, they stayed in a hotel and returned home the following morning. Mom occasionally spoke with Aunt Janice over the phone, but as far as Ink knew, she was in contact with no one else. Long before Ink was born, there'd been a huge falling out that had to do with her marrying Dad and leaving Indiana for good.

"You know," Dad said. "I truly respect your mother. I believe she always has your best interests in mind."

Ink looked up, tried to find Pegasus with the naked eye. Where were the wings? How could it be Pegasus if there weren't any wings?

"Plus, the grass is always greener. There's that to consider."

Ink wanted to say: "Why does she take her pain out on me? Why don't you set her straight?" Instead, he shivered. He rubbed hands along his sleeveless arms.

"Cold, huh?"

Ink nodded. "It sure is."

"We should probably call it a night."

Ink was disappointed but not surprised to hear the enthusiasm—and relief—in his voice. He stood up, smiled the best he could, and disappeared in the house before the tears began to flow.

Upstairs, with Trouble's yapping through the window, Ink paged through the brochure for the California school one more time, like a mourner saying goodbye to a loved one. The glossy students strode confidently under impressive arches, beautiful trees. The boys were strong and well-formed. The girls had smooth brown legs and bright, flirtatious eyes. These students looked like a different order of being—gorgeous aliens who learned in hallowed halls the strange alchemy that would allow them to perpetuate their kind. Ink threw the brochure in the garbage, where, undaunted, these stunning creatures continue to beam. He sighed. Despite his pain, despite the yapping below, Ink fell asleep with a pillow of hope. Perhaps if he did not press for California, he'd stand a stronger chance of getting something else he wanted somewhere down the line.

*

It was the beginning of December, and Ink, despite serious misgivings, asked Timothy to help him study for the big test in Current Events, which loomed like the threat of lake effect snow. They met again in the library after school, where Timothy re-explained to Ink the significance of 1979: the Shah, the ire of the revolutionists, the taking of those hostages. Once, when Ink had the flu, he sat up with his parents as they flipped to *Nightline*, grim Ted Koppel and his pie crust hair. Mom and Dad had never been ones for news. They only received *The Plain Dealer* on Sunday, when the paper was fat with coupons, which Mom spent the next two days cutting out. After watching for a few minutes, Dad got up to turn the channel to Johnny Carson, and Ink, his cold medicine kicking in, fell asleep right there on the couch to the gentle undulations of their laughter.

"You know Kent State, right?" Timothy said. "What happened there during the Vietnam War?"

Ink was relieved he could reward Timothy with at least one affirmative nod. Of course, he knew about Kent State. 1970. Four

124

dead in O-hi-o. Every time he heard that song on the radio, he tingled with pride. It told the rest of the world that Cleveland—Kent was close enough—was worth paying attention to.

"Well, from another perspective, one might say that incident was nothing."

"People died. Young people!"

Timothy nodded. "Yes, of course. But compare that tragedy to 'Black Friday,' the massacre at Jaleh Square."

Ink had no idea what the boy was talking about.

"Another protest—this one in Iran. People fed up with Western influence gathered together to stand up for what they believed. That day, they ended up speaking not with words but with their own blood and bone. And all the while, oblivious Americans were doing important things like watching TV or fussing with their chemically treated lawns."

It sounded as if Timothy was reading straight from one of his strident editorials, and, frankly, Ink was a bit put off. He hoped the boy would find his way back to talking about what mattered for the test.

"Look, let me show you this," Timothy said, pulling out a newspaper photograph from one of his folders. There was a man with a bad haircut, eyes smashed closed with pain. He was holding red hands up to the camera.

"The US supported the Shah because we wanted his country's oil. Did you know we even orchestrated a coup there thirty some years ago just so the Shah could regain power?"

Ink nodded, trying to disguise his cluelessness.

"And so this man in the picture, many years later, is not only angry at his own leader, but at the United States for supporting him."

Ink studied the picture.

"That blood on his hands is from someone he knew. That face, that blood—this is a human being!"

A fleck of spittle struck Ink on the cheek. He didn't blink. He didn't raise a hand to brush it off. He was frozen with fear, thinking again of fatal disease. A bumper sticker he saw the other day read: "AIDS: It Kills Fags Dead." There was that boy in Indiana, hounded out of town a few years ago. He'd been born with some terrible condition, and the blood he received to help him turned out to be tainted. You couldn't get AIDS from a speck of spit—Ink knew this. But maybe you could. After all, diseases mutated all the time. There was so much that doctors still did not know. The more he thought about it, the more he felt the corrosive power of the saliva against his skin.

"A story like this doesn't just fall in your lap," Timothy continued. "You have to go out and find it—a piece here, a piece there. You've got to dig down, ask questions, stitch things together. It requires a real effort to stay informed."

Ink deftly brushed an index finger across his cheek. Now the spittle was in two places, and both sizzled more brilliantly than the burning bush.

"Anyway, I apologize. Lecture over." Timothy laughed, looked down, and seemed surprised to see the notes between his elbows. "Sometimes, it's easy to forget myself."

After Timothy left the library, Ink raced to the bathroom to scrub his face and hands three long times with soap. He would, as a result, miss the next bus home, but it was a small price to pay in order to be on the safe side.

*

Once again, Mom, her sigh like poison fumes released into the kitchen, was going to have to say no.

"But this one is for God," Ink said, calmly as possible. "For my relationship with God."

Ink was enrolled in a course called Spirituality next semester, a requirement of which was a retreat of some kind. He had the option of going somewhere local, like the boring old retreat house on Broadview Road, or he could go somewhere else, like the Trappist monastery in upstate New York.

"Lucas," Mom said after the requisite pause. "Please tell him the kind of snow they get up that way."

Dad seemed embarrassed to have been put on the spot. He did not provide annual snowfalls for the last thirty years. He did not pass along the almanac prediction for February, the month of the retreat. To Ink's surprise, he quietly suggested: "Why don't we let him talk?"

"Think of my soul," Ink said, emboldened by his father's open mindedness.

"Oh, don't be ridiculous."

"People visit monasteries all the time. To escape the distractions of life."

Mom glared at Dad. He went to the cupboard for a can of salted peanuts. Ink didn't know if this were a good sign, or a bad one.

"To be alone and silent so they can really hear what God wants them to do. You know," Ink said, "like your Merton!"

"This does seem to be different," Dad said, tossing the statement out lightly, like a sock into a hamper. Mom pulled her thin, sharp hair over her ears, like she did on those rare times when she was taken aback or confused. She flipped through her recipe box, slapped a card on the table, which seemed to restore some order to her world.

"Stop looking at me," she said to Ink. "I'll talk about this later with your father."

Dad smiled. He shook the nuts like dice before popping one into his mouth.

Ink retreated to his bedroom, for once feeling good—no, excellent—about his chances. But guilt seeped in too, because, if the truth be known, his plea had nothing at all to do with growing closer to God. It was about the need to break out, to be free for a while. It was about trying to hold onto Sandro as a friend—Sandro, whose parents simply said, "Have a great time!" when he told them about this monastic adventure. Away from his soccer buddies, the boy would have no choice but to turn to Ink. They'd talk sports (if need be), tell inside jokes that went all the way back to first grade, make plans for a post-graduation trip to Cedar Point or Put-in-Bay.

Mom went through the customary routine. With Dad, she discussed every part of the information packet Ink had brought home. Sneaking down to the landing of the stairs, Ink heard Dad say loudly and firmly: "Just because you won't go—"

"This is not about me."

"Most things seem to be."

"You need to take that back right now."

"I'm sorry. It's just—"

"It's *not* just!"

The evening ended quietly, with Dad inching open Ink's bedroom door to say they all needed to sleep on it.

The next afternoon, Mom called Mr. Murfin, the retreat director, and for forty-five minutes pestered him for additional information and assurances of safety. She came away impressed by his seriousness, the very thing that made so many boys think him a "total bore." There was a final hour-long deliberation, during which Ink was once again banished to the bedroom. At last, he was called down to hear the final decision.

"We're going to let you go," Dad told him from the other side of the kitchen table. His face was red and damp, as if he'd just shoveled a neighborhood worth of snow. Mom ground her teeth, but when Dad nodded her way, she signed the permission slip like a vanquished general on the day of surrender.

"If you get killed," she said, rattling the form in his face. "I'll never speak to you again."

Ink smiled. He tried to sneak a look of thanks to Dad, but he was busy running a hand over his face. Ink snatched up the slip, pressed it against his chest. "You're such a comedian," he said.

Mom locked arms across her chest. "You think I'm not serious?"

*

Tired from the trip, the boys sagged into chairs and waited for Mr. Murfin to park the van. Alex Wright honked his nose and Sandro laughed, Ink quickly following suit. Nick Distasio furtively devoured a granola bar. Eric Chevalier absentmindedly chipped away at a blackhead with his index finger. Mark Heidel, with a seat of space between him and the others, nodded thoughtfully at the Christ hanging on the far wall. Timothy Bashour, leg across knee, took notes in a small flip cover book.

Mr. Murfin returned, eased his backpack to the floor. He rubbed his glasses in his sweater. "As I'm sure you remember, the Trappists have taken a vow of silence. We're going to try to emulate them in every way over the next few days. We're going to show them the utmost respect. Be quiet. Be serious. Pray a lot. Put yourself in the presence of the Lord."

Nods, nervous smiles, a few eyes dancing from the punch lines of jokes just dying to leap from lips.

The Guestmaster, Fr. Jeffery, entered and shook Mr. Murfin's hand. He wore a long, loose flowing white cloak (Ink thought: death shroud). He was maybe in his forties, with a good head of brown hair

128

imperfectly parted in the middle.

"Good afternoon everyone," he said, using his mouth like a regular human being.

"Lookie what he can do!" Sandro whispered. Ink shook with laughter, thrilled by the attention of his old friend. Mr. Murfin shot him a look that shut him up.

Fr. Jeffery briefly explained the history of monastic life: Martin of Tours, Benedict of Nursia, Dom Augustin de Lestrange, all the way up to Merton (Mom's favorite for as long as he could remember) and God's humble servants here right now at The Abbey of the Genesee. "Monk" the boys were informed, came from Monos, which was Greek for "alone." However, Fr. Jeffery insisted that none of these men over the centuries was ever alone, for God was with them always, "as he is for each of us . . . if we only let Him."

Alone, alone, alone. Could anything be worse? And yet the Guestmaster said it with a beatific smile, as if recalling a special friend. As Fr. Jeffery went on, Ink wondered how so many men throughout human history had been duped into living such a circumscribed life. If you wanted to sacrifice the freedom to travel, the joy of fine food, the loveliness of a girl's body beneath your own, why did you also have to sacrifice speech as well? What in the world was wrong with shooting the breeze when you hoed the garden or kneaded a blob of dough?

Fr. Jeffrey went over the daily schedule, which the boys were encouraged to participate in as much as they wished: Vigil at 2:30 in the morning; mass at 6 am; periods of manual labor and scriptural study; dinner; more work and prayers and simple food before "retiring" at 7 pm. To a room with a bed and a shelf full of books about God, the house quiet as a coffin, blackness filling up the window like water on a sinking ship. *The Titanic*, Ink thought, its bottom ripped apart by the jagged teeth of an iceberg. Ink began to feel short of breath. He put a hand to his heart, but could not feel the beating. He was drowning. He was dead! How in God's name was he going to survive this trip?

The boys were given time to get settled before supper. Ink dropped his bag in the tiny room, sat on a wool blanket stretched across the bed, and opened his folder, which contained the daily schedule, a number of photocopied prayers, and a blank pad for the journal Mr. Murfin required each of them to keep. At random, Ink pulled out Ignatius's "Prayer for Generosity."

He read the words, but he did not want to speak them aloud. To do so, he felt, would be like signing his name on some spiritual dotted line. He didn't mind being taught a thing or two about generosity, but he didn't know if he was ready to "give" or "fight" or "toil" or "labor." Especially without any tangible compensation. Maybe this was a piece of cake for a saint or monk or even a parish priest, but those were near-impossible goals for an adolescent—a child, really—like him to take to heart.

At dinner, Alex beat Ink to the open chair next to Sandro, and Ink, secretly crushed, slouched into a seat across from them, wondering how in the world these two boys had become so quickly close. Sandro was an Honor Roll student. He lettered in soccer, played saxophone in the jazz band, appeared on stage in dramas and musicals. Alex, in contrast, was an obscene, chain-smoking, people-loathing loser. It almost seemed as if Sandro were saying to Ink: "I'd rather hang out with anybody but you."

The two new best friends performed a wordless slapstick routine. Alex, showcasing his creativity, slurped his soup. Sandro dropped his knife three times while trying to butter a piece of bread. Nick, sitting to the right of them, nudged Sandro, mouthing for him to stop; undeterred, the boy inserted a crust of bread behind his lips like a mouth guard. Ink, watching his friend's dancing eyes, started to laugh. Then he couldn't stop.

Out of nowhere, a hand dropped on Ink's shoulder, and he looked up at Mr. Murfin, his stern eyes beckoning him into the hallway.

"What do you think this is?" he asked. "Play time?"

Ink kept his head down, face burning from shame.

"Oh, *now* you're quiet."

"It was Sandro," Ink wanted to cry. "Sandro and Alex. They were the bad ones. They were the total jerks!"

"Look, do me a favor: if you can't be an adult, then at least try to act like one."

Ink nodded. He shuffled back to the table and, with tears threatening, kept his head in his bowl for the rest of the dinner.

That first night, the silence was terrible beyond all belief. But even worse was rising for prayers at two in the morning. The boys, bundled and bleary-eyed, assembled in the lobby of the retreat house and began the half mile trudge to the abbey. Ink crunched beside Timothy across the brittle snow, the world too frigid now for speech. Sandro was up ahead with Alex, but all Ink cared about at the moment was trying to protect his face from the violent wind. Below and to their right was the warm spaceship-like glow of a town. How far away to civilization, to freedom? He imagined making a break for it, sirens wailing, brown-robed brothers clambering to the battlements with crossbows to take their fatal aim.

It was, thank God, warmer in the abbey, although the temperature was far from comfortable. Ink tried to appreciate the service, but the chanting went on and on, each monk clicking on and off his lectern lamp to take his somber turn. It was so tedious that Ink threw his eyes up at the pitched ceiling to study the grain of the individual boards. How could so many men willfully whittle their lives down to so banal a point? In comparison, they made Mom and Dad look like social butterflies. Ink looked to his left and saw that Timothy and Eric were riveted. And Mark to his right—were those tears in his eyes? What were these boys seeing that Ink was not?

The next afternoon, sad and bored and lonely in the retreat house library, Ink picked up *The Spiritual Exercises*, a book Mr. LeMonde had made frequent mention of during that sex class sophomore year. In nearly four years at St. Ignatius, he had never looked inside this slim volume. Perhaps God Himself had put the book in this room, on this particular table, for the distinct purpose of letting him see the light. Ink turned the first few pages, taking solace in even that meager noise. Ignatius presented a different kind of exercise—one designed to eliminate the "disordered tendencies" in his soul.

At mass the last few years, Ink had been guilty of his fair share of "disordered tendencies." He frequently lost track during the Creed, drifted into fantasy land during the homily, allowed his eyes to wander for pretty girls as he offered some sign of peace. And "exercise" made him think with a shudder of his grade school basketball days—the dry mouth, the shaky legs, the side aches from all that up and down, the shots that sometimes drew nothing but air. What if he was just not very good at exercise—spiritual or otherwise? What if he was unable to develop the determination, the drive, the pencil-point focus? He was, after all, a human being, not some kind of awful machine.

Ink glanced at his watch, surprised to learn he'd been

contemplating for a full five minutes. It was a good start, but already his ears cried out for a little INXS or REM, his eyes for an episode of something: *Cosby*, *Cheers*—no, *Who's the Boss*, the one with that raven-haired beauty. Alyssa Milano. Ink took his time with each syllable, made the name into a sexy song. When his tongue touched the roof of his mouth for the third time, there was a stirring in his pants. Grandma always had on hand a package of Pepperidge Farm Milanos—her favorite cookie—when she wasn't in the mood for baking. Ink closed his eyes, and as he imagined taking a sweet bite, the stir below became a stiffening. Ant preferred Cindy Crawford—"a woman, not some little girl." Well, he could have her and the nasty *Playboy* across which her naked body had been splayed.

Six minutes. He was coming up on six whole minutes of silent contemplation, even if the last few had been besmirched by erotic fantasy. His stomach rumbled. All he'd had for supper was a bowl of mushed vegetable soup and two thin slices of bread. Would it kill them to have even one vending machine on the premises? His mouth watered at the thought of barbecue potato chips, a candy bar with gooey filling.

Ink looked back at the book and was about ready to scream when Sandro appeared like a miracle in the study, hands in his pockets, an impish grin on his face. After mass a few Sundays ago, Mom told Mrs. Gismondi that Sandro was "growing up to be a handsome young man," and Ink, for a second, found himself in disturbing accord. He swallowed hard, tried to coolly smile.

Sandro sat down, held up an index finger, and began writing in a notebook he pulled from his pocket. Head swiveling for intruders, he held the page up to Ink: "Are these dudes out of their minds?"

Ink chewed the inside of his cheeks. He looked to the hallway, expecting to see Mr. Murfin, teeth grinding in anger. He looked to the ceiling and imagined throwing up, failing exams, the sudden death of Grandpa over one of their games of chess. Anything to stop from shaking apart with laughter.

Sandro scribbled something else: "I mean, seriously."

Ink called for the pad and wrote: "I can't compline." He thought the pun was hilarious, but holding the page to Sandro's impassive face, he feared he'd killed the conversation just as it was getting started.

Sandro took back the pad. "Hee, hee, good one!" he wrote.

Ink wanted to reach out for Sandro, squeeze his arm, and say something like: "This—this is how things should be." But he knew it would be social suicide to put his feelings on such display. It was enough, perhaps, to share this brief, delightful exchange—let it ripen into a goofy memory they could return to over drinks many years down the road.

∗

On the third and final night of the retreat, after yet another helping of vegetable soup and a half dozen slices of dense, monk-made bread, Ink "retired" to the library. He hadn't seen much of Sandro that day. In fact, at dinner, his old friend had sat with Alex at the other end of the table, furtively playing a note pad game of their own. He picked up *The Spiritual Exercises* again and studied the cover—a woodcut of Ignatius, simple and somber in black and white. There was a black mark on the saint's bald head. When Ink tried to remove it with a thumb, the rubbing action made him think "genie lamp." Sandro had appeared when he picked up the book the night before; was it so farfetched to think that he'd now do so again? Maybe he would sense Ink summoning him and sit bolt upright on his bed, head swiveling back and forth, as if trying to find the source of an unusual sound. He'd go to the door, listen in the hallway. He'd put on his shoes and creep to the stairs, with each soft step a memory of their grade school days wafting toward him like the homey smell of a holiday bird.

Ink opened his eyes. Nothing for a moment, and then—another miracle!—there he was, smiling around the jamb. Sandro stepped into the room, pulled closed the double doors, sat down, and looked to his right and left. He scratched his head vigorously with both hands.

"Ok, here's the deal." Sandro was speaking, his voice low and sure. "Alex and I are going to make a break for it."

Ink raised his eyebrows. He wasn't going to dare a "what?"

"Tonight. 9 pm. We're going to sneak out. We're going into town. You in?"

Ink swallowed. Here was a real opportunity to be with Sandro, to share an experience that would quite possibly bind them together forever. But at what cost? Surely such a thing could not escape the attention of Mr. Murfin, and he would blow his top. There would be weeks of detentions and, most likely, suspensions as well. Mom and Dad would have no choice but to ground him for weeks. Informed of

133

his transgression, college admission committees would file his application materials in the trash. Before he knew it, he'd be as down and out as Uncle Lare.

Sandro looked peeved. "Stomp once for 'yes' and twice for 'no.'

Ink shuffled his feet on hardwood floor.

"Speak!" Sandro said.

Ink shook his head, lips pressed together. He tasted soup on his tongue.

"Suit yourself," Sandro said before vanishing through the doors like a ghost.

That night in bed, Ink listened for Sandro and Alex in the hallway—the muffled laughter, the creak of the stairs, the soft click of the front door. 9:00. 9:05. 9:10. He hadn't heard a thing, but they would have to be gone now, trudging down the snow-encrusted path to the main road, hands in pockets, breaths puffing before them. Maybe they'd be excited for a while, imagining the legendary story they'd bring back with them. Then the cold would set in and they'd begin to realize that a mile is a long way to walk when it's nine degrees and there are still maybe two miles to go. Then there'd be silence— only the breathing and the sniffling and the crunch, crunch, crunch against packed snow. Numb toes. Exposure of fingers and face. Frostbite.

Ink had made a good—a safe—choice. He was grateful for even this narrow single bed, the simple white sheet and drab wool blanket. It was warm enough here in this room, and if he just went to sleep now, he'd be able to kill a good chunk of time that still remained before release. The problem was, he couldn't sleep. He thought about trying some more contemplation, but he didn't want to get out of bed for a little exercise on that personal kneeler against the wall. God— that's who he needed to be thinking about. That's who these monks thought about every waking moment of their circumscribed lives. God, God, God, with a few brief breaks for bread and soup and physical work.

But no women. You could use the thing to pee, but that was it. Ink kicked off the sheet and looked through the darkness at his crotch. He recalled The Parable of the Talents, the third man who'd received only one and, afraid of what might happen in his master's absence, buried it in the ground. "You wicked, lazy servant!" the angry master said upon his return. What a terrible sin it was to not use the special gifts one had been given!

One day Ink was going to use it in that other, non-peeing way, and (as if it had heard what he was thinking) the thing leaped to action—begging and pleading, briefs like a gag against its mouth. "Now, now," was its muffled cry. Why couldn't he just reach down and remove the gag? Why couldn't he offer the poor thing a hand out of its confinement? If a person were in such desperate straits, wouldn't one be morally obligated as a Christian to bring him such relief?

Alyssa Milano, Cindy Crawford. Sandro's girlfriend Cindi—the Cindi who spelled her name with a boner-sized I. She and his friend had been going out now for a year and a half, which meant Sandro must have gone all the way with her by now. "Yeah, yeah, I bagged her," Andy Crabb said last week about this girl from St. Joe's, a cousin of somebody who was said to be hot beyond all credulity. Ink contemplated the mechanics of the act: Where exactly did you put it? How far in did it have to go? And, God, then what? There was, he was pretty sure, something you had to reach, a bell, like a carnival game at the Cuyahoga County Fair.

Cindi Cindi Cindi—the name on his tongue was so much cotton candy. Hair, lips, neck, hips, legs—Ink assembled the girl in his mind part by delicious part. He shouldn't have—this was Sandro's girl, and he was in the middle of a religious retreat—but once he started, he couldn't stop. Ink turned onto his stomach, and his beautiful gift struggled mightily against the mattress. Its desire for release reached epic levels, but there was no way in hell Ink's hand was going to go anywhere near it. Never had. Never ever would. Especially not here, in a place where it must have never happened—a place that probably could not survive such an affront against God.

Sometime later, Ink woke, the room a silent void. In his head was the evaporating image of a soft, warm hand sliding from his grasp. When he sat up, he realized he was soaked down below. Filled with disgust, he clicked on the desk lamp and raked through his bag for the travel pack of tissues Mom insisted he take, presumably for all the tears he might shed while away from home. He tore almost all of them from their sleeve and did his best to clean the sheet, as well as the sticky stupid thing now snoozing between his legs.

*

"I count six," Mr. Murfin said, blowing on his hands. "Who's AWOL?"

"Ink," Sandro said.

"I'm here," he growled. When he'd come out to the van a few minutes earlier, Alex and Sandro were already in the first bank of seats, shoulders shoving against each other in response to some hilarious joke. Ink just brushed past them to the back.

"No, it's Timothy," Alex said. "I believe he's still doing his hair."

With a grumble, Murfin climbed out of the van and trudged back up the drive to the retreat house.

Immediately, Nick and Eric clamored to hear about Alex and Sandro's adventure into town. The boys waved them off for a few seconds, but then Alex spoke in hushed tones about how the two picked their way down the hill and into town. They came across these two girls from the Catholic high school. "Plaid skirts, white socks—you know the deal."

Sandro said, "We said we were monks on the lam."

"They were eager to see our divining rods," Alex added with a laugh.

Nick swished his lips. "Let me get this straight: 10 PM and you run into Catholic girls coming home from school. I'm . . . what's the word Ms. Keane always uses?"

"Dubious?" Eric suggested.

"Super dubious," Nick said.

"Anyway," Sandro said, "they were into us. The thought of monk sex was getting them all hot and bothered."

"We told them"—and here Alex had to grab his jaw to keep from laughing. "We told them, we told them we had to . . . give it to them from behind cause that's the way we'd been trained in the abbey."

"You're so disgusting," Mark said, pulling headphones from his backpack.

Alex turned around, arm curled like a scythe over the back of his seat. "And you're a fat pussy, so let's call it a draw."

Ink glanced at Sandro, whose eyes were running away toward something on his lap.

When Timothy climbed into the van, he made his way to the back, smiling that big smile as he dropped down next to Ink. Alex glanced back and nodded, as if to acknowledge the presence of a few other "pussies" in the vehicle. All the way back to Cleveland, Timothy organized notes and made additional observations on paper for the series of articles about monastic life he was going to write for *The Eye*. Periodically, he'd try out an insight on Ink, who couldn't concentrate on the O'Connor he had to finish for Monday.

"We're men for others," Ink said. "The monks are men for themselves."

"I understand how you would say that," Timothy said. "They're not like us. I'm having trouble wrapping my brain around it. But, you know, it's important to give them benefit of the doubt."

Ink looked to the front of the van, where Alex and Sandro rocked incessantly with laughter. Occasionally, they'd dart glances his way and chuckle all the more. Ink didn't want to be mean, but he wished Timothy would just be quiet, or better yet, move up a row to make Nick or Mark or Eric gay by association.

"The trip has made me think a lot about roles," Timothy said.

"Roles?"

"Roles people play in life." He thumbed through his notebook. "Somewhere, I've got this great quote from Merton—something about the purpose of leaving society is not to escape or avoid people. It's to understand them. That puts the monastic life in a different light."

Ink nodded. He wondered what Mom, that ornery hermit, thought about that one.

"Some people—like me—they need to report. Some people need to teach. Some need to pray. Some need to act. People should do their own thing as well as they humanly can."

Ink shrugged. "I'll take your word for it."

"Why?"

"You're smarter than I am."

"You shouldn't say that."

"It's true."

Timothy smiled—Ink had never seen such wholesome, such encouraging teeth—before returning to his voluminous notes. Ink went back to reading his story—the annoying grandmother, the car accident, the grimly comical encounter with The Misfit. In the end, the grandmother, the only family member left alive, is desperate to stay alive. She calls the murderer one of God's children and reaches out to him, only to be shot in the head. Bewildered, Ink closed the book and stared out the window at the bleak, iced over Chautauqua, which seemed like a frozen mirror of his mood.

*

When they crossed into Ohio, Ink's mood brightened. Ashtabula, Geneva, Painesville, Mentor—the exits flashed by, and he found himself looking forward to home. Soon, Lake Erie appeared on the right, choppy and gray, but water—the life force—nonetheless. The traffic began to thicken, as cars blinkered to get to the Shoreway or the Innerbelt. People next to people next to people. All this sound and energy, the Terminal Tower ahead of them, dark and hard and durable against a clearing sky. Next to him, a lady flicked a cigarette out her window. Giddy, forgetting himself, Ink waved. For a second, the woman looked like she'd been slapped. Then—a miracle!—she burst into a smile.

At Nick's request, Mr. Murfin clicked on the radio and "Born to Run" roared like a motorbike through the speakers.

"Crank it up!" Alex said, and Mr. Murfin complied with a sigh.

Everyone was jumping. Even Timothy removed his reading glasses and smiled his generous smile. And why the hell not? It was Friday afternoon—the weekend was here, and all was right with the world. As soon as he got in the door, Ink would call Ant and Rick, his good enough friends, to see if they wanted to go bowling tomorrow afternoon. Ten dollars at Carousel Lanes. All you could roll. They'd order nachos with extra ooze and suck down free refills of pop. Ink sang the chorus of the song—the only words he knew for sure. Alex and Sandro might be thick as thieves, but Ink couldn't keep from smiling. He was free; he was once again alive! With each passing second, the cold, dark days at the monastery rolled further out of his way, like a huge boulder from a tomb.

138

Follow Through

(Fall 1989-Spring 1990)

Sun dunked on Ink through a net of leaves and made the bad day even worse. At the cafeteria, he'd devoured two plates of watery shrimp creole—the "last supper" with Mom and Dad—and now his stomach squawked like a squirrel dying in the middle of the road. Saliva filled his mouth, and every few minutes he swallowed hard against the bilious rise in the throat. By the bumper of the old brown wagon, he tried to smile at his parents. This was, after all, the great, long anticipated moment of his escape from home; it was vital to prove that he was up to the challenge of being on his own.

"Well, have fun," Mom said, sunglasses on, lips freshly painted for the road. Ink could almost see the shrug in her voice. And her embrace—an arm flung around his neck, a kiss jettisoned into the humid air behind him—was not the heartfelt gesture Ink thought he deserved. Dad's awkward "Proud of you, son," was disappointing as well. The words (and the accompanying handshake) were limp as canned vegetables, the ubiquitous staple of so many family suppers growing up.

Before he knew it, the old brown wagon was waddling away. When it hit a speed bump a little too quickly, the tail pipe sparked against the pavement. Ink was certain Dad would step out to check for damage; instead, he kept going—over the next bump and the next. At the stop sign, the vehicle leaned right and, just like that, disappeared in front of a large brick building. He spied it one more time, as it followed the curving road out to the intersection of Route 7. When the light turned green, the car lurched to the left and was gone. He had to fight the impulse to gallop after it like Trouble, Mr. Majeski's ageless, yapping beagle.

Over the last several months, there'd been an awful series of battles about the college Ink was going to attend. He'd fallen in love with one in California, but Mom crushed that dream like a black ant scrambling across the kitchen counter. Fine, Ink thought after the initial pain subsided. California was probably a bit far to make his point. But everyone Ink knew from high school was going somewhere else—Ant to Ohio State, Rick to St. Bonaventure, Eric to Miami, Joel to NYU, Sandro to Notre Dame.

"There are plenty of schools right here in town," Mom had said.

So Ink picked one, half-heartedly, then slouched around the house for an entire week after he'd received the acceptance letter. John Carroll was, as Dad explained, "a fine institution," but taking the Rapid to the east side every day was not his idea of going elsewhere. Eventually, complaints began to slip from his mouth. One evening, with the final deadline for applications approaching, Ink pled his case under the whirring blades of the ceiling fan in the living room. Mom retreated to the den, where she folded her arms and studied a squirrel out the window. Dad stood between them in the dining room, turning one way then the other, sending compromises like flares into each room.

"He'd be happy to go to Clerestory."

"I don't even know where that is."

"Just down 77," Ink called into the den. "Maybe two hours." He wanted to go to Clerestory because it was, first and foremost, "away." Also, since no one he knew was planning to go there, he'd have the opportunity to wad up this shoddy rough draft of himself and write someone totally new.

"Not everyone gets what they want," Mom said. "People make sacrifices, adjustments."

"We could look on it as a trial, an experiment," Dad said.

"I'm eighteen!"

Mom turned to the both of them, hands apart in the air, the distance between desire and fulfillment. "Against my better judgment, I let you go to that retreat. In New York. In the middle of winter!"

"And guess what?" Ink said. "Not one bad thing happened!"

"What more do you want?"

Ink wanted to let her have it. "Stop," he saw himself shouting. "Stop taking your family problems out on me!" Instead, sensing the tide was turning, he wisely bit his tongue.

"Can we please?" Dad said. There was an edge in his voice that Ink hadn't heard before. Mom opened her mouth, ran sharp hair around her ears two or three times. It kept coming back, thin blades against cheek and chin. When she finally spoke, it was to say that she needed (as usual) time before she gave her consent, which came out at the dinner table two evenings later as a simple, "What's the use?" Ink was thrilled. He jumped upstairs, where he opened the brochure for Clerestory University and imagined himself into the pictures on every single page. For a few days, he took great venomous joy in seeing Mom mope around the house, silently doing the chores, making perfunctory comments at the dinner table, devoting whatever energy she had left by the evening to her religious books and jigsaw puzzles.

Then Ink was hurt. Then he felt remorse. Then, as days ticked by, Mom's continued silence began to make him seethe. How dare she cast a pall over what should be one of the most exciting times of his life? Many years ago, she moved away from home, drawing the ire of her entire family. Just because her escape did not work out well was no reason for her to spoil such an opportunity for him.

Well, the battles were all over and, despite the awkward parting, Ink felt he had won the war. Mom was out of his life; in fact, he wouldn't see either parent until Thanksgiving, if he could last that long. Now, Freitag Hall loomed behind, a whale ready to swallow him whole. He took a deep breath and plunged inside, clanging up the staircase to Room 402, the number like a secret code to his new and frightening life. Inside, his books were still in boxes, his shirts and underwear in Dad's hard-shelled suitcase. Soon, he would start unpacking. He would go to the dorm meeting. The day after next, his collegiate career would begin.

As he approached the second floor, his stomach capsized. His buttocks clenched. Sweat oozed from everywhere. Gingerly, he made his way down a hallway filled with milk crates and stereo equipment. A shirtless boy, already at home, watched Ink go by, face scary as an unannounced quiz. A wild-eyed mother, making a fist, asked him if he was the RA of this goddamn floor. Ink waved her off, picking up his pace—gingerly, gingerly—sliding around the corner, slamming through the bathroom door and into a stall, where his body did its usual stinking thing.

*

Ink was lying on his bed when the door banged open and a slender boy with tight black hair and a broad nose appeared, peeking over a milk crate of books and papers. Behind him came his roommate's mother and two sisters, all of them chatting in Spanish.

141

"Ho . . . la," Ink said. He'd been practicing the greeting for weeks.

The girls giggled. The boy put down his crate and offered a hand. "Diego Rodriguez," he said, in perfect English.

The mother beamed at Ink. "For you," she said. She uncovered a plastic container of shiny, sugar-sprinkled half-moon pies and implored Ink to grab half a dozen. "Empanadas," she announced.

Stout and severe, the father appeared in the doorjamb like a cloudy day, keeping one dark eye on the sound of a heavy metal anthem that barreled down the hallway. The man nodded at Ink, which he interpreted as permission to indulge.

Still weak, his stomach burbling, Ink chanced a bite. "Ummm," he said, smiling as broadly as he could.

Mrs. Rodriguez clapped her hands. "Calabaza," she said. "You know?"

"Pumpkin," Diego said.

Ink nodded. He held up the pastry. "Very good," he shouted.

The older sister—a precociously beautiful girl who was maybe twelve—did a perfect impersonation of Ink that sent the younger into a fit of giggling. The father, moving into the room, spoke sharply to his daughters until the mother, intervening, coaxed a fissure-like grin from his lips.

Ink found this all delightful—evidence of a family that truly got along. He stood in the middle of the room with a smile on his face until it dawned on him that the playful moment had long since passed. Diego was shelving books and his mother was trying to fold a foil pan of something into the compact fridge. The father had gone back to the door to scowl at the music down the hall. The little sister was at the windowsill, prancing around a plastic unicorn, while the older one had climbed the ladder to the top bunk (his bunk!) and made herself at home. She wore a short skirt, and when she bounced one knee over the other, Ink saw way too much leg. Standing behind the door of his wardrobe, he began to feel like an intruder—and a letch.

So he escaped—down the stairwell again to the main floor, which was filled with students and parents trying to make heads or tails of room assignments. The weather was gorgeous, but he was afraid to go outside, where guys and girls were lying out or tossing Frisbees, their laughter bold and confident. Earlier, as Ink had walked with his parents back to his dorm, it seemed that everyone knew everybody else. Greetings blew like seeds across the quad. Brightly dressed girls in flip flops slapped up to grinning, wide-shouldered boys and threw arms around their necks. Ink got the impression they'd all been here for quite some time, bonding, getting oriented behind Ink's back. Maybe he'd misread the date on the letter from the Dean of Student Life. Maybe the Dean had purposely tried to keep him in the dark.

In the basement of the dorm, Ink discovered vending machines inside an unoccupied laundry room. He bought a can of ginger ale, hopped on a washer, its lid cool against the back of his legs. The windows were at ground level and angled open, and Ink watched the brown sandaled feet and calves—smooth or hairy, huge or sexy— striding by. The morning after next, he'd be compelled to join that terrible march. He looked away, right into the eye of a dryer. Queasy again, he watched underwear tumble and twin around pants, heard the happy plink of change that came with each rotation. He had half a mind to crawl inside—risk violent sickness for the warmth of the womb.

*

Ink arrived early to the floor meeting that night. Boys filled in around him, slouching into soft, multicolored sofas and chairs. Six hours into their college experience, and everyone seemed to chat as if they were best buddies in the world. Ink, humiliated by his isolation, sought solace in a Hemingway book he brought along. Periodically, and with increasing anxiety, he glanced up for Diego. Wasn't his roommate obligated to sit next to him—to be his friend until the real ones came along?

"Hey man," came a voice from above. Ink, jarred from anxious thoughts, looked up in time to see big bare feet soaring over his head—feet and calves and gym shorts, a long body in a rippling white t-shirt. The body landed in the chair next to his with a tremendous poof of cushion. "Drellishak," the boy announced, hand extended, like he was a TV cop or something. Danny Drellishak. To Ink, he had the face of a drug-using comedian—slightly bloated, dilated eyes, lips wavy as a tilde. Well built, sporting a military crew cut, he was undoubtedly a jock of some kind. A few moments later, they were joined by Danny's roommate, who identified himself only as Sherk. With two red rails of sleep running across his cheek, he looked like he just stumbled out of summer hibernation. Every two minutes he licked his fingertips and ran them over his crazy, interrogative sweep of hair.

143

The meeting began when the resident assistant, a broad-faced senior with spiky hair, came through the common area door, a stack of pizza boxes in his hands.

"Good evening everybody," he said, voice like a gym teacher who thought he was coaching pros. He placed the pizzas on a table. He put his hands on his hips and pursed his lips. "I saaaid, 'Good evening, everybody!'"

"Good ev-en-ing every-body," Danny sang, fingers like batons.

"My name is David Vanderberg, and I'm known around here as a straight shooter. Tonight, you listen to me for fifteen minutes, you get yourself a slice or two of pie. Kapiche?"

A stunned smile spilled from Danny's face. Sherk, his eyes closed, made a sound like a Guinea pig. Ink looked down at the floor, afraid he was going to be wrongfully punished for insubordination.

"Remember," Dave said nearly a half hour later. "I'm not your friend, but I am here for you. You've got a problem—an annoying roommate, loud music blaring during quiet hours, midterm stress, lady issues—you come and see me. Kapiche?"

Danny hummed the theme to *The Godfather*. Laughter rippled through the room.

"Is there a question?" Dave said, narrowing his eyes. Ink noticed patches of sweat under the RA's arms.

"May we have the pizza?"—this from a gaunt, studious looking boy at the front of the room.

Dave smiled magnanimously. "You may have the pizza."

The boys milled around the room, flaccid, lukewarm slices drooping from their hands. Danny and some of the other boys turned furniture around to the TV for some preseason football—Browns vs. Steelers. Ink spotted Diego, but his roommate just smiled and retreated to the room. Painfully alone, Ink studied the Van Gogh reprint on the wall. He could relate to these nervous, fiery trees burning toward a sloppy swath of dark blue sky. Trying to maneuver the slice of pizza into his mouth, he dropped his book to the floor.

"*The Sun Also Rises*," a dusty-haired boy said, picking up the book.

"No, these are some of the early stories. Nick Adams."

The boy shrugged. "We read the novel in high school. It's all I know."

Awkward silence. Ink looked back at the trees running a fever on the wall.

"I'm Jesse," he said, and he'd come to Clerestory to study abnormal psychology.

On the TV, a Browns receiver let a sure touchdown go through his hands. The boys in their chairs howled with displeasure.

"You've come to the right place."

Jesse laughed, and Ink felt he'd scored a point. "Call me Ink," he said.

"Oh, you some kind of writer?"

"Just a reader," he said, holding the book to his heart.

There were several replays of the dropped pass, each followed by more hoots and howls. The announcer said, "Footsteps? You got to block out contact and look the ball all the way into your hands."

The two boys shook. They talked about movies, music, the daily horrors and humiliations of high school. Jesse mentioned he was from Indiana, and Ink, without thinking, said, "My mom's family's from there!"

Jesse brightened. "Oh yeah? Whereabouts?"

Ink froze. Logansport? Frankfort? Something like that, he thought. The thing was, Ink had been to the town only twice, the last time maybe ten years ago. He remembered a huge expanse of land, a sky of shredded clouds that seemed to press right down upon them. Hide-n-seek with cousins in endless rows of the corn. A game of Wiffle ball in a field that fell away toward a ducky-crazy pond. He reddened, explained as best he could that his mother and her family, for reasons that went back to her own college days, were barely on speaking terms.

Jesse nodded, swallowed the rest of his pizza. "Sounds like my Dad," he said. "He almost killed his brother-in-law at my high school graduation party."

"Why?"

"Something stupid. Politics, I think."

Ink laughed. "Yeah, that'll do it."

They talked themselves back to music. Ink admitted to liking pretty much whatever he heard on WMMS, The Home of the Buzzard, the best station in Cleveland and in all of America. Jesse was interested now not so much in specific bands and songs but in the guitar, which he recently began learning to play. This summer, he'd been immersed in the blues—Clapton, Hendrix, and Stevie Ray Vaughan. He went on at length about producers, studio musicians, little known album tracks, and all Ink could do was drop in the names of the few songs he knew. After a time, he simply nodded, smiled, made himself agreeable as possible, beating back the bat-flapping fear that this nice boy might move on to someone else more musically astute. He wished he could just stop him now and say, "Will you be my friend?" and Jesse, since no one else had yet made such a request, would say yes. "Best friend?" Yes. "For all four years? For life?" Yes, and he would sign his name on a dotted line, and Ink would come out of this evening assured of at least one good thing.

*

Late that night, there was rabid pounding on the door. Diego glanced up from the fat tome splayed before him on his desk. Ink, a foot on the ladder of the bunk, felt the hot grease splash of fear against his face. He thought: Dave the RA, a hot pot raid, a detention, a write up—whatever they called them here.

"Open up in the name of the god almighty law!" the voice shouted.

Diego returned to his book. Ink cracked open the door, wondering what he could have done wrong.

It was only Danny Drellishak, shirtless, sweatpants riding low on his hips. He bullied his way into the room, and Ink, to his dismay, found himself admiring the boy's wide shoulders, his powerful, well-sculpted arms.

"So these are your digs," Danny said, eyes flitting around the room.

Ink turned bashful. He swallowed, offered the boy an orange pop from the fridge.

Danny did a drum roll on his hard, flat stomach. "What do you have to mix with it?"

Ink shrugged. "Apple juice?"

Danny walked over to Ink's desk, fingering books and going through drawers. He picked up a few figurines—a cleric holding a mitre, an orc wielding a broad sword—Ink still kept from his *Dungeons & Dragons* days. "Gee, can I play?"

146

Ink reddened. His underarms prickled.

Danny took the orc, swung it at the holy man, knocking him off the desk into the garbage can with a ping. "Another one bites the dust!" Next, he drew a finger across the blank cinderblock wall. "Love what you've done with the place." Ink had a rolled up poster of Hemingway in his wardrobe. A gift from Aunt Ruth, the poster was a famous shot of the writer in middle age—smug, hoary headed, ridiculous in a bulky sweater. Thank God he hadn't yet put it up.

Danny farted, loudly and for a while, then snapped it off, a bullfighter's cape in the air. Through the fingers he flung at his face, Ink saw the boy turn to his roommate and say, "What's your story?"

"I'm Diego."

"Good story. Edge of my seat." Danny picked up a family photograph from his desk. "What are you in for?"

"I don't know what you're saying."

"Do I need a translator?"

Ink was afraid to look at Diego.

"What are you majoring in?"

"I'm a double major," Diego said. "Philosophy and Spanish."

"Spanish," Danny said, studying the photograph more intently. "You? Isn't that like cheating?"

Diego smiled, brilliant white teeth in his round, brown face. He crossed his arms. He seemed amused—charmed even. Danny waited for a response, but Diego just sat there, the smile hovering. He did not even blink.

Danny pursed his lips. He prodded the picture with an index finger. "This one . . ."

"My sister Rosa."

"Ah, Rosa! How old?"

"Thirteen."

"Up and coming," Danny said, tongue gliding across upper lip.

Ink trickled out a laugh. It was a conscious choice he made, a risk, a bid for the kind of alliance he felt needed to make in order to survive in this scary new world. Danny acknowledged the reaction, which was an excellent sign. Ink glanced at Diego and was relieved to see the boy was still smiling. Diego was a good guy, affable as could be. He was almost sure his roommate would understand and cut him a break.

The next night—the night before classes were to begin—Danny burst into 402, waving a copy of the *Directory of Freshman Students*.

"Hot off the presses," he declared.

Ink was playing chess with Jesse while Jacob, a portly, bespectacled boy from across the hall, munched corn chips and said "You don't want to do that" every time Ink touched a piece.

"Give me three more moves," Jesse said, zooming a rook across the board to put Ink's king in check for the sixth straight time.

"Who the hell are you?" Danny asked.

"I'm Jacob. Jacob Shimp. Everybody calls me Jake."

Danny smiled. He looked the boy up and down. "You look more like a Cobb."

"Been called worse," Jacob said over the laughter of the others. He offered corn chips to Danny to show there were no hard feelings.

After Jesse checkmated Ink, the boys turned with relish to the directory. Ink's picture, much to his chagrin, was the most humiliating thing on Earth. Teeth jammed together, eyes squinty—he was striving to be cool, but it looked more like he was straining to go to the bathroom. Fortunately, the boys couldn't have cared less about his face. This evening was all about the girls. With Danny leading the way, they went through the booklet carefully, photograph by photograph, each offering a score on a scale of 1 to 10. Many of the As and Bs weren't half bad: they averaged out as sixes or sevens—not quite hot, but definitely cozy warm. There was one definitive zero, whom Danny claimed had "a lunchmeat face," and the group spent considerable time trying to determine exactly what kind of lunchmeat she was. Salami? Dutch Loaf? Pickled Pimento? Danny had them in stitches when he clapped his hands and declared, "Head Cheese!"

There was one consensus nine, although it was one of those tricky glamour shots and, as Danny cautioned, you never could tell for sure about a chick except in the cold light of day. Some faces scored threes or fours, but again, Danny cautioned the others against believing their eyes. "Jury's out," he said. "You just don't know what's going on below."

A spirited debate ensued. Cobb would go to his grave a face man—the eyes, the shape of the lips, the contour of cheekbones. Danny was an advocate for the body, saying, worst come to worst, all you had to do is "turn them over." Jesse fighting off a laugh, said, "you're terrible," to which Danny responded, "Okay, you ask them to please turn over." They all busted up. Hand over his mouth, body shaking with laughter, Ink had to agree that Danny was indeed terrible but in an odd, terrific way. He admired the boy's brazenness, the courage it took to let loose with whatever happened to bubble up to his lips.

Danny rattled the booklet to get their attention before reading aloud the profile of the "next contestant":

Name: Julie Columbo
Major: Communications
Interests: Mysteries, family, kids, travel

"So serious, this one," Jesse said.

"I don't like this nose," Cobb said. He removed his glasses. "There. Much better."

"She could have done something with her hair," Jesse said.

To Ink, the girl looked nervous, unsure of herself. The nose was a problem, for sure, but there was a skittish warmth in her eyes that made her vaguely interesting. Empathetic, feeling every bit the gentleman, he scored her a 6.5.

"Hey, what's with the decimals?" Danny said.

Ink put up his hands. "Okay, okay. Six." He could live with that.

"I respectfully request a recount on that Basilevsky chick," Cobb said, bouncing his voice along each syllable of the name.

"Cobb has a weakness for the Bulgarian weightlifters," Danny said.

Everyone laughed. They went on and on, offering assessments after slugs of cola, through mouthfuls of corn chips. Occasionally, they came across a pictureless profile, which, Danny assumed, meant that the girl in question was too hideous to present.

In the middle of the Ss, Xavier, Jesse's roommate, came in looking for the guy who swiped his Pet Shop Boys CD.

Danny smiled. "You might want to check the fag floor, my friend."

Xavier was an all-state swimmer. He had tight black curls, and big, earnest eyes. Ink had met him briefly the night before, and even then he thought the shape of the boy's body—straight and narrow—was the best way to explain him. He put his hands on his hips now and said, "Excuse me?"

"Perri Simmons," Danny said, whacking the booklet. "Give us a score."

Cobb explained the rules, the scoring system, such as they were. Xavier refused to even take one glance. His chin was up in the air, as if trying to keep brackish water from lapping at his face.

"What's wrong with you?" Jesse said.

"It's crass. And besides, there's only one girl in the world," Xavier said, fingers on his cross. Everybody laughed, and Danny politely escorted him from the room. This was no place for a boy who'd already kissed away the best years of his life when he gave his high school sweetheart a diamond ring.

The rating game raved on. Like a preschool teacher, Danny held open the book, turned the pages, read the names and vital stats. Ss, Ts, Vs and Ws. They joked, they judged, and once or twice more paused in silent awe. Ink was sad there wasn't another volume; he could have played this delightful game all night.

*

For the first two weeks or so, there didn't seem to be much to do. Five classes, an hour or so for each; a generous but not unmanageable amount of reading; the occasional writing assignment, brief pieces designed to keep them honest. There was time to sit out on the quad and dream after the girls passing by. Time for long, meandering dinners in the cafeteria with Jesse and Cobb. Time for pool or MTV in the student center lounge. Time for nighttime fun on The Bell, the strip of clubs and restaurants that grinned around the Buckeye River. Time for late, late nights with buttered toast and David Letterman. Time to sleep in on Sundays and still be able get to the last mass of the day.

On the Tuesday of the third week of classes, Ink's confidence was sky high. By early afternoon on Wednesday, however, it was a smoke-tailed plane corkscrewing back to earth. He still suffered pinpricks of homesickness, intestinal pains from too many grilled cheese sandwiches and greasy fries, heartache from the pretty girls who had no idea he occupied space in this world. But what did all of

150

this matter now, when without warning his very survival at school was at stake?

The situation became so dire that Ink had to skip dinner the following night just to get his act together. He spent forty-five minutes plotting out the remaining weeks of the semester. Only then did he start breathing a bit more easily again. First things first: the Psych exam. He pulled out the syllabus and was surprised to find that, somehow, he'd fallen two chapters behind. He read about the sixteen types of personalities, and when he could not figure out which one he was, he did not feel so bad about his failed plan to make himself new. He looked over notes Jesse had let him copy, made flashcards of every key term. If he did what the study skills people told him at the beginning of the semester, he would be a success. Just as he began to make good headway, Danny, whom he hadn't seen for a while, burst into the room, a piece of paper like a wounded bird in his hands.

"You clean this up for me, okay?" Danny handed Ink a page of handwritten notes that he was supposed to turn into a typed personal experience essay, three to four pages, by the following morning. Danny would have done it himself, of course, but he had two dates that night—as he said, "a 7:30 and a 10:30 show." He was gone before Ink could tell him "yes" or "no."

Ink was of two minds. He could just set it aside and tell Danny "Too bad" when he returned in the morning. It would be the right thing to do—the thing that would make God smile down at him at mass that Sunday. It might also be the thing that would kill whatever kind of friendship was beginning to form. Ink could write the essay, score the boy a decent grade, and then hope Danny was the kind of person upon whom debt would weigh. Maybe next week, maybe a few months down the line, Danny would burst into the room to announce: "Dude, have I got just the chick for you!"

In the grand scheme of things, there were much worse things a person could do: theft, assault, rape, murder. And if Ink only did this once, just once—and if he went immediately to confession, did his penance and more—this sin (this peccadillo, really) would, after an otherwise perfectly pious life, be nothing more than a microscopic sauce spot on the otherwise white dress shirt of his soul.

"It haunts me," Ink began simply enough, although the statement struck him as something he might say years from now, sickened by the guilt that seized him the moment he put pen to paper. He stood up.

He found a towel to dry his stomach, which was suddenly soaking with sweat. He memorized a dozen more psychology terms before reluctantly returning to "Danny's essay."

Sometime later, Diego returned bleary-eyed from his library carrel—his second dorm room. "How's it going?" he asked.

Ink glanced at the clock: 2:43 am. "Fine."

He thought about asking Diego if he'd received a new batch of those pastries (whatever they were called), but his roommate just as quickly slipped back out the door, toothbrush and towel in hand. What Ink wouldn't give to be getting ready for bed after a hard (and honest) night's work. What he wouldn't give to be fresh and cool and clean, dropping off to the hum of the box fan in the window. He turned back to the essay and started to sweat again. How absurd—how utterly implausible—Danny's story was!

Diego returned. "You have a paper due tomorrow?" he wondered.

Ink nodded, afraid to meet his roommate's eyes.

After Diego went to bed, Ink swallowed his incredulity and went on with the story. He described how the car in front of Danny smashed through the guardrail and tumbled into a ravine. The driver was a young pregnant woman, her brand new husband serving overseas. Disoriented, bleeding from the forehead, she could not escape her belt. Danny bounded down the embankment, saw immediately what the trouble was. He chewed—chewed?!—through the harness and began to haul the woman to safety. On the way up the slope, Danny stepped in a hole and broke his leg. Undaunted, he hoisted the frantic woman on his back and hopped up and up and by the time he reached the road the bone (in his notes, Danny had written "lemur") was sticking through the skin. At that moment, the car (of course) blew sky high. As the pieces rained down in the distance, Danny's realized that, although his football career was ruined, he had saved a human life. He had, as the boy himself had scribbled in his notes, "done a small real good in the world."

The professor was going to take one look at this and laugh; then, he was going to suspect plagiarism. Under the harsh, hot lights of the interrogation room, Danny—so cool with his peers—would dissolve into a pool of guilty tears. He'd surrender Ink's name, and Ink would be thrown out of school as well. Aghast, Mom would refuse to take him back in and Dad (being Dad) would go along with it, hands quivering in pockets. In a panic, he'd have no one to turn to but Uncle Lare, who'd offer him a soiled mattress in his unfinished basement. He'd follow long days typing up cover letters and resumes with longer nights under a bare bulb at a weak-legged kitchen table, a bottle back and forth between him and his uncle. From there, how long would it be until he put a bullet through the head?

Ink stood, went to the box fan, and raised his shirt to get some relief. What to do, what to do? He glanced at the clock just as it winked to the next red number. Time was passing, and like it or not, Danny would be back, demanding to see the finished product. He sat down. This stupid essay, the exam, two chapters in his history text, a speech on the pros of euthanasia—never in a million years was he going to get it all done.

But to his amazement, he did. And what was more, he had time for a full one and a half hours of sleep before the door began to shake from pounding. Diego, blanket like a royal robe flowing down his back, shambled to the door.

"Boner dias, senorita," Danny said, clapping Diego on the back.

Diego smiled affably before sitting down at his desk to begin his reading for the day.

"Okay, where's the goods?"

"On the desk. The blue folder." Ink was exhausted and more than a little angry at Danny's presumptuousness. He bit his tongue, though. After all, Danny was Danny, and Ink—if he could dare to be honest with himself for a second—was thrilled to have been of use.

Danny scooped up the folder and examined the contents. He nodded once, twice. "Commas! Complete sentences! I owe you, man."

The door slammed, and Ink turned to his blank wall, waiting with dread for Diego to start asking questions. All he heard, though, was the coffee maker's morning pee, the periodic sound of a page being flipped. Ink turned over and over, a pig roasting on a spit in hell. The shifting springs sang like so many demons enjoying the show.

*

"Can you believe it?" Diego said. "I am—it's just so incredible." His roommate smiled and shook his head, eyes glued to the TV.

Ink swung back his wardrobe door to watch people streaming through a checkpoint, prying out chunks of stone, passing around bottles of champagne in front of grim-faced police. This was the Berlin Wall. Many of the particulars were lost to him, but Ink knew enough to know that, for all intents and purposes, the Cold War was over. The terrible battle of Us vs. Them was at long last drawing to a close. Soon, he theorized aloud, there would be one big happy Us.

"It's certainly a beautiful idea," Diego said.

"What do you think is going to happen?"

"Well, it's complicated. Transitions are never easy."

Ink thought of his first weeks at college—the loneliness, the abject fear, the certainty he wouldn't last another day. And now, even as he was dealing with a fresh avalanche of work, he'd gone a long way toward making Clerestory home.

"Whatever happens," Diego said, "it probably won't be what we expect."

The two had been roommates for more than two months, and this was the most they'd ever talked. Ink felt the need to say something more, and to say it well. He wanted to dig more deeply, challenge Diego with historical precedents, with arcane particulars. But he didn't know a thing. Maybe it was for the best. The night before, Danny had asked Ink to breakfast. His roommate was ready to talk, but now was not the time to get distracted. If Ink dawdled any longer, he'd be late; if he was late, Danny might be gone, or sitting with the more important people around whom he usually hung.

On the way to the cafeteria, Ink found himself thinking about walls. Too often, he thought, there was a wall in front of him. Whichever way he turned—BAM! —there was another, high and wide as the eye could see. When he was frustrated enough, he'd bang against a wall, taking away a few red slivers of brick for his pains. On rare occasions, he'd try to scale the one in front of him for a peek or a hello. But the effort—that, and the fear of being shot down—was usually enough to keep him in his place. He consoled himself with the thought that there must have been at least a few East Germans who, inured to their difficult lives, were in no great hurry to spill into the West.

"John!" a voice called out behind him.

Ink didn't turn. John was his middle name—the name he'd gone by years ago. And besides, there were thousands of Johns in the world. And besides, the voice was distinctly female. Who did he know that was a girl?

"John Alt . . . Ink!"

Against all known laws governing the operation of the universe, there was a pleasant-looking brunette jogging his way, oblivious to walls. Short, bouncy hair made an energetic frame for her cherubic face, which was bright and cloudless. When he realized who it was, he couldn't get out her name.

"It's Nina . . . Nina Sissyan!" she said, presenting herself with a tilt of the head, palms like serving trays in the air.

"Hi . . . Nina." The greeting came out wrong. He sounded embarrassed, caught red-handed. In grade school, Nina had been part of what Macho Maldonado, his old nemesis, had referred to as the Holy Trinity. There was Bethany Hyde, of course, a blonde who even now had the occasional power to wet Ink's dreams, and Bernadette, the tall redhead, freckles like cinnamon on her face and shoulders. Brown, blond, and red—to Ink, they'd always seemed like the flag of a country he'd never be privileged to visit.

"This is so totally amazing!" Nina was perspiring, a little out of breath, down-to-earth in red running shorts and a March of Dimes T. She was shorter than he remembered, maybe a little thicker in the legs. To Ink's dismay, there was even a pimple on the side of her nose. As she went on about herself and how she ended up at Clerestory College, Ink tried to remember the last time he had seen her. In high school, on the rare occasions Mom gave him permission, Ink would meet up with Lance Duda at ten o'clock mass, where'd they'd make jokes about the liturgy and size up girls as they passed by in the communion line. Nina had moved out to the suburbs after grade school graduation, but he had seen her maybe two years ago at St. James, teetering in on heels between her flour-white mother and Hawaiian-looking father, taking a pew three rows ahead of them. When the time came for a sign of peace, she turned and beamed, shaking a peace sign finger wave. Had the wave been for him? For Lance, who had more of the rugged look that would make girls swoon? Maybe it had been a flirty gift to split between them.

Ink asked now about Bethany, whom he hadn't seen since Christmas mass three years ago. Hadn't he heard? Jay Miller, Bernadette's pothead brother, got her pregnant, and she dropped out of school to move in with him. According to Bernadette, another baby was on the way, but Jay said this one was definitely not his. It was so sad, Nina said. Bethany had been so smart and so beautiful. The truth was, she added with a nervous laugh, in eighth grade, she used to wake up every morning to the sin of being jealous—"insanely jealous"—of her. "And, well," Nina concluded with a sigh, "now that I'm no longer jealous, I feel even worse!"

Ink winced. He'd adored Bethany without lapse since first grade—blond hair, strawberry lip gloss, fingernails like Red Hots, all those cheerleader scissor kicks. In his dorm room desk, he kept the class portrait from eighth grade, when he had the unbelievable good fortune to be able to stand right behind her. He remembered being mesmerized by the creamy spill of hair, the smell of the shampoo, which made him think of a juicy half of a grapefruit, with sugar generously sprinkled on top.

Nina covered her mouth, and through her fingers beamed another smile, an apology for being rude. How have you been? she wanted to know, and Ink, still reeling from the news, from this unprecedented presence before him, struggled to produce meaningful words. In time—after several awkward seconds—they came and soon, to his amazement, he pieced together the rudiments of a story to tell.

"Well," Nina said. "St. James is certainly well-represented at Clerestory U!"

"Yes."

"It's," she said, sliding a strand of hair behind her ear. "It's really good seeing you again."

"You too."

"I'm sure I'll see you around."

Ink watched her jog away, elbows out, hips swiveling, buttocks like a hypnotist's watch. He wondered why he and his friends hadn't come across Nina the night they went through the *Directory of Students*. Could they have just missed her? Maybe she enrolled too late to be included in the publication? If her photograph had been included, what score would he have given her? She had big, kind eyes, a toothy, capacious smile, a touchy-feely way of making you feel you were among the most important people in the world. In a word, she was sweet. So did that make her a six? A six point five? Would the score be higher if it were Sunday, if she had appeared before him in one of her bright colored dresses . . . and heels? Maybe there was something about Nina that made her impossible to score.

Ink was jarred from his thoughts by a powerful weight against his throat. He could not breathe. Frantically, his eyes spun, spying two big hands fast around his neck. He kicked, he threw out his arms. The hands disappeared.

"Jesus . . ." he coughed, turning into the roar of Danny's laughter. "You scared the hell out of me!"

"Mission accomplished," Danny said with a shrug. "Who's the babe?"

Ink looked at Nina, tiny now between the trees on the other end of the quad. "An old friend, I guess." A seven maybe? With those legs, an eight was probably out of the question.

"Nice," Danny said. He didn't lustfully draw out the word. Surprisingly, he did not add a noun like "tits" or "ass." He simply said "nice," as if commenting on the weather—partly cloudy, unseasonably warm, a high of 55. For Danny, this was an admirable show of restraint.

The walk to the cafeteria with Danny was an unprecedented thrill for Ink. The boy nodded, shook hands, or hugged almost every other person who passed them, stopping four or five times to talk about some wild pirate-themed party at the football house the night before last. A broad, neckless man gave Danny a nod and a wiggle of his vacuum brush moustache.

"Linebackers coach," Danny said with a bitter laugh. "Dude recruited me, and now I don't even get a "What's up?""

A group of girls cried out, quickly gathered around him, desperate to be hugged, desperate to touch their lips to his face. He chatted, touched, made ribald jokes that gave them giggles. They left, chatting excitedly to themselves, satisfied beyond their wildest dreams.

Even though Danny introduced him to no one, the fact that Ink stood next to this campus icon was a clear sign of how well Ink was connected. All he needed to do was keep close and before too long (he dared to hope), some of Danny's darling groupies would begin to ask who he was. It was not so far-fetched to think one or two would want to get to know him, even if—at first—their interest was little more than a strategy to get to Danny. It might take weeks—the better part of a year—but one day, at least one of the girls would see Ink for the sweet, sensitive boy he was.

"So," Danny said, grabbing a tray in the cafeteria, winking at the hair-netted co-ed for a scoop of eggs, "will you do it?" Danny touched Ink's shoulder. "For your good old buddy?"

"What? What are you talking about?" Ink had not been listening; somehow, he had a stack of pancakes on his tray, bacon strips like shriveled up ears on either side.

"I've got all the sources. I've got quotes on note cards. All you got to—"

"Wait. You want me to write another paper for you?"

"Don't say it like that."

Ink swallowed hard. Danny hadn't come around for weeks and when he did, it was not because he missed Ink's brilliant company but because he wanted to put Ink to use. He was livid, but when words formed on his lips the tone was all wrong. "I can't do this," he said, his voice dripping with whine. "It's not fair of you to ask."

"Come on, man. Don't cry on me."

Ink stuffed his mouth with pancakes. He looked away, saw a plain jane girl thumbing through a paperback. A minute ago, he wouldn't have noticed enough to pity her; now it seemed as if she were having the time of her life.

Danny stood up and Ink, his jaw stopping, waited for further humiliation.

"It's okay. I see you found your morals."

Ink swallowed his lump of food, and Danny left, stopping at a table of tittering girls. He set down his tray, made wild gesticulations. They looked up, eyes wide, teeth resplendent. Ink suspected he was the sad subject of conversation. Soon the rest of the campus would know how weak he was, like orange juice from the cafeteria dispenser. In vain, he looked to the entrance for Jesse, for Cobb, for Xavier, for even that sleepy pothead Sherk—for anyone to sit across from him, and prove to the world that he was not alone.

*

Two weeks into the new semester, the real cold arrived—thick and hard, angry and relentless. Each day tried its damnedest to impress the one before. Heavy winds. Near-horizontal sleet. Ice formed like hard skin over campus walkways. From his window, Ink watched ski-capped, fleece-swaddled students walk backwards to avoid the wind.

One boy, tired of battling the powerful gusts, sat down on the walkway between Freitag and Smith, legs crossed, backpack like a tombstone in his lap. An hour later, wild snow arrived. Small, charming flakes whizzed around for a while and then things began to pick up. Huge chunks flopped against the window and Ink, paging through biology notes, was filled with a sort of Christmas coziness. He yawned. He closed his eyes, imagined blinking tree lights, the sweet smell of Grandma's homemade apple kuchen.

At the sound of the phone, Ink jumped, banging his knee on the bottom of the desk.

"We leave at 6:15," Stash said.

"What? Ow! They're saying eight inches by midnight."

"Sharp."

Ink had hours ago figured their plans had been cancelled. "There's a travel advisory," he said, as if that would clinch the argument.

"What are you telling me? Why don't you take a deep breath and tell me what you are right now saying about yourself?"

Ink blushed. "I'm just saying."

"Do not make me tell you what you are."

"Okay, okay, I'll be ready."

Ink returned to his desk and paged absentmindedly through his biology book, pausing when he came to "phagocyte," a word that groped him like a molester. He closed his eyes. "Those are cells that swallow other cells," he said aloud. "The garbage and all the foreign junk that gets inside." In high school, he'd only known the term as Fag's full and proper name. Had Stash been ready to call him a fag? A pussy? Something worse? He knew enough to know that, if Stash insisted on a plan, you kept your mouth shut. You simply had to go along for the ride.

Ink had met Stash quite by accident at the end of last semester, when, heading out of World History class, he spied a glossy accounting textbook under a chair up front. He was certain it belonged to that tall, quiet blonde—Debbie something, a girl who turned out to be at least two full points better than the six he and his friends had awarded her at the beginning of the semester. There was a phone number inside the cover and when he returned to his room, Ink looked at it and looked at it, trying to suppress the heat rising under his arms. After a series of panic-stricken false starts, he dialed the number. As the phone rang, he found himself short of breath, head dizzy with vaguely imagined outcomes. Then a gruff voice—"You are speaking with Stash," it said—and Ink understood that the book's owner was the guy who always argued with the professor after class about the evils of big government. As his name suggested, Stash sported a thick, dark mustache, one that frowned precipitously over his lips. When he spoke, it looked to Ink like a furry bird trying to flap from the ground. He often wore a ten-gallon hat and alligator skin boots that clicked menacingly as he walked. Sometimes, he sported a bright red handkerchief around his neck. Rugged? Perhaps. Bizarre? Without a doubt. Good looking? Ink was going to have to say no way.

After the next class, Stash followed Ink out the door, thanking him again with a ridiculous "much obliged," asking if Ink knew how much a book like that cost. "Can't say I would have done the same," he said, shaking his head. They got to talking—or, rather, Stash got to talking and Ink, glancing longingly at the stairwell door, got to listening. He shifted his backpack from shoulder to shoulder as Stash went on about his paintball club. He told Ink about how to load the guns, about how you lured the other guy in for the kill. Ink had always thought paintball would be fun—dressing up in fatigues, slithering under bushes and serpentining across open fields, plunking some unsuspecting jackass in the back with a hard fat glob of red or blue. In high school, Ink had played quite a bit of *Dungeons & Dragons*. His main character, Prosper the Paladin, had survived many dangerous missions in harsh, dice-determined worlds. He had a hunch, though, that such information would not impress his new acquaintance.

"I've got to go," Ink said, thinking of the class he was already five minutes late for.

"No problem. I'll walk with you."

To be polite, to make things less awkward for himself, Ink asked more about paintball—Where did he play? Were there tournaments? What kind of guns?

But Stash was done talking about paintball, which was just, after all, a silly game, something whose real purpose was to keep him sharp for his "once-a-month maneuvers."

"Oh, you mean like Army Reserve?"

"Are you kidding? Tell me right now you are kidding, and I'll spare you my invective."

Ink laughed out loud to make it clear just how much he'd been kidding.

Stash wanted to make it perfectly clear that there was a growing number of people who had no time or patience for the government of these "so-called United States." He was not one of the stupid, castrated sheep that the rich and greedy were just going to send off to God knows where to save people from he didn't care what. The government, in case Ink didn't know, was there for one reason and one reason only: "to press its huge spiked boot against your scrawny neck." And the second amendment, the one that gave *all* citizens the absolute right to bear arms, was about the only thing that was going to save them—"common folks, you and me"—when push at last came to shove.

Ink nodded. They were at the door to his class.

Stash stared at him from under the brim of his hat. "Do you think I'm not serious?"

Dangerous or ludicrous? To be on the safe side, Ink decided it was best to see Stash as the former.

*

At 6:15, Ink was at the back entrance of Freitag Hall, picking with his tennis shoes through the snow holes of earlier adventurers toward Stash's idling Horizon. He climbed in the back where Evan Cole sat, squeezing a black stress reliever that reminded Ink of a caret jabbing into the space where a missing word might go.

"Welcome to The Doommobile," Evan said.

"Final examination," Stash said, turning around, arm strangling the headrest. "Essay question: 'In 500 words, explain the extent to which Mr. Evan Cole is both cowardly and effete.'"

Evan squeaked his stress reliever, and Stash, seemingly satisfied with the answer, turned away to put the car in gear.

Ink had met this Evan only a few nights ago, when Stash dragged him to Open Mike's, the "anything goes" place down on The Bell. There had been a stand-up routine, a dramatic reading of Pi, and then skinny, unassuming Evan, who, thumbs in pockets, admitted that juggling "meant the world to him." He took five frozen peas from a Ziploc bag and got some drunken laughs as they plinked to the stage after a couple of tosses. When he moved onto Brussels sprouts, the laughter quickly gave way to jeers. That was the point where he took out three long bread knives and proceeded to amaze them all.

The Horizon swished along the ring road to the rear of Dolan Hall, where Robbie Petersen was supposed to be waiting.

"This is not optimal," Stash said, laying on the horn.

Ink's stomach flopped. He took a deep breath and told himself to have a little faith, to give these new acquaintances a chance. "Your first friends at college are great," a psychologist from the counseling center said at a floor meeting to start off the semester. "They're golden. But try to meet their friends, and then the friends of their friends. In other words, make contacts. Expand your network. Get out of your comfort zone." All of Ink's "first friends" seemed to have done just that: Jesse was more often than not jamming with fellow musicians in the basement of the student union. Xavier, when not in the pool, was with church friends doing things like giving a women's shelter a new coat of paint. Danny was off at the football house, emptying beer bottles with pie-eyed compatriots; Cobb had found a bunch of video game loving geeks and spent all his free time riveted to a screen. Diego, although seemingly friendless, had made many new companions on the shelves of the library stacks. And Sherk? The last time he'd seen the sleepy-eyed boy was during one of his Bowl Patrol stops at 402, when he offered Ink "one hit for two itty bitty bits." With everyone else occupied, it was either a night out with Stash and his gang or a night in front of cop dramas on a twelve-inch TV.

Stash laid on the horn again, and Robbie appeared, smug in short sleeves, a Vikings ski cap on his head, hands on his hips and legs apart like Superman. Ink had never met this boy before, but something about the face—perhaps it was that Nike swoosh of a smile—made him think there would be trouble. He swung open the front door with a flourish.

"I'm going to ask you to stop and explain exactly what you are doing," Stash said.

Robbie poked in his head, tossed a smile around the car. "What the hell are you talking about?"

"In back."

On the passenger seat sat Stash's cowboy hat, looking like a mushroom that might well be poisonous. Robbie reached to push the hat aside.

"In back," Stash said.

Grumbling, Robbie did as told, pushing against Evan, the boy who had invited him on this expedition. Evan smiled weakly. He squeezed his stress reliever three times in a row. As the other boys got settled, Ink tried to slide closer to the door, but there was nowhere left to go.

With great difficulty, Stash maneuvered onto Route 7 and at last they were on their way to Pittsburgh, where this "lovely girl" (at Open Mike's the other night, Stash passed around her picture, and no one disagreed) was throwing a party at her off-campus house. "Now you realize this is a special school," Stash explained. "Only the finest ladies may attend. They are unused to but not unreceptive to the presence of men." Ink bit his tongue. In his mind's eye, he saw a lollipop swirl of heels and short bright skirts, big hair and juicy red lips. For a few moments, he forgot all about the snow and ice.

"If you don't step on it a bit," Robbie said, "they'll be graduated and gone."

Stash said, "I'm going to laugh at that because I am in good humor at this point in time." He cracked his knuckles. He turned up the radio. "'If Tomorrow Never Comes'—that's Mr. Garth Brooks," the DJ said. WBMB The Bomb was in the middle of forty commercial-free minutes of country music favorites, but before spinning a classic by George Jones, the DJ had to announce, once again, a severe weather advisory for all of Central Ohio. "I'm looking outside the studio window and all I can say is: Stay home! Batten the hatches. Do not—I repeat—do not become a statistic!"

On cue, Stash slid through a red light, and Ink pressed knees against the back seat until the car stopped a few feet from a phone pole.

Evan offered Ink his stress reliever. "You just squeeze the life out of it. See how many times in a row you can get the ends to touch."

Ink shook his head.

"This is nothing," Robbie announced. "A dusting." He sucked a stick of wintergreen gum into his mouth to show the extent of his concern.

The Horizon crawled up the wide arc of the interstate entrance ramp. Evan crushed Ink against the door. Girls, he chanted to himself. Girls, girls, girls.

The back tires began to lose their grip. The car was sliding, spinning. A guardrail appeared.

"Holy—!" Evan cried.

"Weee!" Robbie said, thumping the headrest with a palm.

The pretty Pittsburgh girls flashed past Ink's eyes, and when they were gone there was Mom, tight-lipped, hands folded, sitting in judgment at the kitchen table—Chief Justice Mom, who could recall at a moment's notice all kinds of precedents of careless people who lost their lives well before they were supposed to. Like that boy in grade school, Frankie, for example—the one who drowned in a foot of water. In an hour, Mom would get the phone call that would say her son was dead in a horrible crash. She would nod and thank the officer. Back on the sofa, she'd turn on the eleven o'clock news, see the mangled carcass of Stash's Horizon, and smile with grim satisfaction.

When impact failed to occur, Ink inched open his eyes to see that, against all odds, they'd made it to the highway, were merging with the few intrepid vehicles that slipped and slid around them. Ink took a breath, tried to take things one moment at a time. He focused on the slow, sad country song on the radio. Verse, chorus, verse, chorus. A green sign emerged from the furious shakes of snow. One mile to the next exit. Nine tenths of a mile. Eight tenths.

Stash clicked his tongue. "I'm going to admit that conditions are not optimal."

They could stop, Ink thought. They could get a room at a motel. Two rooms. And Ink would even pay—surely, gladly. If only he'd filled out the credit card application that appeared in his mailbox a week ago. He could see the form in the garbage can, buried under a thick rain of coffee grounds. "Dear Increase," the letter had so thoughtfully begun. *Dear* Increase. The company, he understood now, hadn't really been interested in his business; they had only wanted to save his life!

Robbie thrust his head between the bucket seats. "You think this is bad? Spend a winter day in my hometown."

"Is that right?" Stash said. Evan put a hand on Robbie's shoulder. The other hand worked the stress reliever—squeak, squeak, squeak, like a series of doors in a haunted house.

"I'm from International Falls," Robbie said. "That's way up there in Minnesota—by the border. Go there sometime and see what cold and snow are all about."

Ink followed the slippery path of the slide guitar on the radio. He was no fan of country music, but the song, it was clear, was the work of a professional musician; it knew exactly where it was going and was arriving there without a hitch.

"My people don't need coats," Robbie said. "Hell, up there, wearing coats is an old wives' tale." The boy went on to tick off all of the hearty outdoor activities he and "his people" enjoyed in the city stuck to the roof of the United States. He laughed—"Oh man, we know how to have our fun," and that fun included (he kidded them not) frozen turkey bowling. "I use a 16 pounder. Just like the PBA."

"Is that right?" Stash said. "And what, pray tell, is your high game?"

"Would you believe a 279?"

"No, I would not believe such a thing."

"A 730 series."

"No one rolls a 279 with a Butterball."

"Actually, Perdue is my turkey of choice."

Stash was mumbling now; to Ink, the words sounded sharp, admonitory. Was he scolding himself? Trying out a comeback for the ages? Or was he just getting ready to blow?

"Like most things, it's all in the follow through. You gotta kick that foot and shake hands with the pins until they disappear in the pit."

Ink thought of grade school, basketball jump shot drills, Mr. Bishop saying, "Bend that wrist! Follow through! Your knuckles should be watching the shot to the rim." Bend the wrist? Really? In eighth grade? When "homo," "gay," and "faggot" poured so easily from the mouths of boys eager to put others forever in their place?

Stash snapped off the radio. He turned down the heat. For a few moments, there was only the hingy cringy sound of Eric's stress reliever.

"We have the most snow per capita—"

"You need to be quiet," Stash said.

"If you can't hack it, I'd be happy to take the reins."

Stash reached over to the passenger seat and stroked his hat.

Evan, with a wavering voice, wondered, "So . . . are these girls pretty?"

"It sure is windy out there," Ink said, seeing the driver's burning eyes appear in the rearview mirror.

"You doubt my word?" Stash said. "There is a compelling argument to be made that I am risking my life for you, and yet you sit there, cozy as can be, and suggest that I'm chauffeuring you in adverse conditions to another state to meet a mere pack of dogs?"

"I was just asking," Evan said.

"All you need is a hat—keeps in 90 percent of your body heat."

"There will be no more comments or questions."

"A good old-fashioned ski cap—"

Stash found Robbie's eyes in the rearview mirror. "For your own good and the good of others, you must cease and desist," he said. The tone was calm, but the driver's left eye twitched.

Robbie smiled. "Not one of those lame ass—"

"Hey Stash," Ink said, voice breaking. "Could you maybe . . . possibly turn the heat back up?" Ink's feet were becoming numb. The snow he'd tried to dodge by the dorm had long since seeped through his shoes and socks. He would have worn the waterproof boots his grandparents had given him for Christmas, but they were caution tape yellow and robin egg blue, embarrassing even for a third grader. Dad would have suggested that he wear them and bring tennis shoes along in a plastic bag, as if this were a thing eighteen-year-old boys could do without serious repercussions.

"I am unable to honor the request at this point in time," Stash said.

Ink wiggled his toes. It was a good sign he could feel them. But for how long?

"Embrace the cold," Robbie said. "It's the human condition."

Evan began chattering about the news the other day, this special called "Memories of the Wall." They interviewed a guy—an American, a high school kid—who had a little too much to drink one day and stumbled up to the wall, binoculars in hand, to have a good look at the enemy. The guy raised a hand, made the peace sign, and the guard looked down on him with a face of "total stone." Undaunted, the American continued to peer through the binoculars "Something had to give, right?" Evan said, laughing nervously. Finally, the soldier spread two fingers along the side of his gun. "How cool was that?"

"The Cold War is over," Ink said. "We're all going to be best friends."

"Nothing is ever over," Stash said. "Everything simply goes underground. Things lie dormant for a time until an event brings them forth again."

"I've been waiting for years to get a crack at those East German women," Robbie said. "Lose myself in all that armpit hair."

"We have to be ready. Judgment is nigh."

Robbie put hands to head. "Nigh? You are a freak, dude," Robbie said. "I'm sorry, but I call them as I see them."

"You know," Stash said. "That hurts me. My feelings are hurt. I say this calmly, with both hands on the steering wheel. But the question is: for how much longer?"'

"A Jesus freak—the very worst kind."

The Horizon slowed. It moved to the shoulder and crunched to a stop. Stash opened the door and the wind, eager for the opportunity, tore inside for a tour. Ink looked at Eric, who worked the stress reliever like a garlic press. The next thing Ink knew, the passenger side window next to Robbie was filled by the skinny, jeans-clad legs of Stash. There was a pocket knife in his hand, and he moved it like a beckoning finger. "Come on now," he called. "Let's go."

Ink sucked in his breath.

Robbie laughed. "Put that shit away," he said.

Stash tapped on the window. The tip of the blade, the way it jumped and touched the glass—delicate little landings, Ink thought, like Katarina Witt skating for gold. Then the door was open, and Stash was dragging Robbie out by the purple sleeve of his Vikings jersey.

"Don't, don't!" Robbie cried, and it seemed he was worried more about a tear in the shirt than a knife in the chest. Stash obligingly let go, and Robbie stumbled and slipped on what was left of the shoulder. Evan dropped his stress reliever and made no move to pick it up. Ink stopped wiggling his toes and buried his mouth and nose beneath the zipper of his coat. He closed his eyes, trying to remember words to any prayer at all. A few seconds later, the door slammed and a jolt forward snapped his neck. Ink opened his eyes to see that they were moving again. There was plenty of room in the backseat, yet Evan remained frozen where he was.

This was a joke. It had to be. Stash would drive another two hundred feet and stop so Robbie could jog up to the car and climb back in. "Ha, ha, ha," the boy would say. "Good one, dude!" In ten minutes, the snow would begin to abate, and they'd all laugh about the time Stash, that crazy cowboy, scared the living shit out of Robbie Petersen by letting him gorge for a bit on the cold he loved so well. But Stash kept the car crawling through the slush and whizzing snow. Stop! Go back! Ink cried to himself. He stared at Evan, tried to will him with his eyes to grab the wheel and save the day.

When the next green sign appeared, the Horizon veered again to the right. For a few terrifying seconds, Ink thought Stash was preparing to throw another passenger out of the car. Instead, he kept going, climbing slowly up an exit ramp. What did this mean? Where were they headed now? Evan finally moved, turning to Ink, eyes doing a tentative dance of relief as Stash pulled under a gas station's sunny yellow sign.

"Ink," Stash said, his voice shivering. "Be a friend and fill us up with the regular unleaded."

Ink nodded. He popped out of the car, wanting to be good, eager to distinguish himself as obedient. He stood by the pump, watching the rapid tick of numbers on the screen. The wind cut through his suede jacket and wet slop seeped through his shoes. A banner advertising fresh brewed coffee whipped above him.

With a sympathetic shudder, he imagined Robbie plunging through the snow in his tennis shoes and short sleeves, stumbling up to the interstate to wave cars down, eyes black with horror, ears the color of new potatoes, an eighteen-wheeler splashing gray icy sludge over the poor boy's body as it barreled by. He imagined him moving still, one foot after another, slower and slower toward the large green sign in the distance, a few more steps before he stopped for good, one leg up, an arm thrust out for help that would come too late.

Ink's ears became as numb as his feet. He put nose and mouth back underneath the zipper, trying to keep warm, of course, but also trying to avoid the angry eye of God. In high school, Mr. LeMonde told the boys there were two kinds of sin. Sins of commission were those deeds you actually did: speaking ill of another behind his back, cheating on your wife, gunning down an a-hole who cut you off on the highway. Sins of omission, in contrast, were the result not of horrible acts but of horrible failures to act. Ink had done nothing wrong tonight, but to the voice in his head that screamed "Do something now!" Ink said, "Why?" If he did act—if he tried to, say, wrench the wheel away from Stash or something, what's to say that wouldn't make things worse. Stash (with the help of Evan, that coward!) would overpower him, tie him up, and toss him in the trunk. Maybe they would dump his body in some icy pond. To die in such a way—to die for a stupid jerk who couldn't control his mouth— wouldn't that be the real sin?

If only he'd stayed back at school. He could have made another pot of coffee, crammed in a few more desperately needed hours of study for his big biology exam. He could have wandered over to the student union to watch Jesse jam with his blues-crazed friends. He could have tagged along with Cobb to Dempsey Hall for a video game all-nighter. With all of these good choices—these safe choices— before him, Ink had ended up picking the option that was going to leave a young boy dead. By early afternoon, the police would be pounding on his dorm room door. They'd barge in, grab him, drag him past a stunned Diego and down to the station. He'd be placed in a small, harshly lit room with chain-smoking detectives in loose ties and rolled up sleeves, one sitting down as the other coolly strolled back and forth, composing himself for the next phase of the interrogation. "I didn't do anything," Ink would cry. One of the detectives would nod while the other would shake his head in disgust.

The sudden thunk in the line told him the tank was full. He trudged to the cashier's window, and with shaking hand placed the bill in the tray. It occurred to him that he could dash off a note— "Help, I'm with a crazy man. Please call cops!"—but he had no pen and paper. Or, he supposed, he might simply tell the cashier what was going on. More than likely, the guy had a gun in there, underneath the register. He'd probably used it before.

"Here you go," the cashier said, sliding the change under the bulletproof glass.

"Oh . . . yeah. Thanks," Ink said. He clutched the bills and coins in his fist and turned away, unable to believe his last chance had just past him by.

"Hey man," the cashier said, "you do know they're closing the freeway."

"Closing?"

"A big pile up or something."

"Closing," Ink said, just to savor the word—the unexpected deliverance it offered. He nearly danced back to the car to tell Stash, who took the news surprisingly well.

"Yes, yes, it was simply not meant to be," Stash said, eyes on the road ahead, voice oddly loud and bright. He drove across the bridge over the highway and slipped down the westbound entrance ramp. They were going back, back, back—and Robbie would be spared, and Ink's soul would be wiped clean. Ink glanced at Evan, who reached down for the stress reliever and began squeezing more stridently than ever. What could be the matter? They were less than a mile from the abandoned boy, and soon he'd be back in the car, frozen to the bone, no doubt, his pride shattered to pieces. But he would be alive.

Unless, of course, Stash had no intention to stop for the boy. Unless he was planning to cruise on by, letting Robbie shout and give chase, stumble in a drift and lay there dazed until sleep—his final sleep—threw its thick, icy blanket over his head.

Ink pressed his face against the side window. The median was a petrified white snake, wide enough and long enough to swallow the entire world. Beyond it, in the eastbound lanes, there was not one vehicle on the road. And beyond that, there was the dark, sinister sharpness of evergreens. Not a single sign of human life. Ink took a breath. Robbie may well have moved. Maybe he immediately began walking, was nearing the station where they'd just filled up. Maybe someone had offered him a ride.

"There!" Evan cried, pointing toward the window, hand by Ink's face like a comet.

There, there, there he was—Robbie, in the median, a marvelous squall of snow rising up around him. Ink, unable to help himself, slapped his knees with joy.

"Stop . . . now," Evan said, his voice bold over the squeak of the stress reliever. "Please."

Ink was surprised when Stash obeyed, slowing down, easing off the road, as if there had never been any doubt about what he was going to do. Ink looked into the rearview mirror and caught a glimpse of Stash's full moon pupils.

From a distance, Robbie looked as casual as could be. As the

Horizon rolled up to him, though, Ink could see he was shaking badly. His hands were jammed in his pockets, and his elbows flexed like wings. Stash remained in the car, both hands on the wheel, a bus driver making a routine stop. When the boy climbed back in and softly closed the door, the car swished back onto the highway. Robbie's head rolled slowly against the back of the seat. His eyelids fluttered, his teeth danced crazily. In a few minutes, he began to breathe evenly. In a few minutes more, he slid the ski cap from his head and shook snow onto the floor beneath him. He sucked snot into his nose with a ferocity that made Ink jump. Finally, the tendril of a smile broke through to the surface.

"God*damn*, that was refreshing!" he said, reaching forward, slapping Stash hard on the shoulder.

"Please, please," Evan said. "Not again."

Ink braced himself for the inevitable: Stash whirling around, a quick slash of the knife across Robbie's neck, dark blood burbling up through his mouth, the kick and thrash of the boy as he tried to clear some space to die. Oddly, Stash neither made a move nor said a word. He just kept the car creeping along the empty snow-covered freeway, hands at ten and two. Ink glanced in the rearview mirror and saw that those swollen pupils looked about ready to crest. Ink was relieved. He laid his head against the seat and listened as Robbie slowly warmed back up to his subject, citing more of the ample joys of outdoor life in the upper Midwest.

When Ink searched again in the rearview mirror, Stash's eyes were nowhere to be found. For a moment, he thought the driver himself had disappeared, but there were those hands—those thin, reddish fingers—still at ten and two.

Ink tried to put a better name on what he was feeling. It was more than relief. That was certainly part of it, but the feeling was blended like soft serve ice cream with something richer, more pleasant— something tingly and warm that, after he saw the sign for Clerestory, made him want to break into a smile.

Pleasure—yes, that was it. Pleasure because the lawless and ludicrous cowboy in the driver's seat had suffered a failure of nerve. Pleasure because he'd failed in the most egregious way to follow through. With anyone else, perhaps Ink might have empathized. After all, how many times had he himself panicked after getting in over his head? But Stash was Stash—or so he claimed to be. There was not supposed to be a depth that could be over his head.

"That's enough now," Stash said, but the words, spoken quietly—almost politely—seemed less a threat than a matter of form.

Ink looked past Evan at Robbie, sitting there, comfortable as could be now, going on about the Vikings, the last game at The Met. "A real heartbreaker," he said.

Ink wanted to laugh. After a harrowing interlude, the world was returning to normal. Even the snow was beginning to abate. In less than fifteen minutes, he'd be back in his room, the great beautiful routine of the semester stretching out again before him.

"I'm from Cleveland," he declared, eager now for Robbie's approval.

"Yeah, yeah, you know what I'm talking about. Bad weather, a history of sports futility—Red Right 88, The Drive, The Fumble. You and me, we're made of the same, stern stuff." He winked at Ink. "We don't take shit from an ass."

Ink blushed. He looked back through the space between the seats and saw those red chicken hands still melted into the wheel at ten and two. What did the guy—this utter fool—in front of him deserve now except his unbridled scorn? Robbie, on the other hand, was the night's true hero. If Danny had been here, he would have dubbed him "one cool dude." And cold. Without question, this Robbie was cool and cold as hell.

Major

(Fall 1990-Spring 1991)

You worked, claw by ragged claw, like a fiend. You hustled your behind to class. You took notes until your hand was numb and followed directions to a T. When you weren't sure what was going on, you gathered courage to see the professor during office hours, notebook in hand. Ink was a sophomore, and he, unlike so many of the lost souls around him, had the drill down. It had been a rough first year (2.2 in the fall, 2.6 in the spring), but now he was on a roll in every course except Earth Science—specifically, the lab component. Something about the hands-on stuff always made him look like a fool. But even with one C (surely he could manage that by semester's end), he'd land himself on the Dean's List and Mom perhaps would end for good the talk of transferring to some place in the Cleveland area, where, according to her odd logic, distractions that were crippling his GPA would magically disappear.

At the beginning of the semester, Ink devised his most comprehensive schedule—broke it down by the hour and taped it on the wall above his desk. Up at seven and in bed by one-thirty, after David Letterman, which he watched religiously with Cobb and Jesse and sometimes even Danny, if he weren't off with some babe or his beer bong crew. Every day of the school week, Ink ate a good breakfast, went to class, took a quiet lunch, hit the books, scurried through dinner, and rewrote his notes for the following day. On Saturdays, he read all morning and then, if the weather was nice, went with Jesse to Riverside Park to toss a Frisbee. If the weather was obscene, he watched afternoon TV with an orange pop and a bag of peanut M&Ms, a book in hand for the commercials. In the evenings he went out (usually alone) to The Bean Bag to read a novel and drink flavored coffee. On Sunday, he attended mass uptown, shelved books at the library for five hours, ate dinner with one or more of the guys, and then studied like a monk in his room for the rest of the night. Every once in a while, he'd think of last year's list of attractive Clerestory girls, but he had no time for such foolish pursuits; he was smart enough now to expend energy only on those things that stood a good chance of yielding a positive return.

Of course, occasional distractions buzzed into his world—this thing in the always-troubled Middle East, for one, which throughout the semester would just not go away. Ink didn't read the papers very often; nevertheless, he was convinced that now that the wall had fallen, everything was going to be just fine. However, one November morning, when Ink's mind was full of poets for a Brit Lit survey exam, Diego came in the door with the *Crux* in his hand.

"Now it really looks like war," his roommate said. He showed him the front page, where it said the United States was going to double its forces in the region. The president was quoted as saying that Iraq's actions were a threat to the entire world.

"Saa-dam," Ink said, adopting the president's pronunciation of the evil leader's name. "Saa-dam's going to cave."

Diego pursed his lips. "400,000 troops—that's a lot to send over for show."

"The United Nations won't let us go to war." Ink said, stealing his opinion from the final paragraph of the article.

There was a knock at the door. It was Cobb, dressed in a powder blue bathrobe and holding out an electric toothbrush. "I say," he said, adopting a posh accent, "could either of you spare a squiggle of paste?"

"War or not?" Ink said.

"Pahhdon?"

Ink pushed the paper against his nose.

"Hmm, I say 'coin flip.' Now which of you uses the blue stuff?"

Ink, his voice wavering, tried out his "theory of the cave," to which Cobb responded, "How many people said that about Hitler?" Ink didn't know what to say; to him, the precedent of Hitler was impossible to dismiss.

"I think there are ways to go about things that lead to war," Diego said. "And ways to go about things that lead to peace."

Ink pinched out a worm of gel, making sure not to touch the mouth of the tube to the ugly, fraying bristles of his friend's brush.

"Good show!" Cobb said. Yawning, having satisfied his immediate need, he shuffled out of the door.

Ink took one last slug of coffee. He understood there was a world out there, eager for his attention, but he just did not have "world enough and time" (Andrew Marvell, he remembered, quite pleased with himself). In ten minutes, his Interpersonal Communications class would begin. Then he'd be off to the library for an hour more of studying for his literature exam. Afterward, he had a lab report to edit and print out in the computer lab. It took every bit of energy to keep his own busy world chugging smoothly down its track.

*

The next thing Ink knew, it was early December, and the great, all-enveloping maw of final exam week closed down upon him. In Earth Science, desperate for sleep, he nodded off a few times. He developed an eye tick from all the flavored coffee he'd been drinking. He came down with a cold, and stole a roll of toilet paper from the bathroom to blow his constantly runny nose.

"Time flies," Mom said when Ink called about coming home.

"I need to be out of the dorm on Thursday, by 5pm."

"That's the middle of the week."

"Actually, it's more towards the end."

"Don't split hairs. Your father can't get off work. Can't you take a bus?"

"Can't you give me the money?"

"John, what's gotten into you?"

Ink had half a mind to say, "What's gotten into you?" because there was indeed something inside his mother, a malignant cancer of the attitude, which had been spreading since Ink had come out of the womb, if not before, but had grown exponentially after he'd won his battle to go away to school. He didn't think much about it until he was home on breaks and she seemed surprised to see him doing something routine, like taking a bath or opening the fridge. In the past year, she had taken serious steps to remove most of the evidence of his life within the house. Last May, at the beginning of summer vacation, she'd said: "I hope you don't mind that I took down those posters." Han Solo, Indiana Jones, *Clash of the Titans*. "They're a little young for you, don't you think?" Upstairs, he'd discovered three sealed boxes of clothes and toys against a wall that she was planning to have Dad take to Goodwill. She had been cleaning out the attic, but she hadn't thought it necessary to consult him about anything.

175

During this past Thanksgiving break, Ink decided he had enough. "Mom!" he cried, pulling a stuffed bear from a shopping bag on the bench by the front door. "That's from Grandma and Grandpa—from Germany!" Years ago, his grandparents had gone on a family heritage tour and brought him a Steiff Bear in a Santa outfit. It had been on his dresser for almost two-thirds of his entire life. "This is a part of me," he said, gazing into its wet marble eyes. Mom crossed her arms. She shrugged, saying somewhat cryptically: "You know, not everyone can be saved."

Now, with more than a hundred miles between them, she said, "John, I am tired. Very tired."

"I've got to go anyway."

"Sure you do. Will forty cover it?"

A door slammed across the hallway. That would be Jesse, back from Chemistry lab. It was 5 pm—time for dinner with the boys.

"What?"

"The bus!"

"Sure Mom. Thank you, and goodbye."

Ink held the phone to his ears for a few moments after the click. He closed his eyes. Silence. Blankness. What was Mom doing on the other side of that click? Thumbing for guidance through Merton's *Seeds of Contemplation*? Fiddling with yet another of her puzzles? Preparing an artery-clogging casserole at the kitchen counter? Could she be thinking of her own mother, to whom Ink was pretty sure she hadn't spoken in years? Could she just be standing by the wall in a daze, damp eyes on the receiver asleep in its cradle?

There was a drum roll on the door, followed by Jesse's affable "Let's go!" Ink grabbed the knob, flipped off the light. He wondered why he thought so much now about his mother, when there were so many better ways to spend his time.

Much to everyone's chagrin, the cafeteria had already begun its end-of-the semester recycling: Wednesday's chicken cutlets had become Thursday's Chicken Cacciatore had become Friday's chicken gumbo. Ink, Jesse, Cobb, and Danny made an about face and headed for The Bell. On the quad, Danny bolted up far ahead of them, packed snowballs, and fired back at others. Ink ducked behind a tree as a chunk of snow whizzed by his face. He scooped up snow, spun, and threw wildly, the back spray freezing his face. Two seconds later, a fastball ripped off his cap, and, clutching his "wound," Ink fell grandiosely to the ground. "This—*this*— is what college is all about!" he thought, perspiring despite the cold. This had been what was missing for most of the semester.

Three more snowballs struck him in quick succession. "Ow," he cried, "I'm dead you know!"

"Doesn't sound like it," Jesse said, raining more snow upon Ink's uncovered face.

He sat up, slapped together a fat white bomb of his own. With snow spraying in his face, he tossed it blindly into the night.

At the campus gate, they encountered a small group of protesters. To Ink, they reeked of loneliness. He pitied them in the same way he pitied many kinds of outcasts he'd encountered in his life: awkward, zit-blasted high school boys who sat against back walls with their boring, brown bag sandwiches; emaciated old people who dined alone in fast food restaurants; dark-eyed foreigners who hadn't bothered to learn the language. The Glassmakers were half way decent this year. Why didn't these people go buy a ticket and watch some quality basketball? Better yet: Since it was Wednesday, why didn't they head over to Hangovers for fifty-cent well drinks?

One of the protesters, a long, thin girl in fatigues, lay twisted on the ground in the snow and leaves and mud. She was supposed to be dead, a casualty of war. Jesse ran by the girl, followed closely by Danny who stopped abruptly, leapt in the air like a shortstop avoiding a slide, and pegged his target squarely in the back. Cobb, never one to exert himself, brought up the rear, hands in pockets, black boots kicking absentmindedly at the snow.

"No blood for oil," a ponytailed boy said, as casual as if he were saying hello.

Ink didn't want to be rude, so he glanced at him and nodded.

"See, see, this one knows exactly what I'm talking about." The ponytail strode toward Ink like he wanted him to join the club. He thought of the days outside St. Ignatius, waiting for the bus on Lorain, the homeless people approaching with sad stories and held out hands. Ink waved the ponytail away and went to cross the street.

"Hey," the boy said, "You forgot . . ."

Ink turned, hand to his head, thinking his ski cap might have fallen to the ground.

The ponytail held out cupped hands. He slowly opened them, as if releasing a delicate bird. "You forgot your conscience."

Christmas lights flashed around the window of the Glasshouse Diner across the street. Danny, Jesse, and Cobb were already heading inside, where students lounged in big, cushioned booths, squirting condiments on burgers, ripping apart mozzarella sticks and sweeping them through bright pools of marinara. Ink kept walking—one foot in front of the other. He filled his mind with what he might want to order.

"I'm not going to hurt you," the ponytail called after him. "Not me! It's your government that's always foaming at the mouth!"

*

Much later—too late considering all the work he had—Ink returned to Freitag Hall, reliving the evening, which had been a total blast. At dinner (Ink had a double mushroom cheeseburger), Danny regaled them with "dick raising" tales of drunken girls at the end-of-the-semester Football House party last weekend. Jesse, who'd recently met a girl—a "gifted songwriter"—explained his new-found love for folk music and took with equanimity the abuse the boys heaped upon him. Cobb talked about wanting to write a memoir. The fact that, as Jesse pointed out, nothing much had happened to him except school in his nineteen-plus years on the planet did little to dampen the boy's ambition. Afterward, they played coin operated pool at CGs until the lights went up. Overall, Ink had a grand time, but now all he wanted to do was put heavy head to pillow.

When he opened the door, however, he found Diego glued to a late night news show. His first impulse was to ask him to turn the TV off, but his roommate hardly ever used the room. He sighed (he couldn't help it), grabbed a pop from the fridge, and sat down to watch frosty-haired pundits speculate about what was going to happen with Iraq. Would this crazy dictator bend under the pressure of international outrage? Would the embargo take its toll or would the United States have to lead the coalition into war? If the latter, how might such a conflict affect the stability in the region? One commentator insisted the sanctions were working. Another claimed Bush was "itching to pull the trigger." A third concurred with the second, saying, "You call someone a Hitler, and diplomacy is pretty much no longer an option."

The pundits babbled on:

"Kuwait is no Poland."

"How much of history do we have to repeat before we learn our lesson?"

"Just imagine this lunatic with nuclear weapons!"

At the commercial break, Ink said, "Haven't you had enough?"

"There's so much to sort out."

"Yes, but what can we do about it?"

"Ah, so now you think there will be war?"

"I don't know. Sure." Ink tilted his head at the stack of books on his desk. "I've got more important things to worry about."

"I'm doing this paper on Hobbes for my Moral Philosophy course."

Ink shrugged to show his cluelessness.

"An English philosopher. Seventeenth-century."

Ink nodded. This didn't help orient him much.

"Well, Hobbes said we're all motivated by self-interest. He would give money to the poor not because it was good to do so, but because it would make him feel better about himself."

"Fear of failure," Ink said, flipping open his Earth Science notes. "That's my motivation right about now."

Diego smiled. He nodded his head, and the movement made Ink think of a mouth savoring the meal of his life. His roommate was like that with all the big ideas.

During the commercial break, Ink reminded himself of the layers to the earth—crust, mantle, core. The earth's core, 4000 miles from the surface, was 9000 degrees. Four and a half billion years ago, when the planet was formed, all the heavy stuff sank to the middle. Several months ago, there'd been this humorous story in the news about workers in Siberia who in an attempt to drill to the center of the earth ended up discovering hell. Maybe, Ink thought, that's why people— and, by extension, why nations—could never become close. The deeper you dug towards another, the more trouble there was. But sticking to the surface—to what extent was that a better option?

The pundits returned, and Ink, roused by the possibility that he might get to know his roommate a bit better, closed his book to watch. He'd been surprised when Diego agreed to room with him again, especially because freshman year had been nothing special. The first month, the two said little more than hello to each other. If awake, Diego was usually in the library. On those rare occasions when he was present, he was in his own world, hunched over a book at his desk, the tinny sound of Mozart from ear muff-sized head phones. When Danny would burst in to say or do something rude, his roommate seemed less bothered than intrigued—as if Danny were less a human being than an object for scientific study. After a while, Ink began to wonder about Diego's silence—his unfailing cordiality in the face of all that happened in their room. Was he really that nice, or was he silently damning them all? Did he think he was better than everyone else?

During the recessional at St. Thomas one Sunday morning, as Ink scanned the departing congregants for pretty girls, he felt a tap on his shoulder.

"Peace be with you," Diego said.

"Hey," Ink laughed—surprised, embarrassed. "And also with you." The handshake was awkward—a flaccid pump of fingers—but it was, Ink concluded, an important moment for them.

"I had no idea you were Catholic."

"I try." It turned out that Diego had gone to a Jesuit high school near Akron.

Finally, with something in common, the two boys went to The Bean Bag for breakfast, where Ink apologized for Danny and Cobb and all the things he'd done or failed to do.

"And I ask Blessed Mary, ever virgin," Diego said.

Ink laughed, relieved his roommate caught the allusion to the Confiteor. In the silence that followed, they sipped coffee, chewed their bagels. Diego glanced at the partly cloudy world outside. Nervous, desperate to hold this smart boy's interest, Ink went on about life as a Catholic: those ghoulish, ear-pulling nuns of first and second grade; the interminable homilies; the unspeakable horrors of an all-boys Jesuit high school; the guilt, of course, always the guilt— about every single thing on earth. Diego nodded and smiled, sprinkling in an anecdote or two of his own along the way. Ink had expected a different "seasoning" to these stories, something that would reflect what Ink guessed was his Mexican background, but Diego's experience seemed pretty similar to his own.

"Don't you think the mass is a little bit . . . slow?" Ink asked.

"If you believe," Diego said, wiping his mouth. "Truly believe, I'm sure there's nothing more exciting."

"So you don't believe?"

"I don't know. There are so many other competing ideas. I need to read more, think, try to figure out things on my own."

"What do your parents think about that?"

"My parents . . . we don't see eye to eye on a lot of things."

Perhaps, Ink thought, this explained why Diego seemed mysteriously free of the trappings of ethnicity. He was tempted to press the boy—he couldn't imagine how it might hurt—but something told him to keep such questions to himself.

By the end of that breakfast, Ink felt that they'd at least become acquaintances. Afterwards, whenever he saw Diego at mass (which was not often), he sat with him, tried to see the world through his curious and capacious eyes. Occasionally, they even went to dinner together, although Diego would politely excuse himself if Danny or Cobb dropped down their trays.

The pundits went on with their elaborate blah blah blah. As Ink was rising to go brush his teeth, Danny burst through the door, dressed in blood red boxers, cereal sloshing in a bowl.

"Gentlemen," he declared.

"Danny," Diego said. "Do you think there's going to be a war?"

"A what now?" he asked, dropping into Diego's desk chair and tossing a spoonful of soggy mash into his mouth.

Diego's smile was toothless, cryptic. "Does Hussein need to be removed? I find it ironic that only a few years ago he was our ally—"

"What do you mean?" Ink said.

"During the war with Iran."

Ink had a dim recollection of the hostage crisis. In high school, there'd been that boy, the gay one—Timothy . . . Bashour—who'd tried to straighten out Ink about who was on whose side with the Iran Contra Affair. If a test about this stuff had dropped in front of him right now, though, he'd never stand a chance.

"Saa-dam, right?" Danny asked, scratching his behind. "That's the one we're talking about?"

Ink nodded, happy to know they agreed about how to pronounce the enemy.

"He never had a weapon he didn't use."

"What about the U.S.?" Diego wondered.

"We know how to do things. The world can trust us."

"What about the atomic bombs?"

Danny, his mouth full of cereal, said, "Both my grandfathers served. One lost his leg."

Ink stood by his desk, knees weak with fear. Beyond blinking, Diego didn't move an inch.

"We used those bombs to save the goddamn world."

"Two days," Diego said. "More than two hundred thousand dead."

"Some things have to be done."

"Innocent people."

"Patriots, martyrs . . . How many brave young men gave their lives so you could grow up free and go to school and study *Spanish*?"

"What, by the way, is your major, Danny? I never asked."

"General Studies."

"I would have guessed Corporeal Studies."

Danny's lips became a tilde. "That's a joke. I don't get it, but that's a fucking joke."

Diego turned back to the screen while Danny glowered. Ink imagined the boy during his high school football days, huffing and puffing over a receiver he'd speared for daring to catch a pass over the middle. After many tense minutes, the boy stood up, wiping his mouth with the back of a hand.

"In other news, that's some sweet sister you've got," Danny said, before leaving the room with a bang.

*

Break. Home. Such as it was. Dad had picked him up at the Greyhound station, shaking his hand, beaming, calling him as he always did by "Increase," his obnoxious given name. He asked how finals went, upper teeth sliding across lower as he thought of what to ask next. As usual, he was eager to please. He wanted to give Dad something beyond the perfunctory, but he was tired, and his breath stank of coffee. In the car, the light rock station purring, Ink

182

remembered the previous Christmas, when he couldn't wait to get home—to sink back into that familiar bed, to read on the floor underneath the gleaming tree, to hit the bulging malls with Ant for last-minute shopping, to eat slice after slice of salty spiral ham and grandma's delicious panoply of pastries. Now, he was full of dread, an escapee on his way back to prison.

The heavy bars dropped around him later on that night, during the post-supper malaise, Mom on the couch with her Merton and Dad in his chair with a thick tome of solar system facts. Upstairs at his desk, Ink tried to catch up on a journal he'd kept in spurts since September. He wrote about those protesters, their absurd persistence, their unshakeable belief in the rightness of the cause. He wrote about the delicious meal at the Glasshouse Diner. He recorded Danny's epic tales of the Clerestory party scene—the complicated drinking games, the bathroom propositions to which he gentlemanly assented.

Trouble, as if on some kind of cue recognized only by him, began to yap at the fence next door.

"Shut up," Ink said half-heartedly through the closed window.

How old was that damn dog now? How, after all these years, could it keep up such a racket? Was it as stupid as it seemed or was there some reason why it behaved the way it did? What if the dog wasn't just yapping but trying to call Ink's attention to something—to warn him, away, for example, from the death-like inertia that ruled this house? He opened the window a crack to get a better listen. Maybe, he thought after half a minute, he was reading too much into things.

But then the TV went on downstairs, and he almost screamed "Nooooo!" Instead, he took a breath and called Ant to come and rescue him. Ant had to help his dad finish putting in a new kitchen counter for his mom's early Christmas present, but they agreed to do something the following evening, which was better, because Friday was, well, Friday!

They went "malling," but Ant, to show he was not stuck in the past, added a wrinkle to this favorite high school pastime. "Beachwood Place," he said, fist emphatic against palm. "That's where all the rich girls go." It was just long enough of a drive across town so that when they arrived, each was filled with expectations that could never be met. For the first few minutes, the experience was thrilling. Then Ink began to feel creepy, walking from one end of the place to the other, soft pretzel in hand, his high school friend nudging him every two seconds to sneak a peek at a pair of legs or (their lucky day!) a blatant instance of unapologetic bralessness. How old were some of these girls? Sixteen? Fifteen? In the grand scheme of things, a difference of three years was no big deal, but Ink felt so much older now. And wiser. Like it or not, adolescence was fast becoming a part of his irrevocable past.

"Every girl in here," Ant said. "Later on, they'll be in their underwear or naked, maybe taking a shower." He raised his head as if he were himself in the shower, anticipating spray from the nozzle. "Doesn't that just kill you?"

Ink was going to say that it had long since become exhausting—and depressing—to think about naked girls all the time, but at that moment Ant grabbed his arm and nodded at a pretty one standing alone in the food court. Sleek, blond-streaked hair, pouty lips, leather mini skirt, a Saks bag at her side—she was in every way that mattered way out of their league. But Ant had a fail-proof, three-step plan:

1) Approach the pretty girl in question.

2) Politely ask her the time.

3) Coolly allow things to develop from there.

Ink laughed. Home was no great prize, but if this was the way things were going to be with friends, then it was time to get back to the house, where at least he had his room—a place where he could, without interruption, imagine mid-January, when he'd return to where he belonged.

*

Christmas dinner, to Ink's weary-wise mind, was less of a holiday than another dull rerun: Grandma, sweaty and solicitous, bringing steaming plates of food from kitchen to table; Grandpa, bookending his pipe-fragrant platitudes with beneficent smiles; Dad, offering tedious summaries of yet another space book he'd been devouring; Mom, sentimental from the lights and a half glass of wine, providing pious reflections on the Advent season; Aunt Ruth, showing off her latest boyfriend, this one a mousy public defender; and the dinner itself—the clove-riddled ham, the gooey scalloped potatoes, the flaccid green beans, the apple kuchen—almost painstakingly unremarkable. The only difference this year was that Uncle Lare wasn't around to unnerve everyone with his drunkenness, his contentious politics. Curiously, his absence drew no more notice than a student who dropped a class before he failed. A few days later, Ink overheard Mom make passing reference to his uncle on the phone. "As long as he stays there," is all she said. Ink had no desire to probe. For one, this was a matter for the adults. For another, he was only in town for another two weeks. This, thank God, was no longer his world.

*

The afternoon Ink returned to campus, The Bean Bag was buzzing with talk about the war. The TV was on, sound cranked, and the news anchor was ebullient with the prospect of things at last coming to a head. But there wasn't going to be a war, Ink said to himself again. In fact, wars in general were over and done with. They'd been thoroughly domesticated by history books and PBS documentaries. They'd become nothing more than moving oral stories from shriveled up septuagenarians. It was absurd to think there was going to be war.

And then—surprise!—there was. Bush's deadline for Saa-dam's withdrawal passed, and the bombing began. Those first couple of days, Ink, Jesse, and Cobb squeezed into the crowded coffee shop between classes and watched CNN, transfixed by clips of SCUD missiles sizzling brightly through the air. How fascinating to Ink that, like his grandpa and father before him, he was living in a time of war. To him—to his friends as well—this was a thrilling event, not unlike an epic miniseries on TV.

That night at dinner, Jesse had talked in vague terms about some new songs he'd learned— "different stuff for me," he said, "more emotional, more sensitive, which I think is a good thing." He was drumming up interest for his performance next week at Open Mike's.

Cobb laughed. "All for this granola girl who's captured his fancy."

"Be quiet."

Ink studied his newly transformed friend—the expertly tousled hair, the brand new, sculpted sideburns, which resembled two Velcro Idahos.

"Judy Collins?" Cobb said, wiping his glasses. "Buffy St. Marie?"

"Not my cup of tea, okay? But she's got these amazing originals."

"I bet she has!"

185

"Anyway," Jesse said, ignoring Cobb, "my secret plan is to convert her to the blues."

"You just want to convert her into your bed."

"Danny says that stuff, I let it slide. You just sound like an idiot."

Cobb shrugged and stuffed a fork of fried potatoes in his face.

Having barred the feminine element from his life for the past several months, Ink was not especially jealous about the girl. He was hurt, though, that Jesse had seen fit to tell all this news to Cobb first. It suggested a hierarchy the opposite of what he'd assumed. Jesse tried to change the subject, talking about his on-again-off again blues band and the masters whose work they covered—Buddy Guy and Stevie Ray (God rest his soul!), as well as the oldsters: Robert Johnson, Leadbelly, Blind Lemon Jefferson. Ink nodded. He knew Stevie—that "Stranded" tune was still all over the radio—and Jesse said "of course" before going on. Ink hung on to the monologue by a thread until it snapped and he felt himself falling away from his friend, further and further into the darkness of his circumscribed world. The more Jesse insinuated himself into the campus music scene, the less time his friend was going to have for him. It was high school all over again, when Sandro, his best friend from the beginning, discovered soccer and band and the stage and all the infinitely more dynamic boys and girls who inhabited those worlds.

A sudden commotion at the other end of the cafeteria caused them all to turn. Rhythmic noise, a chant of some kind. Three boys climbed onto chairs. It took a few moments for Ink to understand: "USA, USA, USA!" they shouted, fists in the air. Soon others joined in, some standing, many pounding the tables. The sound thundered around them. Boys at the table next to theirs banged their plastic trays, and cola lapped like black blood onto tables. Several girls even joined in: "USA, USA, USA!"

"Good God," Jesse said, hunching his shoulders.

Ink was wet with fear. What if these chanters began to scan the room and point out those who refused to join in? What if this pure, animal hate turned physical? Ink found himself mouthing the letters at the same time he eeked back his chair, looking around for an emergency exit. Cobb nervously massaged a breast, an action that, in other circumstances, would have made Ink burst out laughing.

And then, as suddenly as it began, the chant petered out. Students stepped down from their chairs. There were a few bursts of laughter and a stray shout here and there, but everyone returned to their meals and the large, long room became a simple, pleasant cafeteria once again.

*

Cruise missiles, scuds, surgical strikes, collateral damage—in those first days, Cobb and Danny bulled their way into Ink's room, the words of war rolling off their tongues as if they were high ranking military officials, in the thick of it, sweating the details, weighing the cost of human lives against the cause, which, lest it be forgotten, was "the liberation of Kuwait." It was like they—neither of them strong students—had discovered a whole new course of study.

"I'm kind of busy here," Ink would say, but the two would sit there, hanging over one piece of furniture or another, eyes and ears devouring the latest from CNN. Ink was annoyed, yet he admired their felicity with this new language, wondered how they could have acquired it when Ink had already grown tired of the coverage: the endless opinions, the daring rooftop reports, the complicated maps. After those awesome first few days, this drama had turned out to be just more of the same.

That Friday, Jesse's folk-singer girlfriend busy at work, Ink escaped with his friend to the mall. "I'm fed up with this war," he said, sliding into some brand new tennis shoes. Jesse sat on a stool with chin in palms.

"You hear Bush is thinking about reinstating the draft?" he said.

"Get out of here!"

Jesse pursed his lips. "It's what I heard."

Ink stood in the new, stiff shoes. He tried to wiggle his toes. Nothing doing.

"Well, you going to get them?"

Ink bounced a few times before the mirror. His old pair had a gash in the sole, and when it rained his sock got soaked. But they were so roomy, so comfortable. Over the past three years, they had become an indelible part of who he was. "I don't think so," he said.

In bed that night, Ink could not get the draft out of his mind. A few summers ago, Dad had taken him to the post office to fill out his selective service card. It had been a beautiful day—a slight breeze, not a cloud in the sky. Afterward, in his embarrassing way, Dad said, "It was—it seems like—only yesterday," and Ink blinked at him, wondering what he was going to keep from pouring out of his mouth. They stopped for fast food, and Ink, not really hungry, ordered a cheeseburger and a strawberry shake. Sitting in the booth, Dad tapping the plastic top of his decaf, Ink felt like he was eight years old. Now, he remembered that card, each letter of his name in boxes like so many coffins. He flipped back and forth back on his bed.

"You okay?" Diego called from below.

"Fine. Sorry."

Ink saw his trembling hands unfolding letter that told him he was going to have to serve his country. He saw himself at basic training, on the front lines, hard sand eating away at his face, leaning against a military vehicle, sharing jerky with a fellow soldier when, out of nowhere—a hail of gunfire, a pants-wetting panic, troops dashing here and there, every man for himself. He saw himself hit twice in the leg, dragging his bleeding, sun-blasted body over endless dunes to escape menacing brown men, turbans like white tornadoes upon their heads. They would overtake him, and he would have to die—slowly and horribly—when all he'd done to deserve this fate was to grow up and do, to the best of his ability, what the adults in his world had told him to do. Sure, he'd voted for George Bush, but that was because the other man, the Willie Horton one, was soft and squeaky-sounding and came from the east coast where, as Mom explained, everyone thought they knew it all. It had been his first election. What in the world did he know?

Early the next morning, unable to shake his sense of alarm, Ink called home, told Dad he wasn't ready to die. Dad, as if he misunderstood the purpose of the call, informed him that the Iraqi army was ranked fourth most powerful in the world. "America is number one, of course, but you must respect your opponent."

"This is not what I want to hear."

"I really don't think . . . Let's put it this way: If I were a betting man, I'd put ten dollars on there not being a draft."

"Ten dollars?"

Dad laughed. "Okay, twenty. But don't tell your mother."

Ink glanced at the window, where a sparrow scratched at the sill. In high school, in European history, they'd watched a film about World War I. At the end, the main character—a soldier, an artist with sketch pad in hand—raised his head from the trench in order to get a better look at a song bird. It was a clear morning, a sweet morning, but the enemy bullet didn't give a shit. It flew, it screamed, it shot the young man dead.

"Son, the war will be over before you come home for Easter."

"One of my friends says it's going to be another Vietnam."

"I remember Vietnam. It was an awful time."

Other men Dad's age—Mr. Gismondi, Uncle Lare—had served in that war; Dad, however, had not. He'd mentioned the reason a few years back, when Ink was at the dining room table preparing a speech about Kent State. "I failed the physical," Dad said. "Me and Jimmy Buffet." He laughed loudly, awkwardly, like this failure was the funniest thing in the world. As Dad went on with his predictions about the current war, Ink winced. It was as if the conversation were being broadcast to the world.

Later, alone before a Dickens novel he had to get through by morning, Ink saw Jesse's rumor again open up its horrible mouth, devouring all of Dad's reassurances. He had to leave the room. He had to leave the dorm. Outside, the cold air filled his lungs. Ink breathed more deeply, trying to take in as much life as his body could bear. A gust of wind made his eyes water, his ears tingle. But all this was good. Everything in the world was precious and fine and now, just as he was coming so splendidly into his own, he was in danger of losing it all.

He kept walking across the green, past the lonely stadium, up to the corner of Old Route 7, where St. Thomas's stood, as if waiting to receive him. He walked in, dipped his hand in the holy water, and made the sign of the cross. A nun in street clothes puttered around the altar, but otherwise he was alone. He slid into a pew near the back. Kneeling down, hands pressed together, he was ready to pray, but he wanted to make this one extra special. He looked up. A weak light trickled down from the bank of small stained-glass windows on either side of the church. Clerestory—Ink remembered the term from art history class his freshman year. In the 1830s, this town had grown up around a soon-to-be-renowned glass works. Then the university people arrived, a group of energetic revivalists from the northeast, and in naming the school used the town's booming industry as a potent spiritual metaphor.

Ink gazed up at those distant windows. To the founders, the light was God's comforting hand reaching down to invigorate His people. To the secularists who would follow, the light meant intellectual insight, the flash of inspiration. Ink prayed. He pled for forgiveness for his sordid thoughts about girls. He apologized for being bored and distracted at mass and vowed to get more involved—serve a holiday dinner, make crafts with the elderly, become a Eucharistic minister. This war was without doubt his wake up call, and he was ready to be a Christian through and through. He looked to the windows for some response to his vow. Any second now, he felt, there'd be a providential shifting of clouds, the pouring down of sun through red and green and blue.

*

March. March Madness. The Glassmakers, followed by the Clerestory student body in fine desultory fashion, finished third in their conference, a passable 9-7. But then, miraculously, the team got on a roll and won their conference tournament to earn an automatic bid to the NCAAs, the first time in twenty-four years. The students, the town, and all of central Ohio went mad with joy.

Ink had always been the occasional sports fan. He cheered when there seemed to be a reason, but he had little patience for the subtleties of most games. He'd watched the Browns with Ant and his raging parents as the team suffered heartbreaking losses in back-to-back years against Elway's Denver Broncos. He witnessed the heroics of Michael Jordan, who sunk the championship hopes of the Cavaliers more than once. But this was different. This was his team, his school bursting onto the national stage. Serious Jackson, the star forward with the ludicrous name, was even a student in his sociology course.

The night of the tournament selection show, Ink huddled with his floor mates around the lounge TV to watch an ESPN story about The Little Mid Major That Could. The Glassmakers were a "textbook team," the reporter explained, that had all the essential ingredients: slithery Dwane Wallace at the point; quick Skip Ambercrombie at the two; Ben Sestak (known affectionately as "The Sleestak" or "Farmboy Zombie") at center; Nate Russell, the rebounding machine; and Jackson, of course, the team captain, the smooth moving jump shooter with unlimited range. It was, the reporter declared, "a team that might just surprise a few people at the big dance." That said, the Glassmakers' first test would be a stern one: the Indiana Hoosiers, a number two seed, from the powerful Big Ten. Calbert Cheaney,

Damon Bailey—these were the kinds of names that appeared on *Sportscenter* every other night. These were the talented young men who played for the monomaniacal Bobby Knight, winner of not one or two but *three* national championships.

The next morning, Ink tuned in to the local sports talk show to hear more about the matchup. Big Red vs. Little Red. "David vs. Goliath," Hank Zamora, the voice of the Glassmakers, declared. "And we all know how that one turned out."

Diego smiled as he buttoned up his shirt.

"You're not excited?" Ink said, a bit peeved by his roommate's smile, which sometimes struck him as condescending.

"It's . . . interesting. I'll say that much."

"It's *historic*."

The college bookstore sold t-shirts—"Lights Out, Knight!"— and they were gone in less than twenty-four hours. Homemade banners rolled out of fraternity house windows. Gregory the Glassmaker, the team's bespectacled mascot, ambled around campus distributing prizes to those who could answer trivia questions about the school. As the week went on, professors set aside lesson plans to discuss keys to victory. Students snatched up seats on busses chartered for the game in Atlanta. For the rest, large screen TVs were going to be set up in each of the cafeterias, with free soft drinks and nachos for all.

Danny, whom nobody had seen in weeks, appeared at Ink's door Thursday afternoon, and insisted they all watch the game somewhere up on The Bell, since that was where all the action would be.

"What happened to you?" Ink asked, stunned by the condition of the boy's face—a black eye gone purple, a brownish gash above the brow.

Danny yawned, and Ink's nose shrunk from the smell of sweat and powerfully bad breath. "Pulled an all-nighter," the boy said with a laugh that seemed lighthearted enough for Ink to set aside his concern. Danny wouldn't be Danny, he thought, if he wasn't throwing them all a curve.

That evening, Danny was transformed—freshly showered, eyes feverishly alive, looking and smelling like his old self. He led the gang across the quad, dropping racy anecdotes behind him like breadcrumbs on the lawn. When they reached the campus gate, he ordered everyone to stop and admire the founder's statue, which had been draped now in Venetian red. "Oh great founder," Danny said, bowing his head, squeezing his hands together. "You who laid the cornerstone in 1836 and I who laid Mary McConnell 1991—"

"Seriously?" Cobb said, completely impressed. "McConnell?"

Danny held up a hand. "We who are part of the long, grand tradition of fucking around meet together on this auspicious occasion as complete equals, except for the fact that you're dead and nobody gives a damn. Yet in your death—your plain and perfect deadedness—it is you who has the true connection with the almighty Goodhead."

"Godhead," Ink said, unable to check a laugh. He longed to be so brash and assured; he wished he could compel an audience. To be honest, though, this bit—this routine—also unsettled him. Six weeks ago, in the beginning of that unexpectedly brief war with Iraq, Ink had turned in a panic back to God. Now, guilty about how quickly his faith had flagged again, he wanted to take some vocal offense. He glanced at Cobb and Jesse, but they just stood there, hands in pockets, grinning indulgently. If only Xavier, the pious one, the chaste cross wearer, had come along, he would have definitely made his feelings known.

"You, great dead one," Danny went on, "we ask you to ask the Him of Hims what we mere mortals must do to help our team win."

Danny fell silent. The wind gusted, and the red cloak flapped around the stone neck of the giant, green-nosed founder.

"Wait," Danny said, flinging his arms, clobbering Cobb in the side of the head. "I'm getting something . . . a message . . . a command." And what he was getting had to do with the huge stone ring that stood across the brick walkway. This ring had once held a rose window, a relic of the original chapel the town founder had built. Long ago, however, the glass had been a victim of drunken vandals; after it was repaired, it was moved to the safety of the campus art museum. Now, as Danny explained, the stone hole that remained was nothing less than a doorway to an alternative universe in which, against all odds, the Glassmakers would be victorious.

"Everybody, jump through," Danny said. "Founder says."

"I'm going to draw the line," Cobb said. He had his glasses off, checking to see if Danny had bent them.

"Would it help if we greased the sides?" Jesse said.

"Not funny."

"Just do it!" Ink said, wanting the whole bit to be over already.

And when they did—each of them, Cobb making it through with plenty of room to spare—Danny announced that all of the magic was on their side. "Those Hoosier fucks don't stand a chance!"

It was thirty minutes until tip off, and Ink just wanted to get a table somewhere with a good view for the game. But Danny had yet another idea. He led them past all the bars and eateries on The Bell to a nondescript door that stood beside a nail salon. In a few moments, the door buzzed, and they climbed up warped, beer-stinky stairs to another door that was thrown open as they approached. Muddled music greeted them: The Allman Brothers? The Dead?—whatever was playing, it was the soundtrack for drugs.

Some sleepy-eyed guy—"Wetzler," Danny said, hand on the boy's cheek—let them in before weaving back to the couch. On the coffee table were a pipe and paper and a bag of something one might sprinkle over pizza. Ink had a pretty good idea what it was.

"During the day," Wetzler said, "the fumes from the salon drift up here." He rolled some of the pizza topping in the paper and licked the cigarette closed. "Hardly need this shit."

"Listen," Danny said, rubbing his hands together. "We just have time for a bit o' the High Life."

"Sure, man," said Wetzler, swinging an arm lazily toward the kitchen. "Word to the wise: last I checked, D-Con was in there with one of his roly polies."

The only evidence of recent human occupation in the kitchen was a half-drunk wine cooler and a black skirt hanging like a dead flower over a box of Froot Loops. Cobb picked up the garment with thumb and forefinger and danced it over his head. "Welcome ladies and gentlemen to the Barnum and Bailey—"

"Cobb, you could stand to lose a roll or two," Ink said. Over time, he'd learned he could (anyone could) attack Cobb with impunity. The boy was completely immune to insult.

Danny opened the refrigerator and passed out bottles. Ink said "no" and made sure to say it loudly, in case the place was bugged. He was, after all, almost a year away from being legal. If the cops barged in for a bust, they'd have no choice: they'd have to let him go.

"Nice set up you've got," Cobb said, raising his beer to Danny.

"The fraternity of washed up high school ballers—we're a tight little group," Danny explained.

"You played basketball?" Jesse asked.

"Football. In fact, I was once a prized recruit of this very noble institution. Now I'm just another crippled dude who can drink his weight in gold."

Danny poured three-quarters of a beer down his throat. Cobb swished a swig like it was mouthwash. Jesse took a nip, and made a face like a rat with stylish sideburns. Ink was proud to realize he was better than them all.

*

Hangovers, everyone's first choice to watch the game, was packed because they had pre-game specials, a new basketball cage, and a halftime bikini contest. Disappointed, the boys shambled across the street to Giottos and scored the only table left in the place.

"John Alt!" the waitress said. Ink looked up from his menu to see Nina Sissyan, brown eyes beaming, strands of hair wandering out of a silky bun. It had been weeks since he'd seen her, and only then at a distance—across the quad, from his chair in the cafeteria as she entered with a gaggle of sorority girls. "Hey Danny," she added in a less ebullient tone.

"When did you start working here?" Ink asked. The question came out petulantly, a kind of accusation, which it probably was, since the subtext of it was: "How in the world do you know Danny Drellishak?"

She shrugged, and Ink thought of a shield raised to deflect an arrow. "Have to pay the bills."

"Listen, Nina, I lost my appointment book." Danny patted his pockets to prove it. "Can you tell me again when we're supposed to get it on?"

She pressed her lips together. She scribbled on her ticket book and slapped his hand with the slip.

"Ha," he said. "Hell *will* freeze—to make up for all the global warming. And then you're going to be so screwed."

Ink looked down at the menu again, offended, embarrassed, angry and, most of all, ashamed for not saying something to express his disapproval. When Jesse finished giving the order, Ink looked up to see Nina looking almost plain, her trademark smile nowhere to be

194

seen.

"Anything else?" she said, thwaping pad with pen.

Danny put his hands behind his head. "Nah, we're all good."

As she turned to leave, Nina swept her eyes over Ink. It might have meant nothing, but Ink burned from the heat of judgment for the company he kept.

The pizza arrived in time for the twelve-minute time out, the Glassmakers down by five. Ink, having pushed Nina to the back of his mind, scooped up a piece of Greedy Meaty pie and craned his neck at the screen just in time to see Sestak tip in a Jackson miss. Then, just a few seconds later, Wallace stole a pass and went in for a reverse jam. Danny, Cobb, and Jesse shot out of their seats. Coach Knight, lumpy in his red sweater, barked from the sidelines, threw his fists in the air. Ink had a hunch that things might never be so good again.

At halftime, the Glassmakers—unbelievably—were up by three, but it felt—after the incredible run—like a whole lot more. The boys joked and blabbed and kept an eye and ear on the heart-warming story about Serious Jackson: bleak, mid-winter shots of Youngstown projects, a single mother wiping away tears, a father in prison for second degree murder, a cousin shot down for snitching. Born Darius Anthony, the Clerestory star was renamed "Serious" by friends who were impressed by his dedication to both basketball and school. He was, the reporter said, "the epitome of the student-athlete." The piece ended with soft piano, with Jackson surrounded by grade school kids he read to once a week.

"Hard to find a better young man than that," the studio host declared, shuffling papers on the desk.

"Christ that was beautiful," Cobb said, taking off his glasses to wipe his eyes.

Jesse said. "You're fat as hell, but you'll never be half the person he is."

They turned to Danny, waiting for his sage comment, but he just nodded, eyes distant, as if he were re-seeing something special he had done in the days when he was capable of doing.

At the commercial break, Danny disappeared, and Ink spied him a few minutes later at a table of pretty girls and square-headed boys by the window overlooking Bell Street. He was holding forth about something, and they were either laughing or preparing their mouths for the next punch line. A fleet of amber shot glasses descended upon the table, and Danny, who was not even legal, splashed two back, a move that (as with all his other moves) gave his audience great joy. He placed hands on the shoulders of two different girls, each of whom gazed up at him with cheese-melty eyes.

Not for the first time, Ink wondered why someone like Danny continued to hang out with them. The boy had many friends at Clerestory—in fact, he seemed to know every other student who strolled across the campus green. Guys would stop to share a funny story or a complicated handshake. Girls would charge up to him right out of the blue and throw long gorgeous arms around his neck. He'd put his palms out, as if to say "What can you do?" Even the wary ones (like Nina, Ink frowned to himself) betrayed some sign of interest: a slight blush, a twitch of the lips, a glance back after passing. Danny was popular. Danny was king. Why didn't he tell plebeians like himself to get the hell lost?

"Foul! Foul!" Jesse cried, shaking Ink's arm as if he were to blame. "Russell got raped in there!"

Ink looked up at the screen. Bailey went to the line for Indiana, trimming the Glassmakers' lead to two and then one.

Time ticked down, and the game went back and forth. Joyful fans throttled each other after a Clerestory basket or steal. Livid boos and hisses filled the place when the calls went IU's way. With eight minutes left in the game, the Glassmakers were up by five. Coach Knight yanked his point guard and berated him while the boy sat stone faced on a chair with a towel around his neck. Each time the camera panned back to the scene at the bench, the restaurant exploded with cheers. At the next time out, the guard went back in, and Clerestory's lead began to evaporate. A turnover here, an ill-advised three there. Cheaney slid by Serious on two straight trips. On the second, the Glassmakers' star player came up holding an ankle.

"Don't be a pussy!" someone roared. Ink turned to see one of the wide, square-headed boys at the table Danny had visited, his face smashed with anger. The girl to his left laughed, looked around, and dutifully sopped up spilled beer with a wad of napkins.

"Time to take it to another level," Jesse said at the next time out. Ink nodded, appreciating the profundity.

"Warrior time," Danny said. "That's what my high school coach used to say. And he'd make us smack our lips with a hand and go "woo, woo, woo, woo."

Ink smiled. "How'd you do that with a football helmet on?"

"You know, I thought about that. I was one of those intellectual athletes. But, the thing is, Coach tells you to do something, you find a way to do it."

"You have to be stupid to play sports," Cobb said. "I mean, no offense, but . . ."

"It's a chance to test yourself," Jesse said. "See what you're made of."

"I already know what I'm made of," Cobb said, squeezing the flab of his stomach.

"Think about it," Danny said. "Imagine a tie game, the outcome in the balance and there are a hundred, two hundred thousand people who really really care. Family, students, alums, the coach, the AD, the president of the university . . . bookies . . . townies with nothing else to do with their lives. You're lucky enough to be out there, on this incredible stage, ten seconds left in the game. You juke, you cut, you lose your guy. You go to the hole, you jump, you let the ball roll off your fingertips. It rises, spins there in space. It comes down. Nothing but net!"

Cobb stifled a yawn.

"Who the hell *doesn't* want to be the big fucker on campus?"

Cobb blinked. With a middle finger, he scratched himself between the breasts.

"You could just as easily miss," Ink said, thinking of his own on-the-court horrors.

"Yeah, yeah, rim and out. Airball. If you think it, it will happen."

The Glassmakers and Hoosiers went down to the wire. Back and forth, back and forth. As the clock wound down, the rims seemed to shrink. Serious took a three pointer—CLANG! Crombie attempted a runner in the lane and the ball went in and out. With twelve seconds to go, Clerestory was down by two with the ball at midcourt. Serious set a baseline pick to free Wallace in the corner. He caught the pass but hesitated, startled by how open he was.

From the table by the window, a familiar voice screamed: "Shoot the goddamn ball!"

With a Hoosier closing, Wallace let the ball go. It spun off his fingertips, over the outstretched hand of the defender—up and up in the air and down, thunking off the back of the rim. Bodies shoved and banged and leapt. Somehow, Sestak came up with the ball. Three seconds left. He pivoted for a shot but was stripped. His arms kept going, moving wildly toward the rim. He collapsed in the lane. No call. The Hoosiers, hands to the heavens, stormed the court to celebrate.

Ink and his friends slumped at the table, staring at the remnants of pizza—a few brittle crusts, some burnt crumbles of ground chuck, a snot smear of cheese across the dull metal tray.

They cursed and complained until the postgame interviews, which began with Jackson, still dripping with sweat, bending down towards the reporter's mic, speaking calmly, as if the loss had been suffered by some other team half way across the world. He thanked God, "from whom all blessings flow." He thanked the Clerestory fans. He praised his team, who gave it all they had, and he congratulated the Hoosiers, against whom it had been an honor to test themselves. As usual, Serious said all the right things and in the most elegant way. When the interview was over, the school's star player held up two fingers and gently said "Peace" to the camera.

"Peace? PEACE?" The square-headed boy from the window table was out of his chair. He jabbed violently at the screen. "You are a Serious piece of shit!" he cried. This time, the manager quickly appeared and gestured at the door. Another boy, his facial geometry more subtle, stood to calm down his friend.

Outside, dejected students who'd spent too many hours in bars stumbled this way and that. Occasionally, someone let loose with a grief-stricken howl. When a TV tumbled from a third story apartment window and exploded on the asphalt below, Ink imagined all kinds of terrible things: smashed windows, looting, bullets, and bright blood. He wanted to get to the safety of his dorm—as quickly as possible.

Jesse could not keep from going on about that painful last play. "That was a foul. Clear as day. But you know—we all know—IU's going to get the benefit of the doubt every single time."

Danny, hands in his pocket, seemed surprisingly reflective. "I thought they might have sprung Serious for a shot."

"I don't know much about the game," Cobb said, "but nothing much is going to happen if you just stand around, like he did at the end."

"He was just trying to get other people involved," Ink said, although he secretly agreed with Cobb.

A drunk, lanky boy appeared behind them and said, "We call that 'shrinking from the moment.'" His friend, dragging the boy ahead, added, "like a dick in winter."

Danny frowned as they passed. "They did what they could," he said. "They almost did it."

"If you hadn't forced us through your magic circle," Cobb said.

"Yeah," Jesse said. "That was the real killer."

"SER-EEE-OUS!" Down at the corner of Bell and State, the huge, smash-faced boy was being held up by two of his friends, both of whom fought laughter while telling him to take it easy. Several feet away, the girls stood in a circle, mumbling fearfully to themselves.

Danny, hands in pockets, began to walk toward the group.

"SERIOUS. SERIOUS? SERIOUS fucking nigger," Smash Face said, struggling to free himself.

"Come on, man," his friend said.

"Hey, hey, watch your mouth," Danny said.

Alarmed, Ink shuffled behind Cobb and began to pray.

"Danny D! Hey! Why so angry?" This other boy—the caretaker—approached, unable to shake all the slyness from his smile. "You best walk on by. We got it under control."

"Tell him not to be an asshole."

At that moment, Smash Face broke free from the wall. He pulled down his shirt, drew a hand across spumy lips. There were no more words. He went right for Danny, his huge right arm arcing like a jump shot across the body. Danny moved aside and the boy crashed face first to the sidewalk. The girls screamed. The caretaker burst into laughter.

"Get him out of here," Danny said.

"Easy dude. We're on our way."

From a couple blocks away, there came the sudden blip and whir of sirens; red and blue flashed across their bodies. Cobb and Jesse had inched away to the corner. Ink froze where he was, a rabbit in the grass.

The drunken boy started to rise. "I'm bleeding," he moaned, studying his hands.

"I should cave your goddamn head in," Danny said, talking around the caretaker who was now chest bumping Smash Face toward the street. When Danny turned, he looked directly at Ink. There was a long career of murders in his eyes.

*

Peace. Quiet. A cozy little pocket of time, the hour before the first classes of the day. Ink sat in the empty first floor student lounge of Halloran Learning Center and sipped his flavored coffee, felt the black stuff already working its magic. He peeled back the baking cup of a plain corn muffin and pinched a bit of it into his mouth. He opened up his fat Norton anthology and found his place among the thin pages of teeny tiny print. The caffeine had a way of making every single word delicious.

Across the hall, the door to the English suite banged shut, which meant, in all likelihood, that Dr. Marks had arrived for the day. 7:20 am. Ink read another page and then, backpack over shoulder and cardboard cup in hand, opened up the door, walked past the secretary's desk (she wouldn't be in until eight), down the corridor, suddenly self-conscious about the cuffs of his jeans, one slapping against the other, as he moved past the closed doors—Dr. Campbell, Dr. Long, Dr. Giordano, Dr. Sikma, Dr. Durbin-Foster—toward the one at the end, open a crack, the faint strains of classical music making Ink doubt his ability to sit one-on-one in a room with a man who knew just about everything.

"Oh, Mr. Alt. Hello, I didn't see you there." Dr. Marks laughed— a lovely habit, regular as breathing.

"Good morning, Dr. Marks."

"Do you need to see me?"

"I'm supposed to declare . . ."

"Why of course!" he said, clapping a book closed in his hands. "Another sheep coming into the fold. Many are called, but few are chosen, eh?"

Ink smiled. Dr. Marks was the good grandfather to many. Hoary headed. Arm palsied from a childhood disease. Magnanimous with his time. Some of the girls, like annoying Katy Fuster, thought he was a letch and passed around stories about squirmy office visits, but Ink

200

hadn't seen any evidence of it. To him, Marks was simply a wonderful professor of literature.

"Well, come in, come in!" he said, shuffling back into the office, kicking a plastic bag before him and snatching it with his good hand out of the air. He pushed three paperbacks off a chair and said, "Sit, sit, sit. Don't mind the mess."

The office was small, lit by a flickering florescent bulb and a desk lamp without a shade. Books were shelved and stacked and strewn, spread open or face down on the floor or desk. There were papers too, of course—in two stacks like a sliced in half deli sandwich on the stained desk calendar. Inexplicably, two gnarled sweet potatoes rested at Ink's feet. He sat down, looking at the photographs hung around the room. Marks had been a serious stage actor in his youth, and there were wonderful black and white photographs of him as Hamlet and Macbeth. Occasionally, he still hobbled around the stage for minor roles in campus productions. Once, Ink overheard this girl—Tamika Johnson, an English and Theatre double major—tell her friend that, "Acting is easy: You don't have to be yourself." On the surface, that sounded like common sense. But what, exactly, were the steps you needed to take to get beyond yourself?

Declaring a major turned out to be far less thrilling than he'd hoped. No grand ceremony. No program. No music. No laying of a sword upon the shoulders. Just a form in triplicate, a signature, and a suggested reading list. Still, Ink was thrilled, even as he felt a twinge of guilt for not finishing that one long Henry James story in the professor's "Short Fiction of the World" course. To understand after several rereadings what exactly was going on in a given paragraph only to be confronted with another dense wall of prose—it was too much to bear. On the one hand, he felt sorry for John Marcher and May Bartram, the two characters trapped inside this vast prison of verbiage. What had they done to deserve so cruel a fate? James might have provided the answer somewhere in there, but Ink hadn't been especially eager to know. On the other hand, did these two fools deserve anything more? All Marcher did was wait and wait and wait for whatever it was he figured was going to pounce. May, for her part, just stood stupidly by his side for all those years. All over campus, girls dangled from boys for reasons he strained to fathom. Fat, smash-faced, verbally abusive, no matter: girls clung as if their lives depended on them. The pretty ones too. The downright beautiful ones. And yet not one single girl, pretty or plain, had thrown her arms at Ink, the one boy on campus who would revere the right girl like the queen of the universe.

"Well," Marks said, slapping his hands together. "You are now officially a major!"

Major. He liked the sound of the word. It had the heft of commitment. It reminded him of war—something decisive, irrevocable, a sign that he meant business. Without question, this form was an irrefutable sign that he had come into his own.

On the other side of the wall, the day had come to life: students treading through the hallway, the muffled conversations, the opening of the outside door (perhaps the secretary a few minutes early). Ink wondered if he and Dr. Marks would ever meet in this strange, clumsy, quasi-intimate way again.

"I'm expecting big things from you," Marks said, giving him a soft, moist hand to shake.

"I'll do my best," he said, the words lame to him because they were so sincere.

Back in the hallway, Ink stood in a daze as students moved past him, chatting and sipping coffee, sealed away in their headphones. There seemed to be something inadequate—something trivial or even wrong—in what they were doing. Only Ink seemed marked for special distinction. If he tried even harder, perhaps he could be one of the special ones for whom Marks and the others would make real time. One of those students the professors would rave about in recommendations, one whom they would tearfully embrace on graduation day, one with whom they would forever keep in touch. This was the true beginning of his college career. Of his life! The middle and the end—who was to say the days that followed could not look like anything he desired?

Of Age

(Fall 1991-Spring 1992)

Oh, and there was one more thing: "Grandma," Mom sighed, "slipped last week on her front stairs and broke her hip."

"Last week?" Ink cried. "Why didn't you tell me?"

"I'm telling you now. Everything's okay."

"Except the broken hip."

"You're not here. Sometimes I forget."

Three years after the fact, Mom couldn't pass up another opportunity to make him pay for leaving home for college.

"'Slipped,' you said. It's September. You've got snow up there already?"

She sighed. "Slips happen. Isn't that what you kids always say?"

Ink laughed. Slips happen—yes, that was a good one. And true. You didn't know it until you were flat on your back or worse— drowned like that boy in grade school. Frankie . . . Frankie McGooken was the name. His death had been a terrible shock at the time; now, ten or eleven years later, Frankie had become, to paraphrase the end of a book he'd just finished reading, part of the background on which Ink would paint his dreams.

"Anyway," Mom said. "I've got nothing more to report."

"Think hard now. I don't want you to miss anything."

"She'd appreciate a card."

"Of course I'll send a card. What do you think I am?"

A kick at the door, and Jesse popped into the room, Frisbees flapping like elephant ears against his head.

"Goodbye," she said, and Ink imagined Mom standing at the kitchen table, trying out a puzzle piece here and here and there.

"Goodbye." Ink put a finger to his temple and pulled the trigger. Jesse laughed, hand over mouth—exactly the way Ink hoped he would.

"I'll give your father your love."

Ink sighed. "You want me to speak to him?"

"Do what you like. You're an adult now."

"And so are you."

When Ink hung up, he unscrewed the imaginary bullet from his brain and plunked it in the garbage can.

"Let me guess—your Mom?" Jesse said.

"My nemesis." The sentiment sounded good—it got another laugh—but Ink wondered how much he meant it.

"Well, put on your ol' fishing cap."

Ink took a disc and balanced it on his head all the way down the stairs. Last weekend, Jesse (newly single again) had shown Ink how Frisbee golf could be a kind of terrestrial angling, with strolling girls as the unwitting fish. It was simple: You picked out a "hole"—say, the birch in front of Dolan Hall or the oxidized nose of the founder's statue—and cast discs toward co-eds strolling by. More often than not, they tip tapped after the lure, thinking you'd just made an errant toss. That was your chance to run and reel them in. Ink shook his head in admiration, having never heard of a better plan in his life. Jesse, only half joking, said that he might have found a project for his senior research.

On the way to the quad, the boys ran into Cobb, walking with his new fraternity buddies. Last spring, Cobb had joined one of the Phis and lived now in a dreary, Romanesque house on the north end of campus. "Tell me why I did this again?" was the line he used on his old friends the first day of the semester. But now, standing between his two brothers, he looked the picture of contentment.

"Disc golf?" Jesse asked.

"Will there be perspiration involved?" Cobb scratched a palpable breast.

"Sadly, yes."

"My body is a temple."

"God help the faithful!" Ink said.

The brothers smiled, but Cobb waved off the insult and reminded them about the improv show at Open Mike's, featuring his multi-talented girlfriend Susan. Ink had seen a picture of this Susan in the program for the *Streetcar* show last spring. "Unbelievable," was all he could think. Ink said he wouldn't miss it for the world. Jesse said he most certainly would. Cobb made a praying motion, like he was splitting the difference, and strolled away with his friends.

They played nine holes, and Ink tried to keep from being annoyed by Jesse as he went on about his next musical venture with "a group of guys who actually knew what the hell they were doing." The closest either of them got to a bite was when Jesse lofted a beautifully errant drive that skidded to a stop on the brick walkway about twenty feet from a brunette in heels and jagged denim shorts. In a flash, his friend was off, pulling up in front of the girl just as she bent to pick up the disc. Jesse put his hand to his chest and although Ink was far away, he thought she might be laughing. What was he saying? How was he holding her attention? Ink had known Jesse since freshman year, and over that time he'd had three steady girlfriends, this despite the fact that he was no better looking than Ink. For God's sake, the boy's teeth weren't even straight. Maybe it was the wavy hair, the way it spun out from behind the ears. Maybe it was those two meticulously sculpted Idahos stretching down the sides of his face. By the time Ink caught up with him, the girl was gone. "Boyfriend," he explained with a shrug. Ink was relieved; for the time being, all was right with the world once again.

*

Open Mike's was packed by the time Ink and Jesse arrived, but they were able to squeeze in at a table with Cobb and the two frat brothers they'd met earlier in the afternoon. Susan came out in a Dalmatian pattern mini skirt and a bee hive do for a short standup routine comprised of observational stuff about life in the dorms. "Hey, hey, boys, girls, tell me: how far do you all go with this sharing thing? A blouse? All yours. Jeans? No problem! Underwear? Hmm, a little personal, but why the hell not? Toothbrush?" She rubbed a finger against her grimace. "Freshman year, believe it or not, my roommate stumbles in stinking one night and says, 'Susie Su, be a dear and let me borrow your toothbrush?' This girl's just gotten back from some massive frat blow out. How the hell do I know where that mouth has been?"

A smattering of laughter.

"I mean, right? You hear what I'm saying?"

Cobb sat back in his chair, a proprietary smile on his face. Ink looked at his friend. He stared at Susan—large breasts, shapely legs dropping out of that hot spotted skirt. The two of them together had the same effect on Ink as a Dennis Miller joke. Try as he might, he just couldn't get it.

During a break between performers, Danny appeared, head freshly shaved, silk shirt undone to his sternum. He stood at the entrance, scanning the room, probably trying to figure out which group he was going to grace with his presence. The Cure was laying down a beguiling off-kilter groove on the jukebox. To Ink, it seemed the perfect soundtrack for the boy.

He hadn't seen Danny since the first day of the semester, when he ran into him on the way to class. Sherk, his roommate for the past two years, had officially dropped out—"up in smoke" Danny said, thumb and forefinger to his lips. Danny lived now down on the far end of Bell Street, up above the nail salon with Wetzler and a few other hobbled jocks on the six- or seven-year plan for graduation.

After slapping a few backs at the bar—after splashing down a complimentary shot—Danny wandered over to their table. Ink stood immediately to surrender his chair.

"Where've you been?" Jesse asked, more out of a sense of duty, it seemed, than of curiosity.

"Ice cream social. A sorority thing. All you can lick."

"You're disgusting," Jesse said.

"It was for charity!"

At a Christmas party years ago, Uncle Lare told the family that there were all kinds of drunks: happy ones and somber ones, quiet and belligerent and obscene ones, joyful and jealous ones. "I'm mostly a sulker. I brood about doing things. Bad things." Ink considered a category for Danny. Under the influence, he just seemed to be more Danny. Off-color. Outrageous. Angry. Danny squared. Or cubed.

"What you pussies been up to?"

Ink told him about Frisbee golf, and Danny listened distractedly, rubbing bloodshot eyes with index finger and thumb.

"You know," he said, "my cousin is a cop, one of Canton's finest. I asked him once: you ever let go a pretty woman you pulled over for speeding? Bastard didn't want to answer, but I kept him drinking shots until he smiled and said, 'Yeah, sure. I'm a human being.' I asked him why. I mean, did he honestly think she was going to do something in return? To, you know, show her gratitude? I said, 'You knew she wasn't going to open the door and give you the blow job of your life. You knew she wasn't going to come to the station after your shift, all cleavage and heels, and give it to you good, right? Right? Right? Therefore, just give her the goddamn ticket!'"

"Who the hell is this guy?" one of the frat boys asked.

"Are they ever going to let you have it?"

"Susan's pretty funny," Ink said, lying through his teeth.

Cobb nodded. "She has, as she says, 'a comic wisdom beyond—'"

"Answer the question," Danny said, slamming the table, spilling drinks.

The frat boy, scowling, flicked a turned over cup, striking Danny in the chest.

"Danny," Jesse said. "You are now officially being a jerk."

"Exactly," Danny said, sitting back, dropping his chin toward the dark stain on his shirt. "That's my whole fucking point."

*

More and more these days, Ink obsessed about girls the way Trappist monks obsessed about God. Every waking moment, images avalanched into his brain: painted toenails, smooth legs crossing, the freckled slope of breasts disappearing into a low cut top, a tongue between full red lips, a rump in Spandex wiggling across the quad. As a freshman, he'd come up with a list of his dream girls, a top twenty-five, like the rankings for college basketball teams. On occasion, he'd returned to the list to make the necessary concessions to reality. The true beauties, with their flawless faces and baby skin and long, fruit-fragrant hair and thin bright dresses blithely flapping against long tanned legs—they had to be struck from the list because he simply didn't stand a chance. The uglies and the fatties, of course, were ruled out as well—for the opposite reason. That left two other categories: the girls who made up for plain faces with some attractive anomaly (half way decent legs or pert, prodigious breasts) and what he'd come to think of as his target group—the shy, socially awkward, easily embarrassed ones with good skin and nice teeth and passable curves that might draw attention if they dared to come out from behind bad hair or bug-eyed glasses or all those layers of baggy, monochromatic clothing. In every class, there were invariably a few of this sort whose lack of self-esteem oozed from their pores. The best of these were freshmen, strangers in a strange land, not yet having met the two or three good friends they'd need in order to feel at home. The scent of such vulnerability often drove Ink wild with desire.

Perri Simmons had never been at the very top of his rankings—she was, metaphorically speaking, no Duke or Carolina or UNLV—but for a few years now she'd hovered between twenty and fifteen. She was tall (a bit gangly, alas), with a pleasant face and a thin blond ponytail that swung energetically at the air. A tennis player for the university, she was even a kind of minor celebrity. He could not sit down next to her in class without sweating profusely. When she said "Good morning" to him in her sleepy amiable way, he could barely breathe a "hi."

One morning, about a month into the semester, Ink went from awed admirer to knight in shining armor. The class started off with his usual awkward greeting. Then, for the most part, he forgot about her, as he furiously scribbled down the key points of the lecture. Near the end of class, Dr. Durbin-Foster stalked up and down the row, returning exams that, for the most part, he didn't think much of. Ink, much to his relief, received an A minus. To his right, Perri stared at a bright red 8 X 11 F. Embarrassed, Ink slipped book into backpack and stood up to leave. Still, the girl sat there, green eyes glistening with tears.

"Are you alright?" Ink asked. The question came instinctively, before he remembered the girl's lofty status in his mind.

"I'm ruined."

"No," Ink said. "It's one test."

When they walked out of class together, Ink tried hard not to reflect on the magnitude of the moment. Down the hallway, out the double doors, into the sun and across the quad, she went on in fits and starts about Ralph Waldo Emerson. To her, each of the writer's sentences was a puzzle, an impenetrable mystery—she didn't know how anyone in his right mind could be an English major. Ink nodded, murmured commiseratingly, all the while gauging the reaction of students passing by. Were the boys greening with jealousy? Were other girls seeing him in a whole new brilliant light? It was hard to tell if anyone even noticed him at all.

"How do you do it?"

"What?"

"The words. They seem to make sense to you."

This was his opportunity to say something striking, and he offered up a chunky verbal stew of ums and ahs and wells before saying, "I think—don't quote me on this—that Emerson aims for the heart. You've got to, um, find him there."

She looked at him, eyes shining. She dug a tissue into her nose. "Do you think you'd have the time, sometime, to help me out? You know, when the next exam comes up?"

"Sure," Ink said, trying immediately to rein in his enthusiasm with a second—a much more nonchalant—"sure." It was as if he'd gotten the girl's phone number, as if she'd asked him out to dinner and a movie. By the end of the day, Ink had nearly convinced himself that he and Perri were an item.

*

After three lengthy study sessions at The Bean Bag, though, Ink began to get frustrated. Perri always looked sleepy—disinterested, ready for bed. Did she act like this on the tennis court, a first serve rocketing her way? Of course not. Because tennis was something she was passionate about.

"If it's love," Xavier told him at dinner one evening, "You'll know soon enough."

Ink looked at the good and good looking boy, officially loathing him now.

"She's just using you," Jesse theorized, stabbing half-heartedly at his salad. "Classic life preserver." Jesse had yet another new girlfriend—this one a vegetarian—and he said, in all seriousness, that he planned to respect her wishes. Ink looked at his friend's dinner bowl—the shredded carrots, the sprouts, the sesame seeds, the felled forest of broccoli—and wanted to gag.

"At least I don't have to pretend I'm someone I'm not."

"Hey, hey, don't take this out on me."

Perhaps Jesse was right. After the study sessions, all Ink had to show for them was a cup of flavored coffee, which Perri bought for him at their last meeting. Maybe she thought that was payment enough for his services. Not that she should have felt obligated to do anything more than say "thank you," which she did. Ink was more than happy to help someone—anyone—better appreciate the power of the world's literary gods. But still. By now, *something* should have happened: a lingering look, a squeeze of the hand, a peck on the cheek.

Ink refused to give up. With a little sage advice, he was certain he could break through, waking up Perri in the way that Thoreau, that crotchety chanticleer, implored his readers, past and present. After classes the following day, he went down to The Bell and popped his head inside Hangovers. It was the hour before happy hour, and Danny, as was his habit lately, slouched in a dark corner like a mafia don.

"What in the world is that?" Ink said, pointing to the book in Danny's hands.

"Hey, I can read with the best of them." He put a finger on the page and inched it to the right, slowly mouthing the words.

"I've got a girl problem," Ink said.

Danny smiled at him with glassy eyes that looked like they'd been crushed under heels. For a moment, Ink was concerned. Was he grieving? Was he stoned? Crazy? Simply running on little sleep? Whatever the issue, the boy seemed to be hanging in there. And if he were in real trouble, there were countless girls on campus who'd die for the chance to be his mother with the hopes of something more.

Ink laid out his predicament, and Danny nodded, stroked his stubbly chin. "Perri Simmons!" he said. "I tried to crack her once."

Ink was offended, but the feeling was tempered by his sense that he'd just shot up in the estimation of the world. "The thing is," he said, "sometimes, she looks at me, waiting for what I'm going to say. Her mouth's a little bit open and the hair is falling across her face and, I don't know, I want to just, I don't know—"

"My boy's really dying for some action."

Ink frowned. He waited for Danny to put down his beer before he said, "Sure, why not? It's about time."

"Coming of age?"

"That's right."

"Tired of coming into your own?"

"That's hilarious."

Danny downed his beer and winked at a passing waitress for another. "Look, it's really, really simple. You want to buy another goddamn textbook, when all you have to do is follow your instincts."

Ink waited.

"But you're not that kind of guy." He folded a cocktail napkin into a tight little square and slid it over, a pharmacist parceling out a pill. "Start lower. Pay your dues."

Ink looked down at the spine of his friend's book, which rested before a small pool of spilled beer. *The Savage Mind.* He wondered if Danny might be working in secret on the sequel.

*

Katy Fuster was, in Ink's mind, the "little lower" his friend had in mind. She was frumpy, with slush colored hair tied up in a bun and big round glasses, skin loose under the arms. She had huge, hungry eyes, though, and Ink was hopeful that would mean something when he dumped her into his bed. A talented English major, she sat on the other side of the room in his short story survey, not so much attending class as setting up shop. When the session ended, she had to put away her text, her notebook, and the pile of library books from which she occasionally read passages in order to earn Dr. Giordano's praise. There was also the empty travel mug of tea, the bagel wrapper, throat lozenges, and an arsenal of moisturizers. All of it, after great effort, fit into her backpack. One day, Ink waited and waited and waited and stood up when she did, smiling, bolstering his confidence with the thought that his teeth were straighter than Jesse's.

"Welcome to the communion of your race," he said, a pick up line that was original, even if it didn't make much sense.

The girl's big eyes shrunk. "I don't like Hawthorne."

"Are you crazy?"

"I find his daughter is much more interesting."

"Whose daughter?"

"I'm going to write my paper on Rose Hawthorne—her conversion, what she did for the poor and the powerless."

Ink smirked. "She's not one of the writers on the syllabus."

"Hawthorne was a wimp. A do-nothing."

"He's one of the greatest writers this country has ever produced."

"He had that custom house job and whined about it until they threw him out. Then he whined about it some more."

Ink walked in a daze with her all the way over to The Bean Bag, where, against his better judgment, he bought Katy an herbal tea and let her go on about the virtues of her wonderful Rose.

211

"Who else do you like?" she asked, more of a challenge than a question.

"Well, you know, the writers we're reading." He shrugged. "The greats."

Katy snorted. She railed against the tyranny of the literary canon. Last week, she asked Dr. Campbell if he was going to teach Toni Morrison in his contemporary literature course next semester. "'Who?' he said, while running for cover behind his precious podium. Morrison won the Pulitzer Prize a few years ago, and all he can say is, 'Who?'"

"A different writer wins that prize every year. You can't put them all on the syllabus."

"He's just interested in dead white guys."

"Wait, Toni Morrison . . ."

". . . Is a woman. She's black. She's from Ohio."

Ink hung his head. Katy was no great prize, but that fact did little to make him forget he was oftentimes an ignorant fool.

When Katy informed him a few days later that Dr. Giordano had rejected her plan for the paper, Ink was full of secret glee.

"No big deal," she said, her lips puckered in determination. "I'll write the paper for myself."

Ink found such assertiveness off-putting, yet she kept talking as if this were her crowning glory. As they walked across the quad, she moved on from Rose Hawthorne to Elizabeth Cady Stanton, to Seneca Falls, to the long struggle for the right to vote, to the epic battle for equity in the workplace today. Ink reconsidered her drab, makeup-deprived face. He looked down, eyes following the potato sack of a dress to the thick bare legs and big black boots. Suddenly, everything clicked. The attitude, the clothes, the shamelessly unadorned face— this girl was a lesbian. A lesbian! Just his luck.

*

The next one—Judy Something—was not even a Katy Fuster, although she'd nearly done the trick. A bit of acne, a faint, musty smell behind her ears—Ink didn't care. She was a girl—one of those desperate freshmen—and he had, after the requisite pizza and a movie, managed to find himself on top of her in his dorm room. He was kissing her, digging fingers into flesh like it was sugar cookie batter. At one point, she elbowed him in the temple, but he shook off the sharp pain and burrowed more deeply, discovering to his dismay a nominal breast. When his eyes returned to her face and saw that page boy hair, the light fuzz beneath her nose, for one terrible moment he thought: boy in disguise, some crazy Shakespeare thing. But that was—it had to be—his brain trying to rob him of this pleasurable pull and plunge. He dug elsewhere, lower, tried like mad to get a good angle on the zipper of her pants. He had the tab between thumb and forefinger, and he ripped and ripped but the thing wouldn't budge. And Judy wasn't helping any, squirming all over the bed.

Suddenly: a furious pounding on a door down the hall. SNAP!— the spell was broken. Judy pulled away, scurried up toward the headboard, a fish through his grasp. His face struck her hipbone, her knee, her foot. Before he knew it, he was left clutching a big ball of sheets.

"You want to," Ink said, and he knew because he'd watched her for days in the commuter lounge, looking up sadly from her brown bag lunch at her peers, all of whom had someone to talk to. When he went up to speak with her, she nearly choked with joy upon her bruised apple.

"I changed my mind," the girl said, tears welling.

"No you didn't."

"I want to be respected."

Ink got on his knees. "I'll respect every inch of you."

"No."

"I will."

"I won't," she said.

There was an inebriated giggle in the hallway, a vicious riff of Zeppelin. Someone roared, "Turn it down, asshole!"

Ink sat up, squeezed his head in his hands. Could there be any more humiliating way to become oh for two?

*

For days, Ink slunk to classes, feeling the eyes of everyone upon him. A laugh across the room became in his mind a response to a joke about how he couldn't laid. On the third day, he woke with a tightness in his chest that felt at first like fear; the dull ache in his jaw, however, made him realize it was anger. It did not help that later in the afternoon Judy passed him on the quad, laughing with some new-found friend, oblivious to his presence in the world. He turned, watched her flat ass until he realized that wasn't going to make him feel any better at all.

The following Monday, he had another study session with Perri. It was almost 8:30. Diego was gone already (Why didn't he just move into the damn library?), and Ink would have to hustle if he was going to be on time. Why shower? Why brush his teeth? Why comb his hair? On the off chance his luck might suddenly turn, he did each of those things and more: dabbles of cologne here and there, a series of mouthwash rinsings, a few Q-Tip twists to the ears.

They sat at a corner table in the library stacks, heads close together, slowly but surely working through "Song of Myself."

"'Dash me with your amorous wet,'" she said, trailing a pen under the words as she read them. "Now what does that mean?"

He waited for her to say that she was kidding.

"Well?"

Ink swallowed. "'Amorous.' You know what that means?"

"That's love."

"Okay, good." His throat was dry. Perri ran a few strands of hair behind an ear. Was she flirting with him? What else could such a gesture mean?

"So Whitman uses a lot of, let's see, imagery. Imagery—those are details that appeal to the senses: you know, sight, touch . . . taste."

He glanced at her lips, wet from the ginger ale she'd just put down. His eyes fell to the slope of her breasts before sliding back to the printed page. He returned to other, less explicit passages as a way of building up courage. Whenever he spoke at length, Perri had the habit of letting her eyes drift to his forehead. It made him self-conscious and stumbly in his speech. Lint on the brow? A zit? A smear of food? Throughout his explanations, he made surreptitious swipes at his forehead, trying to remove whatever it was.

"So basically, Whitman's talking here about, let's see—"

"Ejaculation!" Perri cried, eyes flashing for a moment. Then she sat back, trapping a giggle with her hands.

Ink looked at her. They laughed. It was a great moment—a breakthrough of sorts—but Ink couldn't dare fill the awkward silence in a similar vein.

"Who's your favorite tennis player?"

"Steffi Graf."

"Ah," Ink said, nodding knowingly. "Fraulein Forehand."

She laughed. "Hey, that's right!"

While shelving books at his work study job last week, Ink found himself in the sports section. On a lark, he drew down a few books about tennis, paged through them in haphazard fashion. Before long, he was taking careful notes. Steffi Graf won Wimbledon in 1991. She could play on clay and grass and hard courts. Navratilova (the lesbian one) took the title the year before. In a tennis magazine he found on the periodical shelf, he read a profile of Monica Seles, the one who squealed like a pig. She won the most recent U.S. Open. Like Perri, she was left handed. He'd crammed these facts and more inside his head and now, by the grace of God, they returned when he most needed them.

"Do you play?"

"Occasionally," he lied. "Not for a while."

She cocked her head. "Let's hit some balls next week."

"Sure," he said, the image creating a stir in his pants. "That'd be great!"

Smiles, nervous laughter, the sudden buzz of a light overhead.

"Anyway," she said.

"Yes, well, the good, grey poet . . ."

"Exactly."

They returned to Whitman, to his sexy words pouring out across the page. Perri was more attentive now. She scraped her chair closer to the table, leaned her fragrant body towards his face. Ink suddenly felt large; he contained multitudes.

*

The following week, they met at the indoor courts. While Perri stretched out, Ink—heroically avoiding the temptation to gawk—studied the facility's rules, which were posted directly above his head.

It turned out that Perri was on the tennis team for a reason. She hit the ball hard, with terrific accuracy. Ink flailed about, sending his shots into the net or onto other courts, when he wasn't missing the ball altogether. He tried to smile, but managed only to grit his teeth. When he popped up like a ball player, he joked, "souvenir for a lucky fan."

She gave him a good-natured laugh. It seemed to be a sign that she wasn't holding his incompetency against him.

"Set your feet," she said. "Like this." She spread her legs, bounced in place, the pleats between her thighs like a curtain at a theater. He tried to focus, did as she advised. When she fired the ball his way, he swung. He whiffed.

"Helps to keep your eyes open." She smirked, turned, the smooth flick of the ponytail leaving him short of breath. "No mercy now." Ink watched Perri at the baseline, pounding the ball five times before flipping it into the air, shirt rising from the stretch to reveal her belly.

The ball sizzled toward him. Ink came over the top of it, and sent it down the line, leaving Perri a statue in the opposing service box.

"Wow," she said, hands on hips.

Ink was shocked. Somehow, though, he had the wherewithal to say, "More where that came from."

She smiled. They played another half hour, and he never scored another point.

Later, at Perri's suggestion, they met up for dinner at the Glasshouse Diner. Ink was at a booth fiddling with a menu when she came in, tall and freshly showered, frizzy hair down on her shoulders, long painted fingers on the purse strap across her breast. He thought of his list of girls, tapped her figurative bottom like a ball player into the top five.

She ordered a Caesar salad and Ink, starving but afraid to seem piggish, ordered a turkey club. While waiting for their food, they talked about the Romanticism course. She admitted she'd signed up thinking they'd be reading romance novels. "You know, Danielle Steel and stuff." Ink made an effort to laugh good naturedly. Talk drifted to other topics: Pete Sampras, whom Perri adored; REM, Ink's favorite band and—what would you know?—hers too; *Pretty Woman*, a movie he couldn't believe she liked. It was amazing how one thing led to the other, fluid like a long, leisurely volley, neither trying especially hard to score. Afterward, Ink walked her back to the dorm, all the while glancing around for a witness who might later be able to corroborate this unprecedented event.

"Well, good night," she said, and Ink watched her tap up the front stairs of the dorm. "It was fun," she added with an open-fingered wave, right before the door clicked closed behind her. A little abrupt,

Ink thought. If not a kiss, wasn't a little lamplight lingering in order? Ink walked away, collar up, head down, consoling himself with the thought that he could almost safely say that he was now in the game.

*

"The History of Leisure"—Ink knew that the course was going to be a breeze. A good thing, since he only signed up because Perri said late last fall that she was going to take it. When he arrived in the classroom the first day back in January, he stopped in front of her desk, two coats of faux surprise painted on his face.

"Hi," she said, smiling blandly, as if he were a total stranger.

Ink had helped the girl survive the Romanticism course. "A B!" she'd cried, her Christmas Eve call like an early holiday gift. And then, he hadn't heard another word from her until this perfunctory hello. She lived in Michigan, so it was not as if he'd expected her to come to Cleveland every weekend for a date. But if, despite his repeated requests, she wasn't going to give him her phone number, the least she could have done was call a few more times. She could have said "I miss you." She could have said, "When we get back, we'll stroke a few more balls." He thought he'd come so far with her, but what exactly did he have to show for nearly three months of work? A cup of coffee? An afternoon of tennis? A handshake at the net? Generic chit chat in a diner? Ink opened his mouth to complain; instead, he found himself asking in a somewhat pouty voice, "You going to be around later?"

"Um, I think so."

He was tempted to say: "It's not an existential question." Instead, he sweetly inquired, "Would you, I mean, like to do something? Have a coffee?"

"I've got a lot of studying to do."

"It's the first day of class."

The professor strode in, out of breath, unzipping his coat, brushing snow from his hair. "No offense kids, but days like these I dream about retirement. Florida, a view of the gulf, a kiwi daiquiri. To hell with winter." He wormed out of his coat and slapped it down on the floor, as if it were a creature that had surprised him from behind. "To hell with winter," he said again, raising his hands. "Everybody now!"

"To hell with winter!" the students said, laughing, looking quizzically at each other.

217

Ink slouched to a seat in the back, dragged out his books. In front of him, Perri scrunchied her hair. A boy to her left leaned in, and her head bobbed in assent. The professor wrote the word PLAY on the board. He wanted to know what it meant, and he was serious—"serious as my heart attack." Ink scratched his only pen on the back of his notebook, but nothing at all came out.

*

The semester moved on, tentative toddler steps at first then, three weeks in, the track meet began. Novels, papers, quizzes, exams. Ink was well-acquainted with the rhythm and completed his work in a diligent manner. He thought about dropping the Leisure class, but every Monday, Wednesday, and Friday, he kept taking his seat in back, a steaming cup of flavored coffee in his hand. He tried to focus on the professor, who talked with great, dark humor about, among other things, the various blood sports of the colonists. Dog fighting, rat fighting, cock fighting. "'Cockers,' they were called," the professor said, hands out to gather the inevitable titters. As hard as he tried to pay attention, Ink found his eyes drifting toward Perri. He watched her write. He watched her stretch. He watched her stand, bend to reach for a dropped book. He took note of what she wore each day and how the article of clothing rested against arm or leg or rear. If the professor had given him a midterm on the parts of Perri, he would have earned a perfect score.

One afternoon, staring into the bakery case at The Bean Bag, waiting for a new pot of Irish Cream to brew, he heard a familiar voice behind him say, "Anything good?"

He turned, and there she was—tall, smiling, in a green form-fitting turtleneck. It took Ink a moment to notice her eyes—the dusky crescents underneath. Had she been crying?

"Are you—?"

"I'm great. How you've been?"

"Why do you want to know?"

"Look," she said. "I'm sorry." Perri gazed out the window. "I've been busy with some, well . . ." She swallowed. She swooped hair around her ear. "Some personal issues."

"My birthday's tomorrow," he said, an announcement that made him feel desperate and small.

"Really? I love birthdays! How old?"

218

"Twenty one."

"Oh, the big one! How are you going to celebrate?"

Ink was going to go out with the guys, and Danny, clapping a hard hand on his back, promised it was going to get "butt ugly." "No real plans," he said.

"You've got to celebrate!"

He tried to read her eyes instead of her breasts. "Maybe I could come over."

She smiled. They arranged a time.

"Who's got the Irish Cream?" the barista cried, holding it in the air like a chalice. Ink took the cup and smiled "goodbye" to Perri. On the way out the door, he tried to be thrilled. He tried to convince himself that victory, long denied, was on the horizon.

The next day, when Ink returned from breakfast to grab his books for class, the phone shrilled. He was running late but picked it up, a wild fantasy that it was Perri—Perri just wanting to hear his voice—taking shape in his mind.

"John, your father's in the hospital."

"What?"

"He had a little episode this morning," Mom said, voice wavering. "I thought I'd tell you right away."

"What do you want me to do?" This afternoon, he was planning to meet Danny and Cobb for happy hour at Hangovers. Afterward, he arranged to go to Perri's, where something, damn it, was going to happen.

"He'll be in at least one night for observation."

"What do you want me to do?" It was his birthday—the only twenty-first birthday of his entire life.

"You're an adult."

Ink looked at the fire exit sign on the back of his door. A clear path of escape was marked out in red.

"Happy birthday, by the way."

"Yes . . ."

Ink had a car now—an old, jaundice-colored Nova that bled oil and antifreeze and occasionally refused to reverse. He crossed himself every time he climbed behind the wheel. He could have easily told

Mom the car was in the shop—that it needed brakes or shocks or a whole new transmission. Instead, he heard himself saying, "Yes, yes, I'll be there. I'm leaving within the hour." He tortured himself by driving down Bell Street, studying the sleepy facades of Hangovers, Open Mike's, CGs, Ad Nauseam, and all the other clubs that would later in the day come roaring to life: By the light at the interstate, he stalled, and, key between thumb and forefinger, mumbled a prayer that the car wouldn't start again. But of course it did. And of course he managed to get to Cleveland in good time, without further incident.

Mom met him at the door with a dripping dishrag. A nod, but not a single word of thanks. He followed her into the kitchen, where the kettle was beginning to whistle. Ink made himself a cup of instant, as Mom explained what happened.

"He was getting ready for work, nothing out of the ordinary," she said with a sigh. "All of a sudden, he starts holding his chest and says, 'I don't feel so good.' Then, and you'll appreciate this, he says, 'well.' He could have been having a heart attack, and he takes the time to correct his grammar!"

She laughed, a response so uncharacteristic that it made Ink once again wonder about the landscape of her mind. If the long silences and separate occupations were any indication, she and Dad did not get along so well. Now, though, with this sudden scare, had she remembered to love? When Dad returned home, would she press against him? Kiss him desperately? Would they fall into bed together and make love to celebrate the tenuous miracle of life? The thought made him queasy.

"Want to walk?" Ink asked. It was a cold, windy day, but Metro General was just three blocks away.

"I'll take my chances in your car," Mom said.

For a long time, Mom had been suspicious of the neighborhood. In the past few years, the few neighbors they did know—the Frears, the Russos—had moved to the western suburbs. "Heading for higher ground," Mom liked to say. As they drove up the block, Ink looked at the barely familiar houses—the flaking paint, the bloated furniture on saggy front porches, the plastic toys scattered across overgrown lawns. The corner store, owned forever by Mr. Bozak, a bald spindle of a man who wore white button down shirts, was now, according to Mom, run by "brown people and drugs." Ink didn't want to agree. He didn't, and he wouldn't, even though he was secretly glad they'd taken his car to the hospital.

"Increase, it was good of you to come," Dad said with his usual embarrassing formality. He was sitting up in the bed, smiling, hands folded on a blanket, the picture of perfect health.

"Are you okay?"

"Yes. I'm fine. They've been running tests. It isn't the heart— they said it's in fine working order."

"The doctor mentioned something about anxiety," Mom said.

Anxiety! If that was enough to put you in the hospital, Ink would have never seen the light of day for the last eight years.

"So," Dad said, a smile spreading. "I heard it through the grapevine that it's someone's big birthday."

Ink closed his eyes. He imagined cinnamon schnapps at Hangovers, Perri Simmons answering her door wearing nothing but a smile.

"This is a little something for you."

It was, of course, a schmaltzy card, full of scripted sentiments. Inside, there was a check for fifty dollars.

"We thought money was what you want the most at this point in your life."

"Thank you. I'll use it on something important."

Dad wrinkled his eyes and pursed his lips—more infuriating sincerity. "Son," he said, "it was good of you to come."

Ink nodded. Damn right it was good—good because it hurt him so much. What else could his sacrifice have been besides the gesture of a saint?

*

Ink's bitterness about his ruined birthday was rinsed away two days later by his first legal beer—a sweaty bottle of Heineken at Hangovers. The first one was on Danny, the second would be on Cobb—back and forth, as Danny explained, "until you throw up real good." After the second beer, which made Ink a little queasy, Danny, with a wink at the waitress, ordered up some shots. Ink glanced at his watch. It was 4:30 in the afternoon.

"Relax, buddy," Danny said. "We're just getting started."

"Don't you have a date or something? Aren't you going out with somebody?" Ink asked.

"Well, sad to say, me and Lucinda are done."

"How long was this one?" Cobb asked. "Two weeks?"

Susan, the gorgeous but not especially funny comedienne, had dumped Cobb the week before, but Ink, sensitive to his own frustrations, chose not to chide him about it.

"Hmm, how long, how long?" Danny did quick calculations in the air. He audibly carried the 1. "Let's see, seventeen days."

"Have you ever had *one* serious relationship?" Cobb asked.

Danny frowned. "You know I don't enter into women lightly."

"You're sick," Ink slurred.

Danny shrugged. "Looks like you're the sick one, dude. If you blow, do me a favor and watch the Chuck Taylor's."

"I just, I need to slow down." Ink closed his eyes again. Saliva bubbled in the corners of his lips. He found himself vaguely envious of Jesse, who was down with the flu in his dorm room.

They took a break for food. Ink ordered a fat bloody burger with cheddar and double bacon and a jumbo order of curly fries, both of which he greedily devoured while listening to Danny's elaborate tales of his most recent conquests. Ink nodded. He smiled. He said "Oh" when he was supposed to, but the little part of him that was still sober felt that the monologue was, at least in places, both tedious and offensive.

When Ink finished eating, Danny clapped his hands. "Okay, time for the exercise portion of the program."

They went to the dartboard, a coin operated game with little color coded darts that were impossible to control. Behind them, the waitress set down a tray with three more beers. Ink's stomach recoiled.

"Thanks, hon," Danny said, a big bill folded between his fingers. She began rooting in her apron for change. "Keep it," he said.

She smiled. It was Danny. For him, they always seemed to smile.

Danny slid quarters into the dart game. "Okay now, see that red thing—"

"The bull's eye?"

"Imagine, if you will, a certain something else."

Ink's nose wiggled with disgust.

"The eye of God!"

"Gross!" Ink put his hands over his ears. That small sober part of himself—a mere speck now—wanted to tell Danny to just stop already.

"Is an arm gross? A hand? A finger?"

Cobb belched. "If you prick it, does it not bleed?"

The speck disappeared, and Ink couldn't help but laugh.

Danny threw first and came within a hair's breadth of the black. Cobb's dart flew wildly but stuck in the fat part of the twenty. Ink, a little unsteady, pumped his arm a few times and then let his dart go. It stuck in the wall two feet below the board, quivering for a moment before flopping to the floor.

Cobb laughed so hard that beer lapped from his glass onto his loafers. Danny lazed an arm around Ink's neck. "That's alright, little man. You'll get her next time."

"Maybe you should close your eyes," Cobb said.

"Think of Nina," Danny said.

"Give it a rest," Ink said.

"Who?" Cobb asked. "Does Ink have himself a girl?"

"Nina, Nina, Nina. She's one of his old flames. Much better, I think, than that Perri chick."

Ink waved away the words—a swarm of flies at a picnic. "She's just someone I went to grade school with." He'd seen her only a handful of times this year—the last time she was wearing a pink sorority sweatshirt and running shorts. Her hair was tied back in a bun, revealing that pleasing round brown face. "Cute" was the word that always came to mind. She was someone it would be nice to be cozy with on a couch.

"You know," Danny said, knees bent, fingers rocking his dart. "If you don't want to . . ." The dart flew, and the plastic point stuck in red. "I will! Ha, ha," he cried, turning his throwing hand in a fist.

Ink pushed his friend between the shoulder blades, and Danny, exaggerating the impact, fell against a nearby table, beer splashing to the floor. Cobb's responded in equally stylized fashion—a stagger back, wide spread fingers polishing the air in front of his face. Danny turned, teeth bright, eyes blazing with approbation. "Ha, ha!" he said. "I love your passion. That's the way for my little man to be!"

Laugher ate away all of Ink's anger and outrage. He collapsed face upon chest against his friend, who took him under the arms and dragged him to a chair. Head in hands, he saw for one lucid moment that he was wasted. And then, like that, he was gone.

*

There was light. There was talking in the room—a measured, dispassionate monologue. Ink caught the words "world" and "victory." His mouth was a desert, his head smashed up with pain. He'd gotten in God knows when, swallowed down pain pills with two glasses of water, and stumbled up the ladder to his bunk. He blinked, looked down now. He was surprised to discover his body in clothes.

In time, the monologue assumed the form of a news report.

The door opened, and a familiar young man appeared, blue towel wrapped around his waist. Yes, everything was coming back to him. Ink was at college. He was a second semester junior. He lived in Freitag Hall. Diego, his roommate these past three years, had set the alarm clock to NPR.

Ink sat up, spun his tongue to try to form saliva. To his relief, the coffee had just finished dripping.

"Good morning," Diego said.

"Um . . . not especially."

Diego's sympathetic smile hurt his eyes like a blast of sun. Ink drew his shirt above his face to hide from it, but the smell of smoke nearly made him gag.

"Sorry I didn't join you last night. Big Ethics exam today."

Ink scrubbed hands through his hair. "It's okay." Actually, it wasn't okay, but Ink, hungover as he was, didn't have the energy to muster up much anger. In fact, he felt sorry for Diego. Holed up perpetually in that library carrel in the fourth-floor stacks, where even the most studious seldom dared to tread. Denying himself a night out on the town with friends, the unparalleled pleasure of a good, strong buzz.

Diego handed him a mug of coffee, and Ink, feet dangling over the bunk, took a sip and tried to make sense of the news report. UN forces, he gathered, were going into Croatia, which used to be a part of Yugoslavia. Sarajevo was mentioned, a city he knew because that's where a recent Olympics had been held. Macedonia, Croatia, Slovenia, Bosnia—everybody and his brother was declaring his independence.

224

Some of these people were Christians, others were Muslims. That, evidently, was a problem. Baker, the secretary of war or state (Ink could never keep them straight) was over there now. He was on the case.

"This is not good," Diego said, slipping on his clothes.

"They'll figure it out." This was one of Ink's longest and dearest held opinions. The Berlin Wall had fallen, the Soviet Union had crumbled. The threat of nuclear annihilation had all but gone up in smoke. Meanwhile, America had remained what it always had been: a strong, blindingly bright beacon of democracy. If everybody had what people had in the United States, Ink theorized, he was almost certain there'd be world peace.

"We'll see," Diego said.

Yes, in due time, they all would see. But, as always, first things first: aspirin, a long, hot shower, another cup of coffee to try to clear the brain for a full day of work.

*

The sole purpose of dragging his beer-soaked body out of bed at seven am had been to see Perri in Leisure class. Just his luck, though: she was not there. Without an object worth his study, Ink spent the hour drawing concentric circles on his notebook. They reminded him of bull's eyes. He felt a little better after sticking each of them with his pen.

Two nights ago, as soon as he returned to campus from his brief trip home, he'd tried to call Perri, in order to explain why he hadn't met up with her as promised. Her phone, however, just rang and rang. Was she out, trying to determine his whereabouts? Upset he'd stood her up? Maybe she had simply forgotten about their plans. Whatever the case, he was sure he had taken at least three steps back in the relationship. As he brooded, it occurred to him that he might be able to use Dad's hospitalization to gain some traction with her. "I could have lost him," he imagined himself saying, slumped upon her bed, voice quavering, eyes moistening with tears. "And, you know, it's really made me think about . . . the human condition." She'd be moved by that portentous phrase Diego liked so much to use. She'd tear up, slip her arms around him, press him back onto the mattress. She'd know, without another word, that she was in the presence of a real man, mature beyond his tender years.

225

In the afternoon, he left a message with Perri's roommate, who annoyed him by asking with a full mouth, "Wait now, who are you again?" Then he waited in his room for the call. He watched a soap opera. He skipped dinner and ate a whole cylinder of crackers and a half a dozen squares of cellophaned cheese. He sat against a wad of pillows on his dorm room bed, writing in the journal he'd been keeping in spurts. He was angry at a lot of things, but mostly it was "the sheer obesity" of the afternoon that drew his ire. "I will not call again, I will not call again, I will not call again," he scrawled in his book, a bad school boy hard at work on his punishment.

He made a pot of coffee and picked up the novel Aunt Ruth had sent as a gift—*The Awakening*, a literary classic to which he'd not yet gotten around. After a few slow pages, during which the female protagonist proved herself to be dour and petulant, Ink nodded off, only to be roused some indeterminate time later by rap music down the hall. Bad, black coffee sat heavily on his tongue. He wiped his lips with the back of the hand, trying to imagine how much lower he could sink. Next door, the phone suddenly rang, and the first thing Ink thought was that Perri must have misdialed. Hang up, try again, don't give up, he said to himself. The phone grew silent, and Ink waited. He counted to a hundred, but there was not another ring. He slouched under his covers and turned in tears toward the wall.

*

The following night—insult to injury—Danny came to Ink's room with slip-slidy eyes and a somnambulistic blonde to ask if he could use his room for a while.

"Seriously?"

"Wetzler's in the middle of his semi-annual pornathon."

Ink looked back into his room. "I need to study."

"We've got no place to go." Danny lowered his voice. "Like Mary and Joseph."

"Is that my problem?" Ink intended to sound firm, to stop Danny right in his tracks, but his voice snapped in two.

"Come on, man," Danny whispered, squeezing his shoulder. "Aren't you flattered I thought of you?"

Ink looked past him to the girl in the hall, whose head rested against the glass of a fire extinguisher case, her painted mouth agape. Her satin blouse was already unbuttoned to the bra. Pretty, of course.

Sexy.

"Come on, Danny," she mumbled. "We going to or not?"

Danny raised his brows; Ink closed his eyes. "Just give me"—he glanced back at the girl—"a half hour."

Ink sighed.

"Twenty fucking minutes!"

Ink plodded downstairs to the first floor lounge and stared at music videos. Women, women, women—they were everywhere, showing off legs and breasts and butts, twisting into positions that almost made him cry. When he returned to his room, the message board hanging on his door had one marker-smeared word: "DONE!"

Ink put his hand on the knob, pulling first then turning, forgetting how the door worked. When it opened, he smelled sweat and perfume and booze. The sheets on his bed were in the shape of a drizzle on an obscene dessert. He felt used. Violated. Fed up.

*

In a booth at CGs, Ink sat rigid, pen stuck on a bare sheet of notebook paper, a plate of limp fries and a draft beer sweating all over the table. How long must he wait for something of his own? Twenty-one already, and nothing to show for it but a wrestling match with a girl who wasn't worth his time. "Once," he wrote, the black dripping thick onto the page. "Once, I want bare shoulders, hard nipples, soft thighs. I want all that screaming, sweating, and clutching. Then, the explosion . . . the sweet pouring out." In that moment of climax, Ink was convinced something astounding would occur—a revelation, an epiphany, a (as he phrased it in his notebook) "reforging of the very core of being."

"Fuck," he wrote, tracing over the word again and again, each time pressing the pen more firmly against the paper until the point tore through. He finished his beer and yanked the page from the notebook, squeezed it in his hand. Once. Twice. And again for good measure.

*

Buzzed, bloated with both anger and desire, Ink rapped on Perri's dorm room door later that night.

"Oh hi," she said, neither surprised or disappointed. Her face looked different—a smattering of freckles, small squinty eyes,

227

bloodless chapped lips. It took him a few moments to realize she was wearing no makeup at all.

"I've been trying to call you," Ink said, speaking carefully. "I had to go home the other day. My father. He collapsed."

"Oh dear! Is he ok?"

"He's fine," Ink said, swallowing hard from an attack of nerves. He was, without question, a complete coward. He'd come to the room with that foolproof plan for sympathy—he'd rehearsed it, in fact, several times in his mind—but now that the time came to put it into action, he panicked. "It turned out to be nothing," he said. "But my mom thought I should go home."

"You did the right thing."

He shrugged and pulled out a box of chocolates from behind his back.

Her eyes widened. "From Broussard's?"

"Well, you must have a birthday coming up."

"Believe it or not, it's today!"

Ink thought a moment. "Today? February 29th?"

She laughed. "That's right. I'm still five years old!"

"Let's play house" was the line that slid to the tip of Ink's beer-loosened tongue. Something, however, told him to say, "Want to hang out?" instead.

She annoyed him by glancing at the clock on her desk. "For a bit," she said. "Find me something with a jelly center."

"You actually like those?"

"I may be the only one."

It was a god-awful struggle to open the candy. Ink turned the box over and over looking for a tab on the cellophane to give him a start. He scratched with his meager nails. He took out his dorm key and started to dig at the wrapping. Nothing doing.

"Let me work my magic," she said, gently taking the box from his grasp and slitting the plastic with a pretty nail.

"I would've been here all night," he said, only aware of the deeper meaning of the words after they'd tumbled from his mouth. Their eyes met briefly, but he couldn't tell what she thought of such a possibility.

While she tested a series of necklaces against her blouse at the full-length mirror, Ink studied the chart on the other side of the lid. "Carmelaide?" he asked.

"Umm, that'll do."

He brought the box to her, watched her bite into the creamy square and laugh when she had to scoop filling with a finger into her mouth. "It's good!"

Ink sat down at her desk, looking for the square with the most striking candyscape. Perri went back to the mirror and began to apply eyeliner.

"Going somewhere?" he asked.

She nodded cryptically as she drew lipstick across her mouth, sculpted a knee-weakening dip in the upper lip. When she finished, she patted her lips with a Post-It note and stuck the yellow square on his cheek.

"Here's a kiss for you."

Kiss! Kiss? In their time together, all he'd gotten was one measly handshake. Now, out of nowhere, she was throwing out the word "kiss." Was this some kind of promise of future passion? It had more the scorch of torture. He thought of the condom in his wallet—one-twelfth of Danny's birthday gift to him. What would it really cost her in the end, ten minutes of in and out?

For something to do, he clicked on the TV. There was some charity event—a pet telethon—and two elegantly dressed news anchors stood in front of a row of volunteers waiting for phones to ring.

"Aww," Perri said, sitting on the bed and crossing her legs. "I tell you right now, the first black lab I see, I'm really going to lose it."

He waited for few moments and then sat next to her. He could not believe his boldness, but Perri, engrossed in the program, didn't seem to notice.

"Another?" he said, offering the box of candy.

She reached, felt for another piece, eyes never leaving the screen. He watched with her for a time, did his best to be patient. He never knew how much Perri adored animals and when he asked her about it, she told heart-rending stories of how she'd help wounded or abandoned strays, bringing them to the vet, calling her indulgent mother for money for the shots, the casts, the operations—whatever it was they needed. Afterward, she'd bug friends and acquaintances, sometimes even strangers on the street, and find homes for them all. As she spoke, an idea started forming in Ink mind. A question, really, the question that had sprung to his tongue several minutes before.

When the commercial break came, Ink, still clinging to the buzz from his beers, decided to go ahead and ask. "Do you," he said, swallowing for more courage, even as he realized drink and desperation had made him a total fool. "Would you . . . like to play house?"

Perri looked at him, lips moist with fresh lipstick, green eyes widening.

He tried to smile without shaking. "That's what five year olds do."

She smiled, tentatively, but then those eyes escaped to his forehead. Undaunted, he leaned into the freshly made up face. Her lips did not pucker, but neither did they run. He closed his eyes, and then there he was, resting against her face, his lips beginning to move around hers. Tender, he reminded himself. Tender. After a few moments, he withdrew, applauding his gentlemanly restraint. When he opened his eyes, he saw a face that was serious and sad. He went in again, more aggressively this time, thinking perhaps that was the key. It took some time, but Ink felt a counterforce that he thought, for a thrilling moment, must have been passion. A few seconds later, sure she was simply doing him a favor, he gave up and slumped forward, pointing his eyes toward the telethon and taking in the absurd parade of animals across the screen. After a time, he assessed her profile, looking for signs her interest has begun to wane. Ink had been here for an hour and it was about high time for the TV to be off, the lights down, and Perri straddling him, her groin hungry against his own.

"Have a heart," the anchor said, trying to keep the animal's paws from her dress.

Ink felt like a dog, something ugly like the one right now prancing on TV—a dainty Pekinese, its face looking like the rolls of skin on a fat person's neck. With head down, he rose and slumped into the chair by her desk. He told himself not to whimper.

A commercial came on, and Perri went back to primp in the mirror. With nothing better to do, Ink plopped a local phone book in his lap and began paging through it—the As, the Bs, the Cs. So many names, so many people—and just in this puny town. How many were getting laid? Right now? Not just the beautiful people, but the homely ones too—people with big noses; people whose faces were red and purple with acne; people with body odor and bad breath, skin rashes and V.D. Could it be that hard? After all, women wanted it just as much as men. He'd seen them through the tall, curvy windows at Ad Nauseam, thrusting hips at guys they hardly knew, letting them put hands on their thighs and behinds as if they were simply shaking hands and saying good to meet you. Sex was just an appetite, as natural as eating.

"Come here," Perri said, and when he looked up he saw a softness in her face that, although encouraging, didn't seem to fit the mood. If he was not mistaken, he even saw a twitch of resignation on her lips.

"What?" Ink said petulantly, still clutching the phone book.

She returned to the bed and patted a patch of mattress next to her leg. "Just come."

Ink shuffled over to the bed where she smiled at him.

"What?" he said, a little softer now.

She put a hand on his shirt and began to pull it out of his jeans.

"What?" He swallowed hard, gazing into her sad green eyes.

"Shhhh," she said, unbuckling the belt, brushing fingers against his stomach hairs before sliding them down, reaching beneath the rising surface of his boxers.

"Jesus," he whispered, still looking at her eyes, which had lowered to focus on the task. Her hand was cold, but soft, so soft that he didn't know how he could bear it.

"Oh God," he said, eyes wide and full of reverence.

Perri bestowed upon him a Mona Lisa smile. He moved to her, wanting the lips again as well. She kissed him once, quickly. She pressed her nose against his.

"Call now," the voice on the TV said. "Save this dog."

Ink opened his eyes, looked down at the flapping belt buckle, the fabulous punching inside his briefs, assuring himself that yes yes yes this was happening beyond a doubt as his legs began to tingle, tingle until they disappeared into an ecstasy of numbness. This was absolutely everything, the best moment of his life—the unprecedented point toward which the whole world had been heading. Perri shifted her body, keeping the motion going as every single particle of his being spilled into this, this thing, smashing against this final obstacle—bam, bam, bam—and when he broke through he'd be a different kind of person—older, wiser, a man. Stroke, stroke, stroke. The enormous, pent up force drove one more time against the barrier before bursting out of him, pouring and pouring and he didn't care where, let the world drown in the damn stuff if that was how it had to be.

Just as quickly came the disgust. "Stop, stop, please let go," he said, remembering Perri, the room, Whitman and his "amorous wet." He slid off the bed, pulling up his pants as the pale gunk continued to run.

"I'm sorry," is all he could think of to say. "This was wrong. You . . . shouldn't have."

Pushed back—blocked again and again during all his animal pursuits—the weight of God now collapsed full force upon him. How selfish he'd been. How monstrous! Oozing remorse, he made a panicked vow to go to confession to cleanse his miserable soul. From here on out, he'd become a perfect saint.

"It's okay," Perri said, smiling sadly, sitting up, surreptitiously wiping her hand with a wad of tissue.

The telethon went on. Ink listened to the pleading announcers, the occasional ringing of the phones, the desperate chirping of a poodle next on the adoption block. Ink pushed shirt into jeans and feverishly latched his belt. Perri, oblivious to his shame, let her eyes drift back toward the TV. He could feel the penis in his briefs, soft now, listing to the right: a tired old man, he thought, or maybe a baby's runny nose.

The End of History,
Once and for All

(Summer 1992-Spring 1993)

The tedious, coffee maker drip drop of summer: with the flood gates of senior year bowing against the surge, Ink figured it was for the best. During the days, he worked the call box at the Sears in Middleburg Heights. When the tape spit from the machine, he ripped the ticket and weaved with the two wheeler through the fumy stockroom to find merchandise. Back at the freight elevator, he slid the microwave or washer or whatever off the blade of the cart, punched the up button, and returned to the Faulkner that was blowing his mind. When a coworker asked what in the world he was doing, he said, "Adding mind to a mindless occupation." He loved that one—loved the fact that this would go a long way toward securing a reputation as the one young man of substance in a department store of drones.

The first few weekends home, he met up with Ant and Rick—boys who less than four years ago he could not live without. They drank cheap pitchers at Carousel Lanes, shot pool with warped sticks, and nudged each other at the sight of a half way decent girl bending to pick up a spare. Afterward, they enjoyed a nightcap of drive thru burgers and fries. Summer fun, Ink would dutifully remind himself, toothbrush in mouth in front of the bathroom mirror, stomach squawking like the door to his piss-colored Nova.

In July—a bolt from the blue—Sandro called. Once his "best friend in the world," he was back in town for just a week and had time for a quick cup of coffee at the Coventry Arabica. He arrived late, wearing a black silk shirt and designer jeans. His hair resembled a furrowed field, glistening with rain. He talked a lot about music—obscure, small-label, critically acclaimed groups he'd been following long before they'd been noticed.

"Nirvana?" Ink said.

"Sure, sure, Nirvana," he said, disappointed if that was the best

Ink could do. Sandro talked about fraternity life ("You don't know what you're missing"), his winter mission work in Mexico ("We made a real difference"), and, of course—how could he forget?—the trip with the school band to the Cotton Bowl ("Sometime I'll tell you about this Mindy—what years of piccolo playing has taught her to do"). Ink had little to talk about except the intricacies of point of view in *As I Lay Dying*.

"Yeah, I heard of it," Sandro said with a shrug. He turned a page of the *Scene* magazine, reading quietly for a minute while Ink studied the "For Rent" posters on the cork board behind him.

At the counter, his friend said, "It's on me." Ink slouched behind him while Sandro chatted up the spritely barista. Only after he was home did he have possible names for what he'd felt like the whole time: a baby brother, maybe a charity case.

In early August, Ink was surprised to see Nina with her family at mass. They'd moved to North Olmsted—to St. Richard's parish— several years ago, but the family had returned to have Fr. Nadolny celebrate the parents' twenty-fifth wedding anniversary. They took up the gifts—the portly, Hawaiianish father in his too-tight suit, the svelte pale mother in heels and a flower print dress, the younger brother crabby in a white Oxford and tie, and Nina, of course, in a yellow sundress and high heels she couldn't quite work. "Cute" was the word that again jogged through Ink's mind. On the way back from communion, he risked a nod. When she saw him, she gave him an O-shaped smile and a furtive wave from her hip. In the vestibule, feeling like a school boy between Mom and Mrs. Breen, Ink didn't know whether to dread or welcome Nina's approach.

"This is *so* amazing. I was *just* thinking of you!" she said, a hand in the air between them.

She was taller than usual—almost eye to eye—and closer to him than she'd ever been in his life. He'd never been a fan of short hair, but those Cleopatra bangs, the sleek sweep of hair towards her chin, made him shift and sweat so much it took him a few moments to understand that she was passing along an invitation to a party next week, a grade school reunion thing. Celeste Aaron—remember her? Well, her aunt was letting her use her house in Rocky River, right on the lake, a private beach and everything! Sandro was going. Lance too. Maybe Macho—"not that you're much a fan!" She was even "in talks" with Bethany Hyde, the love of Ink's elementary school life. If she could swing a baby sitter, she said she'd drop by for a bit.

Ink rolled up the church bulletin in his hands. He had a vision of bikinis and fruity red drinks and skinny dipping on a dare.

"You really should come!"

"I'll have to see." The party sounded exciting, but Ink was annoyed by the seemingly accidental nature of the invitation.

Nina grabbed away his bulletin and wrote her number in the open space beneath the ad for Ripepi's funeral home. "Call me," she said, fingers to ear and lips, before clicking after her parents.

"That Nina's always been such a pleasant girl," Mom said later, as Ink stood by the kitchen counter, shivering in the central air, waiting for BLT bread to toast. He turned to the table, where she sat with *The Plain Dealer*, getting an early jump on the day's massive crossword puzzle.

"What is she exactly?"

"What do you mean?"

"She's definitely . . . ethnic."

Ink didn't know how far east in Europe one had to travel before reaching a country whose inhabitants, upon moving to the United States, would now be considered minorities. Was she Romanian? Turkish? Ink thought again of her father. Pacific Islander?

"Nice smile," Mom said without looking up.

"Is Dad ever coming down for lunch?"

"Beautiful skin."

"Is Dad—"

Mom sighed. "He's his own person."

Something had been happening to his parents for years. They still ate dinner together and went to eleven a.m. mass and muttered banal courtesies to each other at customary points during the day. In the evenings, they still retired to the living room, Mom slouched on the sofa to read one of her religious books, and Dad with perfect posture studying the stars in the Queen Anne chair. To end the evening, they'd watch in silence an hour of TV. If they seemed close, it was only because they scrupulously avoided talking about the things that would underscore the distance. A lot of it had to do with family tensions: the disturbing behavior of Uncle Lare, Mom's side of the family, which, with the exception of an older sister who called on rare occasions, pretended that she did not exist. But perhaps the real problem was just marriage itself, the day-in day-out that was bound to do anyone in. When Ink complained to Ant about his parents' icy relationship the week before, his friend said, "Better than throwing shit." Maybe, but Ink would have liked to see a firework or two, just so he could judge for himself.

Dad came down for lunch, and they ate their sandwiches. Ink thought it might be more pleasant to have a picnic in an office elevator. Later, Dad went out to trim the hedges, and Ink, bored out of his skull, went out to help. They started on opposite ends of the bushes, stopping occasionally to mop faces with shirts. When they began snipping right next to each other, Dad smiled, tipped back his Indians cap. "I'm dying out here," he said, wiping his brow with a palm. Ink thought of bombing comedians—the hot lights, the cold, brick wall behind them, the deafening silence. He wanted to say something to bail out him out; instead, he just nodded and leaned deeper into the bush, tips pressing like a crown of thorns against his chest. It gave him something else to think about. For the time being, it was better than going back inside to freeze.

*

On the night of the party at the lake, Ink was under the blankets on his bed, Pearl Jam in his ears to block out Trouble, the yapping dog that was still going strong after all these years. Ink looked down at the church bulletin resting in his lap. There was something about Nina's five—the way she'd flipped it like a ponytail in the back—that made him catch his breath. He imagined the scene: Nina in a nice one piece, legs tucked demurely under her bottom; Sandro, an arm around the neck of his latest babe, saying "Notre Dame, Notre Dame, blah, blah, blah"; Macho, arriving fashionably late, reeking of cologne, the girls rushing to surround him; Bethany, bags under the eyes, sloppy around the waist, a snotty boy in tow.

He got up and brushed his teeth. He slathered deodorant under his arms. He put on one shirt then another, but each looked equally dumb in the mirror. He sat on the bed and watched the clock's red numbers for half an hour. Finally, he picked up *The Sound and the Fury*, his next classic in the cue. With each dense and difficult page he labored through, he became more convinced of the fact that he knew how to spend time better than just about everyone else in the world.

*

236

The start of fall semester meant so many things: an escape from the frigid solemnity at home; the return to the classroom, buzzing with big ideas; black coffee and cool talk at The Bean Bag; Saturday night club hopping on The Bell. Ink returned to campus filled to the brim with entitlement. He was, after all, a senior. He knew campus and town like the back of his hand. In an important way, he owned them. How pathetic were these newcomers, sweat cascading down their faces, campus maps spinning like kaleidoscopes in shaky hands, wide-eyed parents sagging under the burden of plastic crates of books and toiletries. How wonderful to know the drill—to smoothly be able to slip back into a world he'd finally gotten the best of.

But even before he plugged in the compact fridge and arranged books by course upon his shelf, Ink knew that Freitag Hall was not the home he had once known. Jesse had made a last-second decision to live off campus with new, "awesome" bandmates who were committed—*really* committed—to their music. Cobb, despite his incessant complaining, was determined to stick things out at his fraternity house. Danny had signed on again to live with Wetzler and an ever-revolving cast of brain-addled boys. Even Xavier, the straight-laced boy he'd eat dinner with in a pinch, was gone now, living by himself in Dolan, the quiet dorm on the other end of campus. Diego roomed with Ink again, but as usual, he lived a hermitic life in the library stacks. There were his English major "friends"—Scott McAveney or Tamika Johnson—but with them he often felt he was in a competition for which he was ill-prepared.

The upshot was that Ink was alone; in many ways, it was like freshman year all over again. That first evening, he felt the burn of humiliation as he walked with a tray of food through the cafeteria, every table having the impromptu party of a lifetime. To make matters worse, many of these kids were freshmen—they'd paid no dues and their faces seemed annoyingly free of pain or doubt. Ink sat all the way in the back, at the far ends of tables with small groups of outcasts who tried to pass for normal—a mullethead and two metal t-shirt friends; a girl with underarm hair and a dreadlocked beau; a trio of black wrapped girls, conversing ferociously in a language he wouldn't dare to guess the name of.

Ink began arriving at the cafeteria twenty minutes before it closed, when there were fewer students and he would look less conspicuous eating alone. One evening, while filling his cup at the pop dispenser, someone shouted his name. He turned to see Scott beckoning him to a table, where he sat with Tamika and—much to his chagrin—dumpy Katy Fuster. Last year, for a time, Ink had tried to get from her what he could; however, the episode had been a disaster. Afterward, he'd kept his distance, certain she'd expose him in front of others for the creepy loser that he was. With trepidation, he approached, orange drink sloshing onto his tray.

"We're having an argument," Scott said. "And we need you to cast the definitive vote."

"You've got an odd number already," Ink said.

"This is one of those third world democracies. I'm going to vote at least twice."

Smiling, Ink sat down.

"Katy says Hemingway is . . . what's the theoretical term?"

"Horseshit," she said, glaring at Ink from across the table.

Scott laughed. "That's right. And Tamika agrees, although her assessment is a bit more . . . diplomatic."

In the American Modernism course, they'd had an animated discussion about gender politics in Hemingway's short fiction. Ink smiled, nodded, burger bun gummy in his mouth. There was no real advantage in siding with Scott, who would, as he did with most things, laugh it off. He would never side with Katy because her goal in life was to shoot down the male writers they studied with her vast arsenal of feminist opinions. In Ink's mind, she took great, angry joy in bringing up female writers they'd never heard of, writers most of their "dead white guy profs" were "afraid" to teach. Tamika was nice enough, with kind eyes, a generous smile, and an endearingly husky laugh. When she played Bennie in *A Raisin in the Sun* last fall, he had been surprised to start thinking about her as attractive. But every time he studied her after that performance, the words "attractive" and "black" held a drag race in his brain, and the latter always seemed to win by a nose. Because he felt terrible about the outcome, Ink always made sure to be nice and respectful towards her.

"Hemingway is," he said, pausing for a drink. They all looked at him, eager to hear what he had to say. It was a rare moment of power. "Hemingway," he said, "is our country's greatest short story writer."

"He's a misogynist pig!" Katy said, stabbing at her salad.

"Just because he presents women being treated poorly," Scott said, "doesn't mean he hates women."

Tamika said, "'Hills' is to me like this great short play." She held a cup of tea in both hands to her lips. "The dialogue is amazing. The subtext."

Ink nodded, remembering a paper he wrote about this story in high school. There was so much in it that he'd missed the first, the second, and even the third time through. So much tension roiling beneath the surface.

"In one of my theater classes last semester," Tamika continued, "we performed an adaptation. That 'Please, please, please' line at the end—it's so powerful when you hear it out loud."

"I actually feel sorry for the woman," Scott said.

"Me too," Tamika said.

"Uh oh," Ink said, slapping a napkin in front of his smile. "The feminist front is crumbling!"

The four went around and around, talking boys and girls, men and women, patriarchy and victimhood. Phallocentric writing, l'ecriture feminine. Who was right and who was wrong. Who was good and who was evil.

"It's not that we want to be better than men," Katy said at last. "We just need you"—and here she nodded at Ink and Scott—"to be more, I don't know, human."

Scott stood and bared his teeth. He hunchbacked his tray towards the conveyor belt.

Tamika laughed, and Ink, more self-consciously, followed suit. After an eye roll, even Katy broke reluctantly into a smile.

*

The Modernism course switched to poetry, the baffling fragments and juxtapositions of Eliot's *The Waste Land*.

"What do you think?" Dr. Sikma asked.

Everyone was intimidated by this young, newish professor: his glistening, concise hair, the expensive cologne, the goatee, the dark, perpetually dubious eyes. He'd been brought in to develop a graduate program and made it clear to his students the first day that in this course, he was going to treat everyone as if this were the first class for their Master of Arts. Ink looked down at his notebook, pretended to write even though there were no terms on the board to be recorded.

When Ashley Grace pronounced the poem "total garbage," Sikma shook his head and said, "I won't accept such a lazy dismissal. It's the height of ignorance."

Ashley's mouth dropped open.

"Next time, please think—really think—before you speak."

Sikma looked around for other hands, and, seeing none, continued: "Everything you believed when you came in here—it should have been thrown out long ago. It's not good for now. It doesn't rate. After you've studied this stuff, after you've seriously considered what these writers have to say and why they had to say it in their own inimitable way, then you can go back to your old ideas and sweep up what's worth saving."

"Like Eliot?" Katy asked. "Like what he's saying at the end of the poem?"

"Ah, someone gets it," Sikma said, a sardonic smile breaking across his face. Katy turned and caught Ink's eye. She beamed, and he pinched his face in her direction.

For the rest of the semester, Katy seemed to "get it" just a little more than Ink. Response papers, midterm, oral presentation—on each assignment, Katy scored slightly better. When he was not around, he was sure she gloated—sure that she took out her graded work in front of Scott and Tamika to explain in detail all the ways she came out on top. He began to go to dinner at times when he knew the others would not be present. When Katy asked him after class one day to come to an organizational meeting for the literary magazine, he said, refusing to look at her face, that he was busy. He was determined to keep his distance from them all.

*

"Is it a competition?" Jesse asked. It was late November, and Ink was sitting with Cobb and Jesse at the Glasshouse Diner devouring baskets of fried vegetables and cheese.

"It's just," Ink said, holding up a brown finger of mozzarella. "It's just that she's always so sure of things. So smugly certain."

"Perhaps," Cobb said, "our young friend is in love."

Ink smiled. "Don't you have a face to stuff?"

"You just have to be your own person."

Ink looked at Jesse. His friend was a psychology major whose senior research had something to do with rejection and self-esteem. Was 'Be your own person' really the best he could do?

*

As the semester drew to a close, Ink's anger cooled. There was a comprehensive final exam in Modernism, and if he hoped to survive it, he'd need Katy's help. Once again, he swallowed his pride and began sitting with his English friends for dinner. He endured Katy's diatribes with little or no resistance. When Scott asked him to be part of their study group, he of course assented, even bringing with him to the student center lounge a box of chocolate chip cannoli from Giotto's.

"You're my hero!" Tamika said, smiling brightly at him. As they reviewed the literature and quizzed each other, Ink found himself glancing again and again at Tamika. Objectively speaking, she was much better looking than Katy. Plus she was warm and gracious. He tried to imagine going out with her on a date. He tried to imagine kissing those lips.

"Should we go on to Stevens?" Scott asked.

"Yes, yes," Katy said, eyes filling with venomous joy. She did not, as Ink expected, go on about the poet's supposedly sexist views; rather, she praised him for so artfully exposing as a fraud the "master narrative of Christianity."

Ink cringed and he, somewhat lamely, mustered a defense of tradition. But truth be told, mass had become a real chore for him. If he remembered God during the week, it was usually when an examination loomed, when emaciated, fly-haloed children appeared on the evening news, when he was nodding off in his dorm room after a surprisingly good dinner.

"'Death is the mother of all beauty,'" Katy said, alluding to "Sunday Morning," her new favorite poem.

"No it isn't," Ink said. Church might be a chore and God a forgotten friend, but there was no way he was going to let some smart-ass girl sit there and trash the afterlife.

Katy laughed and, in Sikmaesque fashion, praised Ink for his exquisitely conceived rebuttal. She went on to talk about Stevens' courageous romanticism. "He doesn't need Jesus. He doesn't even need an Oversoul. This world is more than enough."

"Didn't he convert on his deathbed?" Scott said with a wink.

241

"'Let be be finale of seem,'" Katy said, lips sealed with smugness.

Ink fumbled and fumed through another response, but as he spoke all he could see was that foolish, hapless man from Jack London's famous story—the one who tried to start a fire under a tree weighed down by heavy snow.

*

Shortly after the beginning of the new—his last ever!—semester, Ink sat with Diego in The Bean Bag to watch the new president's inaugural speech.

Today we celebrate the mystery of American renewal. This ceremony is held in the depth of winter. But, by the words we speak and the faces we show the world, we force the spring. A spring reborn in the world's oldest democracy, that brings forth the vision and courage to reinvent America.

Despite the cold, despite the magnitude of the moment, there was Bill Clinton offering the world his perpetual smile—bemused, cocky, wry, not unlike a ball-capped boy at the back of the class. Ink couldn't help smiling to himself. Clinton was the first politician who spoke his language. He would not soon forget him playing "Heartbreak Hotel" on Arsenio Hall, eyes closed over the saxophone, a presidential candidate for the first time in human history being cool.

"Turn that man off," Mom had said last summer, bulling into the living room with a heaped up basket of laundry.

"*That man* is going to be the next president of the United States."

"If you vote for him, what do you think God's going to say?"

Ink knew Clinton was pro-choice. He knew all the sordid details of the Flowers affair. But as he sat now with his roommate in the campus coffee shop watching the rest of the speech, he thought once again: What did those things matter in the face of such intelligence and energy and, yes, charisma?

When our founders boldly declared America's independence to the world and our purposes to the Almighty, they knew that America, to endure, would have to change. Not change for change's sake, but to preserve America's ideals— life, liberty, the pursuit of happiness. Though we march to the

242

music of our time, our mission is timeless.

Ink sipped his flavored coffee, pleased by how the change in administration coincided so well with his own coming of age.

"It's a new day," he announced. At last, his senior year had found the shape it had been looking for.

Diego wiped his glasses on his shirt. "I suppose."

"You don't believe—?"

"Every new president promises a revolution."

"Well, Clinton is different."

Diego's shoulders did their quick, quizzical leap. It was an old, familiar gesture that seemed to say, "What do I know?" This time, though, Ink detected a trace of confidence, of condescension, as if Diego knew full well he was in the right. He wanted to challenge his roommate, ask him straight out: "Do you like me? Respect my opinions? Do you think I'm just like all the rest?"

Ink left the coffee shop buzzed from caffeine and rich rhetoric. "Our time," "change to preserve America's ideals"—phrases from the speech kept darting back and forth in his mind. He found himself at the campus gate, in front of the old stone ring, the empty rose window through which, a few years before, he and his friends had hurtled, thinking with a wink that they could alter the course of future events. Now, though, Ink was completely serious. He would step through and change for once and for all. He would read the daily papers and watch the news with renewed, religious vigor. When necessary, he'd write long, articulate, impassioned letters to the editor. He would join Clinton's new benevolent army and do his part to fulfill its noble vision.

Then, as usual, the semester took off, and he barely paid attention to the news that swirled around him: gays in the military, health care reform, the violent splintering of Yugoslavia. He was too busy with "Willa Cather: Her Life and Art," the senior capstone course for English majors, which required a twenty-page scholarly paper, a fifteen-minute oral presentation, and a cumulative essay exam. Plus there were three other courses—Renaissance Literature, Early American history, and Anthropology—plenty to keep him occupied. Up early for hurried mouthfuls of powdered eggs in the cafeteria, then off to class. Lunch? Maybe—unless he was running late for the next place he had to be. Occasionally, he ate dinner with Scott or Diego, but most of the time he was alone, too busy to wring his hands about the unfortunate goings-on in the world. Evenings were spent reading and recopying notes, worrying over sentences of a paper in the computer lab. A midnight pot of coffee gave him the push he needed to finish the rest of his day's work.

On the weekends, he met Jesse and Cobb (and, on rare occasions, Danny) at Hangovers or CGs for long smoky nights of beer and loud cover bands and the knee-weakening parade of finely dressed girls. Sundays, he nursed hangovers, completed his work between catnaps at his desk, worked at the library for a few hours in the late afternoon. He managed to get most everything done and pretty well, wiping the slate as clean as possible for yet another insanely busy week. In the frenzy of activity, there was no sane moment to sit back and say, "These are the best days of my life." Only a second, it seemed, to wrap his brain around the idea that "This is one of the last times I'll do X." At times, Ink felt not unlike the central character in an Elizabethan tragedy, still standing tall in Act V, but with the bodies piling up around him.

One night at the end of February, he went to Open Mike's to see the debut of Jesse's blues band, A Little Knowledge. When he arrived, they were already on stage, loud and fuzzy, Jesse's face ablaze with joy as he bounced his palm against the whammy bar of a Stratocaster. The singer, a tattooed man in a muscleman tee, sweat running from his huge bald head, sang in a growly baritone:

No one taught me gee-tar
No one said I could sing.
But I've learned a little knowledge
Can be a VER-y dangerous thing!

As they finished their signature tune, Ink spotted Cobb and Rebecca, Jesse's latest girlfriend, sitting at a table with a couple he didn't recognize. He felt suddenly shy, excluded, and watched the rest of the set—a Muddy Waters song, something the singer said was by Stevie Ray—while sulking over a beer at the back end of the bar.

When the band finished, Jesse leapt off the stage, arms out for Rebecca, who hurried into them.

Beating back jealousy, Ink took a deep breath and approached. "Good job, man," he said.

"I thought I saw you back there. Thanks for coming!"

"Blues is like Latin," Cobb said.

Jesse ran a hand through glistening hair. "What do you mean?"

"It's a dead language."

"You're so full of shit."

Cobb smiled, wiping his damp brow with a napkin. "I take that as a compliment."

When they all sat down, Cobb introduced his date, which, after the beauty of Susan, was a bit more like it. Greg and Brin, the boy and girl beside him, were friends of Rebecca—nice enough people, Ink supposed, but not interested in him in the least. It didn't take long for him to realize he was a hapless adjunct to the evening's fun. He sipped his beer, looked around the room, and nodded as if he were doing important work. Inside, he was about to cry.

"Weren't you seeing that Perri girl?" Rebecca asked, exchanging a cryptic glance with Jesse.

Ink, caught off guard, shook his head. Perri Simmons. Last year, he'd helped her survive a literature class. They kissed a grand total of twice. And, of course, she did that other thing as well, which he realized now was just her gracious way of saying, "Leave me the hell alone."

"We've got to find you somebody," Jesse said, turning to Rebecca, who sucked a blue drink through a curlicue straw. She had shoulder-length auburn hair and large freckles that Ink wanted to eat like candy from her face. He had to hand it to Jesse—each of his girlfriends had been a marked improvement upon the last.

"What about her," Rebecca said, nodding toward the stage, where a big-boned girl in a paisley skirt was tuning her guitar. "I know her a bit."

"Hi everyone," the girl said, voice soft and darling as an eight year old's. "I'm Diamonda Hammond, and I'm a romantic, an idealist, a lover of goodness—of love—in whatever heartfelt form it takes."

"Diamonda?" Cobb said, doing his worst to hold back a smile.

It was simple: Ink did not want 1) a girl named Diamonda and 2) a girl who looked like she'd be more at home on a field hockey pitch.

He knew few things about relationships with the opposite sex, but of this much he was certain: the guy must always be bigger. Not necessarily taller, but if he had to pick one word for the quality he was looking for in a girl it might be "delicate." Not that he'd be dumb enough to say that to Rebecca, who seemed like she could be, like Katy Fuster, one of those girls who would be sure to find his opinion offensive.

Bread, Poco, England Dan—whatever it was, the gooey notes of Diamonda's first song glued Jesse and Rebecca together at the forehead. Cobb tried to move in on his new girl, but she seemed more interested in the singer on the stage. The other couple, Greg and Brin, began talking about an art house film they were dying to see. Ink, knowing when he was not wanted, went to the bar for another beer. He held a five between two fingers, buzzed enough to think this gesture was the epitome of cool. Maybe some svelte beauty would accidentally bump into him. Maybe he'd buy her a drink. Maybe they'd get to talking in a quiet corner, where the lights couldn't reach.

Ink got his bump sure enough, but it was one that would have sent him to the floor if a barstool hadn't stopped him.

"Sorry, man. Don't know my own strength." It was Danny— Danny Drellishak, the one and only. He had loose, wet lips and sleepy, red scratched eyes; in other words, he was drunk as a skunk. Someone behind them muttered "Jesus Christ." A tall, big-armed boy shoved Danny in the shoulder, said, "Well, well, if it isn't the crazy fuck." It pleased Ink to be, however unintentionally, a small part of this disturbance. He didn't even mind when Danny took the fresh beer from his hands and chugged it without stopping for a breath. The boy was the ticket that allowed Ink to return without shame to the table where Jesse and the others sat.

"I have a little question for you all," Diamonda said, giving the knobs of her guitar a few more careful twists. "What's so funny about peace, love, and understanding?"

"Where do I start?" Danny yelled at the stage.

Diamonda glanced over in the direction of the table but was otherwise undaunted. She began to sing about troubled times, about darkness and insanity, the love glow on her cheeks growing brighter with every line.

At the table, Danny rubbed his hands and said, "Well, they're getting awfully close."

"What are you talking about?" Jesse asked.

"You didn't hear? They tried to blow up the World Trade Center today."

"Who?" Ink asked. He almost said "Where?" as well, but figured that would come out soon enough.

"Them. Those terrorist fucks."

"It was all over CNN," Rebecca said. "On the way out, I saw an interview with this woman who said it was like a plane hit the building."

"Wow," Danny said. "Sounds like an excellent idea."

"I have family in New York!" Brin cried.

Danny crossed his arms. "Who are you?"

"I could ask you the same."

"Then why the hell don't you?"

Greg stood up, spilling a beer across the table. "Where do you get off—?"

"How about right here? All over your face."

Everyone was standing now, except for Ink, who, stunned by the sudden turn of events, looked down the thin dark neck of his bottle of beer.

"You need some serious help," Jesse said.

On stage, the strumming stopped and Diamonda, after a dramatic pause, whispered one more time: "What's so funny about peace, love, and understanding?"

"Chill, everybody," Danny said, stepping back, adjusting his Polo shirt. "I'm outta here."

When he was gone, Rebecca turned to Jesse and asked, "Friend of yours?"

"What do you think?" Jesse said, his tone defensive.

"Of yours?" Rebecca turned sharp blue eyes toward Ink.

He shrugged. Freshman year, desperate to matter, Ink had clung to Danny the way Ishmael held onto Queequeg's coffin. He was popular. He was supremely cool. Danny was, well, Danny—a force of nature, an American original. But this year, every time Ink saw him he was filled less with joy than with dread. The boy's obnoxiousness was playful—exciting even—when it worked within certain boundaries, but there were times (more and more often, it seemed) when he could in a flash become cruel. Even hateful.

"You know, this is the beginning of the end." Jesse downed his beer. "It's only a matter of time before bombs come to a neighborhood near you."

"I don't think we need to panic," Rebecca said.

Brin, Ink noticed, was in tears. Greg put an arm around her.

"Why'd they do it?" Ink asked, a question being the only thing he could think to add.

Diamonda was in the middle of another song—something, Rebecca let them know, by the Indigo Girls. The gentle picking and sweet voice were drowned out in places by the increasing din. A sudden shout from the bar made Ink jump. He tried to focus on the song, but through his mind rolled a series of images—lean, swarthy men dressed in white gowns, turbans like ominous whipped cream, mouths screwed up to form the words of their incomprehensible chants. He'd seen enough of them on the news, angry about one thing or another. A few years ago, they'd pronounced a death sentence—a "fatwad" or something—on a writer who poked fun at their religion. It was not enough to voice their displeasure, as Mom did when he'd told her he'd seen *The Life of Brian*. No, these freaks would not be happy until the writer was separated from his head. But so far, they hadn't been able to accomplish their goal, just as they hadn't been able to do any real damage to that soaring tower in New York. Maybe this was not, as Jesse believed, the beginning of the end. Maybe it was a total aberration. Caught with its guard down once, there was no way in hell that this great country would allow such a thing to happen again. His faith in this respect quickly became firm.

The next morning, Ink dragged himself to mass, where Fr. Kennedy, who typically held the congregation's attention with a combination of corny jokes and birthday party magician props, spoke simply and seriously about the attack. He talked about the power of hate and how everyone of us, whether from pride or ignorance or a desire for security, surrendered more and more control to this destructive emotion. "With our own hatred," he said, "we set the tone for the hatred of others." As if anticipating objections, Fr. Kennedy held up a hand and said, "But here's the good thing, the good news" and the good news was there was an opposite force—the power of love, the power of the gospel. If everyone, through compassion and humility, allowed this other power an "honest-to-goodness chance" to grow in their hearts, it would work a real and lasting revolution. In time, the power of love would conquer the entire world.

Ink closed his eyes. He couldn't help it. Last night, after they walked Rebecca back to her dorm, he and Jesse returned to The Bell to ogle the window dancers at Ad Nauseam. Later, they wandered drunk up and down the aisles of Quik Pik for a long, hazy time before settling on roast beef subs and a sixty-four-ounce Mountain Dew to split. Ink must have stumbled in at 3:30 or 4am—who knew? He remembered Diego turning in his bed to the light, squinting up to ask, "You okay?" and Ink, collapsing on his bed, smiled with the satisfaction that could only come from a night of too many drinks.

Ink knelt for the Eucharistic prayer. He yawned into his shoulder. What he wanted more than anything was a long nap—a few hours of sweet oblivion. He could have just slept in this morning, but he hadn't missed mass for the past three and a half years of his collegiate career. Perfect attendance despite exhaustion and pounding headaches; despite the long shadow of schoolwork due the following day; despite the same mind-numbing prayers, the same up and down and all that hard, back-straight time on the kneeler; despite the same saccharine hymns strummed and sung by gawky students with blissful smiles. Unlike his high school friends, Ink went to mass every single week and stayed until the last chord of the recessional song. He was not—he would never be—one of those spiritual lightweights who strolled in right before the gospel or who slunk out a side door right after Communion. He was, in a word, committed. It was something like his cross to bear.

*

By mid-semester, the capstone course had become a real slog. Out of all the great American writers—Melville, James, Hemingway, Faulkner—Dr. Long had chosen to focus on Willa Cather. Ink was sick to death of the plotlessness, the increasing austerity of the novels, the aching nostalgia for the past. The only saving grace was that Dr. Long had permitted him to bring Emerson (one of his literary heroes) into his major essay, which would, if he could get his act together, critique the misanthropic St. Peter from *The Professor's House* through the lens of "The American Scholar."

As often as possible, Ink would get together with his English friends to review lectures and share drafts of each other's work. During one session, he leaned back, messed up his hair, and said, "You know that wedding party? From *My Antonia*? If only she would have fed all of her characters to the wolves."

Scott laughed. "That would have certainly advanced her plots."

"Oh okay," Katy said, crossing arms over breasts. Because Tamika was at a rehearsal for the spring production, she was outnumbered—and, for that reason, even less happy than usual. "This is different from your beloved Faulkner how?"

"Faulkner is, I don't know, far more . . . interesting," Scott said, as if he were letting everyone know the temperature outside. "His characters aren't pining for the past, they're tortured by it."

Ink thought of Quentin and Shreve in that cold Harvard dorm room, trying to solve the mystery of Charles Bon. He always expected to have—at some point—the opportunity to be a part of such a weighty, late night conversation. So far, he'd only been a part of squabbles like this.

"Cather's characters are tortured too," Katy said. "You know, there are different, non-male ways of going—"

"'There's no such thing as was,'" Scott intoned.

Ink nodded, continuing Faulkner's famous quotation: "'Only is. If was existed, there would be no grief or sorrow.'"

Katy shook her head. She started thumbing through a novel for a quotation that might shut them up.

"Did you know she was a lesbian?" Scott said.

"Who?"

"Cather!"

"I don't see what a writer's sexuality . . ."

Ink glanced at Scott. He could feel his lips stretching across his face. A few weeks ago, Dr. Long had spoken quickly and with painful awkwardness about the writer's "intense personal relationships."

"What's so funny?" Katy asked, her eyes darkening.

"Why don't you get on him?" Ink said, thumbing at Scott. "He's the one who brought it up."

Scott threw his hands in the air. "Hey, hey, I'm just passing along information."

Katy slapped closed her notebook. "I've had enough," she said, sweeping up her backpack and cup of tea and stomping out of the lounge.

Ink was glad Tamika had been unable to attend the session. It meant that, after it was clear the girl would not return, he could turn to Scott and match him smile for smile.

That night, Ink stayed up late, forced his way through the rest of *Death Comes for the Archbishop*, a book as dry as his mouth would get before those long-ago basketball games. There was one scene that seemed to perfectly sum up Ink's attitude toward the work. Dining in Sandusky—in Ohio, the eventual home of Cedar Point—Latour tells his good friend Fr. Joseph of his plans to do missionary work in the remote southwest. Fr. Joseph objects to the idea. He does not want to go any farther than they already are. Ink starred the passage. Tomorrow he'd point it out to Scott for a laugh.

Class the next day—to his great surprise—was interesting. When Dr. Long asked for reactions, Katy declared the novel, "a beautiful book. Simply gorgeous."

Ink wasn't sure if the adjective or the adverb turned his stomach more. Perhaps it was the pompous combination of them both.

"I'm surprised," Scott said, raising his hand as an afterthought. "Cather is so old-fashioned, I expected you'd be blasting her left and right."

"Each sentence is a necklace of precious jewels."

"She's writing about Catholic priests," Scott responded. "About colonialism, if you care to face the truth. The importance of faith, of tradition . . . of, of . . . patriarchy!"

"She's exposing the simplistic views of colonizers. She's using religion, *appropriating* it in order to raise art to a higher level. It's like what St. Peter says in *The Professor's House* . . ."

Other students jumped in with observations, and Dr. Long sat down in an empty desk, wearing the stunned smile of someone who simply could not believe his good fortune.

Ink found himself torn. On the one hand, tradition was a stuffed animal—a soft and cozy thing that in a panic he could squeeze. He was a Catholic, a Clevelander too, a Glassmaker, and as a member of each community he enjoyed the comfort that came with being a part of something much bigger. He might be small—a virtual nobody—

but he was also a necessary link to all who were and all who would be. On the other hand, tradition was a terrible burden—a beast whose paw pressed down upon his neck. Emboldened by his careful rereading of Emerson, Ink had been giving more and more thought in the last few months to wiggling out from under this restraint. The question was: at what cost? It was all well and good to be self-reliant, but Ink still clung to the idea that he needed people behind and around him, telling him he was in the right place.

A few weeks later, his conundrum was solved when, after a long night spent revising his seminar essay, he woke to a bright window and an astonishing thought that hung like a carnival banner across his brain: YOU DO NOT HAVE TO GO, it read. YOU DO NOT HAVE TO GO. He lay in bed and watched the digital clock straight through the start of mass. The dorm suite began to awaken: primal groans, slamming doors, expletive-laced greetings, ambitious farts. Through it all, Ink watched with absentminded joy the red numbers change, one after the other. Eventually, he roused himself—showered and shaved, went to the dining room to devour a sausage omelet and a stack of pancakes. He returned to his room and dozed until one, when the sounds of an NBA game reached him from the lounge. With diamond-like clarity, he understood this: I am not going to be harmed.

Ink sat up and smiled. Wasn't this exactly what Joyce had meant by epiphany? He was uncommonly alert, the bold ideas coming quickly now: I am my own person, I will not be just another in a long long line, I will not add one more ounce of weight to the heaping, stinking rubbish pile of the past. He was being honest with himself for maybe the first time in his life. Like Emerson, he was going to stand boldly against all institutions in order to have a self for himself.

Over the next several days, Ink watched with some sadness but much exhilaration as his once-cozy house of faith burned all the way to the ground. He could see the charred beams tumbling through a blinding blaze. The following Sunday, a few embers of guilt and remorse still twirling around his head, he decided to conduct an experiment. He went back to church and said the prayers and sang the songs, wondering if the old feeling might return. In the communion line, Fr. Kennedy said, "The body of Christ," and Ink took the host in his palm, even though the words sounded now like a punch line to some silly grade school joke.

The experiment, Ink concluded, was a spectacular success.

Before he knew it—before he had a chance to prepare—the end of the semester arrived. Again, the panic, the despair. Sleepless nights in the computer lab. Bad black coffee and bleeding cuticles. The rhythmic chanting of terms and concepts for final exams. In a daze, he had to write an essay more or less off the top of his head. The Cather paper, of course, consumed every spare moment: sewing in more Emerson, simplifying a clunky introduction, correcting several citations, making a pronoun agree with its antecedent. The final two weeks of his college career began to remind him of "War Pigs," the Black Sabbath song this guy down the hall blared every Friday afternoon, in honor of the weekend. It was the end of the song Ink thought of, when the instruments sped up and up, turning into a sound like Alvin and the Chipmunks, before the break-neck finish, which always left Ink with the image of smoke curling out of a molten CD player.

His oral presentation of the Cather paper went well. Afterward, Ink, sweating in his tie and long-sleeved shirt, tried to remember how to breathe. Dr. Long placed a congratulatory hand upon his shoulder and, plagiarizing Emerson's note to Whitman, exclaimed, "I greet you at the beginning of a great career!" For a while, Ink stood on the periphery of the group, watching Scott, Tamika, Katy, and others talk excitedly with their parents (Mom and Dad had been unable to come because the old brown wagon broke down ten miles out of Cleveland). He wandered over to the refreshment table and took a chocolate chip cookie from the tray and, for something to do, studied the spines of old Clerestory yearbooks locked up on a shelf. He thought of all the kids within those pages. Candid photos of boys and girls from every year darting across the quad or relaxing in cramped dorm rooms or soliloquizing on stage or bunched together in bleachers to cheer the football team. Studio portraits of seniors on the verge of their futures. Boys and girls who were just getting started and boys and girls who were heading out into the real world. Of course, none of these kids was a kid any longer. Many, in fact, were probably no longer alive, having long since been folded like diced meat into the massive omelet of tradition. He gulped. He felt suddenly claustrophobic.

"Great job!" Katy said, jolting him from his reverie.

Stunned, Ink turned and, after an awkward moment, she shook his hand. "You too, you too," he said, somewhat lamely.

"Would have been better with a sprinkle or two of Hemingway."

"What?"

"Oh, I'm just kidding." Katy gave him a warm smile, and Ink was thrilled to see it, not that he wanted this girl or anything.

*

When the thick smoke of the semester cleared, Ink packed up, moved out for a handful of days, and then returned to campus for Senior Week, the ultimate reward for four years of hard work. It was the culmination of everything—a glorious, stress-free time out of time. The seniors were able to stay in Tyler, the brand new dorm, with its huge, brightly colored rooms, lavish common areas, and balconies. Lying on a comfortable bed, Ink could almost trick himself into thinking he was starting once again, infinitely wiser, better accommodated, and primed to face any challenge that might arise.

He did not kid himself for long. This was, without question, the end of things. All he had to do to understand this was look past the excursions, the cookouts, and the mixers on the senior week schedule and see that chilling word in CAPS: DEPARTURE. To think he'd been so brave just a few short weeks ago, rejecting tradition, striding confidently out from the lengthened shadows of the one institution most responsible for keeping him in the dark. Now, though, he wouldn't mind crouching in the shadow of college for a few more years.

Thankfully, Diego arrived, distracting him from his worries. His roommate set down a tote of clothes and a backpack of books, which he promptly began to arrange on the shelf above his desk.

"What are you doing?" Ink asked with a laugh. "Senior Week does not have an exam."

Diego picked up a book, something thick and obviously new. He opened it to the middle and stuck his face into the voluminous V. "There will be time," he said.

Ink bent down to read the spine: *The End of History.* "That about sums it up," he said, trying for the light touch even as the dark thoughts stretched back over him. When Ink stood, he felt the floor moving beneath him—a table cloth trick and he was the glass that never in a million years was going to stay put.

"You okay?"

"Ink smiled. "I think so."

254

But he did not truly feel better until there was beer, and plenty of it—graduation special, a dollar a draft—at Open Mike's. When Ink and Diego arrived, Jesse and Cobb were pushing tables together in front of the stage. Together, they laughed their way through a series of tedious acts: Diamonda Hammond removing the rage from a number of popular heavy metal tunes; a would-be comic who did a dumb bit about vowels, using the word "assonance" as much as he could; Stockton Rife, a steel-bearded local (and loco), who read a long but occasionally humorous poem called "Those Freshman Dumbfucks, Tender As Can Be." Evan Cole, a boy Ink briefly hung around with a few years before, hopped up on stage, did a handstand, and juggled ping pong balls with his bare feet. During the performances, Ink stole glances at Diego. He'd known his roommate for four years, and this was the first time he'd been out with him in a place other than a church or coffee shop. He seemed to watch everything with an anthropologist's eye; at times, he even let escape the rudiments of a smile. But was he enjoying himself? Did he know how to?

Danny arrived in grand fashion, slapping everyone way too hard on the back. He spilled into a chair and took a deep drink of Cobb's beer. He ordered a dozen burgers because they were two dollars each. A few minutes later, Diego finished his cola, stood, and laid a five on the table. "I think I'm going to turn in," he said, smiling politely.

"To what?" Danny asked with his tilde smile. "A toad? A princess? A real-life Mexican?"

Ink looked down at his drink.

"Easy, Danny," Jesse said, thumbs nervously smoothing down his sideburns.

"Good night," Diego said.

"Your pesos—they no good." Danny crumpled the bill into a ball and shot it into the empty pitcher of beer.

"My money is as good as yours."

"Who exactly do you think you are?"

"Dude, dude, what ails you?" Whenever Cobb had too much to drink, he tended to speak in some strange, affected manner that only he found funny.

"Are you for real?"

"In the phenomenological sense?"

Danny stood, eyes narrowed, jaw set, as if he'd been savagely insulted. Ink, risking a look, tried like crazy to figure out what had been said or done to bring things to such a boil. Part of him longed to see Danny smash Diego against the wall or chuck beer in his face, just to see how—or if—his roommate might react. But Danny did neither; instead, he slumped back into the chair and jammed a burger in his mouth.

Ink watched Diego work his way to the exit. "Um," he said, "what was that all about?"

"Where are all the women?" Danny said, mouth half full of food. He climbed up on the table, which wobbled dangerously beneath his sharp-toed boots. "WHERE ARE ALL THE GODDAMN WOMEN?"

Not ten minutes later, the door opened, and there they were: skirts and heels, short shorts and spaghetti straps and all good kinds of skin.

Cobb bowed his head and kissed the table. He said, "Daniel spake and so in time it was."

*

"You can just sit in the cart if you want." Jesse was squeaking the dorm room door back and forth and Ink, sprawled upon the bed, had the sensation of his skull opening and closing. A few feet away, coffee dripped into the carafe. The radio said it was going to be ninety-two today—sunny and humid.

"Danny's going. Says he has something like a one handicap."

"I bet it's more," Ink said, annoyed by the tinge of awe in his friend's voice. Ever since Jesse broke up with Rebecca, he seemed to be all for Danny again.

"You coming?"

"I'm going to lay low. Save my energy for tonight." Ink flexed what few muscles he had.

After several cups of coffee and a good, long shower, Ink called Scott and they headed over to the intramural field, where a flag football tournament was beginning. Cobb was there to root on his fraternity brothers, a cardboard boat of goo-covered nachos swimming beneath his nose.

"You think Student Life would have come up with something

256

for us non-sportsmen to do," Scott said.

"Cobb snorted. "Like a poetry reading or something? Gee, that'd be a gobs of fun."

"Sure. Why not?"

"A book discussion group, maybe. Tea and crimpets."

"Crumpets," Ink grumbled. "If you're going to make fun, at least use the right words."

"Outside of getting another guy from behind, I cannot think of one single thing more gay than the study of literature."

Scott sighed. "You're the reason our country is the way it is."

Cobb took off his glasses and wiped his sweat-soaked face with a handkerchief. "Seriously," he said, "what in God's name are you going to do with a degree in English?"

"Anything we want," Ink said. "An English major knows how to communicate effectively. An English major is versatile and creative and—"

"Blah, blah, blah."

"An English major can think critically and—"

"Teach. Those who can't do, teach."

With a hint of apology, Scott said, "At some point, I thought it might be nice to take time off, go into the Peace Corps or something."

"Ah," Cobb laughed. "To teach!"

"An English major," Ink said, remembering what Dr. Marks had often told him, "learns to be sensitive to other cultures and appreciative of life in all of its complexity. It's not going too far to say that the discipline teaches a student what it means to be human."

"What it means to be human is to get a job, and I'm happy to report I already have one."

"But you majored in Business!"

"Ink, you make it sound like a sin."

"Well, isn't it?"

When Cobb, suddenly attentive to the game that had just kicked off, did not respond to his eloquent retort, Ink assumed he'd scored a victory. He watched the frat team's quarterback audible at the line, waving his teammates this way and that. He took the ball, faded back, and threw a tight spiral right into the outstretched hands of a receiver.

On the next play, he rolled out and tossed a touchdown pass. He raised his arms, as if he'd expected nothing less than the future he'd drawn up the moment before. Ink thought about his appointment at the career placement office about a month ago. For the longest time, he'd just assumed he'd have a career editing books or magazines or something. But the counselor who looked over the draft of his resume sat back in her twirly chair and said that his experience was "a little thin." He had worked in a retail stockroom. He had shelved books a few hours a week at the university library. He had, however, very little that might catch the eye of an employer. He had, in short, little idea of how to go about things in the "real world."

By the end of the half, Cobb's frat team was up three scores. Cobb, oblivious to a Nike swoosh of nacho cheese from lip to chin, was beside himself with joy. Sweaty and sunburned and highly annoyed, Ink decided to take off before he shoved his smug friend down between the bleachers.

A long shower failed to revive him, but Ink strolled over to the party tent, counting on that first sip of cold, bitter beer to bring him back to life. Unfortunately, for the first hour he was stuck with Scott and Tamika, his two teetotaler friends (Katy, for her part, had refused to attend Senior Week, dismissing it as a "sordid, bacchanalian affair"). Tamika talked at great excited length about some summer stock thing in Massachusetts. Scott, beaming from ear to ear, announced an interview he just scored for a community arts beat reporter job in Cincinnati, his hometown. All the while they chatted, regardless of where they moved, the three seemed to be in the direct line of smoke pouring off the grills. Ink eyes burned. To make matters worse, a sinus headache loomed.

Just when he'd about lost hope, Danny and Jesse arrived, Danny laughing as he mimed what was either the world's worst golf swing or the swipe of an executioner's sword. Ink watched as the two drew cold, golden beers from a keg. At the first opportunity, he told Scott and Tamika that he'd "be back in a few." When he got to the keg, he drank down a beer right away (such small plastic cups!). After filling up again, he took his place by the boys, listening to Jesse laugh through a story of how Danny, out of patience with his driver, went after the ball like an unhorsed polo player, swinging all the way down to the green. They drank some more and some more and then, maybe an hour later, they were at the far end of the tent, a couple other boys Ink didn't know around them, one of whom was flicking out cards as he explained the rules of a game called "Asshole," which Ink, with a beer-buzzed shrug, played, only dimly aware of what to do. And yet, to his surprise, he did almost as well as Danny.

Soon, though, his brain increasingly fuzzy, he said, "Deal me out." When he stood, the folding chair tipping backwards onto the lawn.

"You don't look so good," Jesse grinned.

"Just need some air."

Danny laughed. "If there's an outside to the outside, our boy is sure to find it."

Ink weaved toward the portable toilets, near which Perri Simmons of all people stood chatting with a clean-cut boy in shorts and striped rugby shirt. He had half a mind to take the boy aside and whisper, "This one gives the best hand jobs," but he had to go badly. He propelled himself forward into the land of portable toilets, which were arranged like Stonehenge done in green. Waiting for the door in front of him open, he did a little dance. POTTY DOLL, the label above the door read. Ink giggled—wasn't that the most hilarious thing? He bit the inside of his cheeks, trying to staunch the flow of laughter. The door opened, beckoned, took him into a cramped, foul-smelling twilight. The seat was soaked with piss that missed its mark. The hole was dark and nasty, and his head spun from the terrible smell. It didn't take much imagination to be reminded of another hole, another act, but no, no, no, that other hole—no, *the vagina*—was the world's most sacred place. One day, one day, he would take the journey. He would get there, and it would be dark and warm and lovely beyond compare. God would be present, of course, in the form of a bright, ecstatic light from above, pouring through him. He peed away, full force, like nobody's business. He was happy, happy that he was young—so young—and the necessary parts were there, patient, biding their time, content for now to function in this extremely useful way.

Later—his mind at some point had temporarily lost the gift of sequencing, the understanding of cause and effect—he found himself uptown, head hanging over a beer at CGs then stumbling through frenetic lights at Ad Nauseam, held up by a girl with a sharp nose and a green, glittering top hat that made him think of St. Patrick's Day, only it was not March, it was that other M month—Marpil or Mune.

A pint was thrust in front of him—black, sloshing stuff, the sight of which made him queasy. He wet his lips with froth.

"Lightweight," a voice, another girl's, screamed in his ear.

Ink sat down in a chair, watched for an indeterminate period of time as Jesse moved against a girl who was not Rebecca. He stood again, shaky as a toddler. He felt like he was moving downhill to his friend and he was pushing him, shouting at his turned shoulder, "Not yours, not yours!" before remembering that Jesse did not go out with Rebecca anymore.

"Ink, man, whoa! This is Celia. Went to high school with Danny."

Danny, Danny—of course. That was why he and Jesse were now so tight. Disgusted, Ink stumbled away. There was a break in the music, and Cobb, talking to a humanoid blur, said, "If I could just build one. There are enough suitable body parts floating around, that's for sure."

Ink remembered the Potty Doll and tried to communicate his vision to whoever was before him. People laughed. Hard hands pounded him on the back.

"Go to hell," he said to no one in particular. He knocked over his beer, and boys, several of whom he did not recognize, shot out of their chairs, scowling. A cup of coffee appeared, and Ink, sitting down now, studied the otherworldly arabesques of steam. He tilted his head sideways to read from left to right. Sloppy cursive. No, Arabic. A language about which he shuddered to think.

Somehow, he was with his friends back on the quad, enveloped by a lovely mist. Ink cried out, "I've never felt so alive!" Cobb had his face in a dumpster. Danny screamed the chorus of a popular Nirvana song, over and over again. Then, the stairwell of the dorm appeared, and Ink became mightily impressed with his success—one foot in front of the other, the stunning echo of iron, the squeaky, upward slide of hand on rail.

A burst of light, and for a few blissful moments, Ink was sure he'd passed to the other side. But there was Diego, scooting back from the book at his desk, eyes stretching over the frames of his reading glasses, curious as always, and perhaps a little concerned. Where the hell had he been all night?

"Well, Mrs. Burrito," Danny said to Diego. "Here is your little boy. I want you to know he's been about as bad as bad can be."

Ink fell onto the nearest bed. He could not remember if it was his.

"Did you all have fun?" Diego asked.

"What is el philosophore reading this fine evening?" Danny scooped up the book, and punctuated the sound of turning pages with a series of studious noises and nods. Ink, thinking vaguely of the altercation the night before, protested with a flaccid "hey!"

"Kierkegaard," Danny said. "Never heard of the dude."

"He's quite an important thinker. This book is an extended meditation on an important verse from James."

"Never heard of him."

"From The Bible."

"Never heard of him."

"Danny . . ." Jesse said.

Diego pursed his lips. His eyes blinked expectantly at Danny.

"Sure you have," Cobb chimed in. "The Bible is the one about that Santy Claus the Jews hung out to dry."

"Cobb . . . stupid," Ink said, sober enough to know he couldn't manage a verb.

"Purity of heart is to will one thing," Danny said, trying the proposition on for size.

"That's right."

"Okay, I will one thing," Danny said. "To do young women."

"That's not one thing."

"Women. That is one thing. I'm not interested in men or sheep or dogs, like"—he punched Cobb in the shoulder— "some fuckers I know!"

Cobb grabbed his arm. His eyes struggled to remain amused.

"Women—that's many things. For Kierkegaard, there's no such thing as oneness of pleasure."

"So, you're saying I've got to fuck one woman. One position too, I bet."

"Well—"

"Look, is this dude alive?"

"No."

"Then what right does he have?"

"Lengthened shadow," Ink mumbled, Emerson wafting back at him like a breeze. "One man."

"What do *you* say about the matter, my overstuffed burrito?"

Diego swallowed before speaking. "He challenges me, reveals my weaknesses. In short, he makes me think."

"Fine. You think, and I'll do."

"You seem a little bit angry. Maybe this is bothering you. Maybe a part of you is wondering why it might matter to be—or try to be—pure of heart."

"It makes me wonder why so many smart people are so fucking dumb. Why do they go through their lives trying to talk themselves out of using all the fine equipment they were given—by God, of all people—to use?"

"Purity," Ink said, speaking slowly, trying his damnedest to be articulate. "It only makes sense if . . . there is a God." He closed his eyes. In his condition, that sentiment seemed to him a new and notable gift to the world.

"I want to give this a chance," Diego said. "I may be missing something. The plan is to read more and see what happens."

Danny laughed. He tossed the book back onto Diego's desk. "Man, you guys . . . it's like Final Jeopardy or something. 'Mathematical Equations,' and when you hear 'What's two plus two?' you won't write four. No, no—anything but four. You stand there, the music chiming, the time running down, and think there's no way in hell Alex is going to let me take home twenty-five grand for a gimme of a question. So you write five, scribble it out. Then three and six and finally sixty-nine. The time runs out. Alex wants to see your response. The audience is on the edge of their seats and don't know that in about 1.5 seconds they're going to be laughing their goddamn asses off."

"You've got to believe . . . in something," Ink said. The word "tradition" bubbled on his lips, even as he had a vague recollection of having burned that stuffy house down.

"I believe in things," Danny said, cupping his crotch. "My faith grows with every passing day."

When Diego shook his head, Danny, like a foul wind, was upon him, hands on his shirt, dragging him out of his chair and plastering him against the door. "I should punch you," he cried. Maybe toss you out the window. I want to go on a rampage. Things need to come to a head."

Diego blinked. He didn't say a word.

"Danny," Jesse said, pushing them apart. "For Christ's sake, leave him alone!"

"People say, 'Use your God-given brains.' Well, I've got news for you and the rest of your monkish friends. The body is God-given too, and you should use it, as frequently as possible, with some other God-given body, preferably with one that God has given plenty to. And, and," he continued, throwing arms around the room, "when that fun is over, you use your body again, preferably on one that's even better. Use, use, use. You aren't going to have what you have forever."

"Yes, that's what religious writers—"

"My point is: 'Don't bury your dick under a bushel,'" Danny said. "That's Jizzmaticus, Chapter 1, verse 1. Shortest book of the bunch."

Cobb's laugh turned into an ill-disguised belch.

"What about control? Basic human decency?"

"I just want to say right now that you're lucky, my overstuffed burrito. If she'd been eighteen, I would have humped her sweet ass to Columbus and back."

Diego pushed him away, and Danny stumbled backward, with great exaggeration. In slow motion, he fell, letting out a long "nooooo" on his deliberate way to the floor.

Ink's roommate stood over him, suspended hand vibrating. Jesse stepped in again and lowered the boy's arm. He spoke softly in his ear.

"Punch me," Danny said.

Ink was transfixed by Diego's flaring nostrils. Never, ever had he seen his roommate riled, much less filled with this murderous rage. He had no idea what was going on.

"Stomp my head, you bookworm puss."

Ink sat up, sobering quickly, pillow like a shield in front of his body. Diego did not take Danny up on his offer; instead, he left the room, closing the door behind him, quietly, as if afraid of waking a sleeping friend. Danny threw out his arms across the floor. He closed his eyes and let head drop to chest.

"Lord," Cobb cried out," forgive him for he knows not whom he does."

"Not everything is a joke," Jesse said. He bent down and hauled

Danny from the floor. Ink closed his eyes to stop the room from spinning. He was clueless about the meaning of this exchange but smart enough to know that, in an argument between Diego and Danny, it was his roommate who had to be in the right.

*

Friday night. For months, Ink had been building up in his mind the party to end all parties, but it began as just another party with more bad beer and loud, poorly played pop tunes, boys and girls on the prowl for one last part of a body to grab. Periodically, he wet his lips with beer. He moved his pounding head to shrill music, listened to Jesse's self-deprecating story about a show he and his bandmates played a few weeks ago at Spring Fling, laughed with the others at just the right spots. All the while, he was becoming filled with a terrible loneliness. He'd had his once-in-a-lifetime crack at college, and now it was nearly over. Behind him, metaphorically speaking, were all but the last few pages of a book that, for better or worse, would occupy considerable shelf space for the rest of his life. For the first time, he wondered if there weren't some better group of people he could have known. Better friends—deeper and more considerate, capable of carving indelible autographs upon his heart. He worried that years from now, those he'd come to know would fail to stay with him, fail to have the power to draw him back into the past and make it, upon command, a charming present once again.

Maybe he was overacting. Maybe he expected too much. Maybe, he thought, wetting his lips again with beer, he was simply too worn out by these long hard nights of drink to see the world straight.

"And so," Jesse said, pausing to smile around the lip of a plastic cup. "She says, you're not Danny. That's good enough for me!"

Danny was nowhere to be found, and that was good, because Ink did not know if he had the courage to deal with him. At lunch, Cobb had said, "This is hard for me—to be serious," but he did a passable job of it, providing Ink with an account of what led to Danny and Diego's fight the evening before. It had to do with Diego's sister Rosa, who'd been on campus for an Accepted Students Weekend about a month ago and Danny, drunk out of his mind, discovered her walking back to Wrigley from a mixer with her escort. Of course, the escort, Diane Blaine, knew Danny. And of course, Diane dripped with desire for him and would therefore do anything for him, which included allowing Danny to walk the two of them across the quad to the dorm.

264

Which involved Diane inviting him into the dorm, into her room and onto her unmade bed, where she unscrewed a bottle of peach Manischewitz, which they each drank plentifully from.

"Wait, wait, how do you know all this?" Ink said, squeezing his grilled cheese, watching an orange blob seep out like a tear between slices of toast.

Cobb shrugged. "I seem not to have mentioned that I was there."

"You asshole!"

"Hey, hey! I was monitoring the situation."

Ink had met Rosa a few times, first as a pouty and pretty thirteen-year-old and again, when Diego was moving back in to Freitag junior year, as a sixteen year old in a siren red tube top and a fringy denim skirt. She'd nodded at him, but did not smile—did not say a word. Under no circumstances would he look again in her direction.

"Anyway, Diane passed out, and Danny told me with his eyes to, you know, get the hell lost."

"You didn't!"

"I told him with my eyes that it was going to be a three way or nothing."

"Because you're a pig."

"But not a liar. I draw the line there."

Ink stood. A moment earlier, he'd seen Jesse come into the cafeteria with the lead singer of his band. He'd go sit with them, even if the conversation would be miles over his head.

"Nothing happened, my puritanical friend," Cobb said. "But Danny spread around a tale that was vague enough to allow anyone to assume the worst."

"Diego never said a word to me." Only after he said this did Ink feel the deepness of the wound.

And now, as if sensing Ink was thinking about him, Danny appeared with a flourish in the tent, splashing down at the first available folding chair, chatting up a pretty brunette Ink recalled from one of his courses two or three years ago. Within seconds, she seemed to be all ears.

"Look at him go to town," Ink said, shaking his head.

"Jealous?" Cobb asked. He nudged him with an elbow, made him slop some beer.

Ink had half a mind to "fuck you" his friend into oblivion, but Cobb, after all, was onto something. If he were completely honest with himself, Ink could take the moral high road only because he lacked the brawn and brazenness to sink luxuriously into the moral low road's rut and mud.

"My reputation precedes me," Danny said, hand to his heart.

"You got that right," the girl said, eyes more peeved than playful.

Out of nowhere, a slender blonde in a lemon bikini top slapped up in sandals and bear-hugged Danny from behind. He turned to her with a laugh and a grab, and the other girl turned back to her friends.

From what Ink could discern, if you were a certain kind of boy, all it took to snare a girl was sexy talk talk talk and a don't-give-a-shit attitude because the table was long, senior class was large, and you could just move along to the next girl in line, same strategy, give or take a suggestive word, and there would be a good-enough girl who was too lonely or too horny or too far gone to resist. It depressed him, made him want to drink. He downed the bitter cup and felt his stomach tilt and slide, but he went back to the keg for another because he knew he had to have plenty of the stuff in him, if this night was going to mean in the way he always imagined it would.

*

Golden, magical, brain-transforming beer, the bubbly layer of foam like (to Ink) the hoary head of the wise man. Fat brats with stadium mustard. Eardrum-rending covers of Zeppelin, Bad Company, and other classic rock gods. Fragmented talk with Jesse and Cobb, Scott and Tamika. Awkward stretches when he found himself on the fringes of groups he barely knew, listening to impassioned reminiscences in which he never played a role. The night went on and on, and they were all moving much too quickly through and out of this glorious time. Nina Sissyan, whom Ink had seen here and there throughout the week's festivities, appeared at the table. Drunk, she was even more amiable than usual. When she winked in his direction, he felt more sad than thrilled. He finished off his beer and went to the keg for another. When he returned, Nina said, "I've . . . I've got a story." She stood, pitched forward, was righted by a boy who placed proprietary hands upon her hips.

In grade school (so many years ago!), Nina had been one of those quasi-supernal beings whom Ink couldn't dare gaze at directly. She was no Bethany Hyde, of course, but hadn't Bethany herself fallen far short now of what she was supposed to be? The one true goddess of his grade school days had two kids now—two kids by two different men, both of whom (he'd heard) were equally unsupportive. She worked at a grungy bar on the near west side of Cleveland—The Ugly Broad! Good Lord, was all he could think. The love of his life was twenty-two and already a white trash cliché.

Ink stared into the wise old head of his beer. Nina was different: smart, bubbly, a job already lined up in Pittsburgh with some public relations firm. She was unfailingly kind and always seeming not unpleased to have him in the world. She was in shape—athletic without being mannish. She was attractive too—big, exuberant eyes, nice skin (as even his mother once noted), smile bright as a wedding invitation—but in a way that, for some reason, failed to punch the breath out of him. He added her up again. He carried the one. For the life of him, he could not get the math to work.

"My story," Nina said now, "is called, ahem, is entitled: 'How John—er, Ink—Just Sat There without Doing a Thing.'"

The others—only a few of whom he knew by name or face—laughed and looked his way not with judgment but with a kind of bemused interest. Ink, squeezing out an embarrassed smile, took a huge gulp of beer. Nina began with a "once upon a time" and the time was seventh grade, after school, and Macho and Dave, these two boys who tried to outdo each other with coolness, got into the sports equipment room in the gym and took out the archery stuff. Believe it or not, she said, the arrows, all sharp and pointy, were right there for the grabbing. Anyway, it was not too long before Dave took his position behind one of the gym poles and began shooting these soft arching arrows into the room where Macho still was. One of them struck the door and they both couldn't stop laughing at that. "Me, I'm just there for cheerleading practice and yelling at them to stop, although it's pretty exciting too—at least to my thirteen-year-old self."

Ink remembered this well: leaving the library, heading into the gym by way of the stage, looking for Sandro, his best friend, with whom he was going to walk home. When that first arrow flew, he'd been scared beyond belief. He thought if he turned, tried to flee, one or the other of them would shoot him through the back. Plus Bethany—sweet Bethany—had just entered through the parking lot door on the other side of the gym, and he wanted to see her take off her sweats.

"War. Mano a mano. It's what the boys do best, right?"

The girls in the group broke into gentle knowing laughter. One boy horse-collared his friend, eager to provide support for Nina's assertion.

"And John, the good, the obedient boy, never in trouble a day in his life, is just sitting there on the stage in this stray desk, looking like he's ready to take notes!"

"So what happened?"—this from Scott, who'd at some point joined the circle. "I'm guessing emergency room visit."

Nina put up a hand. She had to go back and describe the major players: Macho, "the handsome little devil," who, between gestures of sincere piety, liked to grab at the girls; Dave, "a stoner in training."

Ink had wanted to see them both bleeding on the hardwood floor.

"You look at the two of them, and you can almost predict what's going to happen. The arrows go back and forth, clattering here and there. Macho pulls back his bow a little further, puts a little more zing on his next shot, and—wah, wah, wah! —there it was, waving away in Dave's hand. My friend Bethany screams, Dave drops his bow and steps from behind the pole, gazing at the blood. I'm crying, I'm like harmonizing with Bethany, and John here, cool as a cucumber, is just sitting there with this satisfied smirk on his face."

"That's cold," Scott said.

Nina took Ink's fingers for a moment and gave them a friendly shake. "John Boy here is not so bad." The crowd waited for more, but Nina shrugged, turned away, and weaved back to the keg. Ink watched the leap and drop of her white shorts, the shiny backs of her legs. He didn't know what to think.

At that moment, the PrimaDonalds—the headliner for the evening—took the stage. The girls all cried for Aidan Malone, the charming front man who played the tin whistle and the mandolin and sang all those weepy Irish ballads in his fabulous brogue. Years ago, he'd been a graduate student in history. He never finished and never left, deciding that there were worse careers than "local legend." Aidan bumped his mouth against the mic. "Testing, breasting, jesting." The crowd roared and, after a screaming count to four, the band crashed out of the gate with "On the Doss," a frenetic reel of their own. After a few false starts, Bridget Neeley, one of Nina's friends, began step dancing, teeth leaping out of her damp, translucent face. Nina, after some coaxing, followed suit in a not entirely clumsy way. Danny, not to be outdone, locked his arms in front of his body and started kicking out his legs like a fiddler on the roof. Ink laughed and finished off another beer, thinking suddenly: this is the life. Why had there not been more of it?

"Whew," Aidan said, the last strains of the tune reverberating in the cool spring air. "Knackered already." He wiped his brow with a handkerchief. He took a deep breath, shot a blazing white smile at some front row ladies, and said they were going to slow things down a bit with "a little old timey gem called 'Carrickfergus.'"

The song came at Ink, slow and thick, a slathering of raw emotion—sadness, longing, acute yet vague nostalgia. The speaker was a wandering man—yearning for Carrickfergus, a quaint town by the sea. He was drunk and full of despair, his death impending.

At the end of the song, Aidan sang, "I wish I was," leaving the fragmented sentiment in the air to dissolve into a last fuzzed out strum of electric guitar.

Ink's arm had become draped around Nina's shoulder; for the life of him, he could not remember how this happened. He looked at her, and she danced her brows. He closed his eyes to keep his balance, to try to process the moment.

Aidan put out his hands to quiet the cheers. He crouched, picked up his beer, raised his cup to the roaring crowd. "Sláinte!"

When Ink opened his eyes, Nina was out from under him, woo hooing the band, punching her fists into the air. In and out of his life these past four years—no, these past sixteen years—Nina had weaved. A smile here, a quick chat there, an occasional pat upon hand or arm. All of these moments, these brief encounters—he was back again at math, his least favorite subject in the world.

With the sad Irish songs dragging down his heart, Ink stepped outside the tent to look up at the star-speckled sky. He was alone, but this time sweetly so, by choice, soaking in the memory of Nina's bare shoulder, her wide-eyed look—fear, surprise, joy, who would ever know? He looked at the campus—the brick walkways, the gorgeous green quad, the glowing gothic façade of Halloran Learning Center, Freitag Hall. These were spaces he could no longer call his own. He bit his lip, and his eyes became misty. But there was something thrilling about the end, the inexorable passage of time. "Death is the mother of beauty," he thought, seeing Katy Fuster's "told you so" face. Maybe Stevens had been right after all. Maybe the end of everything was needed in order for anything to matter. He put cup to lips, and let his teeth rest meditatively against the plastic rim.

Sadness. Longing. The abstractions hung with him over the railing like Dali's droopy clocks. Ink continued to look at the stars, enjoying his mood, his pose, waiting with considerable faith for a girl (Nina, maybe? Was she the one?) to approach, to stand beside him, her eyes lovely in the light. Strands of hair would blow across her face, and she would remove them with delicate fingers. She'd smile shyly, earnestly. Ink would turn away, gaze back at the quad, and in a moment, she'd lean her head against his shoulder. Together, for the rest of the night, they would face a kind of sadness that could never be borne alone.

But this girl never came, and Ink, his eyes on the rear end of Freitag Hall, realized that he'd never enter room 402 again, except perhaps as a balding, potbellied alum brimming with stories his undergraduate guide would not want to hear. Faulkner was wrong: there *is* such a thing as was, and it was right now being stuffed in a huge lock box too cumbersome to bring along. In front of him was death, which, now that he'd had another minute to think about it, was pretty much the mother of shit.

Overcome with self-pity, he wandered from the tent, walked with hands in pockets down the brick walkway back to Tyler. Upon entering the lobby, he saw a girl sitting under a pay phone, cord wrapped around her body like a rope. He froze, not sure if he should acknowledge her or hurry on.

She was sniffing, muttering—"oh, oh, and one more thing . . ."

Ink held on to the horizontal bar of the door that had fallen closed behind him.

"Fuck you," the girl said in a strange, matter-of-fact tone.

He began to move through the vestibule, toward the interior doors that led to the first floor hallway. That's when the girl began to bang the receiver on the floor—one, two, three deliberate strikes.

"Are you okay?" He didn't want to—he groaned inwardly about having to do so—but he felt he needed to say something. When she didn't immediately answer, it occurred to him that she might think he was some drunken loser, looking to take advantage.

"Are you all the same?"

"Excuse me?" He stepped forward, trying to find her face in the shadows.

"Boys. I mean, I know you all have dicks. But beyond that . . ." The girl pressed her back against the wall, bounced one leg over the other. He recognized her—the girl Danny had accosted earlier this evening.

"Well," he said, trying to contain his anger. "Girls are no better."

"We're quite a bit better."

Ink shrugged. The girl rolled her eyes.

"My boyfriend—my *ex*-boyfriend," she said, strangling the phone. "He says, 'Julie, I am always going to be your friend.' I tell him to go to hell, and then he gets so riled up, so damn passionate, it's hard to believe he's not falling in love again. He says, get this: 'Julie, you just let someone try to keep me from being your friend, your very best friend, and watch what I do to them.'"

"Oh," Ink said. He looked at her more closely: vibrant eyes, a pretty neck, a tantalizing comma of cleavage. Slim brown legs, one bouncing nervously over the other.

"You ever give your ladies the 'friend' treatment?"

"Uh, no."

"Every have some girl do that to you?"

"I've never even had a girlfriend."

Julie squinted into the dimness. "Hmm, I can see why."

Ink opened his mouth.

"I'm kidding! It's what I do when I want to cry."

"Well . . . if you're okay, I'm going to go now."

"Sure, sure. Happy graduation. Have a good life and all of that."

Ink looked down, watched Julie stand, tug down her shorts, and place the phone back in its cradle. "Will do," he said, and then all the way up the stairs to his room he tried not to be embarrassed by what he'd said. "Will do"—how stupid, how falsely suave it sounded. Yet didn't she deserve it, given her harsh dismissal of the opposite sex?

Diego had left for home earlier that afternoon, telling him that he was "not feeling especially well." Ink knew by that point what was wrong, but he, failing miserably to be a friend, had done nothing except shake his roommate's flaccid hand. Alone in this brand new room, staring at the now useless itinerary for Senior Week in his hands, Ink had the urge to scream out, to be heard, to be known, to cow someone into granting him permission to start all over again.

*

The morning of graduation, Ink developed a huge headache from the sun. He sat in the front row, squinting, pinching the bridge of his nose, wanting to close his eyes but afraid to since there was only a forty-foot plot of mushy grass between him and the stage, where all the Clerestory worthies sat. He was wedged between two boys who knew each other well. They kept a running commentary on the ceremony, a whispery volley of comments back and forth in front of his face, and Ink couldn't help but see this arrangement as the epitome of his young, socially frustrating life.

The commencement speaker, a famous writer Ink had never heard of, stood after a long, fawning introduction by the dean. The man was maybe thirty-five, old in Ink's eyes—impossibly so. But the girls, he was certain, found this writer dashing, with his thick shoulder length hair and tough guy jaw. Ink crossed his arms, determined to be skeptical.

"Thanks," the writer said, holding up the honorary degree over his head like a heavyweight belt. "Not bad, not bad, for a college dropout." He put a hand to his brow and scanned the crowd. He whistled, impressed by the spectacle or pretending to be.

"The boy to his right leaned across him to whisper to his friend, "Dude's drunk off his ass!"

The other boy, nodding vigorously, put two hands in front of his face.

"Look, dear young people, I don't have much to tell you beyond this: "TODAY IS NOT A BEGINNING!" He tapped the mic with a middle finger. "Did you hear me? IT'S NOT A BEGINNING! It— the whole thing, in case you haven't noticed—has been going on for quite some time now, and if you, dear young people, have been waiting all along for this diploma—if you've been thinking that it and it only is your license to do whatever it is you're going to do, then let me also say this: "YOU ARE ALREADY SEVERELY BEHIND! GET

272

MOVING. TO HELL WITH YOUR PIECE OF PRETTY PAPER. TO HELL WITH THE BENEDICTION. THE PARTY YOUR PARENTS ARE THROWING IS JUST A STALL TACTIC. GO, I Say, GET ON WITH IT RIGHT NOW!"

The famous writer turned and walked right off the stage. He stood in the squishy grass, hands on his hips, soaking in the nervous laughter rippling throughout the crowd. The boy to Ink's left laughed out loud, said, "Worth the price of admission." Ink began to sweat. The university president had had his mouth open for some time; now, he stood, his face white as computer paper. He adjusted his tam and stepped toward the podium, ready to restore order.

At that moment, the writer scrambled back up the steps to the podium. Slowly, he edged his lips to the mic. He scratched his head. He waited patiently for the laughter, the catcalls, the smattering of boos to diminish. Then, he whispered: "Wait, you're not gone yet? Can you give me one good reason why we all are still here?"

Take It for Granite

(Summer 2007)

So many things happened, one after another, and then Ink set off, unfinished and alone, for Cleveland, the shriveled up city of his birth. As he pulled from the curb, he watched his wife uncross arms long enough for an index finger wave. Oblivious, the Corolla's horn bleated like a cheerleader in the face of a blowout loss.

A few hours later, Ink was bumper-to-bumper on the Valley View Bridge, a handful of miles from the place he still called home. On NPR, pundits parsed Bush's Coast Guard commencement speech. More adolescent tough guy talk from the Douchebag-in-Chief. Ink punched off the radio, strangled the wheel in an effort to calm down. To his right stood the two soaring obelisks that announced Cleveland was, for the time being, still a city. Growing up, Ink had seen them as proud sentries, standing fearlessly near the edge of Erie, guarding the northern coast of the United States. But now the one true icon of the cityscape—the aptly named Terminal Tower—looked ashen, abandoned, and in the sludge-colored minutes before noon, ready to call it a life.

*

"Where's Julie?" Mom said, face pinched like a priest behind the screen door.

"Permission to enter?" Even from the porch, Ink could feel the central air gush over his flip flopped toes.

After a sip of ice water, Ink, shaking off a shiver, did his best to explain. The dissertation, as Mom might have guessed, was not going well. He needed distance, a total change of scenery. His advisor had even suggested it (actually, Sikma had said in his black-browed, supercilious way: "It certainly can't make you any less productive"). In the mornings, he'd teach a composition class at Cleveland State; after lunch, he'd strap himself in a chair and "dissertate" until dinner. Over the course of five weeks, he'd bang out "at least two whole chapters." He went on to use what for him was higher math: 4 writing hours X 35 days = 140 writing hours. If he typed 200 words an hour (a modest-sized paragraph—couldn't his worst students bang out as much?), he'd have 28,000 words—two chapters and then some. Eight hundred words a day, not counting any additional words he might plunk down during an unscheduled fifth or even sixth hour of writing. He'd done enough background reading. He had two shoeboxes crammed with note cards. When he was finished, the world of Hemingway studies wouldn't know what hit it.

"And Julie?" Mom asked.

"Julie," Ink said, clearing his throat, downing the water before telling her he was really, really glad she asked. Julie, he said, Julie was most definitely on board with this plan because she knew he needed to just get this thing done. When summer session was over and those two chapters (and then some!) were in the bag, he would head right back to Clerestory, "pedal to the metal," and the two of them, "together," would take off for Cape Cod to celebrate their tenth year of wedded bliss. As these words tumbled from his lips, Ink couldn't help but feel a little impressed: they sounded much better than they did as he'd arranged and rearranged them in his mind on the drive up. Mom dropped her chin—less like a nod than the tink of hammer on nail. At least she didn't ask any more questions.

Dad emerged from the basement, blinking through wire frames, eyes adjusting to the bright light of the kitchen. Thick black lines went up and across his shirt. Graph paper, Ink thought. He had the urge to plot points.

"Increase," Dad said. "It's wonderful to see you." With a nervous spasm of the lips, he took Ink's hand, gave it a bland shake. Dad had always been a slight, uncertain man, with narrow shoulders and pale, spindly legs that always kept him in long pants even throughout countless humid summers. But for the past several years, Ink accused him in his mind of a more substantial lack—an absence of depth, a lack of focus, a spiritual void—which Dad tried to disguise with broad smiles and arcane trivia and time-worn aphorisms. To make matters worse, every time Ink came home (which was rarely anymore), it was almost as if they were meeting for the very first time.

"How are things?" Ink asked.

"Oh, fine, fine." Dad turned to Mom, and Ink saw the Adam's apple bob. "Well, you make yourself at home. There's Great Lakes in the fridge. I'm going to go up and take a shower." He patted his hair.

"Rinse out all this dust."

When Dad retired from the faucet company, he was at a loss about how to spend his time. Initially, he'd seen this new phase of his life as an opportunity to more strongly connect with family. He'd drop by Grandma and Grandpa's to fix whatever was broken. He'd have regular coffee with Aunt Ruth, who was "happily single," and regular counseling sessions with Uncle Lare, who'd remarried and redivorced and would have sworn off women for good if he knew how to make a decent meal for himself.

A few months earlier, Mom had complained to Ink over the phone: "For much of the day, he just wanders around the house, following me with the clothes basket or out to feed the birds. It's like he's five years old, and his best friend's out of town for the summer." There were only so many times a day one could run up to the Giant Eagle for lunchmeat and bread. There were only so many hours one could spend reading books about computers or ring-tailed lemurs or the Hopi people or whatever other subject happened to seize his interest.

Mom couldn't take it anymore: "Do something—*anything*," she told him at last, and, unfailingly amenable, Dad disappeared upstairs to research hobbies on the computer. After running a few options by her at the dinner table that night, he decided to learn what he called "the fine and noble art of woodworking." For the next few weeks, he split his mornings between the library and the Home Depot. One day he arrived home with long spears of wood and a circular saw and got down to business.

"This is good for him," Mom said.

"You know," Ink said, to have something to say. "I could use a good bookcase."

"He'd do that for you."

"Oh, I wouldn't want to put him out."

Unbalanced, the washing machine began to furiously shake, and Mom disappeared into the basement to calm it down. Relieved, at a loss for what to do, Ink lit the stove for coffee. While measuring crystals into his mug, he noticed a plaque hanging over the waste basket by the hallway door:

GRANDMA'S KITCHEN
Tasters Welcome!
Everything Made with Love & an
Extra Spoonful of Sugar

He edged closer, as if the plaque were some poisonous spider that might pincer his face. Where in God's name had this come from and what on earth could it mean? Ink and Julie were childless; in fact, the thought of children was not even shimmering sentimentally on the horizon. What is more, Mom had never bothered him about grandkids—never made so much as a peep. Yet, here, out of nowhere, tacked up for any visitor to see, was this flagrant sign of discontent. He approached the basement stairs, listening to the plink of the washer lid, the nervous clack of clothespins, Mom's slippers chuffing across the concrete floor. Upstairs, the shower thunked to a stop. His father, he suddenly realized, was wearing no clothes.

Ink looked to the front door. Through the translucent curtain was the porch, and beyond that, the stairs, the cracked slate sidewalk to the Corolla, the tank three-quarters full. He could make a break for it. He could be gone in a moment—would be—if he had a single other place to go.

*

Bright and early the following morning, Ink swiveled in a chair in the room of his youth, fingernails scratching the surface of his old cherry wood desk. Meanwhile, his laptop slowly came to life, the icons appearing—one bright, jovial pop after another. A silo of fresh coffee stood at his feet and a Brandenburg concerto tinkled through his ear phones. Surrounding him were countless library books, slips of paper sticking out like the limp tongues of overheated dogs. He sat one of the shoeboxes on his lap. "Just Do It!" the lid exclaimed. He tapped out a sentence—"Late in his career, Ernest Hemingway became ever more fascinated with the theme of gender"—but Dr. Sikma's voice zoomed up right behind it, saying, "This is no longer news." He sighed, backspaced the damn thing into oblivion, and tried again, this time using a quotation by Debra Moddelmog about the novel's preoccupation with sexual transgression. Not especially flashy, but this introductory sentence, invoking the power of a clear authority in the field, felt much, much better to him.

Ink sat back and looked at the blinds, which resembled eyelids peacefully closed; behind them, he knew, the sun glared like a grade school teacher. He stood, yawned, went to the bathroom. When he came back, he sipped strong black coffee and creaked back into the chair, waiting for the good ideas to backstroke through his brain. He took a long shower, thinking all the while he lathered that the scholar's life could well be one of the most difficult lives of all. No, no—of course, nothing could be further from the truth. There were the soldiers, more than 3,500 hundred of them killed in Iraq because of George W. Bushfuck. So what if Iraq had a newish prime minister who would unify the country? So what if the president recently declared a "turning point" had been reached? The car bombs continued. The body count rose—for Americans and Iraqis alike—while people in the States, bored by such details, simply went shopping like there was no tomorrow.

Clean, freshly caffeinated, Ink sat in front of the computer again, his anger about world events more or less gone. He had, after all, his own pressing worries. His professional future—maybe even his marriage—depended on the completion of this dissertation. He tapped away, came up with a couple of lines of uninspired prose. He yawned to clear his brain. His stomach growled, and he conjured up an image of a turkey club, head lettuce and crispy bacon, sweet, firm tomatoes, kettle chips on the side, a tall, ice-clunky glass of sizzling pop. Before he knew what he was doing, he'd typed three full sentences (one of them a doozy, compound complex with a dismissal of a critic snug in its subordinate clause). Sitting back in the chair, he felt he'd earned lunch. Downstairs, he searched the kitchen for something approaching his vision, but Mom, who'd recently turned health nut after Dad's less-than-stellar check-up results, had nothing on hand beyond non-fat cheese squares and pasty whole grain bread.

"How's it going?" Mom asked, slipper-shuffling into the kitchen with a stack of junk mail.

"Fine," Ink said. "I think I'm on a roll."

"How many words did you write?"

He swallowed a bite of sandwich. "It's not always about the words."

Mom smiled; she couldn't help herself: "It's about the pictures?"

After lunch, Ink came to the conclusion that his writer's block had to do with the fact that he still did not know enough about his topic. From a distance of a hundred-plus miles, he felt confident enough to disagree with Sikma, who'd two weeks ago told him in no uncertain iambs: "Put DOWN the FUCKing BOOKS and WRITE the STUpid THING!" He lifted one of the few tomes not yet filled with paper tongues. On the first few pages were thirteen lengthy epigraphs, and Ink dutifully considered them all before starting in on the dense Introduction. Before he'd read a page, the book tumbled to the floor, frightening him half to death. Perhaps what he really needed was a head-clearing nap.

Sometime later, Ink awoke on his bed to the sounds of Mom slapping cabinets in the hallway. He sat up, swiped drool from his mouth with the back of a hand, and blinked at the clock on the dresser. 3:47 pm. The work day was almost over, but he tried not to beat himself up too much about it. This was, after all, just the very first day. In time—certainly in no more than a week—he would find his groove.

*

The next few days, each stupid with sun, followed a similar pattern. In the mornings, Ink planned his composition course. In the afternoons, he struggled to make his thoughts and notes and sources mean something new about Hemingway. He was especially relieved when Monday rolled around and class began. It was good to have somewhere to be—if only for a few hours out of the day. Teaching would make him more aware of the preciousness of his afternoons. With more demands on his time, he would have more focus. He would, in short, get more done.

Ink's students at Clerestory had at least the veneer of sophistication, even if when all was said and done they were so many consumers who'd purchased courses like a pair of designer jeans. The Cleveland State kids were raw, unrefined. Ink started the course with a personal experience prompt— "Tell me about an event that made a real difference in your life"—and that gave them free reign to get the sentimental shit out of their system. As expected, they wrote myopically about the big game or the senior prom or the car crash that killed their best friend on that "dark, fateful night." They appended hackneyed, heartfelt lessons: "I went in as a boy butt, I came out a man;" "As the song says, 'I had the time of my life, and I owe it all to him.'" However, the aphorism that galled him the most was, "Life is short—we should defiantly not take it for granite."

With increasing frustration, Ink filled the papers with red (only one contained long stretches of grammatically correct prose) and wrote a scathing endnote, itemizing every single way the student went wrong. Afterward, his brain was fried. Yet the work made him feel better too, filled him with a warm, intellectual glow. He went back to his dissertation to discover the words were there, tingling on his fingertips. He wrote amazingly well for a good nine minutes, no longer an inconsiderable amount of time.

*

The next evening, 418 good-enough words in the can, Ink met Anthony Gigante at the Winking Lizard down by the arena to watch the Cavaliers, who were playing the Detroit Pistons in what his old high school friend, doing his worst Marv Albert, called "a pivotal game five of NBA Eastern Conference Finals." Ink was already half way through a Dortmunder when Ant burst through the door, sporting a LeBron James jersey, a bright white number 23 against a field of wine and gold.

"What are you, ten?" Ink said.

"Just keepin' it real." Ant thumped fist against heart, an urbanism that made Ink's stomach turn. "All hail to The King!"

The bar was packed, and it took forever for their burgers and wings to arrive. But the game was thrilling, and Ink, never a real sports fan, watched with more than a little interest.

Suddenly, in the middle of the fourth quarter, James—just twenty-two years old—became transcendent, scoring and scoring and scoring some more: jump shots, lay ups, three pointers falling away. After every basket, the restaurant blew up with screams. Ant, a certified public accountant, would jump from his seat, grab his jersey, and hi-five fellow patrons, most of whom seemed little more than half his age. On into overtime The King extended his mighty rule, ultimately scoring twenty nine of the team's final thirty points. With victory secured, even Ink found himself being swept away by old, puerile emotions.

The Cavaliers were up now three games to two in the series, a first-ever trip to the NBA Finals just a single win away. Mouths gaped, tears streamed, total strangers collapsed against each other. "We've just seen history," a professorial man beside them said, shaking his head over a brand new beer. "All the fucking way!" a man in a double-

280

breasted suit screamed, plastering himself against the front window of the bar to the delight of crazy-faced passersby. There was chanting and playful punching before a spontaneous spilling out onto Huron Road and toward the arena, where the thousands who watched on the big screen inside poured out to join the Winking Lizard pilgrims. In front of them, a giant Lebron—King James, The Chosen One—rose up the side of a building, chin to the heavens, tattooed arms stretched to bear hug the world. "We Are All Witnesses," the advertisement proclaimed.

Up by Ontario, a line of drunken middle-aged men fell to their knees, bowing down before the massive image of their hometown star. Ant sprinted up to join them. Drivers in passing cars jabbed horns or stopped to thrust fists in the air, renewing the frenzy of the crowd.

Throughout the years, Ink had made popular culture a frequent topic of his writing courses. He hounded students through drafts of essays about the objectification of women on TV, romantic clichés in pop music, the implicit sexism of toys for children, the athlete as marketing god. Had he been twenty years younger, this spontaneous worship service might have been something into which he would have recklessly (and without reflection) hurled himself. But he was thirty-five—much too old now to embarrass himself, much too smart not to know that this playoff game (the entire NBA, for that matter) was just another part of an insidious advertising campaign designed for the sole purpose of lining the pockets of star players and owners with obscene amounts of cash. Perhaps tomorrow morning he'd treat his students to a rant along these lines. They might enjoy the break from the syllabus. He knew he would.

Back home, Ink weaved into the dim dining room, where Mom was working on her most challenging puzzle to date: Mark Rothko, a swath of red up top, a blotch of black on the bottom. She had the frame completed, as well as a tenuous bridge across the middle. One piece was pressed like a nail into her palm.

"How was the game?"

"We won. The city's going nuts."

"That's nice."

It was more than nice, the more he thought about it. Northeast Ohioans from every walk of life coming together, losing their minds about the exploits of one young man, barely out of his teens. Should he ever finish his dissertation, how many people would get in line to praise his talent and hard work?

"You know," Ink said, nodding at the puzzle. "Rothko went insane."

Mom found a home for the piece before looking up. "I wouldn't always read so much into things."

He went upstairs, half a peanut butter sandwich in his hands, feeling like he'd somehow scored a point. The light in his parents' bedroom was on—Dad, his nose no doubt in a wood working book. In front of him, his laptop slumbered. He sat on his bed and ate, watching for a long time the power button breathe in and out, in and out. The computer looked so at peace that he didn't have the heart to wake it for some work.

*

That Monday, the "take-it-for-granite" girl came to Ink's office, essay like a dead pet in her hands. It was sunny outside, 80ish, yet she wore these huge, Sasquatch boots that grew wildly up to her knees. All Ink could think about was how badly those damn feet must stink.

"I finished tenth in my high school class," she said by way of opening argument.

Ink tried to remain calm, but a morning of piss-poor writing had made him ornery. "Do you understand, for starters, that granite is a kind of rock?"

She didn't say a word.

"When you don't proofread, you show me—you show the entire world—that you don't care about your work. And that tells the world that you don't care about your mind, your thoughts. Tell me, would you come to school without brushing your teeth? Would you pick through dirty laundry for your underwear?"

He stopped, looked away to his computer screen, clacked away on the keyboard, afraid he'd just said something that could get him fired.

"Here is 'granite.' I've found us the exact definition."

The girl ground her teeth. "I know what granite is," she said.

"Then why—why in God's name—would you title your paper, "Don't Take Life for Granite"?

The girl pouted.

"Not to mention that, even if correctly spelled, this is arguably the worst cliché known to humankind."

She blinked at the wall. She shuffled her stinky, monster feet.

"I guess on one level, it makes sense: Life is really hard, and maybe you were trying to tell your audience that you should not let the hardness of life rob you of its beauty or joy. Maybe you were being clever. Were you being clever?"

"I don't deserve this." The girl stood up and stomped out the door without another word. Ink smiled to himself. She was bright enough to be insulted; that, at least, was a start.

He spun back to the computer, waiting for remorse that didn't come. The truth was that, for the last several semesters, he'd found himself relishing such encounters more and more. Adjunct pay was a crime against humanity, but a truly wonderful perk for him was the opportunity to expose the ineptitude of boys and girls who thought they were (by virtue of birth) the most talented and creative people this world had ever known. It was Ink's solemn duty to make them feel (if at all possible) at least a little bit worse about themselves. Balance—perspective—that's what today's self-absorbed kids needed.

Minutes later, Robert Garner appeared at the door, grinning affably. For his first paper, he had written a beautiful, unsentimental, almost grammatically perfect account of his mother's pursuit of a nursing degree, which she completed in bursts between raising three kids and working two "soul-rending" jobs.

"Robert," Ink said.

He smiled, pleased to be recognized by name.

"Sit down, sit down. I wanted to say I was really impressed with your work."

Soon, they got to talking about the importance of education, and Ink listened, unable to believe his good fortune. It was not enough for Robert to take classes and work forty hours a week. It was important for him to get involved. He volunteered ten hours a week at a retirement community. He served food to the homeless once a month. He was a member of the College Republicans.

"Wait," Ink said, his heart sinking. "The College *Republicans*?"

Robert smiled. "My high school history teacher once called me an idiot to my face."

Ink looked down at his red pen and imagined Robert's Republican-colored blood dripping from its point.

"I see myself as mostly a fiscal conservative, although I support some of the social issues as well."

Ink could not help but ask: "What's fiscally conservative about spending billions of dollars to fight a war over weapons of mass destruction that never existed in the first place?"

"This is a war about democracy, about giving oppressed people a real shot at freedom. You can't put a price tag on that."

It was Ink's turn to smile. He rolled it out slowly, so Robert had time to appreciate its intent.

"You don't agree?"

"If you had to go dodge suicide bombs in Iraq, I'm thinking you'd probably change your tune."

"I don't usually dwell on hypotheticals, Professor Alt."

"But just think if Bush found all those WMDs! For one thing, your position might have a little more moral oomph."

Robert blinked. "So . . . you really liked my paper then?"

Ink had to hand it to the boy. If he were only mean-spirited, he'd be a carbon copy of one of those unflappable Fox News pundits who could, seemingly without prick to conscience, wax eloquent about the new purpose of the war as if it had been the one true purpose from the start. Unlike nearly all of his peers, he spoke with assurance, laughed in the rich, confident, controlled way of a successful adult—a CEO, or worse. By all rights, Ink should loathe this boy; in truth, he found himself a little bit charmed.

"Yes, you're a fine writer, an expert communicator," Ink said, handing the boy back his work. "For you, the sky is the limit."

*

It was the end of another day—the laptop said 8:34 pm—and Ink sat on the back porch off his bedroom, cell phone out, thumb over DIAL. Ten days had passed since he'd spoken with his wife, and he thought it was high time to say hello. He placed his thumb upon the button, rubbed it like the side of a magic lamp. What he'd give for a genie wish or two. Instead, all that appeared before him was a smoke-hazy evening from his collegiate past: Julie tearing up under a pay phone in the lobby of a dorm; Ink, standing against the door,

284

transfixed by legs that scissored through the shadows. She mistook his drunken, lustful awe for Christ-like compassion. Because he listened, she found him attractive; because she'd talked so long about her heartbroken life, she probably felt the need to find him later in his room. Ink said "no, no," the word scrambling from his lips before a reason arrived. "No," he said again, and there it was, the reason: she was vulnerable, and it would not be right. "No" as well, because he was untested, and he could imagine only an ugly afterward in which she'd look up at him with sobering eyes that cried, "What in God's name was that?" Ink "No-ed" the door closed, feeling mighty damn good about himself. What had been fear and fatalism became, after a time, the first stage of a master plan.

After the graduation ceremony, Julie found him for a hug. The corner of his mortarboard speared her in the forehead.

"I'm really sorry!" he said, a thumb to her brow, holding it there as if to staunch the flow of blood.

Julie laughed, much more than the incident deserved. She squeezed him again, breasts hard against his gown, breath breezing his neck. Then she went home to Western New York—"Chautauqua Country"—clutching his address and phone number like car keys in her hand. Ink had her name and number on the back of his graduation program, but in those boring, back-down-to-earth days following the ceremony, her laughter seemed less an invitation than a lovely parting gift.

A week later, the first letter arrived, a sticker heart over the flap. "Dear Good Guy," it began, like the case on him was closed. He smiled as he read a humorous account of a job interview, the dysfunction of family members, the isolation of Fredonia, where the best thing going was Interstate 90, East or West. He read her curvy name several times. The sheets of paper smelled of flowers he wished he knew the name of.

Ink went to a department store at Great Northern with a page of the letter and asked the matronly woman behind the perfume counter to identify it. A small container was thirty-two dollars. He looked down at the shapely bottles, shimmering like diamonds. He swallowed. Bravely, he said, "No problem."

"Dear Good Girl," he wrote back in a card inside the package. "This is for you." As he left the post office, he was convinced that this was the most audacious thing he'd ever done.

A few days later she called, thanking him profusely, using the word "sweet" over and over again until he said he might have to make an appointment for the dentist. She laughed, more than the silly joke deserved. They talked for more than an hour about what had already become for them "The Clerestory Years": wild, besotted times on The Bell, acquaintances they had in common, that psych class they'd been in together, the amazing circumstances that had somehow prevented them from meeting until the very last moments of their undergraduate career. "I'm coming for a visit," Julie said out of the blue. It turned out she had an aunt who just moved to the Cleveland area for her job, and the woman was dying for the company of her favorite niece.

So the Good Girl came and The Good Guy was at the Greyhound station to meet her in the middle of the night, to gallantly take her bags, to drive her to her aunt's. He was relieved that his memory of her face and body had been accurate, give or take a blemish. The next night, he splurged on a fancy dinner at Nighttown, a quaint and cozy Irish restaurant on the east side of town. Shy, awkward, unsure of his footing, they went back in conversation to shared experiences they'd already exhausted over the phone.

"Oh my God, do you remember that speaker?" She reached out and touched his hand. The crazy writer?"

"Yes. He said, 'Get out of here already.'"

"It was like we were all already behind."

At the time, Ink had still been working in the department store stockroom. "Do you think we are behind?"

She smiled, leaned toward him, her eyes steady. And beautiful. "No," she said after a pause. "We're right where we're supposed to be."

By the end of the visit—five days of coffee shops and dinners, movies and complicated bucket seat grapplings in the Great Northern parking lot—Ink had fallen thoroughly and (he thought) irrevocably in love.

But now, with considerable bitterness, he'd come to understand his relationship with Julie as a more ambitious kind of falling—not a simple one-time thing, but a falling for years and years: first, *in* love; then, after a time, *through* that love with an ear-splitting crash; then down, down, head over heels (he was reminded of that grim Dickinson poem), into a pitch black something else that felt for months now like the seconds before the final fatal thud.

The cell phone blittered, and Ink, jarred from his reverie, nearly dropped it over the railing to the patio below.

"Why do I have to rely on other people to let me know you're in town?"

"Who? What?" Ink vaguely recognized the voice.

"Your mom. Ran into her at Giant Eagle."

"Sandro! Yes, well . . . I've been very busy."

"How about dinner next week?"

"I, well—"

"I'm sorry, can you hold?"

He tried not to feel slighted. Best friends in elementary school, the two had, after many years, established contact once again. In fact, during Ink's visit home the previous summer, he and Julie spent a long evening with them, preparing pasta, chatting about foreign films over pricey wine, Miles Davis in the background. "We should really get down there to see you guys," Sandro had said as they were leaving. They hadn't done so yet, but that was no surprise: his friend was a very busy man; in fact, he was probably speaking to a client now.

"Sorry. You there?" Sandro asked.

"I think so."

"Next Wednesday, 6:30? Kate's on this absurd vegetarian kick, but what the hell: some of the stuff she makes is pretty damn good."

"Great," Ink said, and he meant it.

*

It was Sunday—a day of rest. Ink stretched out on the couch, nodding off in front of an Indians game. Mom sat down in her rocker, kneading a church bulletin in her hand.

"They're doing well this year," Mom said, nodding toward the screen. "Maybe they'll go all the way—like your Cavaliers."

"The Cavs are down 1-0."

"They could come back. Miracles can happen."

They watched Travis Hafner at the plate. A strike. A ball. A foul back to net. Then, a hard shot—a double to the wall. Ink gave a fist pump full of irony.

"You missed an interesting homily today," Mom said. "It was about people who forget God until they really need him."

"That's nice."

"You know, it's only a matter of time before the bishop shuts us down."

"Long overdue." Over the last twenty-five years, St. James the Lesser had become St. James the Least. Most parishioners had escaped the city—to Lakewood, Bay Village, Olmsted Falls, Avon Lake. Farther and farther from color and crime. There were several young Hispanic families in the parish, but by and large the congregation was comprised of the aged, the grandparents and parents of those who were around Ink's age. The roof of the church needed to be replaced. The air conditioner was again on the blink. Last month, Fr. Nadolny woke up to discover that the copper gutters had been stolen. Last week, a stained-glass St. Francis had his haloed head punched out. The grade school, Ink's land of dreams and fears for eight long years, had been put out of its misery over a decade ago.

Victor Martinez stepped into the batter's box, and Ink shifted, suddenly keen to see something big.

"What's your problem with the church?"

Mom typically worked by indirection, like Dickinson or Frost. But here, to his surprise, was a direct challenge.

"I just don't buy the whole show anymore." If he'd had some warning about this interrogation, his initial salvo would have been better, stronger, more devastating.

"I see."

He sat up and itemized his complaints about the Church: women were second class citizens, homophobia ran rampant among the "faithful," the priests never seemed to meet a little boy they didn't want to fondle or worse. "It's a new day," he declared. "There are new and better ways to see the world."

As he finished his diatribe, the play-by-play man began to get excited. Ink turned back to the TV to see a deep drive to the wall. Boston's centerfielder jogged back and back and caught the ball on the warning track, retiring the side.

Mom stood and said, "You speak like you've been born again."

"I'm awake to alternatives," Ink said. "I think for myself, if that's what you mean."

Sandro had recently moved to Bay Village, a beautiful five-bedroom colonial with a home theater and an in-ground pool and a backyard that gracefully sloped toward the lake. As Ink pulled up the long, sinuous drive, he instinctively felt his shirt pocket for the gilded invitation he would surely need to have.

"Your place is incredible," he said after the tour, which lasted a full two beers.

Sandro slipped his arm around Kate. "We're doing all right."

Sandro was a tax lawyer, and his wife, a sharp dressed beauty, came from all kinds of money. They had two kids—a little league all-star and a lovely ballerina—who happened to be staying with Sandro's parents for the night. His old friend and his wife were doing more than all right; they had circumvented the nastiness of death and ascended high into heaven.

The three settled on barstools at the vast Formica island in the kitchen, sipping drinks and nibbling bruschetta from a silver serving tray. The track lighting, the stainless steel appliances, the sleek marble tile—all of it made him think of some fancy set on a cable cooking show. He thought of his Clerestory apartment, with its stringy beige carpeting the landlord had been promising to replace for three years, the old windows that had to be propped open with hunks of wood, the chipped linoleum in the kitchen, the milk crate bookshelves. Even after all these years, Ink's living space was distinctly undergraduate—not a home like Sandro's, but more of a place to crash.

Sandro, oblivious to Ink's anxieties, talked about the past as if it were a cool friend who was going to be a little late the dinner. Ink nodded, smiled, feeling ill at ease but trying to be happy about the fact that the long-standing relationship with his friend was being confirmed in this way.

"So what's your dissertation about?" Kate asked.

Hemingway, he told them, his anxiety spiking. A posthumous novel. Men vs. women. He trotted out all the buzz words—code switching, social construction, heteronormativity—in order to impress them.

"Look, I'm going to make a simple request," Sandro said. "Please, please, please, don't tell me Hemingway was gay."

"Why?" Kate asked. "What's wrong with being homosexual?"

Sandro laughed. "Nothing, nothing. But that doesn't mean there aren't some players you'd like to keep on your team."

Ink's original idea for his dissertation had been quite different. He wanted to write about his first love: Hemingway's *In Our Time* and the bildungsroman, Nick Adams and his coming of age in a world of war. To deepen the analysis, he thought he could sprinkle in a bit of Emersonian self-reliance. When he explained the idea to Sikma, his advisor leaned back in his chair and threw a pen at a water stain in the drop-down ceiling. Bull's eye. "Look," he told Ink, "You can't just re-notice interesting things. You've got to break new ground. You like Hemingway, write on this," he said, pulling from his shelf a copy of *The Garden of Eden*, a posthumous novel. "Comparatively speaking, there's still not much written on this."

After an hour of bullying, during which Sikma used words like "complexification" and "performativity," Ink left the office with Butler, Foucault, Deleuze and Guattari. Book after book was dropped into his hands, the dense, jargon-darkened work of thinkers that Ink for the most part had been able to put behind him after that horror of a theory course his first semester of graduate school.

"We read this one story in college," Kate said. "The husband and wife are on a safari?"

"'The Short Happy Life of Francis Macomber.'"

"That's it!" Kate said. "At the end now—didn't the woman kill him on purpose?"

"I think," Ink said, dimly recalling the story, "the important thing is that Macomber stood his ground. He shot the bull."

Sandro cleared his throat. "If you want to be a real man, you don't shoot the bull. You *wrestle* the bull."

Ink smiled. Kate brushed her husband on the wrist with a hand, an act of loving admonition.

Sandro shrugged. "Well, that's the story I would write."

After dinner, they moved to the spacious stone patio, sat down inside a festive ring of citronella candles, and the conversation turned unexpectedly to Julie. Kate, eyes out toward the lake, asked: "Is everything alright with you two?"

Ink wondered how she might have found out about his marital

problems. Julie didn't seem to know Kate well enough to call and talk about such things. Maybe Mom had passed along her hunches to Sandro when they ran into each other at the supermarket? Maybe she'd seen him wandering around town alone and read between the lines?

"You don't have to talk about it," Sandro said.

"No, no, it's okay." Ink, tired of keeping things to himself, started at the beginning—the move from Cleveland back to Clerestory soon after their marriage, Julie surrendering with some pain a well-paying job so Ink could pursue his Ph.D. He sold her on resuming the dream of their undergraduate days, but with Sikma's attitude, Julie's employment opportunities (retail, fast food, minimum wage day care), and the stunning fact that Clerestory—when you are twenty-five and six and seven and the people who made it what it was had long since gone—was just another nice enough small town, they found themselves in a world neither had expected. They'd gamely made do, Julie diligent and optimistic in her various employments, Ink racing through coursework and comprehensive examinations. Then this damn dissertation, the bull determined to finish him off.

Ink had been warned by more than a few people about going back to Clerestory for his doctorate, but he'd applied anyway. Because the graduate program was new and in desperate need of quality students, he was accepted. It wasn't until years later, after he'd at last drafted an acceptable prospectus, that Ink understood fully how his advisor was going to make him pay.

"Wait," Sikma said, flipping through the pages of the document and scanning the bibliography. "You're just going to read the Jenks?"

"What do you mean?"

"The novel as published is just one possible version."

"Are you saying I'll need to read the whole manuscript?"

"Of course. That should really go without saying."

"Where is it?"

"You really should know that," Sikma sighed. "Boston."

According to the most recent scholarship of the time, the published version of *The Garden of Eden* had preserved—had protected—the Hemingway Ink had come to know and love. The 2,000-page manuscript was, his advisor suggested, the underside of the iceberg, the shadowy place where the secret, sexually transgressive writer swam in his skivvies. In the last few years, Ink had driven to

Boston twice, each time at his own expense (rental car, a grim hotel in Dorchester, a series of bad fast food meals) and the plan was to go once more—a quick trip, after he and Julie enjoyed their Cape Cod anniversary. If, that was, his wife didn't threaten to leave him for asking.

Sandro drained his beer. "Well buddy, you'll get it done. And she'll come around."

Ink smiled, but only to be polite. What he was really thinking was that his old friend had sounded like a younger, less socially awkward version of Dad.

"Is there anything I can do?" Kate said. "Would you like me to call her?"

The seafood lasagna, the pinot grigio (and the beers before the dinner), the strawberry tarts—all of the rich food and drink made him feel like a fixture in this family. What if he lived here? What if this woman were his wife? The lipstick and eye shadow, the leather jacket and boots—Kate looked fabulous. But Ink found her a little depressing as well. For all her geniality, she seemed at times to be a person who had somewhere more important to be very soon: a high-powered fund raiser, an anchor desk for the local news.

"No, no," he said, unable to look her in the face. "I just need to finish."

Sandro changed the topic to the Cavaliers, who were down 3-0 to the San Antonio Spurs in the NBA Finals. Ink was of the opinion that LeBron was wilting under the intense heat of the national spotlight, but Sandro shook his head, saying, "The dude needs help. He's not going to win a thing with this cast of characters."

Ink nodded. No one could do it alone. No matter how talented. This was a great comfort for him. Next life, he'd be sure to pick a less solitary occupation if for no other reason than that the blame might be spread around.

Kate listened politely to this sports talk for a while and then stood, yawning into her long, painted fingers.

"And what do you think, my dear?" Sandro asked with a wink.

"That there are more important things than sports. Like sleep. Like skimming bugs from the pool." She kissed Sandro on his impish lips, placed a hand on Ink's shoulder, and clocked back to the house.

The two sat there for a few moments trying to fill up the awkward silence with frequent pulls on their beers. Finally, Sandro sat up and said, "Oh, hey, I've been meaning to ask: you still play ball?"

Ink laughed.

"I'm serious. We've got a game a few times a week up at Ignatius."

Sandro pressed him with particulars. It was grade school all over again, when his friend spent years trying to get him to join the CYO team. Ink had ended up playing, but every time he stepped on the court he'd been scared to death of making a shameful spectacle of himself. There were plenty of awful memories, but the one that came to mind now was this tournament game, where Ink, with time running down, found himself at the foul line. A balcony wrapped around the gym, and the fans leaned over the iron railing, faces scowling, hands dropping down zombie-like to try to bat the shot away when he released it. Ink dribbled twice, teeth chattering. He threw the ball up, and it thundered off the backboard. Above the basket, a crew cut boy with bad teeth rained invective down upon his perspiring head. Ink lasted two more trips down the court before pleading with Coach Bishop to take him out.

"One game," Sandro said. "It'll be just like old times."

"That's what I'm afraid of."

"And afterward, the beer is on me."

"Okay," Ink said, feeling thirteen again. "Let me think about it."

*

Back in his old bedroom that night, Ink's loneliness was especially acute. Again, he stared at his cell phone. The first three times he'd called Julie, he'd gotten the machine, the voice in the new message sharp and professional: "Please leave your name, number, and a *brief* message after the tone." Each time he heard the beep, he listened for a few long seconds to nothing before hanging up. Where was she? What could she be doing? Occasionally, she went to happy hours with her coworkers. There was this Tracy, an undergraduate she once called her cubicle confidante. She'd mentioned a Todd too—Todd, who was "a total riot."

The fourth time, after five rings, Julie answered, slightly out of breath. It had been two full weeks since she'd barely lifted that finger for her goodbye.

"Finished yet?" she asked.

"Love you too, Jules."

There was a long pause before she said, "I'm sorry." She asked about Mom and Dad and from there a weak flame of conversation sputtered to life. Several times, Ink thought to ask things like, "What is going to happen?" or "Can we get through this?" Instead, he asked, "So how's the single life?"

"Don't start."

From there, the argument began in earnest. Ink wanted to know why his wife couldn't think to call one time—*one lousy time*—in the past two-plus weeks. Julie ignored the complaint and asked again how the dissertation was going. He said, "it's goddamn going—do you always have to harp?" She wondered—this should not be news to him—how many more years they were going to slog along in limbo. He wondered why she had not grown bored with her long years of bitching and moaning. She wondered if he actually had what it took to make it in the rough and tumble world of academia. As the conversation went on, each thought of new, terrible ways to make their curiosity cruel.

"Go to hell," Ink said at last.

"Um, I think I'm pretty much there."

The line went dead, and Ink tossed the phone to the bed, where it sat like a giant bug on the turned back sheet. He had half a mind to crush it with his fist.

*

With only two weeks left in the composition course, Ink's students showed few signs of improvement. Clichéd openings, stilted thesis statements, mangled sentences, meandering paragraphs, a general suspicion of the world of serious ideas. The few who brought books to class offered little tangible evidence of having reflected on what they had read. Despite his prohibitions, cell phones routinely did their annoying song and dance. Heads bobbed. Ten minutes into one class, a boy in sweats stood and shuffled by him out of the door, leaving a distinct smell of corn chips and urine in his wake. Episodes like this were enough to make Ink doubt the basic humanity of his charges.

Depressed by their anemic effort, angry at himself because of his latest writing troubles, Ink decided one morning to bore them to death with a lecture on effective paraphrasing. Sasquatch boots sulked in the back. Robert kept his head down, writing too assiduously to simply be taking notes. At the end of class, Ink returned the rough drafts of their research papers. He had them writing on a variety of current events: healthcare, genetically modified food, offshore drilling, social security, the Iraq War. He was trying his damnedest to get them past their cluelessness, to offer, with the aid of credible sources, something beyond their knee-jerk reactions to an issue. Channeling Sikma, Ink said, "If these were your final drafts, I would have failed all but three of you for plagiarism." He didn't want to do it—he thought of the hours it was going to cost him—but he decided to hold another round of conferences. "Plan on staying the full half hour," he said. "And be on time. And be prepared. We've got a boatload of stuff to straighten out."

After class, too upset to return to the somber, frigid world of Mom and Dad's, Ink holed up in the university library, figuring a change of scenery might let his ideas start flowing again. He started, as usual, with the words of others, pulling out a dense, twenty-four-page article that was bound to give him plenty of things to write about. Before diving in, though, he rewarded himself with a quick surf of the Internet: a pet food recall, bombs in Iraq and Afghanistan, Julia Roberts—it's a boy! He checked his email as well and was surprised to discover a new message from, of all people, Danny Drellishak. "RPG FROM PAST" the subject line read, and Ink smiled, if only because it helped settle his stomach. Danny had been less a friend than a larger-than-life figure who, for some mysterious reason, deigned to spend considerable time with him throughout his college career. A nobody himself, Ink had been so thrilled to be a particle lodged in Danny's manic orbit. The boy had known absolutely everyone—the babes and brainiacs, the jocks and jokers, the druggies and frat boys. If he had not been universally loved, he was universally known—a force to be reckoned with. Ink was years past being star-struck. In fact, he was horrified at how often and easily he'd been a party to Danny's anger and misogyny. How in those days he'd used it to fuel his own repulsive thoughts and behavior. Still, a tiny part of him glowed now from this sudden attention. Plus the email seemed innocuous enough: "Old times" and "Miss them" and "Let's drink beer" was the gist of it. Ink hesitated to respond—he tried for a time to imagine all possible consequences—and then typed with a sigh a simple "Great to hear from you" followed by a "Let's do something soon."

*

Ink had decided it would look good to be fifteen minutes late to meet Danny, until he was in fact fifteen minutes late and rushing through the door of the Irish pub, sure he'd made a big mistake. He checked each room of the cavernous place, but Danny was nowhere to be found. What if he'd left already, thinking Ink had stood him up? Ambivalent about this meeting, he now admitted he couldn't wait to see this blast from his past. He returned to the bar and ordered a pint. Across from where he sat was a wall filled with every Irish surname imaginable. As he drank, he read the names to himself—Connolly, Foley, Kane, O'Shea, Sheehan—and became filled with a generic yet still powerful sense of sadness. Maybe it was the thought of those dead before their time—Joyce's Michael Furey, sick and soaking below a lover's window; Frankie, Frankie McGooken, his long-ago classmate, the real-life boy (but now, as much a fiction as the other) whose life had been shorter than Ink's between college graduation and now. Maybe it was the potent call of a homeland, even if, to his knowledge, none of his ancestors lived or died anywhere near the Emerald Isle. Maybe too it was just the creamy Guinness already going to his head.

From behind, two powerful hands wrapped around his neck; Ink flailed, turned, tried to escape the grasp, was ready to cry for help. It took him a moment to recognize Danny, who grinned at him now from under a startlingly full head of hair—lavish brown stuff that brushed at his shoulders.

Danny released him, and Ink, finding breath, said, "Jesus Christ!"

"The one and only!"

Ink felt his throat, but he couldn't help but smile. "Is it . . . real?" he asked, pointing at the flowing locks.

Danny frowned. "That hurts, man. After all these years, that's a dagger to the soul."

"Is it real?"

He pulled out his cell, and the next thing Ink knew, Danny was talking to someone to whom he was frequently referring to as "Mom." "Ask her," he said, shoving the phone against Ink's ear. "Go ahead."

Laughing, Ink took the phone and a woman, whoever she really was, confirmed that the hair indeed was genuine.

"So how in hell are you?" Danny asked. Ink remembered the narrow, dangerous eyes, the lips sarcastic as a tilde. Now, his friend's face looked clear, simple, straightforward—a grade schooler on one of the first bright days of September. Ink relaxed and gave him the quick scoop on his life for the last thirteen years. The beer, in fact, made him quite frank: "I'm all done except for the dissertation."

Danny laughed. He wiped foam from his lips. "You're one of those—what do they call them? —one of those All-Butt Fucks!"

Only Danny could make an ABD sound pornographic. Ink smiled, lips helpless against the strong pull of puerility. "Well, what have you been up to?"

"Oh, you know," he said, looking toward the door. "This and that. Right now, a little real estate in the area—flipping homes with an old buddy from the hood." Right now, however, he was "between actual jobs, as they say," and Ink, although curious, didn't ask "How far between?" because he was suddenly afraid that this get-together might really be less about friendship than about cash, and how much Danny might want or need.

But to Ink's relief, Danny seemed more interested in reliving those "Kick-ass Clerestory days." He'd been back a handful of times since graduation, but it wasn't the same. "Wetzler's still there," he said, "above the nail salon, smoking up his Quik Pik paychecks," but so much else had changed. "You know they closed Open Mike's, right?"

"I heard." In fact, Ink knew. He'd seen Wetzler on The Bell more than once—sad and bloated and laboring back to that fumy apartment with a pizza box and a twelve pack of Busch. He almost let it spill that he'd been living down there for the past several years but thought better of it.

Danny was still in occasional contact with Cobb, who lived in New Jersey with a wife that was "shall we say, definitely his speed." Jesse, if he remembered correctly, was somewhere out on the West Coast, a studio musician or something. "And Sherk, Christ, remember him? The dude went back to school, got his business degree from who the hell knows and now he and his hot little woman own this cozy head shop in Yellow Springs."

"Are you serious?"

Danny shook his hair-heavy head. "You never know who people are going to be."

It was good—it was grand—to hear those names again. Ink had lost track of everyone (except Julie, of course) within a year of graduation, but he often liked to think he'd been a part of a special group—a participant in experiences that were unique and unrepeatable. Each time a reunion notice came in the mail, he imagined the moment of his arrival back on campus: his name shouted from across the banquet hall, a playful slug in the arm, a sloppy beer salute. But the reunions had come and gone—the five year, the ten year—and Ink had let them go, his cowardice always bringing him back to earth.

With every sip of beer, Danny and Ink slid deeper and deeper into the warm bath of the past; finally—Ink had lost track of time— the water went cold. Danny took a long drink of stout and bobbed his hairy head, like he was taking in a lecture. Ink, filled with so much nostalgia that he thought he had credits enough for a major, turned teary eyes back to all those Irish surnames on the wall.

"That's one good looking guy," Danny said, nodding up at the large screen TV, where the Indians were staging a late-inning rally.

"Sure," Ink said, not knowing what else to say. He thought of his dissertation, his stuffed Nike box of notes. Rinaldi and Henry, Jake and Brett, David and Catherine Bourne—there was a career worth of evidence that his favorite writer didn't know quite who he was.

"He's black, or something. Look at him. There's no way he's white."

"Does it matter?"

Danny shrugged. "I think life would be easier if there was one skin tone. It could be his—I wouldn't care. I'm very open minded. Just so there's one."

"Isn't variety the spice of life?"

"Variety is a total bitch." Danny drank his stout. "Except when it comes to beer."

"And women?"

"No, no." Danny pressed his lips together. "Through much research, I've discovered they're all the same."

Ink didn't pry. The player in question stepped into the batter's box.

"Grady Sizemore. Dude should be a porn star."

Ink gave Danny an obligatory smile. Years ago, at a Hangovers happy hour, dizzy from a couple of shots of schnapps, Ink would have thought this comment the funniest thing in the world. Now, it was painful to see Danny groping for such material.

Sizemore swung and missed, the bat lunging out beyond the plate before wrapping back around to pat him on the behind.

"Let me ask you something."

"Shoot."

"Promise you won't laugh."

"Sure."

"Do you remember your really good boners?"

Ink laughed out loud.

Danny's lips turned into a tilde. "I'm dead serious. You know the ones. You're twelve, thirteen, and the . . . thing is just beginning to come out of its shell. A smile. An earlobe. Christ, a crack in plaster is enough to set it off."

Ink laughed again, but he wasn't sure he had enough laughs to last for what he feared was an entire bit.

"Right, right—you know what I'm talking about. Who was the best looking girl in your eighth grade class? What was her name?"

It didn't take Ink long to remember: "Bethany."

"Bethany what?"

"Hyde."

"Hmmm, I'm getting an image, and it's not too bad. Ours was, get this: Luscious Fox. Can you believe it?"

"Not at all."

"OK, her real name was Lucy. Anyway," Danny said, erasing the air between them with a hand. "One day, Luscious had to get her math quiz to the desk at the front of the room. The rows, for some reason, were very narrow, and she had to go sideways. She moved past me, her rump bursting in these tight black nylon pants. Did I tell you she always smelled like cherry Now-n-Laters? I'm thirteen, and I'll tell you—I could hear threads of my underwear popping left and right."

Ink tried to hold onto his smile.

"Honestly, that moment . . . I don't think I ever felt more alive."

One time in the second year of their marriage, just after he'd started graduate school, Ink had gone with Julie to a fancy pool party thrown for some big deal visiting writer whose name he couldn't recall. The party was at the dean's house, one of the sprawling mansions north of Clerestory, a stone's throw from the river. There was an in-ground pool, a huge deck with a canopied hot tub. Inside the house, in a vast living room brilliant with sunshine from the skylight above, there was a miniature museum of African art. Giddy in the face of such opulence, Ink and Julie had more than a few of all the crayon-colored drinks. When they returned to their dour little rental, it was still light outside and Julie smelled of sunscreen and strawberry daiquiri and the leather sandal straps over sun-baked toes put Ink in the mind of carnal things. Julie must have been thinking the same because the front door was not even closed before she went at him, lips and hands and groin. They careened off kitchen counter and fridge, laughing (always laughing, he thought with a pang), grabbing and tearing, clunking teeth, performing a clumsy pirouette onto the couch before wrestling all the way into the second bedroom, where an old futon mattress sat still looking for a frame. But who needed the frame now—at a time like this, who the hell cared about a stupid fucking frame?

"Fin-ish me off!" Ink cried a short fabulous while later, and Julie, face bathed in sweat, made good on his plea in so fine and thorough a fashion that he didn't think he would ever stop shooting out, into her again and again so hard and far that he was sure she'd become pregnant with sextuplets. He had been twenty-seven years old, and here he was now, eight years later, a complete fool, giving serious thought to how to rank this sexual experience against the ones before and since.

"How did it happen?"

Ink blinked at Danny. "Sorry…?"

Danny removed his hair and folded it like a letter upon the bar. "Somebody made me old."

The plug looked like a tarantula taking a snooze. Ink chuckled, even though he told himself not to. "What can you do?" he said.

Danny gulped from the beer that had just been set down before him. "I'm thinking," he said, foaming at the lips. "Give me a little more time."

*

For the last several months—at least since Dad's blood pressure and cholesterol stumbled into the "high" range—Mom had become rabidly health-conscious. She demanded that he take nightly walks

300

with her around the block. She subscribed to magazines. She counted calories. She eliminated red meat. She banned the salt shaker from the table. Every dinner was simple and healthy but, in Ink's opinion, robbed of flavor—robbed of joy.

After one particularly bland meal—broiled chicken breasts, steamed broccoli, and plain brown rice—Ink asked Mom, "Do you miss it?"

"Miss what?" She squirted dish liquid into the sink and frothed the suds with a hand.

"Flavor? Taste?"

"Now you don't like my food?"

"Mom . . ."

"I'm trying to keep us alive."

"Thought you couldn't wait to get to heaven."

Mom clunked a plate against the faucet. "Are you going to start again?"

Ink took the plate from her and wiped in thoroughly before stacking it upon others in the cupboard above. Maybe he should have apologized—if the comment was not out of line then it was an unprovoked attack. He was angry, bitter, frustrated by how little he had to show for his work so far. She should understand that. She should sympathize. Somebody should.

"Maybe you should go see what your father's up to."

Ink wiped his hands and went to the basement, where Dad had retreated after dinner to do his work with wood. The basement was dim, the concrete floor damp. Exposed ducts, sporting pink beards of insulation, snaked around the ceiling. Even as a youngster, the place depressed him. When he went to bed at night, he always made sure the basement door was locked, to keep the ugliness below from creeping up the stairs to where he lay tossing in his bed.

The work bench was stacked with dog-eared how-to books. Hammers, screwdrivers, and implements Ink didn't know the name of clung on the wall. Before them was a pair of sawhorses. Against the washer were thin slabs of wood—"pine," his dad said, as if that would make a difference to Ink.

If only Mom had sent him down here with a load of clothes. Turn the dial, stuff the washer, sprinkle in the detergent, sit on the lid with a book until the cycle was done. In college, he'd washed clothes in the dorm laundry room three or four times a week, at different hours of the day, convinced that a beautiful girl at some point would enter the room, and they would get to talking. A date would follow, a proposal, a marriage. Hers would be a big, rich, deliriously happy family that gathered for loud and lovely holiday dinners. He and this gorgeous girl would have children, and they would age no more than five or six years out of deference to their parents, who'd settle in at the ripe old age of thirty or thirty-one. Summer after summer, they'd go to the family house on Put-in-Bay to play board games on the deck, eat hearty breakfasts, tell long, laugh-out-loud stories over wine and enjoy barefoot sunset strolls in sweatshirts across the cooling sand.

"Slip these on," Dad said, handing him goggles. He put them on, tied on an apron that said, "Home Depot." "And these earplugs."

Ink looked at the two knobs of orange sponge. "Seriously?"

"This saw runs at about 120 decibels. Did you know hearing loss can begin at 95?"

Ink pushed the stubs into his ears. What was the point of arguing?

"I'm going to show you how to cut a board." Delicately, he placed the board over the sawhorse. "Ready?"

Ink nodded, and the saw whirred like his thoughts: dissertation, Julie, Sandro, bad research papers, a palatial house on the lake. Hemingway, Danny, LeBron. Dad and Mom. Church, the bulletin from St. James, which had been laying on the kitchen counter when he came downstairs for an afternoon writing break. Today, he learned from the photocopied sheet that he'd missed the Feast of John the Baptist. At the bottom of the page was a quotation from the saint: "Therefore this joy of mine is now complete. He must increase, but I must decrease." He'd been surprised that Dad hadn't circled the passage and taped it on his door.

When the whirring stopped, Ink said, "Jesus was a carpenter's son."

Dad turned to him with goggly eyes. "Pardon?"

"Jesus," he said. It was the only relevant piece of trivia that came to mind, but Dad nodded, as if the information were good to know.

The saw whined again. Tiny chips flew as the blade made progress against the board. This was supposedly going to be a shelf of his bookcase, which he knew already was never going to fit in his hatchback. He'd have to use bungee cords. He'd have to affix red flags to warn other vehicles of the bulky load. When he returned to Clerestory, he'd have to find someone to help him get the damn thing out and through the front door. Was it too late to ask for something else?—a birdhouse perhaps, maybe a plaque for his study that said, "All But Able to Finish."

*

As he pulled into the lot adjacent his old high school gym, Ink remembered failed athletes from the pages of American literature—Brick in *Cat on a Hot Tin Roof*, crutching angrily around the bedroom waiting for the click; Updike's Rabbit, who at twenty-six, still thought he had game, especially when his opponents were young boys; that character from Cheever, the former track star who gets shot by his wife while hurdling a sofa. He'd put on a brave face for Sandro, but there was no way short of not playing that this evening would end up well.

To his surprise, he knew several of the guys: Sandro, of course, who cried out from the other end of the gym, "Ink is in da house!"; Lance Duda, the center from his old CYO team, who slap-shook Ink's hand and said, "Long time, no see!"; a couple of guys from high school whom Ink had recognized by nod. There were total strangers too: ex-football players, a number of younger dudes—quick as hell strangers, with smooth shots and great ball handling skills. At a glance, it was clear that everyone could play.

While they were shooting free throws for teams, Macho Maldonado, the nemesis of Ink's youth, arrived in shirt and tie, dropping his bag by the pushed back bleachers. Ink hadn't seen him in more than ten years, but as Macho greeted the other guys, he swallowed hard, preparing for what was sure to be the climax of the novel of his life. But it turned out that the two just shook hands and Macho (Miguel now) put his other hand on Ink's shoulder to give it an affectionate squeeze. Macho/Miguel was fit, clean-cut, with dazzling white teeth. There was a trace of cologne about him, a scent of peppermint mouthwash. To Ink, this one-time hot shot was suddenly the best guy in the world.

Ink was relieved to have Sandro and Miguel on his team; however, as fate would have it, one of the ex-footballers had decided to defend him. His body was a boulder covered with dark coils of hair. He wore a stars and stripes bandana to keep his hair from flying

303

around. On offense, Ink tried to beat him with nonstop action. He made cut after cut, but he could not shake the guy. When Miguel passed him the ball, he tried to dribble to the basket, but the guy threw his arms out like wings on an airplane, and Ink didn't stand a chance.

On the next trip down the floor, Ink complained to Sandro, "He can't do that."

Sandro shrugged. "Call a foul."

Instead, Ink became frustrated. He boiled inside at the ignorance of his opponent, the blatant injustice of his actions. When he pivoted into a wad of wet underarm hair, he grumbled, "Learn how to play the game." Bad Ass Bandana either didn't hear him or chose to ignore the complaint.

Finally, mercifully, the ball was deflected out of bounds and rolled behind the folded up bleachers. Ink, his hands on his knees, had time to breathe. He also had time to think. Of family. Marriage. Academia. Sports. In what arena could he compete?

"You're doing fine!" Miguel said, hands on hips, the epitome of good health. "Second wind is coming." Ink nodded, smiled, remembered the torture of ladders all those years ago. Inside, he continued to seethe.

The next trip down court, one of the young quick studs shook a defender and sent a no-look pass to Lance in the post. He dribbled once, twice, and as he turned to the basket, the ball was poked away and bounced toward the three-point line; Ink, seeing Bad Ass Bandana lumber after it, made it his life's ambition to get there first. The two met at the ball, Ink bending down as Bandana lunged head first. The next thing Ink knew he was sitting knees up on the court. There didn't seem to be pain, but the world had become slow, full of any number of fascinating components: the floor, the basket, a body here and there, hands on hips. Blood appeared on his fingers—bright, shiny, like liquid rubies. Bandana was lying on his back, leg going up and down like a hairy pump.

A voice from above said, "Man, that's got to hurt." Ink closed his eyes, saw his gray brain sloshing back and forth in a tub of turbid water. When he opened his eyes again, a familiar face loomed like a dirigible over his head.

"Ink . . . are you okay?"

Sandro. Sandro's voice. Sandro's concerned face. His friend held out hands, and Ink took them, beginning a slow, strange, unprecedented ascent. No, no—he'd done this before. Countless times. It was called standing.

"How many fingers am I holding up?"

Why couldn't he be good at something? Why couldn't he be a King?

"Fingers," Sandro said. "Come on. I'll give you a hint: the number's between four and six."

"We are all fingers," Ink said.

Sandro smiled. Behind him a ripple of laughter.

A few feet away, a body crouching like a catcher, fingers doing laps around a temple. Big shoulders. Hairy up to the neck. The Bad Ass Bandana.

"What the hell?" Ink's voice was out there, the words like skywriting above them all. He was moving, shoe in front of shoe, toward the guy, but just as quickly he was not.

"Easy now," another voice said. The smell of cologne meant Macho. Miguel. His old nemesis was holding him back—but gently, like a parent, which he was. Two kids, a boy and girl, Miguel had told him while they stretched. The once-obnoxious boy had become an ordinary guy—a husband and a dad. And Ink? As Sandro led him toward a folding chair, Ink tried to consider the difference between the self he'd been and the one he was now. His mind, though, went suddenly blank and blank and blank—a ream of printer paper spilling to the floor.

*

There was a soft hand upon his bare shoulder. Ink blinked. For a thrilling moment, he thought, "Julie."

"It's been two hours, son."

Dad. Dad saying words Ink didn't know what to do with.

"Actually, Two hours and two minutes."

Ink dug with his fingers at the pain that thundered across his head. His mouth was drunk drunk dry.

"Do you need anything?"

Ink picked up the glass on the nightstand and took a drink. He lowered his head back down to the pillow. "I'm good," he said.

Sometime later, the voice returned: "Son, I'm sorry to bother you."

"What is it?" Ink felt around: cool sheets, cool sheets. Above, his father's face wrinkling into a smile.

"It's okay. Go back to sleep."

The third time, Ink was ready for him. As soon as the door squeaked open, Ink had a "thumbs up" ready. When Dad left, he stared into the black, saw the Bad Ass Bandana diving for the floor, saw his own head like a rocket into the surface of that star-spangled planet. He'd gone after the guy but was stopped (thank goodness!); then, somehow, he was in the emergency room, Sandro on one side and Miguel on the other. Friends, such dear friends! With everything quiet around him, he thought for a moment that he'd stumbled upon the meaning of life.

In the morning, Ink moved tentatively, like a toddler along furniture. His head pounded. He wanted to throw up, but he wanted coffee more. Downstairs, he moved gingerly around Mom, who was sitting in her nightgown at the kitchen table with a cup of tea and thumbing through a magazine of heart-healthy recipes.

"Do you like kale?" she asked.

"What is it?"

"A vegetable."

"Did you just make that up?" He shoveled grounds into the basket, wondered how many words he'd need to write today to make up for how far he was behind.

"It'll help you live longer . . . as long as you don't do something stupid."

Ink opened the cupboard to see what was on the breakfast menu: Cheerios or Bran Flakes. He wasn't that hungry anyway.

"You could have gotten yourself killed."

"Not really."

When the coffee had dripped enough, Ink replaced the carafe with his mug. As he was making his escape, he ran into Dad, who asked him yet again how he was feeling. Good, fine, slept like a baby— he threw out as many responses as he needed in order to get back as soon as possible to his room.

Upstairs, the cursor was a middle finger on the computer screen. Ink popped another pain killer and listened to a reporter on the radio describing in horrific detail the carnage wrought by another roadside bomb in Iraq. That's right, Ink thought, gently squeezing his head between thumb and forefinger. There was a war going on. Still. Every day, it seemed, there was a bomb, ten people, fifteen, twenty-two gone in a flash—men training to be officers, locals having tea in a café, women holding hands with small children at the market. He imagined stunned eyes blinking through rivulets of blood, arms twisted in agony toward the smoke-smeared heavens, limp, dusty bodies being dragged from the rubble. A few weeks ago, there'd been a *News Hour* story about a young soldier who'd been seriously injured by a roadside bomb. His wife spoke with great poise about how difficult life was now. All the while, the soldier lay in a hospital bed beside her, mouth open and wet, eyes inert, mere receptacles for light. The sad tale of human misery went on and on without so much as a chapter break, while Ink leaned back in a cushioned chair in front of his screen, his only job being to come up with eight hundred words for the day. There was little question he had it good—better in fact than most people in the world. And yet, wasn't he suffering as well? Why did he have to feel so bad about claiming a little pain for himself?

*

That Sunday, still woozy from the blow, Ink came downstairs, rubbed his eyes and said he'd like to go with his parents to mass.

"I'll ask you one more time," Mom said, belting herself in. "Are you sure about this? I'd hate to see you get any sicker."

"I will survive."

Dad smiled bashfully at him in the rearview mirror, and Ink felt sad to the point of tears. The blow to the head had sent him stumbling too close to sentimentality. He closed his eyes. He had to—in order to get ahold of himself.

By the time Fr. Nadolny entered alone through the side door of the church, there were perhaps twenty-five people in the pews, sprinkled here and there. Out of the corner of his eye, Ink studied Mom as she sang the a cappella entrance hymn (there had not been an organist at the church for years) and wondered what she thought might move him in this moribund performance that unfolded before them. But since he'd agreed to come, he figured he'd suspend judgment for the time being.

During the readings, Ink, finding it difficult to focus, studied the

307

massive Christ that hung over the altar, ribs forming a kind of tabernacle. When he was a little boy, the wood carved body had scared him half to death. Now it seemed grotesque—even a little self-indulgent.

"What's he doing?" he asked Mom a long, long time ago.

"Dying."

"Does everybody die?"

"Yes."

"Like that?"

"Only the brave ones. The ones who have something to say and do." He remembered her response being as much a challenge as an explanation.

Fr. Nadolny, grayer and rounder but still possessing that other-worldly capacity for longwindedness, began his homily with an anecdote about Thomas Merton, whose *Seeds of Contemplation* books had long been staples of Mom's after-dinner reading hour. The monk's brother, John Paul, a lost soul who thought he'd find himself by signing up for the war, came to visit Merton at Gethsemani, desperate to become a Catholic before heading overseas. As the priest spoke, Ink thought about high school, the senior year trip to the monastery in upstate New York. It had been sixteen, seventeen years, and still Ink had not forgotten the bitter cold, the abject loneliness, the eternal silence, which drove him and several of his fellow students to silliness. Mr. Murfin, the retreat director, had been livid. No detention. No threats to report them to the principal. He just told Ink, "It's time to act like an adult." The shame of the memory made him tune back in again to Fr. Nadolny, who was still going on with his Merton story—John Paul's hasty instruction and baptism, the poignant parting, the brother's plane going down over the English Channel before he ever got a chance to serve.

"This is a powerful tale," the priest said. He looked around for a few moments, as if the other words he'd wanted to say had escaped out the door. "This is a story of how God's love and grace can come to us at any point in our lives—even in the nick of time!"

At communion, Ink stood—out of habit at first and then, when he remembered what he was doing, out of a desire to be provocative. Mom, still kneeling, stared up at him, eyebrows like cathedral vaulting.

"You're going?"

"Aren't you?"

Mom shuffled out of the pew, and he followed her down that well-worn marble path. Dad, for mysterious reasons of his own, stayed put. As he approached the priest, Ink waited for all the old ghosts to return, but they remained suspiciously aloof. Sure, he remembered first Friday masses with the entire school, the Stations of the Cross, Fr. Nadolny calling students up around the altar for the blessing of the Eucharist. He remembered jokes, suppressed laughter, the comic faces of kids whose names he could not always recall. But such memories came to him like information learned for an exam that he had long since passed.

He reached the head of the line. Brightening, Fr. Nadolny held up the host. "John," he said, with a gravity that made it sound like he was issuing a command.

Ink was moved. It had been years since he'd come here for communion. He cleared his throat and said, trying like hell to mean it, "Amen."

When he slipped the wafer between his parted lips, it promptly stuck to the roof of his mouth. All the way back to the pew, he tried desperately with his tongue to pry the foreign presence loose. This was a metaphor, he thought, and he didn't much like it.

"Well, I have to say I'm very happy you went," Mom said when they were back home, preparing for lunch. "Amazed, but happy."

"Blame it on the brain injury," he said.

"God works in mysterious ways."

"Just think what I might have done had He tossed me in front of a bus."

Mom smiled—she hadn't lost the ability—before folding over a section of the newspaper in order to indulge in her Sunday afternoon ritual: the crossword puzzle. Dad perused the church bulletin, made a few painfully obvious comments about the weather and then, grabbing a diet cola from the fridge, disappeared outside to mow the lawn. Ink tried to concentrate on the arts section, but the coffee he sipped only made him more alert to his nausea, the dull throb in his head. Any good feeling he had this morning was disappearing down the drain.

"Seriously, Mom. What do you get out of it?" Ink asked, taking a bite out of a low sodium turkey sandwich.

Mom looked up from her page of empty squares.

"Every week you go, you sit and stand and kneel, you mumble the prayers. It's like *Night of the Living Dead*."

The blast from the mower changed the atmosphere from playful to tense. Ink put a hand to his brow, felt a headache coming on. He invoked Lyotard, let Mom know that according to the theorist Christianity was simply one of those "grand recits" whose time of tyrannical sway was gone for good. "We live now," he patiently explained, "in an era of little narratives. More than ever before, marginalized voices and perspectives are being heard." He wanted, once and for all, for her to at least consider the possibility that she might be wrong.

"Did you listen to the homily today?"

"Yes, yes, Merton. Your hero. He lived a wild life in his youth, got it out of his system before becoming a monk. He had it both ways, really. Pretty shrewd."

Mom made a few black marks in her puzzle. "You know," she said, "I'm going to keep going to church and then I'll die and go someplace else and you won't have to deal with me anymore."

"Mom . . ."

"Then you and . . . all your people will take over."

"Don't be so . . ."

The mower roared past the kitchen window, but Mom, oblivious, returned to the puzzle. Ink watched her form the letters, one letter per box, each in his tiny cell. Another metaphor—perfect for the circumscribed life of people like her.

That night, he spent way too much time on a handout for his class. But if he didn't, how were his students going to get it through their thick skulls that a thesis needed to be an argument? How were they going to understand how to create effective transitions that would help readers get from one paragraph to another? How were they going to be able to deftly insert secondary source material instead of dropping it like an old TV from a fourth-floor window into a dumpster? When he finished, he opened his dissertation file and stared at the screen bright with a page he'd written the day before. He changed a phrase here, a comma there. He did a word count. He dozed and dreamed—a courtroom in the white, ethereal above, Julie and Sikma entering in black robes, eyes dark, arms crossed in judgment. He woke with a start, thinking with great horror that he was again a young boy, that these dark-clad figures were his real parents.

Unable to get back to sleep, he went to the computer and opened up his dissertation file again. He stared at the screen, trying to will good words into existence. When that failed, he surfed the net: from news (peacekeepers slain in Lebanon) to entertainment (a reflection on the sublime genius of *The Sopranos*) to music (a surprisingly so-so review of Wilco's new CD). Perhaps it was the darkness—the frigid stillness—of the house that made him think of Mom, of Merton, of the so-called joys of the walled-in life. No temptations. No complications. Just rise every morning for the simple job of making your will the will of God. On a lark, he typed the monk's name into a search box and in an instant discovered that Merton, whom he knew little about beyond Mom's books and the occasional words that had trickled down to him at school, was no saint—even after he entered the monastery. In fact, quite late in his life, he'd had an affair with his nurse. A nurse! It was Ernest and Agnes all over again, Ink thought, except for the vows to God and an age difference of *twenty-five years*. Ink rubbed his hands together. He nearly laughed out loud, thinking of Mom (poor soul) and those tainted seeds of contemplation that she'd been pecking like a nervous bird every night for years.

*

The next day, the bad taste of his most recent composition class still in his mouth, Ink returned to his room and began building Babylon with his books. On the BBC, there was a report about a roadside bomb in Kirkuk. A correspondent from an independent news organization was seriously injured, his camera man blown to bits. The host was interviewing someone—a friend, a colleague—who'd come upon the scene a few minutes later. It was terrible, just awful.

The interviewer asked, "Does this give you pause? To what extent will this affect your future as a journalist?"

"I am heartbroken," the reporter said. "I'm going to go lie down for a long while. And cry. These were such great friends! But are you asking me if I intend to leave? To just stop doing my job?"

"In a word—"

"This tragedy is an excellent reason to redouble my efforts, to become even more firmly committed to bringing the true stories of this terrible war to the rest of the world."

"Timothy Bashour there," the host said, "on the latest act of

311

terror in Iraq."

Ink put down the book he'd been thumbing through. Bashour, Bashour—that was the name of an old high school acquaintance, the friendly boy who'd tutored him many years ago. Iran, Grenada, Lebanon, Israel—there was not a place in the world he did not know a great deal about. Back then, Ink paid attention enough to pass the exams. He didn't want to think of how much he might have been like the students he was now trying to show the light.

That night, there was an extended interview with Bashour on *The World*. Ink listened with forehead on praying hands as his old acquaintance recounted the carnage with a combination of grief and unshakable idealism. As the conversation went on, though, Ink detected a real heat, a palpable anger, in the reporter's voice. He accused the West of having attention deficit disorder: "We all know if a war lasts more than a month, Americans will simply turn the channel." Of course, Ink agreed. Wasn't this the very same thing he'd told his students since the beginning of this whole fiasco? What kids needed were a few days not in the library but on the ground in Baghdad. Afterward, they still wouldn't be able to write a human sentence, but at least they'd have done enough research to know not to take their fun and freedoms for granted.

As the interview drew to a close, Ink became uncomfortable. He and Bashour were in complete agreement, yet Ink began to feel as if he were being lumped in by the reporter with the rest of his countrymen. It was possible that he, so attuned to the subtleties of Hemingway's prose, was reading too much into the comments of a man who'd just lost good friends. Maybe too he was feeling himself a bit guilty for how little he'd done beyond bitch and moan about the warmongers of this dangerous administration. Or maybe he was simply beginning to get angry at his old classmate's vitriol. Bashour was doing brave, important work—no question—but it almost seemed now that he was showing off a bit, like those cocky mountain climbers who half kill themselves for the sole purpose of writing books about the ones too weak to make it back down to the green, insipid earth. They say people are most alive when their lives are at risk, but what happens when, suddenly, the bomb blows up and the legs and arms go this way and that? Sure, Bashour was courageous, but wasn't he also stupid, not to mention a bit vain?

*

The student conferences slammed against him with the blunt force of another Bad Ass Bandana. To make matters worse, Bashour's lecture still echoed in his head, intensifying his headache, his nausea. First up was Tiffany Jones, a pleasant enough girl with long fingernails and blond ringlets all over the place. She was writing an argument against gay marriage.

"I've told you more than once," Ink said, pointing to a passage about Adam and Eve. "The Bible is not a legitimate source."

The girl looked at him. "Why?"

"Who is your audience?"

"The Bible is the revealed word of God."

He paged through one of her articles. "Look, you can quote this representative."

"But he disagrees with me."

"You need to take into account all sides."

The girl frowned. "Why is what he says more important than what God says?"

Ink sighed. He zigzagged through paragraphs with his red pen. "Look, for two more weeks, I'm the god here, and what I say is going to have to go."

Each student, with a few exceptions, seemed more incompetent (and more intransigent) than the last. By the time Robert Garner arrived, Ink was in a vile mood.

"What's this?" he said, pointing at the box of donuts in his student's hands.

"The breakfast of your generation."

Ink laughed, relieved that something gave him the opportunity. "I know what a power bar is. Red Bull."

"Indulge before the government takes it away from you."

Ink searched through the pile for Robert's rough draft.

"So what did you think?"

"Fine writing. Excellent, responsible use of source material." Robert had written about something called the Marcellus Shale, an expanse of sedimentary rock that contained an abundance of natural gas. His argument was that by further opening up this area in New York, Pennsylvania, and even Ohio, our country could travel very far along the road toward energy self-sufficiency. What he wanted, Ink thought crudely, was to give corporations free rein to burrow ever deeper into our country's lovely pants. "Overall," Ink said with a sigh, "nice work."

Robert smiled at the compliments.

"And, for what it's worth, I couldn't disagree with you more."

"What's not to like about energy independence?"

Ink waved him off. "So how are you enjoying your war?"

Robert was still confident of success. Democracy would prevail. As he spoke, Ink felt another wave of nausea.

"What are the latest numbers?"

Robert looked at him.

"You know, the death toll."

"In Iraq?" The boy pursed his lips. "The price of freedom is high."

"But not high enough that you might want to join the fun?"

"I have a cousin—"

"I know, I know: You go to war with the army you have."

"Excuse me?"

"Oh, everybody has a cousin," Ink said, waving his hands between them. "And you're praying for him and sending tins of chocolate chip cookies once a month. You know, it's extremely easy to be pro-war when you're not the one who's being blown sky high."

The anger felt so good, like slicing into rare steak and watching the red juice run. For the last three weeks, this young boy had been crafting an argument for the further rape of the planet. He was convinced EPA restrictions held back the country more than they protected its people. He was dubious about the long-term catastrophic effects of global warming. He believed the Constitution made quite clear the individual right to bear arms. Despite the car bombs, despite the corruption, despite the fact that there had not been a *single fucking* Weapon of Mass Destruction, the boy was still behind this damn war in Iraq! Deftly, he'd made all the necessary shifts in thinking the administration had demanded. Making matters worse, he was dangerously articulate on every one of these issues. Somewhere down the line, Robert was bound to become one of the powerful who would oversee the world's demise.

"What the hell," Ink said. "Think what you want."

"It *is* America," Robert said, wincing a bit.

"Yeah, yeah . . ."

"Are we going to have our conference?"

He handed him the draft. "You don't need it."

After a few moments, the door snapped shut, and Ink squeaked his chair around in circles. He'd scheduled himself a twenty-minute break for lunch, but all he could do was stare at the deep pores of the cinder block wall in front of him. Six more conferences to go, and then he'd be free.

That night, Sandro called to check on him. "Want to play next week?" he asked.

"Um, no."

"Got to get right back on the horse."

"No, I'm pretty sure I've been struck down for good."

Ink took a pain killer, tuned into the news, and tried to craft coherent prose. In addition to updates on the dead and injured journalists, there was other sad news Ink could do nothing about: more car bombs, of course; failed immigration reform; floods taking lives in England and Pakistan. He went back to his Babylon of books. There'd been, he realized, too many small paperbacks near the base of the tower. That was a definite problem. Better to shift them to the top, even if their due dates were much later. Better still to make two stacks, and so he did. When he finished, he stood back to admire his handiwork. He counted to ten, all the words and concepts and interpretations gathering as a black cloud in his head. He took a deep breath and knocked the towers together like heads, smiling as they tumbled to the hardwood floor.

Downstairs, his life a complete disaster, he sought solace in a sandwich.

"Everything okay up there?" Mom asked, coming into the kitchen with an empty cup of coffee.

Ink sat at the table with crappy non-fat cheese and was reminded of a story—Hemingway, of course, "Soldier's Home," the shell-shocked Krebs staring at bacon fat while his mother tries to save his soul.

"Did you know," he said, his mouth full, "your Merton, he had an affair!"

Mom tugged at her short, sharp hair. "People are human."

"Oh, that's always the excuse."

Mom spent a long time rinsing her mug at the sink. He took another bite of tasteless sandwich. He was starved, but was more hungry for something else from Mom: an apology, a sag of the shoulders, a tear or two. Something that would let him more fully experience the victory he was sure he had scored. When he got tired of waiting for such a sign, he said, "Don't worry, you still have your Jesus."

She turned to him, eyes sharp but not angry. She worked her hands in a towel. "You know—you might want to know—that I converted."

"What? Really?" Ink swallowed hard. "From . . . from what?"

"Well, before your father came along I was pretty much a nothing."

Mom had dropped out of college, a handful of credits before graduation. She married Dad and left her entire family behind in Indiana. It was too much to lose without getting something besides a bland husband in return. The story that Ink quickly told himself made a stunning amount of sense.

"Why didn't you ever—?"

She looked at him. "Why didn't you ask?"

Ink shrugged. Mom had never been the kind of person to start a conversation with.

"Passing judgment, I suppose, is easier?"

"Mom, you should talk."

"Maybe. Would you listen?"

"That's not what I meant."

"Oh . . . I see." She turned back to the sink to run the faucet, to slap a rag against the one or two dishes that weren't yet clean. Ink sighed and took his sandwich to the living room, where light from the front window poured on the sofa that had been for years Mom's after dinner home. The brown cushion was shiny with wear and bore the deep imprint of her behind. Moving closer, Ink noticed a sprinkling of flakes—potato chips. A secret indulgence? He supposed he should feel sorry for her. Long ago, she'd made a series of quick changes in her life, none of which proved to be very good. It made sense she'd cling for so long to what she had, regardless of what she believed.

*

"Hey, hey, you check out your alumni magazine?" It was Danny again—this time on the phone.

"No." Ink was driving across the Lorain-Carnegie Bridge. Towering above him were stern, massive Art Deco sculptures—the so-called Guardians of Traffic. Below was the industrial hideousness of The Flats.

"Do it. Look in the back. In Memoriam."

"I'm on the road."

"They have me down for dead. Four months running! I'm speaking to you from beyond the grave."

"How? What—?"

"Cobb, that fat bastard. He sent a bogus obit."

Ink laughed.

"Dude's come a long way," Danny said. "My hair's off to him."

"I'd love to chat, but I'm on the way to teach—"

"Whoa, whoa, whoa! You can't hang up on me. I've got real news! Important things to tell you! I'm going to pick you up this afternoon, and we'll go grab a beer." Beneath the old boldness, there seemed to be something else—worry perhaps, maybe even a bit of desperation.

"Sure, why not?" Ink said. One more time. It was Friday—what better way to wash away the bad taste of incoming research papers than a cold craft brew or two?

*

As Danny pulled up in front of Rhodes Tower, Ink wondered how someone "in-between jobs" could afford a brand new Lexus. Instead of asking questions, though, he focused on what he'd come to think of as the task at hand. He assumed they were going to go someplace nearby—E. 4th St., the Warehouse District. He'd have the requisite drink or two, nod and laugh when required, and then Danny would drive him back to his crappy Toyota. After they'd been on 480 a while—Garfield Heights, Warrensville, Bedford, out of Cuyahoga County—Ink figured his old friend might be headed for some bohunk strip club for a happy hour lap dance. By the time they approached the turnpike, he had become officially concerned.

317

"Okay," he said. "What's your news, and where are we going?"

"Remember how we always talked about blowing out of town?" Danny said, smoothing down his fake head of hair.

"No."

He slapped Ink's thigh. "Think of this as a new twist on the old buddy road trip. The academic and the asshole, hijinks in kooky small towns, bizarre love triangles . . ."

Ink laughed, although he wished he hadn't. After all of these years, there was still nothing Danny enjoyed more than being "too much."

Danny slowed for the toll booth and grabbed the ticket that shot out like a tongue.

"You know, I've got work tomorrow."

"You teach on Saturday?"

Ink glanced down at the leather bag between his legs. Inside were twenty putrid papers to mark, as well as the partial draft of a dissertation chapter that was dead in the water. He put a finger to his brow and tried to rub away the beginnings of a headache.

"Okay," Danny said. "Here's the deal: you're being kidnapped."

"Is that so?"

"Yes. Now, here's the news," Danny said, and the news was "good, great"—so great in fact that Danny had to better prepare Ink with a host of other adjectives and assessments. Only after Ink feigned sleep did Danny announce that he had been in communication with "the hottest of your old flames."

"My old flames," Ink said derisively.

"That bubbly one. You went to grade school with her. Nina…"

Nina Sissyan. Memories of Senior Week splashed before him: the girl, smiling and unsteady, telling with great verve the story about him that seemed to be the epitome of his life; later, somehow, he had his arm around her—fingers on damp spring skin; later still, there'd been a shared look—something slightly more gaze than glance. On and off throughout the years, he'd turned these meager moments over in his head, like a burger on a grill, each time the color of the meat deepening without ever becoming done.

"We've been chatting online," Danny said. "Old times, good times. You know, for some odd reason, she never liked me much. But when I told her the other day the two of us were going to visit, she said, 'Anytime!!'"

"And so—"

"She typed two exclamation points. One for each us!"

Danny went on to explain that Nina was a consumer reporter now for the NBC affiliate in Philadelphia. "She knows who's selling spoiled milk! She' knows all the dishwasher no-nos!"

Ink groaned.

But, but, but, she was much more than that, Danny said, holding up a hand. She promoted healthy living through recreational cycling. She ran 10Ks for this charity and that. She was, "for Christ's sake," *an author* of a cookbook for heart-healthy living. In short, she'd become "a responsible community leader, a model citizen."

And, Danny continued, this lovely and compassionate young woman, believe it or not, was still single after all these years! Last year, she'd been one of *Philadelphia Magazine*'s most eligible bachelorettes. The more Danny talked up her charms, the more inclined he was to go after her himself, especially now with his full head of hair. But he, if Ink couldn't have guessed, had matured; he no longer—or hardly ever—thought only of himself. "In fact, I'm like that Samaritan in the Bible, and you are, so to speak, the guy who's going to get laid out on the road."

"You do know I'm married."

Danny frowned. "Man, can't you just play along?"

"Don't get me wrong. I'm grateful—"

"We'll just drop in and do some shots or something."

"Drop in? To Philadelphia? That's 400 miles."

"True," Danny said, "but I drive crazy fast."

*

They sped along, ninety miles an hour, although it didn't feel like it in such a luxurious car. They blew by Ravenna, the Brady's Leap service plaza, the exit for Warren, Ink wondering all the while what would be the point where the plan petered out. Soon, the Lordstown Chevrolet Plant appeared on their left, the smattering of cars in its vast parking lot making Ink think of the last rotting teeth in the mouth of a very old man.

"My father worked there," Danny said, aiming his chin at the window. "Last year, they got rid of the third shift, gave him and a thousand of his closest friends the gift of early retirement."

"A good deal?"

"Sure, if you don't mind being told when your life's got to end."

"Retirement is a new beginning, a chance—"

"At a certain age, who the hell is built for new beginnings? My father was built for hard work, and when he wasn't allowed to do it anymore, he just went to shit. Sat on the sofa and watched the wild animals of Africa tear each other to shreds. Drove my mother fucking nuts."

Ink thought of Dad sawing wood alone in a basement hairy with insulation. "Past tense," he said. "I take it now he's dead?"

"Blew his mind out in a car."

"What?"

"No, no—he just up and died, like the Bojangles dog." Danny swerved around an SUV waddling along in the left hand lane. "Should've used the shotgun, though."

Ink's headache grew. His nausea returned. "Some people still like to think Ernest Hemingway died cleaning his gun."

"The writer guy?"

"That's the one."

Ink thought of the desk in his room, books collapsed around him, notecards in disarray, the cursor on the screen beating like a heart in the face of the terrifying blank expanse beyond.

"Ugly way to go," Danny continued, "but better than wimpering like a puppy through the last years of your life."

*

They roared into Pennsylvania but had to slow for construction for the next six miles. Danny looked for something to do with his hands. He bit his nails. He tapped the wheel. Barrel after barrel flashed by without a worker in sight. Finally, there was a yellow digger snoozing on an embankment. He reached for the dial, found sports talk out of Cleveland—post mortem about the Cavaliers, swept by the Spurs in the NBA Finals: "So, maybe this is our lot as Clevelanders," the host said. "To deal with the ineptitude, the heartbreak, the plain bad luck. Because if we can't win it all with a King, maybe it just ain't ever going to happen." Silence—a dramatic pause. "Call now, come

320

on people, and tell me I'm full of it!"

Later, driving through Alleghenies, even the country music began to go crinkly. Danny punched buttons, found a popular AM talk show host blowing on about Iraq, specifically the "widespread sissification" of soldiers who had the temerity to complain about the length of their deployments when they were the ones who signed up for the war. A caller concurred. "My father, God rest his soul," he said, "he married his high school sweetheart and the next week was on a boat to Europe to fight the Nazis. Years later, all he would say about the experience was, 'I did my duty.'"

Ink glanced at Danny but couldn't tell from his profile how he was taking it.

"Let me clarify one thing," the talk show host said. "I came down on our soldiers pretty hard a few minutes ago, but the fact of the matter is that they're being put up to this by the obnoxious voices on the left who complain about the supposed lack of foresight, the shortage of necessary equipment. The incompetency of Bush and Rumsfeld."

"Exactly," the caller said.

"War is messy. War is complicated. War, in a word, is hard."

"A hundred amens," the caller said.

"And all of these criticisms from the left, they undermine the war effort. They are blatantly anti-American. I've been saying so for years."

"What a jackass," Ink said.

Danny looked at him. "You know, they say suffering builds character."

"Yet another lovely justification for perpetual war," Ink said.

"No, no, think about it: suffering builds character. And character's a good thing, right? If you have character, you are mature and have principles and all of that shit."

Ink thought of Jesus—the strange, quixotic way of the cross. There was a time, of course, when the message held him in its thrall.

"I could see someone saying that a noble goal in life might be to *cause* suffering."

They sped into a tunnel, where the radio quickly gagged with static. Ink squirmed in his seat. He turned to Danny, who looked menacing—a devilish guide down this dark throat of an underworld.

When a drop of moisture splotched the windshield, Ink jumped in his seat.

"That could be one of those, those moral goods. The best kind of charity. Right? Am I off base here? You're the professor . . ."

The Lexus broke back into the sun, and Danny looked normal enough again, hands at ten and two, eyes on the road, the hair plug perfect on his head. In college, Ink had grown used to Danny's unpredictable behavior, his offensive jokes, his outrageous opinions. Was this middle-aged man next to him still that same Danny, or someone even worse?

"I think it's time to turn around," Ink said.

"Not having fun?"

"Work. I've got serious work to do." He kicked the leather bag at his feet. The papers grinned at him from the stuffed sleeve he couldn't zip closed.

"Can't exactly do a U-Turn. It's against the law."

"Next exit then. Toll's on me."

A few minutes later, a sign for a service plaza appeared.

"How about a break instead? Danny said.

"I really want to go home." Home—the word tasted funny on his tongue. Did it mean the frigid familiarity of Mom and Dad's? The emotional death trap of the cramped apartment in Clerestory? The lovely, peaceful place that existed solely between his ears? Why home, of all places? Why not away—away from everybody and thing? California. England. Clean the slate. Start over a new and better man. Years ago, he'd had his longings, if not his chances.

"Break first," Danny said, the first word delivered hard, like a fist.

"Break," Ink said, a student crying uncle during an exam.

Danny slowed, veered, swivel-swerved up the ramp before lurching into a spot right near the door. "There! Happy?"

*

They stood in line at a fast food restaurant while Danny mouthed descriptions from the menu sunning down upon them.

"Hey," Ink said, "I've got to go to the bathroom."

"You're a big boy."

Standing in front of the urinal, Ink tried to make sense of what was happening. By his own admission, Danny had "kidnapped" him; however, he didn't seem concerned about letting Ink out of his sight. Danny had said a number of alarming things, but now he was out there drooling over pictures of cheap burgers and fries. Ink thought again of the car—the brand new, tricked out Lexus. Was "flipping homes" such a lucrative enterprise? What if this fancy vehicle were stolen? What if Danny had torn out of Cleveland because the police for some ungodly reason were closing in?

Ink zipped and moved to the sink, where his pocket clunked against the counter. He reached down, patted his leg. His cell phone! It had been such a recent purchase (a necessary evil, although he'd never admit such a thing to his students) that he often forgot he owned it. He imagined calling Julie to calmly inform her he was in serious trouble, that this in fact might be the last time he'd ever speak with her. He could listen for the catch in her voice, picture her frantic pacing around the living room that for these last few weeks she'd had all to herself. She'd speak his given name— "Increase"—her voice tremulous, full of passion he assumed had shriveled up years ago. After a pregnant pause, he'd purse his lips, stare down the challenge of the restroom exit sign, say "I love you," and thumb the phone button, killing their connection.

Back on the road, Ink's feverish anxiety took a back seat to hot fast food. With each bite of burger (the furthest thing possible from Mom's bland, bad stuff), he felt happier, stronger, relieved he'd resisted making that phone call to his wife. Imagination, his lifelong idiot friend, had run off for a while with his common sense. Everything would be fine. Just fine. It was Friday, after all—TGIF. Why couldn't he just enjoy this weird, spontaneous ride?

"I have this nephew, three years old," Danny said, fry like a lizard tongue slipping into his mouth. "Braden. 'Draw a picture,' he says. 'Of what?' 'Outside.' So I draw a picture of outside—fluffy trees and clouds, a big happy ball of sun, a few stick people doing the nasty on the grass below. I take my time. I do my damnedest!"

Ink nodded. He thought of one of his current composition students—Leo something or another. The boy was a hopeless case: sorely underprepared, overwhelmed by a full course load and a job as a dishwasher at a chain restaurant, becoming (if that were possible) less literate by the day.

"Then Braden comes weebling into the room with chocolate

brown, his favorite color in the world, and smears the crayon back and forth across all my hard work. I bite my tongue. I want to say, 'What the fuck?' He's just laughing to beat the band."

"He's a toddler."

"But that's everybody is what I'm saying. That's a micro . . . a meta—you know, whatever the hell it's called. The point is, everybody is just burning to do the same damn thing. You know, on some . . . bigger canvas."

"I don't think that's true."

"Nutshell!" Danny cried. "Maybe I'm thinking 'nutshell.'"

"You want to hear a story about Nina?" Ink asked.

"We've been doing this kind of character-building shit for centuries . . . since the dawn of time, right? Maybe our only hope for real change is to ratchet things up. Have a real blow out, so whatever the hell is snoozing away upstairs will have no choice but to wake up, put on some goddamn clothes, and come on down to say, 'Enough'!"

"I don't think—"

"Maybe too, I'm just throwing this out there . . . maybe if the suffering, if the horrors could be committed for no stated reason . . . Let the act go without saying." Danny parodied the sign of the cross—head to groin to finger in the nose. "Go without saying, my son."

"Are you serious?"

"Maybe." To Ink, Danny's hands became fists around the wheel. "I'm thirty-five. I really want to have it in me to be serious."

The fears of twenty minutes ago came rushing back. Ink now believed Danny was not taking him to Nina but preparing him to serve as witness—or perhaps even accomplice—for some unconscionable act of terror he'd planned for The City of Brotherly Love. Some people were one way for the longest time—one way, one way, one way and then snap! —a brand new self was born. Not just the good guys—St. Augustine, St. Ignatius, St. Paul—but the roadside bombers too, fast tracking their way to paradise. And the murder-suicides as well, dying for the whole ugly show of life to be done: that vet in New Orleans last year; just last week, the wrestler, Benoit. Drastic change was the story of saints and killers alike. Who could know for certain which way people were going to break until they did?

Danny weaved in and out of traffic. They sped past a green sign for Breezewood.

"When I was, I don't know, nine or something," Ink said, trying to shift the conversation from its disturbing course. "We . . . we, you know, took this trip to D.C., me and the parents." It was a lie—Mom, a devout homebody even then, eventually quashed the plans by saying, "That's much too far to go." That didn't stop Dad, who'd traveled there as a teen, from reciting with trembling voice an assortment of odd facts about "our nation's capital."

"Did you know," Ink said, "during the War of 1812 the Brits burned the whole town down, White House and all? Madison had to—"

"What's your point? Your story?"

Ink shrugged. "I don't have a story. The sign we passed made me remember."

"Breezewood," Danny exclaimed. "The Town of Motels!"

Ink smiled. All those years ago, he'd sent away for brochures— tourist sites, scenic drives, accommodations. When the material arrived, he devoured it greedily in his room. He told Dad that, to make things easier for Mom, they could break up the trip by staying overnight in Breezewood, a couple hours from the city. Dad clapped him on the back, and Ink got his hopes up, although he was nine and even then should've known Mom would at some point pull the plug.

"Let me guess," Danny said, hand out to paint a picture. "D.C. was all well and good, but what you wanted to do in the very worst way was to explore the magical world of Breezewood. To see all the people coming and going—north, south, east, and west. The crossroads of America. And your parents, those selfish bastards, kept right on going."

"Yeah. Maybe." Ink laughed in spite of himself. "That's a good story."

"What I hear you saying—what I'm reading between the lines— is you want to stop for the day. You want the dream you missed out on. You want to get a room."

"No . . . God no."

"Ink, I've loved you since the day we first met."

Just like that Danny had become again the innocuous clown.

"What I'd really like—"

Danny waved a hand in the air. "I don't want to hear it. I owe you this much."

The motel room was austere. There were two single beds, a desk with uncertain legs, an old TV like a giant square basketball on an index-finger stand. On the far wall was a surrealistic oil painting of a ship on a roiling sea of deciduous trees. The frame was crooked, and it looked to Ink as if the crew were going down to a fruit-infused demise.

"Romantic, huh?" Danny said. "Maybe we could push the beds together."

Ink laughed. He wanted to respond in a way Danny would appreciate even as he plotted the precise combination of moves he would need to make to come out of this situation alive.

Danny flopped onto the bed and turned on the TV. "Hey, maybe we can pick up a Philly channel and see Nina in action." He flipped through a few stations before being distracted by a cooking show. The host, a generically attractive blonde, spread fingers across a counter while introducing her guest, who was going to show the studio audience how to make, of all things, sauerkraut cupcakes.

With great trepidation, Ink took a seat on the other bed.

"One whole can?" the host squealed, watching the guest shake the pale, vinegary strands of cabbage into the mixing bowl.

Danny shook his head. "I'll be damned."

A few moments later, he again began punching the remote: a women's softball game; bloody streets in Baghdad; a florid televangelist, hands like a medieval king on his chair's wide velour arms.

"Well, now what?" Ink asked.

"Hey, by the way, who'd you marry? Some Clerestory chick?"

"Julie . . . Julie Colombo."

Danny bobbed his head in what seemed an approving way.

If Ink survived, there was that anniversary trip to Cape Cod. In a cozy bed and breakfast, humbled by the eternal ocean plunge outside their window, they would between sips of wine come up with a plan to save their marriage. They would emerge from that trip with a renewed sense of purpose—with the understanding of the precise things they needed to do for each other in order to make their life together into something it was always meant to be. Success would require hard work—a willingness to talk, to apologize, a desire to listen, an eagerness to take suggestions to heart. It would require a mutual acknowledgment that they, not unlike the ship on the wall, had hit strange and difficult waters, but that there was plenty of fruit around them for the picking.

"Bet you didn't know that *I* was married," Danny said.

"Really? Who? What happened?"

Danny lay back against the headboard, made a basket of hands for his head. "Since Clerestory, I've been a whole hell of a lot of things."

Ink thought he had at last enough material to flesh out Danny's story from college graduation to the present: a few years of horny, bachelor days; a wild wedding, the girl as good as drawn from a hat; a quick child or two; a series of drunken affairs; the loss of a half way decent job; the death of his father, whom he probably truly loved; his wife packing bags and moving with her children to another, safer state. Out of work, out of a father, out of a spouse and kids—out of a world in which his puerile exploits made a difference—Danny was now at his wit's end.

"Are you okay?" Until he could escape, the best thing Ink could do was try to help.

"You mean 'fit as a fiddle'? As opposed to 'royally fucked in the head?'"

Ink glanced again at the tilted ship. He noticed that someone had markered in a few shark fins on the leafy trees. He didn't know whether that should make him laugh or cry.

"Remember, the alumni mag says I'm dead now. I've been liberated! Anything I do now doesn't really count."

On the TV, Barack Obama was speaking about Guantanamo Bay: "We're going to lead by example—by not just word but by deed. That's our vision for the future."

Obama: here at long last was a genuine leader in the making, a voice the country had never heard before. He was more than his liberalism. He was more than his race (although Ink was convinced that the election of a black president would certainly speak volumes about how far this country had traveled). He was nothing less than the personification of human decency. If he could win the primary against that warmonger Clinton, Obama would win the presidency and pull the country out of its moral tailspin with his colorblind "politics of hope." He was someone who would not just do things but do *good* things. He would transform America; as a result, he would transform the world.

"Here's your real man of character," Ink said.

"I guess." Danny stood and went to the door. "Look, I'm going over to the ol' country store for a couple of toothbrushes. You're here when I get back—fine, great, we'll go onto the next scene of our hilarious buddy flick. If not, I'll go it alone. I'll adapt. I'm a pro at that."

He closed the door softly, and Ink stared at the shiny knob, which looked to him like a miniature crystal ball. Throughout his life, he'd encountered so many of these brash, unpredictable types: that Baske boy in grade school; Crabb, the gridiron goof; Uncle Lare, the angry, impotent alcoholic; that ludicrous cowboy Stash. These were people he'd learned to keep his safe distance from—boys or men who seemed capable of the worst. And yet, and yet, what really had they done? When push came to shove, hadn't they all been like old Mr. Majeski's dog Trouble, much more bark than bite?

At a loss for what to do, Ink sat down at the desk and sketched out choices in his head:

A) Go to Philadelphia

B) Contact the proper authorities

C) Subdue the enemy

D) None of the above

As a lifelong student, he'd been taking exams for as long as he could remember: true/false, fill in the blank, short answer, essay, and oral. The most terrifying of them all, though, was the multiple choice test—the one with the answers right in front of his face. It was an ancient fear, going all the way back to those early days of grade school when it was just him and his pencil and the clock running down. Even if he was certain of a given answer, three questions later he found himself ruined by a violent fit of second guessing.

What to do? What to do? His first impulse was to go with A. For him, it was a familiar road—the path of least resistance. If he didn't lose his cool—if he took all of Danny's antics in stride—there was a very good chance the two of them would be roaring into Philadelphia by noon tomorrow. Maybe there'd be time for a look at Independence Hall, the Liberty Bell. Then they would meet Nina at some downtown bar after she got out of work. She would be dazzling, of course, moving quickly towards him, eyes bright, her brown, well-toned arms open for a warm embrace. After a lovely visit, he could go home and become an adult again.

B was a much less complicated option. It would only take a minute to call the proper authorities, another minute for them to arrive and slap Danny in cuffs. But what crime had he committed beyond an obscene and reckless running of the mouth?

And what about C? With no experience in subduing enemies, Ink pondered how it might be done. Should he crash that absurd painting over Danny's head as he came through the door? Back him into the bathroom with a soft bristle toothbrush? After a long career of diffidence—after years of debilitating self-consciousness—Ink wondered if he might be capable of at least attempting one courageous act.

But he could not forget about option D—the always tantalizing "none of the above." As a scholar, Ink had a deep appreciation for ambiguity; however, as an ordinary person in dire straits, he longed for simple and definitive instructions from some transcendent being. Higher or lower—at this point, he was in no position to be picky.

Ink went to the window and pinched the curtains aside. No sign of Danny, which meant there was still time to hazard a guess. His mental pencil tapped back over the options, all of which were fraught with incredible risk. Unable to commit, he returned to the desk and dragged the research papers from his bag. Each was a thick, depressing packet with a draft and a final version and photocopied sources. He began reading the one on top: "In today's society…" and wrote "NO" in thick red pen. In the next sentence was a quotation without a page number. The third sentence—a run on. He came across Tiffany Jones's paper and was depressed to see the Bible referenced three times on the first two pages. A headache loomed. How many times had Ink told his students not to do this or that? How much time had he spent with them on documentation, on making sentences that were if not pleasing to the ear than at least grammatically correct? And the simplicity of the arguments! Despite his passionate lectures, many of these papers were so much either/or. Men vs. Women. Black vs.

White. Straight vs. Gay. Us vs. Them. After all of his hard work, these papers read like chapters of a long and garbled joke.

He thumbed through the stack for Robert's, which he knew would be good. He read the first few pages—unified, well-supported, eloquent paragraphs about a drilling process that meant nothing less than the wholesale destruction of the country's environment. He thought of the Garden of Eden—not the Hemingway novel, but the one at the beginning of it all. Pristine sky, dew-jeweled greenery, crystal clear falls, a naked man and woman, that stupid asshole of a tree. He tried to remember the end of his own long ago innocent time. Third grade? No, fourth—the year that poor boy Frankie had died. With his ordinary brain, with his wait-and-see self-consciousness, how in the world did Ink manage to make it all the way from there to here?

He went back to the window just in time to see Danny striding across the black top between convenience store and motel, paper bag like a baby in his arms. A couple—middle aged, dark-skinned—approached him, apparently for directions. Danny nodded, laughed—he soon had them responding in kind. When he drew a great circle in the air with his hands, Ink could see sweat stains under his arms.

Returning to his mental exam, Ink settled on D. He colored in his choice as thoroughly as he could, making sure not to leave any stray marks outside the imaginary bubble. When finished, he began to breathe more deeply, more calmly. Anxiety dropped from him like scales from his eyes. He let the curtain fall and went back in a better mood to the next paper in his stack.

Abortion! Along with capital punishment and euthanasia, it was a topic he'd expressly forbidden. He scanned the first page, trying to make heads or tails of it, then flipped to page two, surprised to see paragraphs degenerate into sentences, fragments, notes, a random observation here, a block quotation there. On the fourth and final page was a Post-It note that said: "5:37 AM—Sorry, I tried but can't develop." The author of this debacle was Drew Maywell, a quiet boy with eyes that would yawn out of his head at moments that seemed to call for neither fear nor surprise. The kid never said a word in class; what was more, he'd missed both of his conferences and failed to submit a rough draft. In the history of formal education, had there ever been a more obvious F?

The door opened, and a knife of light plunged across the floor. Ink sat up straight, as if he'd been struck. D, he'd concluded, was the answer of the emotionally mature. Did it matter, though, that it was also the letter grade reserved for those who passed by the skin of their teeth?

Danny stood before him, with his stiff, fake hair and punkish tilde of a smile. From the paper bag he drew a small square package and flipped it like a coin upon his bed. "Here's to new beginnings!"

Condoms. Ink's stomach turned, but he braved a smile. "You're very funny."

"I couldn't resist."

"Well, maybe you can do better."

Danny blinked. His lips swished disconcertingly.

"Me too!" Ink added, standing up, palms out to show he meant no harm. "I can be so much—"

"No, no, man. You're good enough for this world."

Danny reached noisily back into the bag and Ink, although he tried not to, held his breath. For better or for worse—regardless of the next surprise—he supposed he should stick with the mark that he'd made.

About the Author

Michael Cocchiarale is Associate Professor of English and Creative Writing at Widener University. He is the author of two collections of short stories—*Still Time* (Fomite, 2012) and *Here Is Ware* (Fomite, 2018).

About the Press

Unsolicited Press was founded in 2012 and is based in Portland, Oregon. The press works feverishly to find stellar writing from authors around the world. Unsolicited Press publishes a range of traditional and experimental fiction, poetry, and nonfiction.

Learn more at www.unsolicitedpress.com.